BLACK
MOUTH

BLACK MOUTH

RONALD MALFI

TITAN BOOKS

Black Mouth
Print edition ISBN: 9781789098655
E-book edition ISBN: 9781789098662

Published by Titan Books
A division of Titan Publishing Group Ltd.
144 Southwark Street, London SE1 0UP
www.titanbooks.com

First Titan edition July 2022
10 9 8 7 6 5 4 3 2

A CIP catalogue record for this title is available from
the British Library.

Printed and bound by CPI Group (UK) Ltd, Croydon, CR0 4YY

This one's for Kangas.

"There is no magic in recovery."

—ALCOHOLICS ANONYMOUS

I

THE LAND OF
THE LIVING

CHAPTER ONE

DETOX BOOGIE

1

One week after our mother committed suicide, my brother Dennis was taken into police custody while walking along the shoulder of a winding mountain highway wearing nothing but a pair of saggy white briefs and what I can only assume to be an empty expression on his face. He had made it six miles out of town, which meant he'd been walking for hours beneath the blazing summer sun. When the police found him, he was dehydrated. His face was lobster-red and glistening, his chest and shoulders blistered with sunburn, and the hairless bulge of his belly, which drooped over the frayed waistband of his underwear, was jeweled with sweat. He must have looked like some ripened tropical fruit, freshly washed. The only exception was his feet, which were bare and powdered in road dust. With each step he took, he stamped asterisks of blood onto the pavement.

I learned all of this—about Dennis walking along the highway in his underwear as well as our mother's suicide—from a police detective out of Sutton's Quay, West Virginia, who had somehow managed to track down my cell phone number and dropped me a line. Admittedly, the timing wasn't great. I was fresh out of rehab, a condition of my continued employment with the Ohio foundry where I had worked for the past six years. I was operating a crane transporting a steel casting ladle of molten metal when the ladle adjustment failed. No one was injured, but the damage was considerable (as was the cost of cleanup and repairs), and that section of the foundry had to be shut down for a number of days. Len Pruder, my shift supervisor, pulled me into his office on the day it happened. He was a squat, potato-shaped fellow with bad hair plugs. He stuck his face in mine, so close that the tip of his nose grazed my lips, causing me to draw back.

"You're drunk, Jamie," Len said, nostrils flaring. His swollen red eyes ticked back and forth as he studied my face. "You goddamn son of a bitch, you stink like a brewery. You're lucky you didn't kill someone. Pack up your shit and get the hell out."

So I packed up my shit and got the hell out. Two days later, however, I received a phone call from the floor manager, an ex-Marine named Yaeger, who invited me to a meeting. I agreed, then immediately felt ambushed when I showed up: Yaeger, Len, and some well-groomed people in suits all sat on one side of the large wooden table in the foundry's break room, patiently awaiting my arrival. The people in suits were lawyers, I soon realized, once they started popping the brass clasps on their briefcases. When one of the suits asked me if I'd been drunk while operating the crane—"inebriated" was the word he used—I said I had probably been hung over, since I'd spent quite a few hours at Donovan's Pub the night before, but that I didn't think I'd still been drunk. When one of the suits asked if I frequently came to work hung over, I said no, not really, although maybe sometimes. Truth was, I was sitting there right in front of them with a bellyful of lead and a hangover that felt like someone was using a tack hammer to the back of my eyeballs. Because, hell, when you get fired from your job, you go out and get shitfaced, right? Anyway, I must have sounded reliable, or at least genuine, because the suits nodded at my response and seemed content. Yaeger, still sporting a military crew cut that made it look like someone had taken a push mower to the top of his head, actually grinned. Only Len Pruder, seated directly opposite me at that creaky wooden table in the foundry's break room, scowled. His face had gone the color of a pomegranate, and his jowls quivered.

"This isn't the first time," Len spoke up. He looked on the verge of having a stroke, and there was a vein as thick as a McDonald's drinking straw pulsing on the side of his head. "This guy's a liability. He's gonna wind up killing himself or someone else. Sometimes he doesn't even come in for days at a time, and we gotta scramble the schedule to get someone else on the floor to cover—"

Yaeger raised a hand and Len Pruder went quiet. The lawyers at the end of the table looked nervous and uncomfortable.

As it turned out, the steel casting ladle hadn't undergone a safety inspection in over three years. I guess a more industrious guy could have flipped the script and walked out of that meeting with a sizeable cash settlement, but I was happy to leave with my job reinstated.

"One condition," Yaeger said, drumming a set of boltlike fingers along the scuffed wooden surface of the table. "You gotta do a stint in rehab, Jamie."

"I don't have the money for something like that," I said.

"It's covered under your health insurance. Drinking and getting fucked up—it's considered a *disease* nowadays. Like cancer."

I watched the suits bristle collectively at this, but they did not interject.

"Anyway, it's company policy," Yaeger went on. "No way around it, if you wanna stay on the floor."

"You'll need to attend regular Alcoholics Anonymous meetings, too, Mr. Warren," said one of the suits as he thumbed through a stapled packet of papers.

"How often is regular?" I asked.

"Daily, at the very least." The guy had a pinched, birdlike face, and an Adam's apple like a desk call bell. "Company policy stipulates ninety meetings in ninety days."

"That sounds like a lot. People really go every day?"

"More, if they need to."

"My insurance pay for that, too?"

"Those are free," Yaeger told me. "Been to a few myself."

I thought about it for maybe three seconds.

"All right," I said, because I needed this job. "Sounds fair."

Len Pruder looked like he wanted to launch himself across the tabletop and choke me out.

A few days later, I went into rehab. It was a twenty-eight-day program, the shortest one they offered, and the woman I spoke with over the phone assured me that I was very lucky. "There's usually a very long waiting list to get in," she said.

"I didn't realize these places were so exclusive. Should I rent a tux?"

The woman on the phone did not find me funny.

I expected an institutional setting, one with stark white walls, crisp bed sheets, and caretakers wearing hospital scrubs. In reality, what I got was more like a VFW hall partitioned into various rooms, every wall paneled in imitation wood, and not a stitch of carpeting in the place. There were crucifixes and inspirational phrases in picture frames on nearly every wall, and a small janitorial closet that doubled as a chapel, where you could pray to a plaster bust of the Virgin Mary or grab a push broom and sweep the floors, depending on your mood. Upon my arrival, I filled out some paperwork then was taken to a room by a middle-aged woman with brash streaks of gray in her hair and blackheads nestled in the corners of her nose. A half-dozen cots were lined up here in military fashion. The whole place was characterless, except for the acoustical ceiling tiles, which were decorated with the swirling yellows, oranges, and browns of water damage.

The first couple of days were fine—I ate my meals, watched television or read books, played board games or ping pong with my fellow inmates in a drab, wood-paneled recreation room that stank of cigarette smoke and the headier, semisweet fragrance of ass crack. There were five other men in the place, each one battling their own personal demons—arms blackened with collapsed veins; mouths empty of teeth; body odor as acrid as volcanic spume. One fellow, thin as a rail spike, walked around with a perpetual smile on his face while his squinty little eyes dribbled a never-ending supply of tears. He would ghost from room to room like that, his expression never changing. I began to think of him as the Weeping Walker, although I never said this to his face. In fact, I steered clear of him altogether. So did everyone else. He was too creepy to engage with, so everyone just left him alone. The Weeping Walker didn't seem to mind; he just kept on weeping and walking.

Nights were restless, but that was nothing new to me. I'd never been what you might call a good sleeper, although the nightmares that had haunted me in my youth had, over time, retreated somewhat to the shady corners of my subconscious. I would lie there at night, listening to the orchestration of snores and farts from the other guys in the room, unable to fall asleep. But it was nothing I couldn't handle, if it meant saving my job.

But then something changed. I began to notice the mesh wiring over all the windows—and not just notice it, but to *obsess* over it. I was suddenly, mercilessly, reminded of a place where I'd spent nearly a year of my youth—an empty place full of black circles, circles, circles. My skin grew itchy and felt too small. Claustrophobia tightened its muscular coils about my body. I imagined blood on the soles of my feet, and drying in russet streaks along my pant legs. Those restless nights turned into marathons of insomnia while my head filled with nonspecific terrors. I stared at the moonlit ceiling tiles (patterned with the shadows of wire mesh) with eyes that blazed like headlamps. Those swirling water stains conspired, in my mounting paranoia, to heckle and terrorize me as they began to slither across the ceiling. I became convinced that *something* had insinuated itself beneath my cot, slotted there like a peg in a hole, where it lay in total darkness lightly plucking at the grid of bedsprings in the cot's metal frame. After several nights of this, I got rid of the frame and slept with my mattress on the floor.

Some change was taking place inside me. I grew irritable, unsettled, twitchy. I found I couldn't keep my hands from shaking. I felt both loose and tightly wound at the same time. I stopped eating. I screamed at the woman with the streaks of gray in her hair. Terrified of the dark, I slept only in the daytime, discarding even my mattress now and opting to sleep directly on the floor, which felt cool against my steaming flesh. The headache that was gradually boiling inside the crock pot of my skull was a constant, never-ending torture; I frequently sobbed with the heels of my hands pressed into my eye sockets for fear the expanding force of that headache might jettison my eyeballs from my skull. I vomited so regularly and with such intensity that my stomach felt like a balloon someone had pumped full of hot gas. Pissing myself became my favorite hobby.

At some point, I was removed from the general population and relocated to a room no larger than a broom closet. An aging hippie with a long gray ponytail and an REO Speedwagon T-shirt tossed my duffel bag onto a fresh cot. I stared at the cot with renewed horror. Only when the hippie clapped his hands—a sound very much like the pop of a starting pistol in that suffocating little room—did I look away from the cot and over at him. The hippie leaned toward me, gazing straight into my eyes. Was this lunatic trying to hypnotize me or just peer deep into my soul? I recoiled from him, my stinking, sweat-dampened shirt sliding along the wall until I found myself trapped in a corner.

"Boy, you're riding the ride now," said the hippie. His teeth were tombstones.

That first night in my new room—what felt to me, in my unhinged state, like solitary confinement, or maybe even a coffin—I heard a *different* sound coming from beneath my cot. Not the muted *thwang!* of those plucking bedsprings, but the wet *thhhk-thhhk* sound of an infant's mouth suckling at its mother's breast. This image—of a child breastfeeding—appeared at the center of my head with such inexorable force and unshakable clarity that it carved through the pulsing fog of my headache with all the authority of a lighthouse beacon.

Gathering what strength I had left in my shaky, foul-smelling, unreliable body, I rolled off the cot and backed away to the far side of the room. (Given the size of the room, this meant I was only about six feet from the cot.) There was a single window in the room, a high and narrow rectangle of glass through which a channel of sodium light bisected the darkness and painted a distorted orange panel on the floor. A part of that orange panel bled beneath the cot, and I could discern, with a deepening sense of dread, that there was *movement* down there—a shape alive. I could still hear the noise, too: *thhhk-thhhk-thhhk.*

Until now, and despite the discomfort I had felt in this place as my body detoxed, it had never occurred to me to *leave.* I was here under my own volition; if I wanted to pack up and get the fuck out, there was no one who would stop me. Now, however, hearing that suckling sound and seeing that indistinct movement beneath the cot, the urge to flee was all-encompassing. Had I trusted myself to get as far as the front door without collapsing from a combination of exhaustion and terror, I might have done just that. But I didn't.

Instead, I took a step toward the cot. I was hoping my approach would silence that suckling sound, the way crickets go quiet when you draw near. But that wet and greedy sucking did not stop. And with it arrived the vague whiff of smoke. I took another step. Then another. A knot formed in my throat as my shins came to rest against the cot's metal frame.

A figure wrapped in a swirling black cloak materialized in the darkness beside me. A voice in my ear, whispering straight through to the epicenter of my soul: *Do you want to see a magic trick?*

"No," I said aloud, but I reached down and gripped the mattress with both hands anyway. No dramatic flourish, no sense of showmanship—I simply yanked the flimsy mattress off the frame and tossed it to the floor, where it raised a cloud of dust into the chute of orange light spilling through the window.

There was a woman lying on the floor beneath the lattice of bedsprings, an infant clutched to her breast. She cradled the child's pale, sloping head while it fed. The *thhhk-thhhk-thhhk* sound of its feeding rivaled the whoosh of blood funneling through my ears, my hammering heartbeat, the reedy hiss of air whistling up through the pinhole of my throat.

Quick as a snake strike, the woman reached out and grasped me around one ankle with fingers that felt like bone.

Stricken blind by terror, I was dragged down into the darkness.

2

My mother killed herself in the master bedroom of the farmhouse where Dennis and I grew up. She had drawn the bedroom curtains, switched on the bedside lamp that was electrically powered but fashioned to look like an antique flat-wick kerosene lantern, smoked a joint, and then ingested an entire bottle of prescription pain pills. Police found her supine on the bed, one eye closed, one leg dangling off the mattress so that her toes just barely grazed the dusty wooden floorboards. She'd already been dead for a week, and the summer heat had sped up her decomposition. The bedroom was dizzy with flies.

As for what specific ailment those pain pills had been prescribed, it was up for speculation. On the infrequent occasions my mother and I came within orbit of each other, she would complain about her diabetes, her arthritis, persistent migraines, unmanageable acid reflux, temporomandibular joint dysfunction, irritable bowel syndrome, vertigo, chronic insomnia, double vision, and all variety of bodily aches and pains. She also had lung cancer (according to the autopsy report), although I assume she didn't know this because it had never come up during one of her pity-seeking diatribes.

At the time of her death, I hadn't seen my mother or my brother Dennis in over four years, and I hadn't been back to that farmhouse since I was a teenager. There was a period when, on a whim, my mom had purchased an old Airstream caravan—one of those things that resembled a giant metal thermos on wheels—and she and Dennis would periodically travel around the country together like a couple of reprobates. At some point on their journey, they would detour to whatever neck of the woods I was holed up in at the time, and I'd spend the obligatory afternoon subjected to my mother's myriad complaints about her failing health while she inhaled an entire pack of Pall Malls and sipped cheap vodka from a paper cup. Dennis would show me photos of their road trip on his iPad, the screen gummy with fingerprints, always sitting too close to me, the heat that radiated from his meaty forearm dampening my shirtsleeve. These visits usually took place in a park or RV recreation area (neutral ground), some barbecue carryout containers spread out on an old bed sheet in the grass, bottlenose flies dive-bombing the potato salad and getting snared in the quagmire of gluey barbecue sauces. At the conclusion of each of these visits, Mom would give me one of her perfunctory little hugs, and then Dennis would gather me up in his big arms, squeezing my guts while yanking me clear off the ground. Yet like all of my mother's capricious endeavors, these cross-country road trips were short-lived. (I think the Airstream was ultimately repossessed, too.)

The Sutton's Quay police detective who informed me of my mother's death was named Aiello, and he spoke in that familiar thick-throated drawl I had grown up to know as Appalachian English. He told me about Dennis shuffling half-naked along the shoulder of the highway, too, and how he had personally responded to the call because he was already in the area. Sure enough, there was Dennis, pink and shiny in the sun, doing the Frankenstein's monster shamble down the highway. Detective Aiello had gotten out of his car and approached Dennis, attempted to engage the peculiar fellow in conversation. But Dennis hadn't responded to the detective or even acknowledged that Aiello was standing there at all; Dennis had simply continued his laborious, barefooted trek along the gritty shoulder of the highway as if under a hypnotist's spell.

Detective Aiello, whose law enforcement career spanned eleven years (although his transfer to the Sutton's Quay Police Department had been fairly recent), had the good sense to realize there was something decidedly *off* about my brother, even without taking into consideration the fact that he was trudging along the road half-naked in the middle of the day. So instead of attempting to slap a pair of silver bracelets on my brother and muscle him into a police car, which would have been a chore, Detective Aiello radioed dispatch for assistance then proceeded to walk with Dennis for about a quarter of a mile. It was hot as hell, but Aiello figured he could use the exercise.

Just as Aiello heard sirens coming over the hill, Dennis stopped walking. He blinked his small gray eyes, and for the first time since

Aiello had joined him on his journey, winced from the sizzling glare of the midday sun. It was as though he had just been roused from a deep sleep. He turned to Aiello, some semblance of clarity filtering back into his small and somewhat childlike eyes. Some of the moisture on my brother's face, Aiello suddenly realized, was tears.

Dennis said something, which Detective Aiello could not readily make sense of. He asked Dennis to repeat himself, and Dennis obliged.

"She. Is now. Dead," said Dennis.

This statement, delivered in my brother's odd and halting pattern of speech, made Detective Aiello uncomfortable. My brother looked like the dude from that Steinbeck novel who accidentally killed a puppy, and his whole lights-are-on-but-nobody's-home affectation didn't help matters any. When police backup arrived on the scene, the officers wanted to wrangle my brother into the back seat of their cruiser, but Detective Aiello didn't think that would go over so well. Instead, Aiello got a blanket from the trunk of the cruiser, draped it over my brother's broad, sunburned shoulders, and agreed to walk all the way back to the farmhouse with him. Hours later, when Dennis and Detective Aiello finally arrived back at the farmhouse, my mother's body had already been discovered, and cops were taking photos of her desiccated corpse.

"Where's my brother now?" I asked the detective. I was on my cell phone in my car, a 1972 puke-green Ford Maverick with vinyl bench seats and a St. Christopher medallion superglued to the dash. It was early evening and I had the windows down, but the air was stagnant and the interior of the Mav felt like the inside of a kiln. I was in the parking lot of the First United Methodist Church on Mill Street in downtown Akron, where I'd been coming for the past week to attend AA meetings. I'd been back to work at the foundry for a week now, too, operating once again under the contemptuous scrutiny of Len Pruder.

"Well, you see, that's sort of been an issue," Detective Aiello said.

"What does that mean?" I asked.

"Well, Mr. Warren, it took us a couple of days to track you down, and we didn't have nobody else to call locally, so—"

"Where *is* he?"

"He's here. At the station."

I cleared my throat and said, "My brother has been staying at the police station?"

"He's fine, Mr. Warren. We had a medic come in, give him a once over. He was dehydrated and there were some abrasions on the bottoms of his feet from walking all that way barefoot, but he was otherwise okay. Thing is, we didn't know what to do with him, where to take him. We didn't think he should go back to the house on his own, given his…well…"

"No," I agreed.

"I was gonna put in a call to the state, see if they'd come and get him, but then I was able to track you down. Figured it'd be better to have you involved instead."

My head was swimming.

"Anyway, your brother is fine, Mr. Warren. He even seems to like it here. And there's always someone around to keep him company. It's just that we didn't know what else to do."

"Is he there now? Can I talk to him?"

"Sure. Hold on a sec."

Then there was Dennis's breathy salutation in my ear on the other end of the line, the familiar halting speech pattern, the edge of urgency at the back of his throat.

"I *saw* her, Jamie," Dennis proclaimed. "She is now *dead*."

I closed my eyes. My body trembled like something hooked up to jumper cables. "What about you, buddy? Are you okay?"

"She. Is now. Dead."

"All right, buddy. All right."

There was a jostling, then Detective Aiello was back on the line. Somewhere in the background, I could hear my brother's high-pitched keening—something like a laugh or a sob or some nonspecific outburst of noise.

"If you do the quick and dirty math, given the coroner's estimated time of death for your mother, Mr. Warren, you'll see that your brother had been living in the house with her for about a week or so after she'd passed."

"A *week*?" My brother had been living in that house with our mother's corpse for a *week*? I opened my mouth to say something but then shut it again. I didn't know what to make of this information. It was disturbing, even for Dennis.

"But again, Mr. Warren, he's fine. Your brother. Like nothing ever happened. Everyone at the station has really taken a shine to him, too. Only..."

"Only what?"

"You'll have to come out here, Mr. Warren," Detective Aiello said. "You'll have to come and get him. As soon as you can."

She. Is now. Dead.

You'll have to come.

Black Mouth had finally caught up with me.

3

It wasn't that I had been spontaneously stricken blind by the sight of the woman nursing the baby beneath my cot, or the very real sensation of her bony fingers closing around my ankle; it was that I'd been overcome by what is known in the business as the Detox Boogie. In other words, I'd suffered a seizure as a result of acute alcohol withdrawal. When I came to, I was sprawled out on the floor of my tiny room, the undersea glow of early morning light leaking through the room's solitary window. The crotch of my pants was damp and the room reeked of ammonia.

I was shaking, my body simultaneously hot and cold. When I rolled my head to one side, a dagger-like pain speared down my neck and detonated across my shoulders.

The mattress was still on the floor where I'd tossed it the night before. There was nothing beneath the cot's frame but scuffed linoleum tiles and dust bunnies.

Peripheral movement caused my head to turn—painfully. The Weeping Walker stood in the doorway, his messy pink eyes leaking tributaries of saline, the edges of his sharp, cadaverous grin expanding beyond the confines of his face.

"Get somebody," I groaned. My voice sounded like the squalling of a rusty hinge.

The Weeping Walker floated away. Moments later, the gray-streaked woman (her name was Deena) and the aging hippie (his name was Fred) filed into the room. Deena helped me sit up and gave me water from a plastic bottle, which I chugged until it was empty without coming up for air. Fred only folded his arms, leaned against the wall, and nodded his head. The look of satisfaction on his face struck me. It was as if he'd been somehow complicit in what had happened to me in the night, and the outcome brought him great pleasure.

"All part of the ride, my brother," he said, and pumped one fist in the air in solidarity. "Welcome back to the Land of the Living."

That was how my twenty-eight days in rehab turned into sixty. I was there when my fellow inmates departed and a new collection of wild-eyed, trembling degenerates took their place. (Only the Weeping Walker remained, and since no one seemed to acknowledge him, I began to wonder if he actually existed or if he was something altogether fashioned from my own imagination.)

I had my cell phone with me the whole time I was in that place, but I never once made a phone call. Nor did I receive any (except for the periodic phone scams, where a robotic female voice who addressed me as Barbara urgently wished to discuss my student loan debt). There was no one in my life to call, no one sitting in a house or an apartment or in a car or on a bus or a plane who cared about what was happening to me. I had no real friends, just coworkers from the foundry who were good for a few beers after work, but I had managed to alienate many of them over the years. I'd wrecked too many cars, gotten into too many fistfights at the local watering holes, blacked out in too many back alleys. My absences from work caused them undue hardship, and they began to distance themselves from me after a while. There were the occasional women in my life, each one too transitory to be called a girlfriend. One woman, whose name I'll respectfully leave out of this sad dissertation, had been special. For a brief period, we'd even lived together. But I had done everything within my power to fuck up that relationship, too.

Sixty days turned into ninety.

"It's like the aperture of the world's growing wider," Fred said one afternoon as we sat playing checkers in the rec room. "You start seeing all your past transgressions under that wider lens and it bugs you out, man. But don't let it get you down. Because, see, that's someone else's life. You're a new man now, amigo."

The idea that I was glimpsing past transgressions resonated with me. Most disconcerting was the inexplicable impression of finger marks in the flesh around my ankle where the woman beneath the cot had grabbed me. Everything else could be written off as a detox-induced hallucination, but this was the one thing I couldn't reconcile with myself.

When I left that place, Deena gave me a hug and said she was proud of me. Fred presented me a handmade hemp bracelet and another fist pump in the air, which I returned this time. The Weeping Walker, somehow still haunting the dimly lit rooms and wood-paneled corridors of that facility, peered out at me from behind one of the wire-mesh windows as I stood on the sidewalk, a grinning ghoul who may or may not actually exist.

Some alcoholics describe coming into sobriety as a metamorphosis. Others have said it is closer to a molting, where they've shucked off their old skins and exist now, wet and radiant and alive, in new ones.

For the first time in my life, I felt like I was filling empty spaces.

4

I promised Detective Aiello that I would head out for West Virginia first thing in the morning—a promise that felt like a lie even as I said it—then I disconnected the call. Across the parking lot, a group of people stood outside the rectory doors of the First United Methodist Church, most of them smoking cigarettes. Emily Pearson was among them, checking something on her cell phone. I watched them until my wristwatch said it was seven o'clock, and they began to file one by one into the rectory's basement for our nightly Alcoholics Anonymous meeting.

Ninety-six days sober—but, as the saying goes, who's counting?

Five minutes later, I was speeding toward my apartment, a bottle of Ketel One wrapped in brown paper on the seat beside me.

I saw her, *Jamie. She is* now *dead.*

At the time, I just assumed Dennis had been talking about our mother.

I was wrong.

CHAPTER TWO

MIA TOMASINA AND THE
SUNSHINE DEVIL GIRL

1

Around the same time I was doing the Detox Boogie on the floor of the rehab facility in Akron, Ohio, an avant-garde filmmaker living in Los Angeles named Mia Tomasina had just sat through a showing of her most celebrated film, *Dead Rabbit*, and was stepping out into the back alley behind the theater to smoke a joint before the Q&A session began.

"Hey. Hey, there! Do you come here a lot?"

Mia looked up from her cell phone, joint smoldering between her lips. A crumbling brick wall dressed in ivy ran the length of the alley. Mia didn't see the woman until she peeled away from the wall, her profile gliding into the sickly orange nimbus of a lamppost's light out on the sidewalk. She was swarthy and feline, something summoned into existence by a collaboration of shadows. Something, Mia instantly thought, not to be trusted.

Mia plucked the joint from her mouth and said, "Who's there?"

"Do you come here a lot?" the woman said again. "What's your name?"

"My name is on that little chalkboard in the lobby," Mia said.

The woman laughed. She scissored the air with two fingers. "You mind if I grab a toke?"

"I'm not really in the habit of swapping spit with strangers," Mia said, which, she'd be the first to admit, wasn't altogether true. What she'd *meant* was she wasn't in the habit of swapping spit with strangers who looked like they were in the habit of prowling parking lots and back alleys for a fix.

"Aw, come on, sis. Don't be like that."

Fuck it, Mia thought, and extended what was left of the joint in the woman's direction.

The woman crossed the alley, putting her bony hips to work, and plucked the joint from between Mia's fingers. Her cut-off jeans were so short Mia glimpsed a bruised sliver of ass cheek when she pirouetted before her, hands arched above her head like a ballerina's. Mia couldn't tell if she had once been pretty or not.

"Yeah, sis, I think I seen you round here before. You must come here a lot."

Mia just smiled at the woman. She'd never been here before in her life.

"Don't you even wanna know *my* name?" the woman asked, still pirouetting. The glowing red tip of the joint rotated in the air as she twirled.

"Sure, why not," Mia said. "What's your name?"

"Sunshine," said the woman. "Sunshine Devil Girl."

"What is that, Polish?"

Sunshine Devil Girl laughed again. Handed Mia back the smoldering stub of her joint. Mia immediately pitched it in a puddle on the pavement, where it sizzled, *sssst*.

"I'm psychic, you know," Sunshine Devil Girl told her. Mia had sunk to the concrete steps leading up to the theater's fire exit by this point, and Sunshine Devil Girl placed a ratty sneaker on the step between Mia's thighs. "Does that bother you?"

"Your foot near my crotch?"

"No, dummy. That I'm psychic."

"No. That doesn't bother me."

"It doesn't bother you that I can see your future?"

"It's not my future I'm worried about."

Sunshine Devil Girl drew her face closer to Mia's. Her eyes were too wide and her pupils looked to be two different sizes, as if she was suffering from a concussion or some other head injury. She wasn't very pretty at all, Mia decided—the girl's face was too sallow, her complexion ravaged by a lifetime of drug abuse and volatile boyfriends. There was a disconcerting sore at the corner of her mouth, which didn't help things.

"*Everybody's* worried about their future, sis," Sunshine Devil Girl told her, rather solemnly.

It was Mia's turn to laugh.

"Seriously, bro," Sunshine Devil Girl went on, ignoring her laughter. "I know what I'm talking about. I've got this gift. You can't bullshit me."

"Okay," she said, hoisting one shoulder in a halfhearted shrug. "But I'm no bro, bro. I'm sis, remember?"

Sunshine Devil Girl would not be sidetracked. "Let me tell you your future. If you're not afraid to hear the truth, it should be no big thing, chicken wing."

"No, thanks. I got no cash on me."

"I don't do it for *money*," she said. "I mean, if you had a pack of smokes, I'd take 'em. Or another joint. I'm not a jerk. And I'd do *other* things for money. I mean, I'll eat pussy or whatever. But I never tell someone their future in exchange for payment. It's bad fucking karma."

"Yeah, hon, you look like the poster child for good karma," Mia said.

Sunshine Devil Girl frowned. Or at least Mia thought she did. "You don't gotta be a cunt about it, sis."

"Whoa, okay," Mia said, holding up both hands in surrender.

"Seriously. Come on, now. Don't be a dick."

"Fair enough," Mia said. "If you don't do it for money, what do you do it for?"

"Posterity."

Mia's laugh was a bit more tempered this time. She started wondering where this woman had come from, how she'd just happened to materialize out of the darkness here in the back alley of this old theater. There was something on the front of her too-small T-shirt—a graphic of a Ferris wheel with a grinning cartoon sun above it. The sun was wearing sunglasses, the phrase *¿Que pasa, amigo?* printed beneath it. *The fuck does the sun need sunglasses for?* Mia thought randomly.

"Come on, sis," Sunshine Devil Girl persisted. "Is it because you're scared?" She bent down and brought her face within mere inches of Mia's, and Mia could smell the marijuana on her breath. Something dirtier, too—a thing that goes down deep. The crusty sore at the corner of her mouth looked like a tiny tortoise shell. "You're scared, aren't you, sis?"

Mia just shook her head. She kept her gaze leveled on the girl. After a moment, she said, "Okay, fine. What the hell. Go ahead and tell me my future. For *posterity*." And she held out her hands, palms up, for Sunshine Devil Girl to examine.

"Nah, sisterhood," Sunshine Devil Girl said, and she executed a clumsy roundhouse kick to Mia's hand. "I'm not a fucking *palm reader*. That's amateur-hour bullshit, sis. That ain't me."

"My mistake."

"See, you gotta *telescope* straight into someone's soul." She stretched her arms again above her head, her T-shirt rising high enough to expose a luminescent white panel of abdomen. Her bellybutton was pierced and looked like a doll's nose, her ribs like a bear trap. Then she brought her hands down in front of her face, each hand making a circle through which she peered at Mia with one eye. "Like looking through a telescope, all right. Or maybe it's like a drill, you know? One of those big spooky drills they use to get oil out of the ground? Only it's not the ground and it's not oil. You hear me?"

"Sure," Mia said.

"I'm talking about your body, sis."

"I hear you," Mia assured her.

"And your hole is so big I could see it from the street," Sunshine Devil Girl said. "Like, from the far end of the alley, even."

"That's pretty descriptive."

"I'm being serious, sisterhood. That's why I just had to come over and jaw with you, you know? Everyone's got an opening— like, a hole straight through to the center of them. Some are small as a pinprick."

"But mine's not," Mia said.

"Yours is like a fucking tunnel in the side of a mountain, sis. And that means I gotta be extra careful. I gotta go far enough down to puncture and pass through the bubble of your destiny without bursting it. I'm like a surgeon that way. Or maybe a plumber. Gotta go straight down to the very bottom of the well. Thing is, I don't wanna fall in and get stuck."

Mia smiled as the girl peered at her through the telescope of her hands. But the smile felt strained and too much like a grimace. That comment about going down to the well? It unnerved her. There was suddenly a bad taste in her mouth, too. Where'd this fucking junkie come from, anyway?

It's not like a telescope and it's not like a drill, spoke up a voice in the back of Mia's head. *It's closer to a camera lens, which is fitting, but it's also something else. Something darker. Something more dangerous. Something that goes straight through the center, all right...*

"Ain't you gonna ask me what I see?" said Sunshine Devil Girl.

Mia cleared her throat and said, "What do you see?"

"It's bleak as fuck, sis. I'll be honest with you."

"What is it, exactly?"

"That's just it—*bleak as fuck*. You hear me? It's all over you. Filling you up like shit water through a pipe."

"All right," Mia said, and stood up. "Thanks for the insight."

At Mia's back, the fire door opened and the event coordinator poked his burly head out. "You got five minutes, Mia."

"Thanks."

The coordinator shifted his attention to Sunshine Devil Girl, who was still studying Mia through the circles of her hands. *Telescope.* To Mia, the guy said, "This chick bugging you?"

"It's cool," Mia said.

"I'm not doin' nothing, dickhead," Sunshine Devil Girl said to the guy, still gazing with one eye through her hands at Mia. "Leave me the fuck alone."

"Give a holler if you need anything," the event coordinator said to Mia, then vanished back behind the door.

"Listen, I gotta go," Mia said, reaching into the rear pocket of her jeans.

"But what about your future?"

"You told me. Bleak as fuck, remember? Thanks for that." She extended a few crinkled bills to the girl.

"What's that for?"

"Not for telling me my future," Mia said. "That would be bad karma."

"Then what's it *for*, sis?"

"For this enlightening conversation."

Sunshine Devil Girl suddenly adopted the countenance of a wary forest critter, some weak and helpless thing that only knew how to eat, sleep, fuck, shit, and sense danger. Yet in the end, she plucked the bills from Mia's hand and wedged them into the too-tight pocket of her jean shorts.

"Have a good night," Mia said, pulling open the exit door.

"Wait!"

Mia turned around. The glow from the nearby lamppost made Sunshine Devil Girl's skin shimmer with an otherworldly radiance. Sickly...yet somehow beatific, too.

"Something's coming, and it's gonna cross your path," Sunshine Devil Girl told her. "Whatever you been running from, it's about to catch up to you. So keep an eye open so you don't miss it. You get me, sis?"

For a moment, Mia could not move. She stood there with one hand clutching the door handle, the other driving her fingernails into the tender meat of her palm. A sudden, curious needling at the back of her brain urged her to bolt down the alley, to jump in her Jeep and get the fuck out of Van Nuys, and not look back.

"Sis? You get me?"

The spell broken, Mia blinked her eyes, shook her head to clear it. She nodded, suddenly feeling like *she* was the train wreck in this little duo. How'd *that* happen? One of those M. Night Shyamalan twist endings.

"Sure," she told the girl. "I'll keep an eye out. Thanks."

"You got it," Sunshine Devil Girl said, already receding back into the shadows of the alley. She blew Mia a kiss. "Much love, sis."

Mia Tomasina watched her go until the darkness of the alley swallowed her up.

2

She was just a junkie with a creative streak, but something about that encounter resonated with Mia. There was no logical reason to be afraid, nothing specific in what the woman had said to trigger anything. Yet she couldn't shake it, couldn't let it go. She spent the following week in L.A., taking meetings, quarrelling with distribution companies, discussing imaginative ways to coax money from would-be financiers, and holding bitch sessions about the industry with her fellow filmmakers over sake bombs at Nagoya. Yet Sunshine Devil Girl's warning persisted: *Whatever you been running from, it's about to catch up to you. You get me, sis?*

It got to the point where she started to ascribe meaning to innocuous things—the bark of Ms. Lopez's dog in the apartment complex every night; the days when her mail came an hour later than it should; the patterns in traffic signals. One evening, after meeting with an actor friend of hers at a bar in Long Beach, she was driving home when the power went out up and down the boulevard on either side of her. The houses all went dark, the traffic lights died, a car alarm started blaring somewhere in the distance. Panicked that she might miss something momentous, she pulled her Jeep over onto the side of the road, climbed out, and stood in the middle of that desolate, powerless street. Looking for...*what*, exactly?

She didn't know.

And too much of this was liable to drive her crazy.

She was booked at a film festival in Utah, but when her flight into Salt Lake City was delayed *twice*, she began to wonder if this was some sort of sign. Were the gods transmitting code to her via airline delays? Still, it was good to leave Los Angeles, because maybe that meant she'd leave her newfound hypersensitivity behind, too.

Yet while at the festival, she found herself assigning weight to seemingly inconsequential things, much as she had done back in L.A.—the number on the door of her hotel room (a18), the timeslot she was given to show her film (11:11, which was a time almost *too* random to be random; it must mean *something*), the curious biplane that kept sweeping across the desert sky every day at noon as if to alert her to some impending catastrophe. Was there some deeper meaning embedded here? Something she'd been warned to keep an eye out for?

"Whiten your teeth with Crest," said the woman on the hotel TV, and Mia thought, *What?*

When she returned to L.A., she had lunch at an outdoor Japanese restaurant with a friend's mom, a woman who was supposedly clairvoyant or some such thing. She was seeking confirmation, or perhaps whatever the opposite of confirmation was, hoping that this woman might untangle the wires she had somehow unwittingly gotten herself knotted up in. She told the woman, whose name was Elsie, about the encounter with Sunshine Devil Girl behind the theater in Van Nuys, and what this girl had said to her.

Elsie laughed garrulously after hearing the story, then affected a pitiable, almost condescending tone as she patted the top of Mia's hand from across the table. Elsie's fingers were bejeweled with all manner of cheap titanium rings, and the sleeve of bracelets along her wrists jangled and chimed like coins spewing from a slot machine.

"Mia, dear, are you honestly saying that some strung-out junkie lurking in an alley in *Van Nuys* has spooked you this badly? Sweetheart, why on earth are you getting so worked up over this?"

It was a good question. One Mia didn't have an answer for. One she kept asking herself.

"It must have been some act," Elsie concluded.

"I don't think it was an act."

"Darling, it's *always* an act."

Mia wasn't so sure.

"Come on, come on," Elsie ultimately beckoned, wiggling her fingers at Mia. (Elsie was already on her third gin and tonic by this point.) "Throw those dainty little paws on up here."

Mia placed her hands on the table and Elsie twisted her wrists so that Mia's palms faced the sky. Gently, Elsie raked her long acrylic fingernails across Mia's palms. It tickled. Mia's own fingernails had been gnawed to nubs, the remnants of black nail polish on some. She felt suddenly embarrassed of her hands.

"Now *there's* a story," Elsie said, running a thumb along the crude speed bump of a scar along Mia's left wrist. Clearly self-inflicted. Mia tugged that hand away, self-conscious of the old wound.

"Right hand for females for reading birth traits," Elsie explained. "Left hand for females for reading the future."

"Is the future the same as destiny?"

Elsie seemed somewhat perplexed by the question. "It's what your future *holds*, Mia, though nothing is set in stone."

"The future, then," Mia said, reluctantly placing her left hand back on the table.

Elsie studied Mia's palm.

Amateur-hour bullshit, Mia thought, and pictured Sunshine Devil Girl pirouetting in some gloomy back alley at the edge of the world.

"Well, see, so this is good news," Elsie said.

"What?"

"Well, look. You see, your love line is long, and you've got two very distinct marriage lines. See here? See? Is there perhaps a certain gentleman in your life at the moment? Someone special?"

Mia laughed. There hadn't been a gentleman in her life since Vince Overmeyer had coaxed her hand down the front of his pants while in the back seat of his parents' car when she was still in high school.

That had been the first and last *gentleman* she'd ever had in her life, thank you very much.

"I don't think this is about romance," Mia told her. "Isn't there, like, a lifeline or something? Something that will tell me if I'm about to die?"

Elsie gawped at her. It was almost comical.

"You're not about to *die*, Mia. Good Lord, the stuff that's in your brain! Is that where all those weird movie ideas come from?"

"How do I know what I should be looking out for?"

"You *won't* know because there's *nothing there*, dear."

"Then why do I feel so certain that you're wrong and that junkie chick in the alley was right?"

Elsie withdrew her hands across the table. If Mia had offended her, that hadn't been her intention. Elsie finished her drink, then stared with disquieting intensity at Mia. She had red freckles in her hazel irises.

"Can I speak candidly with you, dear?"

"Of course," Mia said.

"I don't think you need to be consorting with me or anyone else who deals in the spiritual realm," Elsie said. "I do, however, have the name of an *excellent* psychotherapist."

3

Around the time I was attending my third Alcoholics Anonymous meeting, having been clean and sober for over ninety days, sipping a cup of lukewarm coffee while seated in an uncomfortable folding chair next to Emily Pearson in the basement of the First United Methodist Church on Mill Street in downtown Akron, Mia Tomasina was checking into a rather undignified motel in Lexington,

Kentucky. The room was paid for by the Fans of Feral Female Cinema (a horrible name for an organization, Mia thought) and was part of her stipend for attending yet another showing of *Dead Rabbit*, followed by yet another Q&A. It seemed she made her living more and more these days talking about her movies as opposed to making them. She had hopes, based on the success of her latest film, *Bulletproof*, which had been acquired by one of the notable streaming services of our time, that she might be able to raise half a million dollars for a future production she'd been kicking around, because she was ready to focus all of her attention on her work. Although she'd obsessed over what the strange woman behind the theater in Van Nuys had said to her for nearly two months, she had ultimately climbed out of that strange hole to rejoin the land of the living. That was it: the Land of the Living. A proper fucking noun.

It was a two-day event, beginning on the first evening with a dinner at some restaurant that had clearly once been a Chili's. Perhaps thirty members of the Fans of Feral Female Cinema film group were in attendance, most of them heavyset and odorously off-putting. (There were one or two younger women among them whom Mia found attractive, but she'd learned long ago not to mix pleasure with… well, whatever the hell this was.) The event was tolerable at best, but went downhill when Mia suggested the group rename themselves the Fans of Feral Female Films to at least comport with the whole F alliteration. This proposal was met with blank stares, as if she'd just spoken in some foreign tongue. Anyway, it was nothing a few Scotch and sodas couldn't handle.

The following evening, the group showed a print of *Dead Rabbit* in a dilapidated old theater. When she went outside to smoke a jay before the Q&A, she could see the lights of a carnival in the distance. She watched the great Ferris wheel crank lazily against the night sky, nearly lulling her into a trance. It reminded her of Sunshine Devil

Girl's T-shirt. Before heading back into the theater, she closed one eye and traced the outline of the Ferris wheel with one finger: a circle.

"My movies," she said, "are these really angry, really depraved things. That's a direct reflection of me as a filmmaker. You walk in midscene, you'd think you're watching a snuff film. Or a Nazi propaganda film. Or just someone's psychedelic nightmare imprinted on celluloid. I tried doing the commercial sellout thing but I didn't have the spine for it. Or maybe I had too much spine for it. I don't know. The industry sucks and the people are about as genuine as a three-dollar bill. Anyway, I've never played well with people. Fuck 'em, I say. I'll make my own way."

The women stood and applauded.

As part of their appreciation, they gave her a gift basket of cheap screw-top wine, a keychain, and a Fans of Feral Female Cinema T-shirt (*Official Member*, it said over the left breast). Their questions had been pedantic and grating, or maybe Mia just hadn't been in the mood. Whatever the case, she was relieved when it was all over, and she was able to climb back into her rental car and head back to the motel. She'd be on a flight to L.A. first thing in the morning.

Yet despite her exhaustion, she found herself detouring off the highway and heading in the direction of the carnival, where she spent the next half hour strolling along the midway while picking apart a bright pink ball of cotton candy.

And that was when it happened.

A man stood among the crowd, staring at the carousel as it went round and round. Calliope music shrilled while little kids waved to their parents as the intricately carved horses went up and down, up and down.

The way he stared at those kids on the carousel. Hungrily.

A tornado came blasting through her cerebral cortex. Shrapnel went flying.

She managed to fumble her phone out of her back pocket and snap a few hasty photos before the man vanished into the crowd. She hurried across the midway in pursuit, shoving people aside, scanning the crowd for any indication of where the man had gone. But she could not find him.

Something's coming, and it's gonna cross your path. Whatever you been running from, it's about to catch up to you. So keep an eye open so you don't miss it. You get me, sis?

She got her, all right. Jesus Christ, she got her *now*.

4

Around the time I received the phone call from Detective Aiello informing me of my mother's passing and my brother's peculiar, half-naked romp along the shoulder of a highway, Mia Tomasina went online to locate a lost but not forgotten childhood friend. This man's name was Clay Willis. She hadn't spoken to Clay in many, many years, and wasn't sure he would be happy to hear from her now. She could locate no phone number for him, but she did manage to find an email address.

> *From: deadrabbitmia@tomasinafilm.com*
> *To: cassiusclaywillis@chromemail.com*
> *Subject: hello from planet childhood*

> Clay,
>
>   *I wish I could be there right now as you read this to see the look on your face. Am I a ghost? Am I a figment of your imagination? What I am is a dispatch from your childhood. Remember me?*

I've attached a photo to this email. It was taken the other day in Lexington, Kentucky. No context, I just want you to look at it. If it means something to you, hit me back.

I know how this sounds. I really do.

All my love,

Mia Tomasina

The arrowhead cursor hovered over the SEND button for an eternity. Was this madness? Was this stepping over a line? Was *this* her destiny?

In the end, she hit SEND.

So be it.

CHAPTER THREE

A RELUCTANT
HOMECOMING

1

For nearly two decades, I had been coasting along on a trajectory that, by design, kept me a safe distance from Black Mouth. There were several reasons for this, although I rarely reflected on what any of them might be. That I was running from something occurred to me only on those fleeting occasions when I'd scream myself awake from a nightmare as vivid and substantial as a pair of hands tightening around my throat.

Yet here I was, the Mav's radial tires gobbling up miles of blacktop, windows down, motoring along inside a wind tunnel that was maybe a jet engine, maybe a cyclone. An anonymous interstate that wound through productive little towns, a bumper crop of swimming pools and doublewide trailers, roadside chicken joints and boxcar motels, and roadkill with their bellies unzipped that lay marinating in a goulash of silvery entrails.

My skin reeked. My body felt clammy. I imagined each of my exhalations as a toxic gray fog sputtering from my parched, quivering lips. It was much, much later in the day than I had intended it to be when I'd made my promise to Detective Aiello to come out here. It was almost evening.

At one point during my drive, I pulled into the parking lot of a strip mall and had a drink at a Mexican restaurant. Had two. Just to take the edge off.

At another point, I pulled over onto the shoulder of the road, scrambled out of the car, and puked up my guts into the tall white fronds of grass. A van had pulled up about fifty yards ahead of me, and there was a boy no more than seven years old taking a whiz in the underbrush. He stared at me as I wiped vomit from my mouth with my shirtsleeve then staggered back to my car.

I had spent the previous night a hostage in my apartment, staring at the bottle of Ketel One I had purchased immediately after my phone call with Detective Aiello. It stood on the kitchen counter, its brown paper bag like a pair of pants it had dropped to its ankles. Enticing me. My cell phone, resting atop a stack of paperback novels next to the couch, rang a handful of times during this standoff. It was the same caller each time; I knew this without having to look at the caller ID. Emily Pearson, a fellow Twelve Stepper. First meeting, we had exchanged phone numbers. To give a call if one of us failed to show up. A lifeline.

But it wasn't Emily Pearson I was thinking about in that moment. I was thinking about Black Mouth. I was *perspiring* about it, *trembling* about it. The prospect of returning to that place brought with it a flood of emotion that nearly crippled me. I was trying to fool myself into believing that I could pick up Dennis from that police station in Sutton's Quay and never have to set foot in the Mouth. It was possible, wasn't it? I could hire someone to sell the house remotely, couldn't I? Or pay an arsonist to burn the fucker to the ground. Similarly, I could handle my mother's burial arrangements from afar; there was no need for me to do any of that in person, was there? I'd been deflecting my entire adult life. Black Mouth could call me home, but I didn't have to obey.

I was also thinking about Dennis. He'd spent his entire life in that suffocating little farmhouse. Now that our mother was dead, where would he go? Were there government-funded programs for people like him? What about his doctors? People with my brother's condition generally had a host of medical concerns, and were often dead of a heart attack before they were forty. That wasn't something I was prepared to deal with.

(Of course, there were other things waiting for me back home. Dark things. Things with cold hands and long memories. Things I'd kept packed away in the blackest recess of my mind all these years, that now seemed to be reaching out for me all over again.)

I'm as big as you are, said the bottle of vodka. *Bigger, even.*

I'd like to say I concluded that evening by cranking the cap off that bottle of vodka and pouring it straight down the kitchen sink, but that's not what happened. I recalled a guy from the foundry who'd once claimed that he'd been able to quit smoking by carrying a pack of cigarettes around with him every minute of the day. Whenever he'd get the urge to smoke, he was comforted by the fact that he knew he *could*—that at any moment, if the cravings got too bad, he could just peel the cellophane right off that pack of smokes and go to town— and for some reason, that ease of access, that knowledge that he could do it whenever he wanted because his cigarettes were *right there with him*, kept the craziness from infiltrating his brain. It kept the monsters at bay. It allowed him to delay smoking one of those cancer sticks indefinitely. He just kept saying to himself, *one more minute, one more minute, I'll go one more minute, then I'll have a smoke*, and somehow that was enough to get him across the finish line.

My plan was to stow the bottle of Ketel One in the trunk of the

Maverick, *right there with me*, keeping the craziness from infiltrating my brain. Keeping the monsters at bay. Together, we would speed toward oblivion. Toward the Mouth.

That wasn't what happened.

I drank. And then I popped an Ativan and washed it down with some more booze.

And a thing, manlike, detached itself from the darkness.

2

In the summer of my eleventh year, a monster came to Black Mouth. It came in the night, slinking below the sightline of normal folks, destined to arrive at the threshold of my youth. Perhaps it sought me out the way a bloodhound tracks a scent. Or perhaps it was sheer happenstance, a flip of a coin, a flutter of distant butterfly wings. Events in our lives often have meaning because we choose to give them meaning. Whatever the case, it arrived in the way monsters sometimes do: as a creature in need.

A clash of thunder, a deluge of rain. Some indistinct sense of *wrongness* roused me from a fitful sleep. I rolled over in a bed damp with sweat just as a flash of lightning pulsed against the bedroom window. Briefly, Dennis's silhouette stood in sharp relief against the dazzle of a storm-churned sky. It was the hottest summer in a hundred years, or so the old-timers in the Quay attested, and Dennis and I had taken to sleeping with our bedroom window open because the old farmhouse's HVAC unit was on the fritz. Again.

"Dennis," I said, sitting up in bed. My sheets were soggy with dream-sweat, and the breeze coming through the open window on the storm felt good against my hot, sticky flesh. "What are you doing over there? Get back in bed."

Dennis didn't answer, didn't get back in bed. That was Dennis's way. He only pressed his face against the screen. Rainwater rushed in, sprinkling against his face and chest, raindrops tapping along the windowsill. I climbed out of bed and joined my nine-year-old brother at the window. The floorboards were wet beneath my feet.

"It's just a thunderstorm," I told him, a half-whisper. Maybe the storm had frightened him. Maybe something else had. "Go back to bed."

Dennis was staring out into the yard, across the dark field of desiccated alfalfa toward the edge of our property. It was where the black crest of trees rose up like something massive and prehistoric and deceivingly alive.

I saw it—a flicker of tangerine light dancing between the warped slats of the barn at the edge of our property. Firelight.

Someone was in there.

"Maybe it's Dad," I said, though I didn't believe it. He and Mom had gotten into it earlier that night; she'd taken a Valium and a glass of wine and gone to bed while he'd sped off in his ink-black Pontiac Firebird and hadn't yet come back. The 'Bird wasn't in its usual spot, which was the sandy patch of driveway that separated the farmhouse from the field in a wide loop. Sometimes he stayed away for days at a time, depending on how drunk or ornery he got after a fight with Mom.

"Stay here," I told Dennis, then went to my dresser. I pulled on a pair of cargo shorts and a T-shirt. Dennis didn't even turn to watch me sneak out of the room; he just kept his round face pressed against the screen, as if he might at any moment disperse into a million tiny pieces and pass right through it and out into the night.

I went down the hall and eased my parents' bedroom door open a crack—*rrrik!* I heard my mother's drug-addled snores, glimpsed her pale white form sprawled out across the bed in the darkness. The room stank of those terrible hand-rolled cigarettes my parents often smoked behind each other's backs.

I pulled the door closed and continued down the hall, down the stairs, down into the foyer of the tiny farmhouse where the back door led out onto a screened-in porch. My sneakers were there by the door next to Dennis's sandals—Dennis only ever wore sandals, no matter what—and I climbed into them, quiet as a monk. Turned the deadbolt, *thunk*, then crept out onto the porch.

The rain had cooled the air but had increased the humidity; each inhalation felt like I was sucking oxygen through a damp rag. I pushed open the screen door and peered around the side of the house, wondering if the Firebird might be parked out there in a different spot, but it wasn't. My father wasn't home.

At the far end of the field, that eerie firelight continued to flicker and dance between the slats of the old barn. My dad used that barn to work on neighbors' cars and trucks—it was his "place of business," as he called it, and he didn't like anyone else going out there without him—but he hadn't had any work in weeks. Lately, I knew he had only been going out there to drink, listen to the radio, and smoke those awful-smelling cigarettes.

I stole a breath, stepped down off the porch, and crossed the field. The barn was a massive wooden structure, two stories high, fronted by a pair of corrugated metal doors on two rolling tracks. The doors were usually kept closed at night to prevent animals from getting in, but tonight there was a sliver of space separating them, big enough for a person to slip through.

I entered the barn. Forms took shape—my father's automotive equipment, hydraulic jacks, chests of tools, pneumatic hoses, clutter. Beyond were large boxes of automotive supplies, items he had ordered in bulk from warehouses clear across the country. Romantic, faraway places with romantic, faraway names—Rose City, Elkhorn, Woodvine,

Detroit. There were bales of hay back here, too, because we harvested it throughout the summer then baled it prior to fall, when my father would sell it to other farms or to commercial businesses (who usually used them for Halloween displays). We shared the tractor and baler with Ike Rosemont, another Black Mouth holdout, but my father hadn't used it this year, and the hay inside the barn was old and smelly and from last season. Those bales were stacked toward the center of the barn, a staircase of hay blocks, and it was just beyond those bales that the fire burned.

I crept closer, slinking between my father's boxes of automotive supplies and spools of pneumatic hose, and when I arrived at the wall of hay, my heart was thudding in my throat.

A man stood hunched over a small fire that burned within a wreath of dark rocks on the barn's dirt floor. He was completely naked, his body glistening with rainwater, his flesh devil-red in the firelight. There were clothes spread out on one of the bales of hay, sodden and wet, though close enough to the fire to catch some heat and dry out.

The man looked up at me and I jumped back.

"Hey, there," he said. His voice was smooth as silk, and he didn't sound startled by my presence in the least. He held up his hands to show that he was harmless. "Didn't mean to scare you."

"Who are you?"

"I'm nobody," said the man, and I could see that he wore something over his right eye. An eye patch. "I'm no trouble at all. I'm just a guy passing through."

"What are you doing in our barn?"

"Got caught in the storm. Thought I'd come in and dry off. Maybe spend the night, wait for the storm to pass."

I shook my head. "You can't do that. If my dad finds you…" I let the silence that followed speak for itself.

"Is your dad home?"

"No," I said, then immediately regretted it. "I mean, he'll be home any minute. He'll see your fire."

"All the way out here?"

"Yeah. I saw it from the house."

"Well," he said, crouching even lower on his haunches. He winced noticeably, as if in pain. "That's no good. I certainly don't want any trouble from your dad." He stood then, his body shiny and the color of magma. I shied away from his nakedness, but then looked closer. There was a good-sized scar along his flank, the scar tissue serpentine and angry-looking.

"What happened to your side?"

The man glanced down at his old injury as if he'd forgotten it was there. "This?" he said. "This is a dark bit of business. Maybe I'll tell you about it some other time."

"Does it hurt?"

"Back when it happened. Not so much anymore."

"What about your, um…" I let the question die in the air, deciding it was too impolite to continue.

The corners of his mouth elongated in a wide grin. Or maybe it was a grimace. It was hard to tell in the firelight which was playing with his features, casting him in heavy shadow. I couldn't guess his age, couldn't make out anything distinguishable about his face from where I stood, other than that grin and that eye patch. His hair was long and dark, slicked back on his head and dripping with rainwater, except for spidery tendrils hanging down in front of his face.

"You want to know about my eye," he said, completing the question for me. His accent wasn't from here. It sounded different, somehow. Cleaner. He articulated each of his words, like someone accustomed to speaking on a stage in front of an audience.

I couldn't bring myself to respond verbally so I just bounced my head up and down.

"It was just a silly accident, really. I suppose I've lived through worse in my time." He was suddenly closer to me, within a few feet of the half-wall of hay bales that separated us. "What's your name, my friend?"

"Jamie Warren," I said, then instantly regretted it just like I'd regretted telling him my father wasn't at home a moment ago.

"Are you a dealmaker, Mr. Warren?"

"I…I don't know…"

"Well, let's see. How about we cut a deal, you and me?" He proffered one shiny red hand in the air, as if weighing an invisible currency. "If you'll bring me some food and something to drink, I'll put out this fire and *disappear*." He made a circular motion with his hand as he underscored the word *disappear*. "This way, neither of us gets into any trouble with your old man."

"Some food and something to drink," I said.

"That's it," he said. I realized he was holding out that gleaming, fire-lit hand for me to seal the deal. "That is all I need. Do we have an arrangement?"

I considered this for maybe a full minute. He didn't rush me, didn't even move—just stood there with his hand extended, his singular eye shining in the glow of the fire.

"Okay," I said, and gripped his hand. It was warm and moist, and I imagined I could feel the heat from the fire radiating inside his flesh.

"All right, then." He released my hand. That wide grin was stretching across his face once more. I watched as he retreated back to the fire. "Thank you, Mr. Warren."

Then I was running back through the field, back through the house, into the kitchen. I filled a shopping bag with leftovers from the fridge, then tossed in a can of my dad's Budweiser for good measure. I considered swiping some of my dad's work clothes that were hanging in the laundry room, but decided it was safe just to steal a dry towel from the shelf. I stuffed the towel in the bag with the food, then bolted back out across the field to the barn.

"Here," I said, and reached over the half-wall of baled hay to set the bag of food on the floor.

"You are a *wonder*," the man said. He crawled over to the bag on his hands and feet, peered inside. Reached in, dug out one of the Tupperware containers. Held it up so he could study it before the glow of the fire, then he pried the lid off, drew out a piece of fried chicken, and tore into it like a man who'd just been rescued from a prisoner-of-war camp.

"It's all we had," I said, by way of apology.

"Fit for a king," said the man. While he chewed, he fished around in the bag until he came out with the can of Bud. He popped the tab and took a few glugs. I watched as his Adam's apple ratcheted up and down along the contour of his throat. When he was done, he sucked air in between his teeth then unleashed a belch that sounded like a creaking door. "Want some?" he said, and extended the beer can in my direction.

I shook my head. I knew what that poison did to my dad and wanted no part of it.

The man nodded, took another sip, then set the can down on the ground. He screwed it into the dirt so that it wouldn't tip over. Then he dug the towel out of the bag, and stared at it.

"In case you wanted to dry off," I told him.

"You're a thoughtful boy." He patted himself dry with the towel.

"Maybe if you just put the fire out, you can stay in here until the storm is over."

He paused in mid-dry, the towel pressed over his groin. The intensity of his one-eyed stare was like physical contact.

"That is very kind of you," he said, and I could tell that he meant it. "You've been very good to me, Mr. Warren. I'd like to repay you."

"You don't have to do that," I told him. He didn't look like a guy who had much money.

He tied the towel around his waist then hurried around to the other side of the bonfire, where his clothes were drying on the blocks of hay. He rummaged through the pockets of a damp pair of black pants until he found what he was looking for.

A deck of playing cards.

"Do you want to see a magic trick?" he asked.

This caught me completely off guard, and it took me a second to find my voice. "Sure," I said.

"Great. Just let me see if I can remember how to finagle this old chestnut." He fanned out the deck of cards, facedown, then held them out in front of me. "All right, go on, Mr. Warren," he said. "Pick one."

"I know this trick."

"No," he said, and something in the tone of his voice went flat. "Not this trick."

I stared at the cards, waiting to see if any one in particular jumped out at me. Finally, I selected one and held it against my chest. I asked if I should look at it.

"Of course," he said. "That's part of the trick."

I looked at it.

The card was blank.

I showed it to him. "This card's all messed up. There's nothing on it."

"Is it?" the man said. He was close enough to me now so that I could see the individual pegs of his teeth, the vague creases around his mouth, the stitching in his eye patch. I caught a whiff of him, too—what smelled like perhaps a month's worth of unwashed flesh. "That card represents your destiny, Mr. Warren. Perhaps in time, if you are vigilant and have faith, it may reveal itself to you."

I just stared at the blank card in my hand, not understanding any of what he'd just said.

He tucked the remaining cards back into the pocket of his pants, then crouched down before the fire again. I watched the muscles in his chest and arms flex as he rubbed his hands near the flames then swiped the rainwater from his arms. The sound the droplets of water made as they struck the fire was like oil sizzling in a cast iron skillet.

"It's time we say goodnight, Mr. Warren," he said, rotating around the fire so that his back was now facing me. "Perhaps we'll meet again."

When I didn't move he looked over at me. The rest of his body was suddenly motionless before the fire, the way a deer in the forest might freeze when you step on a twig. I stared at the splayed palms of his hands, long-fingered and radiant white in the dancing glow of the fire. His solitary eye reflected the flames, making it seem as though the fire was actually coming from inside him.

"Go on now," he instructed, his eye aflame.

I retreated toward the barn doors, my own eyes trained on the man until the composition of automotive boxes and tool chests conspired to block him out. My last glimpse of him that night was when he peeled the eye patch from his face and rubbed with a set of chicken-bone fingers at whatever lay buried beneath it.

Back outside, the rain had tapered off, and I took my time trudging back to the house through the sodden fields. When I reached the dirt track that served as our bastardized driveway, I glanced up at the house and saw Dennis's pale moon face still hanging in our bedroom window.

I went inside, turned the deadbolt, shucked off my sneakers, then went back upstairs. In our bedroom, I peeled off all my clothes except for my briefs then joined Dennis at the window. He still had his face pressed into the screen.

"There's a man in there," I told him. "A strange man. He was wet and hungry. I brought him some food. I think he might be lost or something. He doesn't sound like he's from around here." After a moment, I added, "He'll leave after the storm passes. Dad will never know."

And as we stood there, I saw the firelight go dark between the slats of the barn.

I crawled into bed, pulling the covers up to my neck despite the humidity in the air. I must have dozed then for a time, because when I woke up, the sky outside our bedroom window had a different texture, and I had that early morning feeling in my gut.

Dennis was still standing at the window, face pressed against the screen, looking out.

3

Sutton's Quay was the sort of West Virginia mountain town you didn't know existed until you met someone who had escaped from there. Narrow streets, A-frame houses piled one atop the other, a cluster of municipal buildings cowering in the lee of a vast wooded hillside. It had once been a prosperous mining community, but generations ago the old mine had collapsed, burying an entire contingent of coalminers alive and taking much of the western woods and a few of the ramshackle houses on the outskirts of town with it. The result was a massive crater in the earth, formidable as a canyon. The openings of all the old mineshafts were still down there, breaching the loose soil like prehistoric wormholes. In my youth, those mineshafts had mostly been obscured by foliage and by the trees that had learned to grow horizontally from the sloping embankments, each one bowing down toward the center of the crater. From the sky, people claimed those trees looked like fangs, and that the crater itself appeared as a vast, sneering maw in the countryside. It became known as Black Mouth.

My family's farm teetered on the edge of Black Mouth, our back field sloping down into its tamarack-studded throat. I was born a Black Mouth kid, as my father had been. And because that great pit in the earth was supposed to be haunted, Black Mouth kids by their very nature were not afraid.

I am now, I thought, with an irony like giddy terror.

The police station was a surprisingly modern brick building, with a cadre of flags drooping in the breezeless summer air. A middle-aged guy in a gray polo shirt and chinos sat smoking a cigarette on a bench beside a small flower garden. He stood as I approached, brushing ash off one leg of his pants.

"Jamie Warren?" His mouth was overpowered by a jet-black push-broom mustache. "I'm Detective Michael Aiello. We spoke on the phone."

"I'm sorry, I meant to get out here earlier," I began, trying not to stammer or slur my speech. I didn't much care for cops, and I felt this one could see straight through to the cowardly, drunken part of my soul. "I left Ohio as soon as I could. There were some things I had to take care of, some, uh, unexpected…"

"Look, no worries," Detective Aiello said, pitching his cigarette butt to the pavement. He twisted the sole of his shoe on it. "Come on around with me."

We entered the building through a side door and I followed Detective Aiello down an alabaster hallway lined with corkboards and into a bullpen of desks. An air of dry bustle permeated the place.

"Have you been back to the house yet?" Detective Aiello asked me. I began to stammer some response, but he cut me short: "Well, just so you're prepared, the place is in pretty bad shape. Like, it's literally falling apart. A shutter came off a window and nearly took an officer's head off when they were out there to retrieve your mother's body."

I felt a number of eyes on me as Detective Aiello led me through the bullpen and into an adjoining hallway. I paused in my stride when I realized he was leading me through lockup.

Does he know who I am? I wondered. *Is he playing with me? Surely there's a record of what happened in a filing cabinet or desk drawer somewhere in this place. A record of what we did. Does he know? Is he fucking with me on purpose?*

A row of cells lined the right-hand side of the cement hallway, each one of them empty except for the last one. At a much slower pace now, I followed Detective Aiello down the corridor toward that final cell.

Something fluttered out from the open door of the last cell. I watched it fall to the floor, where someone had drawn a circle in white chalk. Something about that circle resonated with me, though I couldn't figure out what it was. As I stared at that circle, a second object came spiraling out of the door and wafted to the floor. A third.

They were playing cards.

"Look who's here, Dennis," Detective Aiello said as we approached the open cell door.

My brother Dennis was thirty-three years old—two years younger than me—and he sat now behind a folding table in the middle of the jail cell, clutching a deck of playing cards in one oversized hand. He had just removed a card from the top of the deck and was about to cast it out into the hallway with the others when, at the sound of Aiello's voice, he looked up at me with his muddy gray eyes. His hand froze, the deuce of hearts clearly visible on the card pinched between his thumb and forefinger.

For a moment, I didn't think he recognized me. It had been four years since I'd last seen him, so I couldn't blame him.

"Dennis," I said.

Dennis's mouth thinned out to a firm, flat line. His stormy eyes narrowed. He dropped the remaining cards on the table, then hoisted his big body up from his seat. The chair legs grated along the cement floor.

"Dennis," I said again, my tongue sticking to the roof of my mouth. My whole body was trembling.

"Jamie. Warren. Is. Home," Dennis said...and then his whole face brightened. He galloped over to me and wrapped me up in his big arms. The force of his hug lifted me clear off the floor.

"It's good to see you, too, buddy," I said, my face smothered against his chest, "but you're crushing my ribs."

He released me, expelled a moist, excited breath in my face, then staggered backward. I looked him up and down—his unruly mop of black curls, his too-small Ninja Turtles T-shirt straining against the bulk of his belly, his stained cargo shorts. He wore clunky sandals on his feet, his thick, hairless legs as shapely as telephone poles.

I looked past him at the assortment of board games, DVDs, and stuffed animals that lay scattered on the cell bunk. Crayon drawings were taped to the cinderblock wall. Beneath the bunk was an old-school boom box, some relic from the 1980s.

"He's been staying in this jail cell?" I asked Detective Aiello.

"We had nowhere else to put him," Aiello said, shrugging. "A few of us went back to the house and got him some things so he'd feel more at home. I hope you don't mind. We didn't know how long it would take to get in touch with someone. With you. Anyway, he seems to like it. And the officers visit when they can. He's been eating all his meals with us in the break room. Everybody loves Dennis."

Dennis broke into a broad smile, the corners of his mouth glistening with moisture. His gray eyes sparkled.

I felt funny, like I was the butt of some complex joke. Or maybe it was that *these* people, these cops, were the butt of the joke—some grand cosmic charade that had unwittingly fooled them into thinking there was nothing terrible here, nothing out of the ordinary, nothing terrifying. That there was no dark, hopeless whirlwind at the center of all of this seemingly innocuous bullshit.

Dennis slapped his hands together, sharp as a whip crack. "Jamie Warren is *home!*"

"Yeah, buddy," I heard myself say. "Sure am."

4

I t was dark by the time we left the police station. I hit the highway and pulled into the drive-thru of a fast-food joint, where I ordered us a sack of greasy burgers and a couple of Cokes. The smell of the food immediately turned my stomach, though Dennis wasted no time tearing into his with enough zeal to squirt a rivulet of oily pink juice onto his Ninja Turtles T-shirt. There was a wetness in the palms of my hands and a dryness at the back of my throat. I needed a drink.

"I can't believe you stayed in that house with Mom's body for a whole week," I said as I pulled back onto the highway. "It's fucking creepy, is what it is. Like serial-killer creepy."

He wiped grease from his chin with the heel of his hand.

"And what's with that little hike along the highway in your underwear? The hell were you thinking, man?"

Dennis stopped chewing, the knob of hamburger cranking to a standstill inside his cheek. He lowered his head almost imperceptibly. "*I-had-a-bad-dream,*" he said, the words rushing out of him in a breathy monotone around the food in his mouth. "In. My sleep. In my walking dream."

"You were sleepwalking?"

Either he didn't understand what sleepwalking meant or I hadn't guessed quite right. Whatever the case, I watched his furtive little eyes shift around, as if he were searching for answers. Searching for clarity.

"You remember telling that detective that Mom was dead?"

"No." The word was thick and round in his mouth. Drawn out, almost: *Nohhh.*

"No? You don't remember telling him that?"

"A girl," Dennis said.

"What girl?"

"A. Little. Girl."

"What girl are you talking about?"

"She. Is now. Dead."

"Who?"

"In a walking dream."

"What's a walking dream, Dennis?"

He just stared at me. Highway lights washed across his broad face.

"Listen, forget it." I was suddenly irritated by the whole goddamn scenario. "Just do me a favor and put some pants on next time you wanna go on a hike."

"Okay," Dennis said, amiably enough.

I spied the lighted vacancy sign of a shady roadside motel up ahead, and wasted no time pulling into the lot. I shut down the Mav's engine, manually rolled up my window, then popped open the door. Before getting out, however, I sensed Dennis's reluctance to follow me. I turned and saw him staring at me, his boom box cradled in his lap.

"What's the matter?" I asked him.

He peered through the windshield and up at the flickering lights of the motel's marquee. He looked apprehensive.

"We're staying here tonight. I need to close my eyes and figure some shit out before we go to the house. So come on."

"I want to go home."

"I'm not going there, Dennis. Not tonight. We'll go in the morning, okay? In the daytime." *When it's safer*, I thought, but did not say.

Dennis said nothing.

"Don't ignore me."

He ignored me.

"This isn't a fucking debate. This isn't a fucking democracy, Dennis. Now get the fuck out of the goddamn car."

He didn't move.

"*You son of a bitch!*" I slammed a fist on the dashboard.

Dennis jumped, startled, but wouldn't look at me. In fact, he turned away from me.

Furious, I jumped out of the car and walked in circles around the motel parking lot for what felt like an hour. My body trembled, my heart was galloping behind the stockade of my ribcage, and I couldn't quiet the cacophony of noises steadily building inside my skull. I needed a fucking drink was what I needed.

When it started to rain, I realized I had run out of options here. I got back in the car, slammed the door, then cranked the ignition.

Without speaking a word, I propelled us through the storm toward Black Mouth, and to the farmhouse where both my parents had died.

5

A social worker once recommended I write down my thoughts in a notebook, or in a series of notebooks, as a way of coping with what had happened. I had always been a voracious reader and displayed an aptitude for writing at an early age, particularly as a means of escape from the real world, so I suppose this seemed logical at the time. But the process of dissecting tragedy through words requires a certain distance for clarity's sake, and at the time this was first suggested to me, I was still a kid drowning in the thick of it.

A house like a blood clot: something snared in the artery of space and time. Or a cancer, metastasizing. Poke a single finger through the brittle bulwark of a wall or a floorboard or a ceiling joist and a black sickness, rancid as bile, oozes out.

"Jesus Christ," I mumbled to myself, easing the Maverick down the bumpy dirt road that led toward the farmhouse. It was smaller than I'd remembered. Dark and vulnerable in the night storm. Not a single light on in those windows, not a single suggestion that anything lived there. Not now, not ever. But that didn't mean the place was empty.

Dennis sat forward in his seat, peering up at the house through the rain-speckled windshield. His eagerness to return was like an electric charge in the air. There was an Econoline van parked in the grass, an old one from the 1960s or '70s, its tires flat. It looked like something you might transport prisoners in. Beyond that was the old alfalfa field, now a black panel of nothingness in the storm. The wooded ridge of Black Mouth, jagged as saw teeth, was out there just beyond the field, I knew, although it was too dark and rainy to see it with any clarity at this hour. Thank God for small favors, as Emily Pearson from AA might have said.

"Jesus Christ, Dennis, I can't believe you stayed here all these years."

It was an unfair comment—absurd, really—because where the hell else was he going to go? This remote farmhouse was all Dennis had ever known, and I was suddenly struck by the notion that to extract him from this place would be akin to amputating one of his limbs.

I drove around to the side of the house and parked the car upon the curling tract of dirt that separated the backyard from the overgrown fields—the exact same spot my father used to park his

Firebird. It was in that moment I realized that all my years away—all my years running from this place—had been in vain. We cannot run from ourselves. There is a history that travels through our blood, a blueprint for the people we are to become. A social worker once told me that no children are born bad, but I knew a different truth. I had more of my father in me than I cared to admit—his rage, his weaknesses, his addictions, his darkness. All of it.

The things that happened down in the heart of Black Mouth that summer had been inexplicable, magical, and ultimately deadly things—things I still don't fully comprehend or even care to dwell on. The things that occurred in this *farmhouse*, on the other hand, were of the human variety, and somehow all the worse for it. I haven't talked much about my dad yet, and there's good reason for that. I suppose I'm working myself up to it. Steeling myself. *You're riding the ride now*, Fred the hippie had told me back at the rehab center in Akron. I guess in more than one way, old Fred was right.

I looked over and saw Dennis watching me from the passenger seat. He was grinning his big childish grin. With some difficulty, I summoned one in return, and beamed it right back at him.

Maybe we could trick each other into thinking this was doable.

6

Maybe no houses are born bad, either. Maybe they're just convenient receptacles for everything we put in them—a box that houses our dreams, hopes, fears, torments, happiness, laughter, grief. They're what we make of them and what we need them to be. Maybe to grant them the power to become anything more is a mistake.

Or maybe not.

I went through the front door and was struck by a wall of dense, humid air, thick as molasses. It stopped me in my tracks. The ancient Honeywell thermostat on the wall registered a balmy eighty nine degrees. Behind me, Dennis stomped up the porch steps, the dry-rotted wood crackling beneath his heavy tread, then thumped past me into the house. My brother didn't seem bothered by the heat in the house, or to even have noticed it. He clomped off down the hall, his boom box knocking chunks of plaster from the walls.

I peered into the kitchen, took in the peeling floor tiles, the drippy sink, the missing panels of wallpaper. A few of the cabinet doors hung at busted angles. It hadn't been a palace twenty years ago, but Detective Aiello had been right—the place was literally falling apart now. There had been no upkeep, no maintenance, no repairs. Whatever had happened here, Mom had just let it happen. She and my brother had been living like stray dogs in a junkyard.

I went directly to the cupboards, opening each one until I found Mom's liquor stash. I knew she'd be good for it. I stared at the cheap bottles of mash whiskey and plastic liter jugs of off-brand vodka while my feet perspired in my sneakers. The back of my throat felt like a goddamn sauna. Yet just knowing these bottles were here helped calm my nerves a bit. *One more minute, one more minute*.

The kitchen overlooked a sunken pit my mother used to loftily refer to as the living room, although it had always been too cramped, too untidy, too much like an annex or a waiting room to have earned the title. Dennis shuffled around in there now, a formless blob in the darkness, his big-buckled sandals kicking up electrical sparks from the carpet until he switched on a floor lamp in one corner of the room. I saw the walls dressed in cobwebs, tattooed in handprints, streaked with all manner of filth. There were gaping holes in the Sheetrock and heavy furniture with shabby cushions. Where the old console television had once been was now a flat screen roughly the size of a ping-pong table. To the best of my knowledge, my mother hadn't held down a job in roughly a decade, so how she had been able to afford such an extravagance was beyond me.

Dennis turned on the TV and activated a DVD player, all with a chunky remote. Rubbery humanoid turtles appeared on the screen, giving each other high fives, or whatever the hell it was called when you only had three fingers to a hand.

In front of me, the hallway tilted like a funhouse corridor. I climbed the stairs, feeling as though I was ghosting through the aftereffects of some profound, debilitating accident.

I broke my arm falling down these stairs. Though it hadn't actually been a *fall*, per se, but a drunken shove from my dad, who had watched me tumble down the stairs, breaking my arm in the process.

There were two bedrooms up here, one on either side of the hall. The door to the master bedroom was ajar—a hermetic chamber where the air did not breathe, sound did not travel, sins were never forgiven. I reached in and ran my hand along the wall for the light switch. A solitary lamp on the nightstand winked on. In its meager glow, I saw the naked mattress, the clothing draped over a chair. The smell of Mom's perfume still hung in the air. I looked down and saw boot prints—probably from the police—crisscrossing the hardwood floor.

The room at the opposite end of the hall was our shared childhood bedroom. The door stood open, and I crossed the threshold, bracing myself for all manner of spring-loaded horror to jump out at me.

Instead, I burst into laughter.

The room had become a veritable shrine to the goddamn Teenage Mutant Ninja Turtles—posters on the walls, action figures on shelves, Ninja Turtle bed sheets covering both twin beds. The entire wall beside Dennis's old bed was papered in crayon drawings—very crudely rendered—of the four Turtles in various battle poses.

I turned and saw Dennis standing in the doorway behind me.

"Christ, Dennis, you're the best."

He lumbered into the room, his rubber-soled sandals clomping against the floorboards, and went straight to the small twin bed that had once been mine. He pulled down the sheets, smoothed them out with his big hands, then retrieved a fresh pillow from the closet.

I went to the window, my head buzzing with memories, a whole flood of them. I jostled the window partway open and let in a sweeping breath of night air. Rain needled at my skin through the rusted screen as I waited for another flash of lightning.

Waited.

Waited.

Then—a flashbulb explosion on the horizon, followed by the gallop of horse-hoof thunder. In the distance, the old barn seemed to glow with an ethereal light. I relaxed the slightest bit when I saw that the barn doors were closed.

The place where I'd first met a man I would come to call the Magician.

The place where my father had died.

Dennis came up beside me. He poked my forearm with a finger that felt like a broom handle. Then he pointed to the bed he'd made up for me.

"Thanks, bud." I felt something tickle the back of my throat.

"Jamie Warren is home," Dennis said, and then he hugged me.

7

That night I lay sweltering in my childhood bed, my mind slowly unraveling. Dennis, wearing nothing but a pair of droopy white briefs that looked like they'd sustained a few blasts from a shotgun, snored in his own bed on the other side of the room. The breeze that sifted through the open window was warm, and it stirred the crayon drawings that were taped to the wall on Dennis's side of the room. The sound kept me awake.

Earlier, I'd gone down into the cellar to see if I could get the HVAC unit to work, but it was no use. How long had Dennis and my mother been living like a couple of squatters in this place? If it was guilt I should have felt at having abandoned them in this hellhole of a house, it was overpowered by my mounting apprehension at having returned.

One more minute, one more minute, and then I was listening to the whisper of feet out in the hall. A weakened floorboard groaned, and I suddenly heard the *thhhk-thhhk* sound of that suckling infant. In my mind's eye, I sat up and rasped the woman's name. But in reality, I was powerless to move or speak.

One more minute, one more minute, and then I was somehow standing in the kitchen, the cupboard opened before me, those tantalizing bottles staring back out at me. I must have lain awake in that toaster oven of a bed for longer than I'd thought, because daylight was beginning to creep over the horizon; I could see it from the kitchen window, a glowing iron brand simmering between the pitch-black arrowheads of distant evergreens.

We're bigger than you, the bottles said.

I know you are, I thought back. *But I'll just stand here one more minute, one more minute, one more minute. After that minute, I'll drink.*

I thought of Emily Pearson from AA, showing me a scar above her right eyebrow. She'd been drunk and tried to cross a busy intersection when the side-view mirror of a passing van had whapped her on the forehead, rending open her flesh and knocking her unconscious in the street. When she'd come to, it was to a hazy semicircle of onlookers staring down at her in horror. *I'm lucky the goddamn thing didn't take my head off*, she'd told me.

One more minute, one more min—

I took one of the bottles down, unscrewed the cap, took a swig. It was like someone breathing life back into my lungs after a drowning.

Somewhere in the house, another floorboard went *creeeeeak*. I leaned out into the hall, but there was no one there.

I took a final drink, screwed the cap back on, then retreated down the hall toward the stairs. Or so I thought I had, but when I looked around, I found myself standing on the back porch. The alfalfa field was aglow with early morning light, the corkscrew trees along the rim of Black Mouth like hieroglyphs carved from wood.

Something in the periphery of my consciousness caught my attention. Not movement, exactly—more like a sensation that I was being watched from some improbable distance. I looked toward the barn and saw that the doors were now open. They hadn't been that way when I'd first glimpsed the barn in a flicker of lightning from the bedroom window earlier that night.

There were a couple of wicker chairs out there on the porch, and some dead plants in terracotta pots. An aluminum baseball bat stood between the chairs, leaning against the house. I recognized it as a relic from my youth. What it was doing out here on the back porch, I had no idea, but I didn't stop to question it.

I went over, picked up the bat, then crept down the porch steps toward the field. Last night's storm had done little to cool the atmosphere, and I was slick as an eel by the time I reached the open barn doors.

Early morning light poked through perforations in the barn's hide, crisscrossing beams of shimmery gold. Gone was my father's automotive equipment, the hydraulic jacks and rows of upright tool chests. Gone was any evidence that my father had ever toiled away in this place, except for the faint yet lingering aroma of motor oil even after all these years.

"Is someone in here?"

Startled by my voice, small black birds roosting in the hayloft ascended toward a rank of exposed beams in the ceiling.

Near the rear of the barn, where large wooden pallets had been stacked on the dirt floor, was my father's Firebird. It was mostly hidden beneath a plastic tarp, sacks of grass seed and mulch on its roof, some farming implements on its hood. I could see the cracked front grille and the squinting orange headlights. The tires were flat and bald.

Something squelched beneath my feet. I looked down and saw I was standing in a tarry liquid substance that hadn't been there a moment ago—that had seemingly burbled straight up out of the dirt floor of the barn.

Blood.

And then I heard it—the wet, gurgling respiration of a man whose chest cavity had been smashed, whose ribs like the spokes of a broken umbrella had impaled the tender meat of his lungs, whose skull had been reduced to a gory raspberry stew. A shadow floated into view, sweeping across the wooden slats that made up the barn's rear wall, disappearing as it passed through the shafts of daylight, reappearing again, the muted thud of heavy work boots on ancient soil...

Would the dead thing reveal itself once again, all these years later? The front of its chambray shirt black with blood, its head gone? Had it been waiting in here for all this time, somehow knowing I would eventually return?

I didn't wait to find out.

I dropped the baseball bat and got the hell out of there.

II

HELLO FROM PLANET CHILDHOOD

CHAPTER FOUR

DEAD RABBIT

The Apprenticeship, 1998

1

When I was eleven years old, my two best friends in the world were Mia Tomasina and Clay Willis. We were Black Mouth kids, and by virtue of that, outcasts among the rest of the kids in Sutton's Quay. And that was just fine by us.

Mia had come to live in Black Mouth when she was five years old, after her parents were killed in an automobile accident. ("Their heads were sliced *clean off* and thrown from the car," Mia once told Clay and me while she dangled upside down from the monkey bars behind the elementary school.) She lived in a dilapidated ranch house with her uncle, a bearded, barrel-chested lumberjack whom I had never heard utter a single word. I suppose it was good of him to take on the role of surrogate parent, although what that actually entailed—aside from providing a leaky roof over Mia's head—was up for speculation. For as long as I'd known her, Mia had prepared the meals, gone to the grocery store to pick up food, and cleaned up around the house. Her attire consisted exclusively of plain white undershirts formerly worn by her uncle, many of them so old the fabric was practically transparent, and they had yellow armpit stains. They were so big on her, she had to tie them at the waist.

Mia didn't really care about her clothes. She had a shelf of books in her room dedicated to death, some with pictures of dead bodies and even mummies in their sarcophagi. She liked watching movies where people got their heads chopped off, even if it looked fake (and it usually did), and every Halloween she dressed up as a walking corpse, white powder on her face with some ghastly black splotches of greasepaint to signify rot and decay. Once, she checked out a medical textbook from the library and it had pictures of autopsies, where the bodies were cut open to reveal a charcuterie of glistening organs. Those photos had turned my stomach, but Mia had gone through every page of that entire book, her eyes glued to those photos, her nose nearly touching the pages. She got in trouble for bringing it to school.

Mia didn't really like people, but she loved animals. She was always taking turtles and snakes and lizards from the woods to her house, where she had a whole shelf of terrariums lined up against one wall of her bedroom. She would keep each animal for a time to study its behaviors before releasing it back into the wild. She claimed she could identify each animal that had once been in her care whenever she came across them in the woods after setting them free, like spotting an old friend at a party. I don't know if that was true or not, but I do know that she loved each of those tiny critters with an intensity that was nearly frightening.

Clay Willis, on the other hand, was born in Black Mouth. In fact, rumors around town suggested he looked the way he did because the Willis farm resided perilously close to the heart of Black Mouth, where all manner of supernatural goings-on supposedly took place, intimating that perhaps some of this bad juju had corrupted Mrs. Willis's pregnancy. Clay Willis had what he called "the vit," or *vitiligo*, which meant he lacked pigment in patches along his body—most noticeably his hands and face. Because he was self-conscious of his condition, Clay always wore pants, long-sleeved flannel shirts and a trucker's cap, no matter how hot it got. Still, that didn't prevent kids from calling him a variety of names. The frontrunner that year was "Skullface," due to the prominent whitish-pink circles of flesh around his mouth and eyes. My father, never known for his empathy, had his own opinion about why Clay always dressed like it was the middle of winter, and it had nothing to do with his vitiligo: "He's black, and he thinks he can hide it."

For whatever dim reason bullies have for selecting their prey, Clay Willis became the target of a particularly merciless group of assholes that summer. Spearheaded by Tony Tillman, who, at two years our senior, was already a teenager, this sordid little cabal never missed an opportunity to make Clay's life miserable. Tillman was the one who came up with the Skullface moniker, which had replaced last year's nickname of Mickey Mouse (due to Clay's stark white hands which looked like cartoon gloves). And while Tillman's bullying tactics had, up until this point, been strictly of the verbal variety, all of that changed on the night the Happy Horace Traveling Circus and Carnival came to Sutton's Quay.

My friends and I had been waiting impatiently for the carnival to arrive since the end of the school year, ever since the advertisements began cropping up in the local newspaper. A week or so before the carnival arrived, flyers appeared stapled to telephone poles around town, the face of Happy Horace, a purple cartoon hippo, grinning maniacally at anyone who paused to read them. I had spent weeks running errands for neighbors just to earn enough money for one of those all-you-can-ride paper bracelets. I wanted to gorge myself on corndogs and cotton candy, and inevitably lose whatever cash remained at the Pitch 'til You Win booth. It would be the highlight of my summer. I couldn't wait. My only concern was that my mother would make me take Dennis, which would ruin my night. But as it turned out, Dennis was terrified of the grinning purple hippopotamus on the carnival flyer, and refused to set foot anywhere near the fairgrounds that week. The carnival was *mine*.

And then there we were on that first night: the three of us encased in a world of flashing red and blue and yellow lights, the smell of popcorn infiltrating our brains, the calliope music, the screams coming off the rides, the buzzing and dinging and cheering at the game booths that lined both sides of the midway. We queued up at the ticket booth where we laid down our hard-earned cash for some all-you-can-ride bracelets, then walked along the midway in awe, the Happy Horace jingle bursting sporadically from megaphone-style speakers on poles throughout the carnival grounds:

> *Happy Horace,*
> *The Purple-Purple Hippo!*
> *The Purple-Purple Hippo!*
> *The Purple-Purple Hippo!*

A clown on stilts strutted by. A child in a stroller shrieked beneath the strobe of white lights strung along the girders of the Ferris wheel. Two teenagers sucked face against a backdrop of giant stuffed bears. It was glorious.

We were on our way to the bumper cars—our first ride of the evening—when Clay stumbled ahead of us and struck the ground hard. His trucker's cap rolled off his head. I thought he'd tripped at first, but then I heard cackling laughter. I turned and saw Tony Tillman and his asshole friends pointing and laughing at Clay, who was still splayed on the ground, looking more confused than hurt.

"There's no freak show at this carnival, Skullface!" Tillman screeched.

Clay rolled into a seated position in the dirt. When he reached for his trucker's cap, one of Tillman's buddies—Dirk Lansing, also known as Dirk the Jerk around the Quay—snatched it up off the ground. He tugged it down on his own head then thrust his arms out in front of him, moaning and shambling around like a zombie.

"Get lost before you scare the kids!" another of Tillman's buddies chimed in.

Clay climbed to his feet. I could see the fear in his eyes as he looked at Tillman and the others. The colored carnival lights splashed across his face, exaggerating the ghostly white circles around Clay's eyes and mouth. In that instant—and I hated myself for thinking this— he *did* look like something from a horror movie.

When Dirk passed in front of Clay, zombie impression still in full effect, Clay made a halfhearted attempt at swiping his cap off Dirk's head. Dirk dodged him, and Tillman and the others erupted with spiteful laughter. As Dirk made another pass, Tillman himself yanked the cap off Dirk's head and popped it on his own.

"Careful, Tony," said another one of Tony Tillman's buddies. "You might catch that leopard-spot disease!"

"Tony's *already* white," Dirk interjected. "He don't gotta worry 'bout *turning* white."

"If you want the hat," Tillman said to Clay, "take it off my head."

Clay sensed it was a trap. He glanced at Mia and me, but found no help there. Then he took a step in Tillman's direction and reached languidly for the bill of the trucker's cap.

Tillman struck Clay in the face.

Hard.

It came out of nowhere, wholly unexpected. A legitimate closed-fisted punch, the kind you'd see in a movie on television. A look of shock flashed across Clay's face as he fell backward onto his ass in the dirt. The colored lights of the rides flashed and blinked all around him.

Tillman and his friends laughed.

"Come on," Tillman said. "That was my mistake, Skullface. Go ahead and take it."

Clay was up on his feet more quickly this time. He grabbed for the cap, and Tillman struck him *again*. Clay didn't go down this time, but he did stumble back. I thought he'd turn away then, but he didn't—he reached for the cap a *third* time, and was summarily struck once more by Tillman. The laughter from Tillman's friends had lost some steam by this point. Tears shined in Clay's eyes, one of which was already beginning to swell.

"I can do this all night," Tillman said.

Clay just stood there, his phantom-white hands shaking at his sides. His eyes unable to keep the tears at bay any longer, streaks of saltwater began to spill down Clay's blotchy face.

"For fuck's sake," Tillman said, pulling the cap off his head and chucking it at Clay. It struck Clay's chest then fell in the dirt at his feet. "That's pathetic. What a fucking ugly loser."

And then, like some magic trick, Tillman and his goons were gone.

Clay stood there, silently weeping. The whole thing had happened so quickly that no grownups had come around to intervene. I didn't think anyone else had even noticed, but then I saw someone in a plush Happy Horace costume seemingly staring in our direction from across the midway. Horace's foam mouth hung ajar, his bulging golf-ball eyes staring off into two different directions at once. In that moment, I was certain that whoever was inside that purple hippopotamus suit had witnessed the whole thing, and that they were deliberating whether or not they should come over to see if Clay was okay. But in the end, whoever was in that purple hippo suit turned away, dancing off in the opposite direction until they were swallowed up by the crowd.

Mia picked up Clay's cap. She dusted the dirt off it then held it out to him. Clay took it without a word and put it back on his head.

He pulled the brim down very low, so that no one would see his tears. Then he turned and headed in the opposite direction of the bumper cars—toward the parking lot.

Mia and I exchanged a look. She had her raven-black hair pulled back in a severe ponytail, the hairline at her temples beaded with tiny droplets of sweat. She was practically swimming in the oversized white undershirt she wore, despite the bulging knot swinging from her left hip.

"Oh well," she said simply enough, and then we chased after Clay.

2

We avoided the carnival for the next two days, but on July Fourth, and with a promise of fireworks on the midway once it got dark, the three of us took a chance and went back. But when we arrived, we saw Tony Tillman and a whole nasty clot of his asshole friends standing in line for the Scrambler. Mia and I looked to Clay to gauge his assessment of the situation, wondering if he'd chance it today for the sake of the fireworks later that evening. His right eye was swollen from where Tony Tillman had struck him, the white unpigmented patch of flesh around the socket having bruised to the color of an eggplant. When he looked at us, I could read the expression on his face shaded beneath the bill of his trucker's cap. There would be no rides today, no fireworks tonight. And although I was disappointed, a part of me was relieved there would not be another altercation with Tillman and company.

"I had a dream that you totally wrecked those jerks," Mia said as we headed down into the wooded crater of Black Mouth, a shortcut to our side of town. She was a bit ahead of us through the woods, swatting at tree limbs with a large stick she'd scooped up along the way. She'd just turned eleven a month earlier, and she'd thrown a birthday party for herself in her backyard. She had made her own cake, too—a slab of gray icing on a chocolate rectangle, specifically made to look like a tombstone. Clay, Dennis and I were the only ones in attendance. Clay and I had pooled our money and bought her a creepy book with a lot of zombie and vampire pictures in it, and Dennis had made her a macaroni necklace, which he had presented to her with such pride that she'd hugged him and even kissed the side of my brother's round, sweaty face. She was wearing that necklace now, the paint Dennis had used on the macaroni leaving a rainbow pattern on the front of her white shirt. "Like, in my dream, Clay, your arms turned into these giant knives and you just went *whoosh-whoosh-whoosh*, and cut all their heads off."

"I would keep the heads and put them on the porch at Halloween," Clay said, grinning.

"Yeah! Put candles in their skulls and let them glow like jack-o'-lanterns," Mia added.

"You guys are gross," I said, but I had to laugh a little bit. It *was* kind of cool.

"Good idea!" Clay shouted. "Then we'd call *them* Skullface!"

Mia stopped, spun around, then marched over to Clay. He stood about a foot taller than her, and she peered up at him almost comically. "My uncle says that if someone is a *bully*," she said, holding up a fist in front of Clay's face, "you pop 'em once real good in the nose. And then that's the business."

Clay and I laughed. Clay said, "That's the *business*? What does *that* mean?"

"Don't be a shit," Mia said, "or I'll pop you in the nose myself."

Clay sighed, then looked instantly miserable. "I'm sorry you guys are missing the carnival. You don't have to hang around with me. You can still go back and see the fireworks tonight."

"You know, I really didn't want to blow all my money at that dumb place, anyway," I told him, which was just about the biggest goddamn lie in the world. "I never win any prizes, either," I added, which was the truth.

Mia had taken the lead again as we walked, passing beneath the archways of bowing trees and chopping at the foliage with her big stick. Every once in a while, she'd call out, "Dare you to touch the Wicker Witch tree! Dare you to touch the Wicker Witch tree!" But then at some point she stopped in her tracks and stood stock still. The backs of her knees were shimmery with sweat in the waning daylight. She was staring at something hanging from a tree.

"What *is* that?" Clay asked, coming up behind her.

It was a brownish-gray rabbit that someone had strung up from a tree branch by its hind legs with a length of twine. I could make out no visible wound—no evidence of what had killed it— but it was clearly dead, its body elongated into a stiffened tubular shape, its eyes and mouth crawling with flies.

"Who do you think did that?" I asked.

Clay shrugged. "Some hunter?"

"You can't hunt in these woods," I said.

"Some trapper, then. Doesn't look like it was shot with anything," Clay said, leaning closer to the carcass hanging in midair. Flies swirled around Clay's head as he stared up at the thing.

"Some mean *jerk* did it," Mia said. "Cut it down, Clay."

"It's already dead."

"We need to bury it."

"I don't, uh, have anything to cut it down with."

"Little children!" boomed a man's voice from somewhere behind us. "Little children, *what have you done?*"

Startled, I spun around and scanned the surrounding woods. I didn't see anyone at first. It was early July and the trees were broad and full, a perfect place for someone to hide. But then I saw a man step out from between a curtain of fir trees, and I felt something leap in my chest.

It was the man who had been hiding out in our barn. That event had taken place on the night Tony Tillman had hit and humiliated Clay, and I hadn't told my friends about the incident because when I'd woken up the next morning to find the barn empty and no remnants of the small fire the man had been drying his clothes by, I had wondered if it hadn't just been a dream. In the light of a new day, it had certainly *felt* like a dream.

The man came forward through the trees. He had his hands in his pockets, his long, greasy hair hanging over his one good eye. That eye patch was like a pocket of black space in the white of his face. He was wearing black pants and a rumpled button-down shirt so filthy I couldn't tell if it was supposed to be white or some striated pattern of yellows and browns. He had on suspenders, too—bright red ones—but his frame was so emaciated that they drooped down the slopes of his shoulders and did little to keep his pants up.

As he drew nearer, we all instinctively gave him a wide berth. When he reached the rabbit, he paused, hands still packed away in his pockets. He stared at the carcass quizzically, head cocked like a dog inspecting something unfamiliar yet tantalizing. There were flecks of dead leaves and tiny greenish sprigs of moss in his lanky hair.

"Why in the world would you kids do something so cruel?" he asked, inspecting the dead rabbit hanging from the tree. I looked down and saw he was wearing filthy black cowboy boots embroidered with intricate stitching, the material so old it was veined with cracks and creases.

"*We* didn't do it!" Mia said, indignant. "Some mean jerk *asshole* did it!"

The man swiveled his head in Mia's direction. The expression in his one good eye suggested the brazenness of her outburst had surprised him, although he wasn't upset by it. In fact, he looked mildly amused.

"Could you cut it down for us?" I asked.

He looked at me. I caught a flash of recognition in his eye, which had looked as black and soulless as a shark's eye that night in the barn, but was in actuality a pale, icy blue. In my head I heard the words he'd spoken to me that night in the barn: *It's time we say goodnight, Mr. Warren. Perhaps we'll meet again.*

"Cut it down?" he said.

"I want to bury it," Mia said. "In a grave."

"Bury it…in…a grave," the man said, as if tasting the suggestion on his tongue. "What a considerate proposition. What is your name, dear?"

"Mia," she said. She had already taken a step closer to the man, her gaze back on the rabbit dangling from the length of twine.

"Is that your full name, Ms. Mia?"

"It's Mia Tomasina."

"In that case, let's stick with Ms. Mia." He turned toward where Clay had been standing just a moment ago. "And my sweaty friend in the flannel shirt hiding behind that tree over there?"

Looking embarrassed, Clay stepped out from behind the tree. "I'm Clay Willis," he said. The lower half of his face glistened with perspiration beneath the brim of his trucker's cap. He nodded in my direction. "And that's Jamie."

The man pulled his hands from his pockets. The cuffs of his shirt were unbuttoned, and they flared out at his wrists as he planted his hands on his hips. Still gazing at the dead rabbit, he said, "Yes, Mr. Warren and I are old friends. Isn't that right, Mr. Warren?"

My throat made a creaky sound. I didn't know what to say. My friends were staring at me.

The man shook his head, as if just now struck by the cruelty of the dead rabbit hanging from the tree. Then he bent forward and tugged up one of his pant legs until his entire boot was exposed. The hilt of a knife poked from his boot. He took the knife out, and with a single slash of its blade, the dead rabbit fell to the ground.

"Whoa," said Clay.

He tucked the knife back in his boot, then picked up the severed length of twine and held the rabbit up to his face to study it.

"How do you think it got up there?" I asked him.

"Who's to say, really?" he responded. "Could be witchcraft. Black magic. A spell to ward off evil." He sought me out with his one good eye. "Or to summon it."

"No way," Clay said.

"Do you think this rabbit is part of something like that?" I asked. "Black magic or whatever?"

He held the rabbit so close to his face I swore the tip of his hawkish nose grazed the mottled flyblown gray fur.

"Hard to tell for sure," he said. "But I don't think so."

"How do you know?"

The man turned and looked at me. I suppose it was a smile that stretched the corners of his mouth, revealing an irregular file of discolored teeth behind his thin lips. He didn't say a word but that smile, which someone else might have found off-putting, seemed to answer my question. Somehow.

"So can we bury it, mister?" Mia said.

The man appeared to consider this. The dead rabbit rotated slowly at the end of the string at his side. Finally, he said, "I can tell you're a woman of ceremony, Ms. Mia. I like that, and consider myself to be something of a ceremonist as well. But I think we can do better than just tossing old Mr. Cottontail here into a hole in the ground. Follow me."

The rabbit slung over one shoulder, the man began carving his way through the trees. His movement was almost dainty, or perhaps innately cautious. I wondered if he had been living down here in the woods since he'd left our barn that night.

"Wait up!" Mia shouted, and ran off after the man through the trees.

"Shit," Clay said. "You *know* this guy?"

"It's a weird story," I said. "I'll tell you later."

"What do we do?"

I thought of Mia trudging through the foliage after that guy on her own, and said, "I think we should follow them."

3

We followed the man to a low, wooded valley. Offshoots of the old mine crisscrossed beneath the earth here, evidenced by the crumbling mouth-like openings in the hillside which looked like enormous groundhog burrows. The openings to some of the larger mines had been boarded up years ago, but there were others that remained open, hidden behind spools of leafy vines and dense curtains of foliage. The eye-watering stench of sulfur rolled out of these holes in the hot summer months, a stink that burned my nose the deeper we went toward the heart of Black Mouth.

Every child who grew up in the Mouth had been warned from an early age to steer clear of them. Never, under any circumstances, were we to go *inside* one of those tunnels. They were pitch black and you could get lost, could wander around for an eternity and never find your way out. Or they might just collapse on you, burying you beneath the town where no one would ever find your corpse. Where no one would ever even know what had happened to you.

As we came upon a clearing, I saw the remnants of a bonfire, a large metal pot with a busted handle, and a few empty food wrappers scattered about the ground. An army-green nylon tent stood beneath the shade of a massive oak. Hanging from a branch of the tree was a black tuxedo jacket with a withered red carnation pinned to the lapel. There were holes in the jacket's elbows and the cuffs were so frayed they looked tasseled. Hanging from a branch above the jacket was a black satin top hat, a thing that looked so old and delicate, I imagined a good sneeze might reduce it to a pile of black dust. There was also some sort of black cape or cloak folded over a branch, equally as shoddy as the other two items.

"You *live* down here?" Clay asked, also noticing the clothes hanging from the tree.

"Temporarily," the man said. He marched right through the clearing without pause. Mia followed, uninterested in anything other than a proper burial for the dead rabbit.

Farther along the clearing stood the opening of one of the mineshafts, a yawning black maw in the sloping hillside. Some other items were scattered about over there as well. I crossed over to the spot and saw what looked like an old wooden vegetable crate, a bedroll, and some empty food containers. There was a deck of playing cards on a mossy deadfall, spread out in a fan.

The man set the dead rabbit down on top of the vegetable crate then went over to the bedroll. He untied it and the bedroll unfurled like a tongue. A tattered blanket of some grimy, indeterminate color was balled up inside. As he carried the blanket back to the crate, a breeze filtered down through the trees, rustling the leaves. The man froze. He looked up, observing his surroundings, the sloping hillsides, the peculiar way all the trees grew horizontally from the walls of the crater and bowed toward the heart of the Mouth. The lengthening shadows that stretched across the wooded loam.

"There's a certain magic here, all right," he said, still looking around. "It strums in the ground. A heartbeat in the earth. Can you children feel it?" Something about that whistling breeze seemed to make him uncomfortable, because he looked around like someone watching a terrible storm gathering just over the horizon. He pointed toward the entrance to the mineshaft, where the breeze had stirred the curtain of vines before its opening to dancing. "These tunnels scream at night."

"That's the ghosts of dead miners," Clay said.

"Dead minors, you say? You mean children?"

Clay frowned, confused. "Coalminers," he said.

"Ah, yes. Charming."

"It's really just the wind blowing through the old mineshafts," I corrected, though I agreed with Clay that it *sounded* like the ghosts of dead miners. I could hear the low, full-throated moans on certain nights coming in through my bedroom window. "There used to be a big coalmine out here but it collapsed a long time ago. A bunch of coalminers got trapped underground and died."

"But not right away," Mia added. She'd learned this story at an early age from Clay and me, and had been fascinated with it ever since. She'd even read old newspaper articles on the incident down at the library in town. "They were all still alive down there for *days*. No one could get them out. And they *did* scream, and people in Black Mouth would hear them day and night, though 'specially at night, because that's when the trapped coalminers would grow so hungry that they'd start to *eat* each other."

"That part's not true!" Clay interjected.

"It *is*!" Mia insisted, her eyes going wide. There was a smudge of dirt across her forehead, severe as war paint. "I read all about it. And it went on like that for *days*, maybe even *weeks*, until one day the people of Black Mouth noticed that the screaming had finally stopped, which meant that the coalminers were all finally dead beneath the town."

"Black Mouth?" the man said.

"It's what this place is called," I told him.

"This town?"

"This...hole in the town," I said, thinking that the best description. "It's what happened when the mine collapsed all those years ago. The whole ground above the mine just went *whoosh*. My dad told me all about it."

"I see," said the man. He covered the dead rabbit with the blanket he'd taken from his bedroll.

"I know what that is," Mia said. "That's a death shroud."

The man glanced up at her. He seemed bemused by her comment. "What do you know about death shrouds, Ms. Mia?"

"A lot," Mia said. "I've read about them in books and seen them in movies, too. You wrap up dead bodies in them before you bury them."

"Well," the man said, "that is true, but this is not a death shroud."

"Then what is it?"

The man didn't answer. We watched him fold over the ends of the blanket. His fingers were filthy, but they moved nimbly. Delicately, almost. As if this was a loved one he was covering in that death shroud (that was not a death shroud) and not some dead rabbit we'd found dangling from a length of cord in the woods.

"What happened to your eye?" Clay asked suddenly.

Without looking at Clay, the man said casually, "What happened to *your* eye?"

Clay brought a hand up to his swollen and bruised eye. "Just some jerks from town."

"Did you do something to earn it?"

"Just being me, I guess."

"Sometimes that's enough," the man said. Then he looked at me. That single blue eye gleamed. "How about you, Mr. Warren? Those same *jerks from town* do that to your arm, as well?"

I didn't know what he was talking about until I followed his icy one-eyed gaze to my left arm. There was a purple bruise outlined in splotchy green along the flesh between my wrist and elbow. "No," I said.

"Then who did?"

"I just fell," I told him, which was a lie I had perfected since early childhood. Some lies were easier to tell than others.

"And how old are you, Mr. Warren?"

"Eleven."

"Bit old for falling down, I would think. But okay, Mr. Warren. If you say so."

A fiery shame flickered somewhere inside me. I never spoke of the things that happened at home, not to anyone—not even to Mia or Clay. Yet for some reason I suddenly wanted to tell this stranger everything, though I felt the moment to do so had just passed and I'd missed my one and only opportunity.

Having finished wrapping up the rabbit in the blanket, the man took a step back to examine his handiwork. He looked pleased with himself. "Mr. Willis," he said. "You're the tallest of the group by a head. Go on over to that tree and fetch me my remaining garments."

"Uh…" Clay said, looking around. "Your what?"

"My coat, hat, and cape, Mr. Willis."

"Right! Right!"

Clay bounded off then returned a moment later with the tuxedo jacket and top hat. He had the long cape folded over one arm, the hem of which dragged along the ground, sweeping up pine needles and dead leaves. He handed the man his jacket then set the hat and the cape on the crate, beside the rabbit carcass currently wrapped up like a burrito in that filthy blanket.

The man slid his arms through the sleeves of the jacket, then ran a hand down each sleeve to smooth out the creases. A cloud of dust enveloped him. When he bent his arms, I could see his shirtsleeves through the elbow holes in the jacket.

Next, he picked up the top hat and placed it at a jaunty angle on his head. Satisfied, he slapped the top of the hat with one hand, and a second cloud of dust puffed out and wafted down over his face. My friends and I laughed, which in turn earned us a smile from the man. He then gathered up the cape—I could see the underside was black silk, or some cheap imitation of silk, with tears and rips in the fabric—and twirled it around his back, fastening it around his neck. Lastly, he produced a pair of silky white gloves from the inside pocket of his jacket and tugged them on his hands. Much like the rest of his attire, they were soiled and grubby. Some of his fingertips poked through holes in the gloves.

He looked ridiculous, to be honest.

"As we discussed moments ago," the man said, holding up one finger as if to instruct a classroom of children, "it's all about *ceremony*. It's all about *presentation*. Do you see?"

I just nodded my head, though I really had no idea what he was talking about. I could tell my friends didn't, either, although they were nodding, too.

Then, with a proper magician's flourish, he whipped the blanket off the rabbit, and we all cried out in unison.

Quick as a flash, the rabbit bolted down off the crate and sprinted off into the woods. I jumped out of its path, craning my head around to follow the rabbit's lightning-bolt surge through the underbrush. A second later, it was as if the thing had never existed.

"Holy shit!" Mia shouted.

"H-h-how…?" Clay stammered. "What did…? I mean, *how*…"

"Magic," said the man. He bowed with some difficulty—I suddenly recalled that old scar at his side and wondered if it pained him—then looked deep into the woods, as if to follow the trail the rabbit had left in its wake. "What do you say, Ms. Mia, dear? Isn't that better than some morbid old rabbit funeral?"

I looked at Mia, who was also staring into the woods in the direction where the rabbit had vanished. Her mouth hung open in disbelief, her dark eyes wide and sparkling. She turned to the stranger who had performed this trick, and said, "That's not the same rabbit! It *can't* be!" Yet despite her insistence, she looked altogether *exhilarated*. "You must have switched them when we weren't looking."

"Did I?"

"You *had* to. The *real* dead rabbit must still be somewhere over there with you."

"Maybe behind that crate," I suggested. I was still somewhat breathless from having witnessed the trick. I kept seeing him whip that blanket away, and the rabbit bolting past me and into the woods. Surely it had been a trick, and a damn good one, yet I couldn't wrap my head around how he'd done it.

The man raised both of his gloved hands. Waggled his fingers, shook his arms. *Nothing up my sleeves, children*. With one foot, he shoved the crate until it pivoted in the dirt to reveal the interior. Empty. No dead rabbit in sight.

"Your sleeping bag!" Clay shouted, springing to his feet. His voice was jittery with excitement. "You hid it in your sleeping bag when you unrolled it and took that blanket out! That's when you made the switch!"

"But wasn't the dead rabbit over here on the crate when I did that, Mr. Willis?"

Beneath the brim of his trucker's cap, Clay's face scrunched up in consternation. He knew as well as I did that the dead rabbit *had* been on the crate when the man went over to the bedroll and took out that blanket. Moreover, we'd watched him as he'd wrapped up the dead rabbit *in* the blanket. At what point had he managed to make the switch?

"You're free to inspect it, if you wish, Mr. Willis…"

Clay hurried over to the bedroll anyway. He dropped to his knees and ran his hands along it, feeling for lumps beneath the fabric. Then he lifted a flap and peered beneath it. Satisfied—though perplexed—that there was no dead rabbit hidden there, he climbed to his feet, brushing dead leaves and twigs from his corduroy pants. "There's just no *way*," he mumbled, hands on his hips, as he looked around the immediate vicinity, like someone searching for a hidden escape hatch. "That was the most *bitching* trick!"

"What about you, Mr. Warren?" the man said, tipping his head in my direction. "Any thoughts on the matter?"

I considered what I'd just witnessed and tried to reconcile it with what, at eleven years old, I already knew about the world. Namely, that dead things couldn't be brought back to life. "I'm gonna say," I began, the notion coming to me all at once, "that it wasn't dead in the first place."

"Interesting hypothesis," the man said. "But didn't you see it dangling lifelessly from that tree, covered in flies?"

"Well, yeah…but maybe that's all part of the trick. Like, you could have given the rabbit some medicine or something to make it *look* dead, but really, it was only asleep. Like when they put you to sleep in a hospital for an operation." *Or when my dad passes out drunk in front of the TV, or out on the porch, or in the barn, or behind the wheel of his car…*

"That is a very astute observation, Mr. Warren, and it certainly does get to the heart of what we consider to be a *magic trick*. The notion of foolery, of misdirection, in other words."

I grinned, satisfied that I had guessed correctly.

"However, your hypothesis would *imply*, then, Mr. Warren, that it was *I* who strung that sorry beast in the tree in the first place, all with the intention of performing this trick for you three. Which is an impossibility, of course, because I would have no way of knowing you three would be down here in these woods—this, uh, *Black Mouth*—today to witness it, am I right? I am, after all, a magician, Mr. Warren. Not a fortune teller."

He was right, of course. I found I had no suitable response to this.

"So then the only plausible conclusion we must draw," the man said, "is that it was no trick at all."

"But...but then *how*?" I asked.

The man removed his top hat and swept it across his hips as he bent forward in a bow.

"Magic," he said.

4

We spent the rest of the afternoon with the Magician, as he performed tricks that we could not figure out. They were mostly card tricks, but he could also summon gusts of wind and draw the leaves down from the trees with his mind. He could read our thoughts, guessing whatever number we thought of. Silk scarves and coins appeared out of thin air. For the grand finale, he lifted his top hat from his head and—swear to God—a tiny bird darted out and settled high up in one of the nearby trees. My friends and I went nuts. By the time the fireworks detonated far over the trees at the Happy Horace Carnival that evening, we hardly noticed.

"If we come back tomorrow, will you show us more tricks?" Mia asked.

"That is a distinct possibility, Ms. Mia," the Magician began, "but I must first ask a favor of you children, if we are to continue along this path together."

We were all eager to do whatever the Magician asked of us. We told him so.

"I must ask that none of you speak about me to anyone outside of our little circle here. That you do not mention me to a parent or another friend. To keep my presence here in this...this *Black Mouth*," and he spoke these words with a notable inflection of distaste for some reason, "a secret between the four of us. What I'm saying, children, is to not tell anyone that I'm staying down here."

"We don't have any other friends," Mia said.

"We won't tell anybody," Clay added.

"Wonderful!" the Magician said, and he clapped his dirty white gloves together, startling us all. "Then I've got much to show you..."

CHAPTER FIVE

SCAR TISSUE

1

We laid Mom to rest on an overcast afternoon. Dennis and I stood before the grave while the priest spoke his priestly words. My face was unshaven, my body vibrating, my flesh reeking. Two bolts of bourbon churned queasily in my belly, and my mind was fuzzy with benzodiazepine.

When we returned to the farmhouse, there was a woman in a sleeveless Iron Maiden T-shirt, skintight jeans, and high black boots standing on the front porch. I was still trying to puzzle out who she was when Dennis broke into a frantic run in her direction. His ill-fitting chinos sliding down far enough to reveal the upper part of his ass crack, a Rorschach of sweat having soaked through the back of the only dress shirt I was able to find in his closet, those goofy sandals still on his feet (only now with socks), he threw his arms around the woman standing on our porch, lifted her off the ground, spun her around.

"Oof, you're cracking my ribs, Dennis!" the woman said, though she was laughing.

"Jamie!" Dennis shouted at me, that radiant smile on his face. His voice was redolent with a childish glee. "Jamie! Mia is *home*! Mia is *home*!"

Mia?

The walk from my car to the front porch felt like an eternity. I saw an ugly orange PT Cruiser with rental plates parked around the bend of the dirt track, just beyond the Econoline. On the porch, Dennis had released the woman from his patented bear hug, and was now thumping her happily on the back. That achingly wide smile was still on his face.

Mia Tomasina?

I took in the punky hairdo, the constellations of hoops and studs in each of her ears, the tattoos high up on her arms and across her exposed collarbones. She was wearing aviator shades, but took them off as she slowly descended the porch steps to greet me.

"Mia." Her name felt like a lead weight in my mouth.

"Hey, Jamie." With those aviator shades off, I could see that it was her. Those dark, piercing eyes. Even as a kid there'd been a depth in her eyes, a hidden and secret knowledge that always made her seem older than she was. "You look really spooked, man. I hope you're okay with me showing up like this."

On the porch, Dennis shouted, "Mia! Is! Home!" He jumped again and I heard the rickety porch boards creak beneath his feet.

"I'm speechless," I said. "I mean, I don't know what to say."

"How 'bout we say nothing? We just hug it out?"

Before I could respond, she came in and wrapped her arms around me. I did the same, though a bit more tentatively, placing one palm against the thin fabric of her T-shirt and the eager knob of a single vertebra. I inhaled every aspect of her that I could in that split second before she pulled away—a smell of cigarettes, mostly.

"What are you doing here?" I asked her.

"I wanted to get in touch with you, but I couldn't find anything online. Last I knew, your mom was still living here, so I thought she might know. But Jesus Christ, Jamie, I didn't expect to find *you* still living here…"

"I don't live here. I'm in Ohio now. I just came back for…" I paused, not wanting to ruin this moment. Not wanting to make it more emotionally confusing than it already was.

"For what?"

What the hell…

"Mom's funeral."

She looked at me more closely, taking in the shabby black suit I was wearing, the only suit I owned. The half-quart of booze shuttling through my veins was the only thing keeping me from crumbling to the ground in a pathetic heap.

"Oh shit," she said. "I'm sorry, Jamie. I'm so sorry. I didn't know…"

"It's okay."

"Talk about shit timing."

"Never," I told her.

Thunder rolled through a bank of dark, menacing clouds that had been inching across the back field since earlier that morning. I felt a few raindrops plink against my face.

"Let's get inside," I said.

2

"Christ, it's like a sweat lodge in here."

"Sorry. Air conditioner shit the bed sometime before I got here."

Dennis shouldered past us and jogged down the hall. His heavy footfalls detonated on the stairs as he raced up to his bedroom, and I swear to God, bits of plaster rained down from the rafters.

Mia went down into the living room where the windows faced the back field, the far side of which sloped down into Black Mouth. A ridge of spiky, leafless trees was visible, marking not only the horizon but the southernmost rim of the Mouth. I knew she was trying to get a good look at the Mouth, perhaps to assess whether anything had flourished down there since the fire, but it was impossible to see from here. She'd have to go *deeper*.

"It's like a giant pit of ash now," she said.

"Did you see it?"

"I drove by it. I couldn't bring myself to get out of the car. You'd think after all these years, something would have grown."

"I can't believe you're here," I said.

"Never thought I'd come back." She was still staring out the window.

"You said you were trying to reach me. What's going on, Mia?"

She turned and faced me. Despite the makeup and the piercings, the punk-rock hairdo and tattoos, she suddenly looked like the young girl I had been best friends with so many years ago. She took her cell phone from the rear pocket of her jeans, pulled something up on it. Seemed to hesitate for a moment, but then handed me the phone.

On the screen was a photograph of a man wearing an eye patch. My blood ran cold at the sight of him.

"There's a few more photos," Mia said, "but that's the only one where you can see him clearly."

It took me a moment to find my voice. "Mia, where did you get this?"

"I took it. This was in Lexington, Kentucky, a little over a week ago. I just looked up and there he was, standing in the crowd."

My hand shaking, I gave Mia back her phone. I suddenly felt loose, like all my limbs might detach themselves from my body.

"I didn't know what to do," she said. "I still don't, to be honest. I even emailed the picture to Clay, hoping he might have some suggestions…"

Hearing Clay's name caused my knees to go weak. I leaned against the wall before I collapsed. "You spoke to Clay?"

"Well, not really. He never responded. So I just hung around Lexington for a while, hoping I might see the son of a bitch again. It wasn't until this morning that I realized I wasn't too far from Black Mouth. I figured, well…what the hell?"

She turned and looked back out the window. Her arms were down at her sides, and I could see a thick, angry scar bisecting the flesh along her left wrist.

It was the sound of Dennis's heavy footsteps on the stairs that broke the silence. He poked his head around the wall, his beady little eyes gleaming. When he saw Mia standing by the window, he broke into a broad smile again then clomped over to her in his sandals. It was as if he'd forgotten she was here.

"For you," he said, holding up a necklace made of uncooked macaroni.

"You were always full of surprises," Mia said, and her eyes ticked over to me for a moment. "Can you put it on me?"

She turned around, sweeping her hair off the nape of her neck. Tongue poking from one corner of his mouth in concentration, my brother carefully placed the necklace around Mia's neck. It took him a couple of tries to snap the clasp, but he eventually got it.

Mia turned around and struck a pose—one hand in the air above her head, the other on her hip. "How does it look?"

"Mia. Is. *Pretty*."

"You're such a charmer, Dennis," Mia said…and then she leaned in and planted a kiss squarely on my brother's sweaty forehead.

3

The three of us ate dinner at a Chinese restaurant out by the highway. I had popped an Ativan back at the house, and was currently working my way through my second extra-large can of Sapporo. The combo was not recommended, according to the drug's warning label, but I found it brought me down to a level where I felt, if not in control, then at least lulled into docility.

"I stopped by my old house today," Mia said as we finished our meals, and I thought it sounded like some kind of confession. "Or what was left of it. Sped past it like a drive-by shooting. I'm surprised someone didn't clear the land and rebuild."

"No one wants to live out there." In the booth beside me, Dennis was chugging a bottle of Yoo-hoo, his throat clicking with each swallow.

"Yeah, well, it wasn't any better after we moved away," Mia said.

"Where'd you go?"

"Where *didn't* we go? Uncle Joe went to Farmington, and I joined him once I got out of that detention facility."

"Where's Farmington?"

"Good old Rush County, Indiana. But that gig didn't last long, so then we were off to Okfuskee County, Oklahoma—the kids there call it Oh-Fuck-Me. And then there were the shit-spot cities in New Mexico, each one of them a confused blur to me now—Truth or Consequences, Sunland Park, Taos. Wherever Uncle Joe was able to find some work. Or thought he could find work."

"At least you got out of here."

"Trust me, it wasn't all roses. Uncle Joe resented me for having to leave this shithole town, if you can believe that. He never really got back on his feet after we left. It was just a cycle of terrible shit, and I felt responsible for all of it. It was like, once that first domino fell that summer, everything else just came crashing down behind it. We were on welfare when Uncle Joe decided to get drunk and wrap his truck around a telephone pole. He died instantly."

"Shit, Mia, I'm sorry."

She shrugged. "After that, I played the foster-home roulette game. You can imagine the kind of foster parents who are cool taking in a teenage girl carrying around my kind of baggage. Not exactly the stuff of Hallmark movies. Those foster parents, they're either religious nuts or the dad wants to stick his hand down your pants. Sometimes both. I guess after a while of that bullshit I just got tired of hating myself. So I got a razor and opened up my wrist."

She stretched her arm across the table, exposing that wormlike lump of scar tissue. Dennis set his drink down and stared at it.

"One quick slash. It was practically painless. All those stupid medical textbooks I used to obsess over as a kid — remember those? — and there I was, quite literally peering down into myself for the first time. The Visible Woman."

"Jesus, Mia. What happened?"

"I freaked out. Saw all that blood and lost my shit. Ran across the street to a salvage yard where some guys were jerking around on a forklift, my arm bleeding all over the place, and started screaming for help. Before I passed out, a couple of good ol' boys tied a shirt around my arm, tossed me in the back of their truck, and drove me across town to the nearest trauma center."

She slipped her arm back beneath the table. "My point is, it wasn't just about what happened to us that summer. That was just the event that caused a chain reaction of misery. All these years later, and I feel like I'm still trying to outrun it."

Keep running, I thought. *Don't stop. Don't look back.*

"Don't you ever think back to that summer?" she asked, her voice a bit lower now. Her eyes volleyed between Dennis and me. "Don't you ever look at it as an adult instead of some dumb, naive kid? Think about what that guy really was…"

"I don't really know what he was," I said. And I meant it in a way that even Mia couldn't understand.

"I want you to go to the cops with me," Mia said. "If I go alone, I'll sound like some nut. But if you come with me—if we corroborate each other's stories from that summer—then they'll have to take us seriously. The two of us can—"

"Stop." My hands were shaking on the table, so I slid them into my lap. "I can't do that, Mia. I don't want any part of it."

"We're *already* a part of it. Maybe now we *finish* it. Me driving around Kentucky by myself looking for the bastard won't cut it, but the police, they can see if they can track this guy down, hold him fucking accountable for what happened that summer..."

"That was *us*, Mia. *We* were accountable for what happened that summer. And I don't want to relive that shit."

Slowly, Mia shook her head. There was a pained expression clouding her dark eyes. "Jamie, it was all him. He was a monster, man."

I flinched noticeably at that word. *Monster.*

"Please," she said. "I need your help."

I felt Dennis's eyes on me, heavy as anvils. I refused to look at him. I refused to look at Mia, too. I just stared down at what remained of my meal on the table in front of me. "There's just too much going on right now," I said, my voice barely above a whisper. "And even if there wasn't, Mia...I just can't. I'm sorry you came all this way for nothing."

"All this way? It's like I didn't even have a choice, Jamie."

"I'm sorry, Mia. But I can't do this with you."

Mia leaned back in her seat. She kept staring at me, and I kept refusing to meet her gaze. I thought I could hear her heart beating from across the table. After a while, she signaled for the check.

Keep running.

Don't stop.

Don't look back.

Despite the pills and the booze, my heart was racing.

4

Mia dropped us off at the farmhouse beneath a night sky misted with rain. She got out of the car with us, gave Dennis a hug, then we both watched him lurch up the porch steps and disappear inside the house.

"Did you want to crash here for the night?"

"In that sweatbox? No, thanks. I've got a room out by the highway. I guess I'll grab a flight back to L.A. in the morning."

"What are you gonna do with that photo?"

"I don't know yet. Maybe I'll take it to the police myself. Or... fuck, I don't know." She looked me over. "What about you? What'll you do now?"

"Pack up first thing in the morning and get the hell out of here."

"And Dennis?"

"He'll come back to Ohio with me for now, I guess. Until I can figure something out. Someplace for him to go."

"Good old Dennis," she said.

The cocktail of beer and anxiety meds that had kept me sedate throughout dinner was orchestrating a mutiny now inside my head. "Whatever you decide to do, Mia, I just hope you'll be careful."

"We could figure something out together." She sounded hopeful.

I just shook my head. "I'm not looking to chase anything. I've spent too much time trying to bury it. And I'm a fucking mess because of it." I showed her my hands, wracked with tremors. They didn't seem to faze her.

"You don't have to be afraid anymore. It's all just scar tissue, man." And then she leaned in and kissed the side of my face. Her hair was cold and damp against my cheek, and I inhaled her cigarette scent once more before she pulled away.

A moment later, she was gone.

5

Something happened later that night. I could blame it on the bottle I killed on the back porch after Mia drove off and Dennis went to bed. I could blame the benzodiazepine shuttling through my system. I could even attest that the mixture of booze and meds made me weepy, and I'd spent a good portion of the night drowning in despair, shaking from fear, and questioning my reality. But I don't believe any of those things were the cause.

(Do you want to see a magic trick?)

A sound like an echo, like a memory—a baby crying out from somewhere in the house. I staggered through the darkness, my eyesight blurry. My head was stuffed with foam, and my body oozed sweat. Things taunted me from the periphery of my vision. I kept pausing to gaze hypnotically into the holes punched into the Sheetrock.

"Sarah?" My voice fell flat in the darkness ahead of me. On the heels of that, my body stiffened, my scalp tingled, and I croaked out, "*Dad?*"

I waited for something terrible to come shambling out of the darkness.

Then I was wavering drunkenly at the top of the stairs, unsure how I had gotten there or what I was doing. Sweat tickled my neck. I smelled smoke, and it terrified me. I heard that suckling sound again—

"*Ugh...*"

—and I whirled around in the dark, my vision lagging seconds behind, only to become aware of a terrible presence crouching in that darkness with me.

And then I was freefalling down the stairs, *whump whump whump*, and crashing to the floor. A bolt of lightning rocketed up my right arm. My skull felt pulverized. Lying there on the floor at the bottom of the stairs, I squeezed my eyes shut until I caught my breath, willing the pain out of my body. I imagined my father's heavy work boots as they thunked down each step, the wet rasp of his mangled respiration.

As I rolled my head to one side, I opened my eyes and saw—or imagined I saw—a pale figure retreat from the upper landing, eyes glowing the way a deer's eyes will in the sweep of headlights.

And then darkness swallowed me up.

6

When I opened my eyes again, it was morning and I was staring at a rabbit. Whiskers twitching, ears scissoring in the air, it was seated on the floor of the hallway in a column of daylight, judging me with its black oil-spot eyes.

I was still sprawled out across the floor at the bottom of the stairs. My head was throbbing and my right arm ached. When I touched a set of fingers to the fresh lump on my forehead, they came away sticky with blood.

I groaned and then rolled onto my side. This sent the rabbit bolting down the hall and out the open front door.

Open front door?

"Dennis?"

No answer.

The house felt empty.

Why is the front door open?

I struggled to my feet and staggered out the front door, cringing at the harsh daylight. Someone was swinging a sledgehammer inside my skull. Just as I wobbled down the porch steps, I looked up and saw a vehicle turning down the dirt driveway. It kicked up a rooster tail of dust as it approached, and stopped just a few yards from my own car. It was Mia's rental, the orange PT Cruiser.

I just stood there, confused and in pain, leaning against the railing at the bottom of the stairs.

Mia climbed out of the car and came over to me. She looked as confused as I felt. "I was pulling out of the motel this morning, and I saw him just walking up the road. He seems okay now, but he was… Jamie, your head is bleeding."

"I'm okay," I said. I looked past her and realized that Dennis was sitting in the passenger seat of her car.

"Jamie, there was something wrong with him." She was looking over her shoulder at Dennis, too, through the glare of the windshield. "Like he was in some sort of trance or something. When I tried to talk to him, he said something about someone being dead."

I wandered over to the car, pulled the passenger door open. I felt like I was trudging through the swampiness of a nightmare. Dennis's dull-eyed countenance gazed up at me. He was naked except for his underwear, his body powdered in road dust and streaked in dried sweat.

"Should he see a doctor?" Mia asked.

"What's going on, Dennis?" I asked him, my voice shaking.

"*Sheeeee*," he croaked. "She is now dead."

"Who?" I asked. "Who's dead? Mom?"

Dennis just stared up at me, his mouth agape, his thick tongue working.

One more minute, one more minute…

I heard Mia's boots coming up behind me. When she spoke, it was just barely above a whisper. "There's something else. I heard back from Clay. He wants me to meet him. He's in Kentucky, Jamie. He said he got my photo and found out something important. But he wants to discuss it in person."

One more minute, one more minute…

She slipped her hand into mine.

"Will you come?"

From the passenger seat of Mia's rental car, Dennis answered for the both of us: "We. Will. Come."

CHAPTER SIX

TRICKS OF THE TRADE

The Apprenticeship, 1998

1

That July, I spent as much time as possible with the Magician down in the heart of Black Mouth. I didn't want to be home. My father had never been what you might call an upstanding guy, but things in the past year or so had gotten pretty bad. His drinking had eventually cost him his job with the refinery over in Shepherd, which meant my mother had to pick up double shifts at the Kroger in town. For a brief time, he worked as a mechanic at the local garage in Sutton's Quay, but even those dim-eyed grease monkeys had a limit to how much hot-tempered, drunken bullshit they were willing to put up with. You could only leave so many wrenches under the hood, could only forget to tighten so many lug nuts after replacing a tire, before the laws of probability thumbed its nose at you.

They say some drunks are bad drunks, but in my father's case, even that was an understatement. A darkness overtook him when he drank, pulled him down, swallowed him whole. He became a thing inextricably trapped in a cycle of his own self-perpetuating horror.

My mother coped with it by learning to become a punching bag. She also became an alcoholic in her own right, and who could blame her?

I learned to cope by perfecting the first magic trick I had ever come to know—the patented Jamie Warren Disappearing Act. I got good at slipping away, fading into a shadow or dark crevice, ditching beneath a bed, inside a closet, hiding out in the barn. If I was able, I'd take Dennis with me—now you see us, now you don't. But I couldn't always be there to help Dennis. So out of necessity, he developed his own peculiar brand of self-preservation.

The previous spring, Mia had given Dennis a box turtle she'd found in her backyard. He'd kept it in a shoebox under his bed at first, but then he emptied out the wooden chest at the foot of his bed that was supposed to hold our underwear and kept the turtle in that. Every day he fed it vegetables and bugs and plucked the wet, almond-shaped turds from the wooden chest with a look of distant pride on his face. For some reason I could never figure out, he named the turtle Breakfast Time.

What had infatuated Dennis so much about the turtle was its ability, when frightened, to withdraw completely inside its shell. It even had a little hinged panel of shell that folded up to protect its head. When Dennis first witnessed this, he shrieked with laughter until his cheeks burned red and his eyes filled with tears of joy. The turtle did this less and less as time went by, having grown accustomed to Dennis's care, but on the occasions when it still happened, Dennis's joy was no less enthusiastic as it had been that first time.

At some point, Dennis began to do the same thing as the turtle. Whenever our father raged, Dennis would retreat inside himself, his glittery eyes growing dim and unfocused, his body curling into a fetal position with his knees clutched tightly to his chest. When I'd first witnessed him do this, it frightened the hell out of me. I shook him and spoke his name until he snapped out of it.

It took me a while to realize this was Dennis's own version of the patented Jamie Warren Disappearing Act—a way for him to temporarily remove himself from the same plane of existence as our father's volcanic rage—and after a time I became more accustomed to it. It was just Dennis, hiding inside his turtle shell. Nothing more than that.

2

It started with card tricks.

The Levitating Queen, the Hermann Pass, the Zarrow Shuffle, the Four Burglars. To me, they had sounded like old-time dance steps at first, but after watching the Magician perform each one, his dirty but nimble hands manipulating the deck, those names had taken on an almost mystical quality in my mind. I begged my mom to bring me home a deck of playing cards from the Kroger where she worked, and when she finally did, I disappeared into my room, tore open the cellophane wrapper from that sleek deck of red Bicycles, and practiced all the tricks, over and over again, that the Magician had taught my friends and me. I wanted to perfect them. I wanted to *impress.* Often, Dennis sat cross-legged on the edge of his bed, watching me with a lackluster gaze in his eyes. Whenever I got one of the tricks right, however, he'd perk up, eyes going wide, his big hands colliding in hasty applause.

"The key to a good card trick is misdirection." The Magician said this to my friends and me on more than one occasion. "You fool your mark into looking over *here*," he said as he held up his left hand, "when the real action is actually over *here*," and then he held up his right hand. A flick of his fingers and he was suddenly holding the king of spades. "Just don't make it *look* like you're misdirecting."

Mia was the best at performing these tricks when we first started out. What made this even more impressive was that her hands were so small, so there was less real estate for her to mask the trick. Of course, once we knew how the trick was done we could anticipate the misdirection, but she still managed to astonish us with how utterly *dexterous* she was.

"You'd make one hell of a pickpocket," the Magician once told her.

"Clay's got that double-lift trick down pretty good," Mia said, never one to hog all the attention.

"Is that right? Let's have a look, Mr. Willis."

The thing about Clay was that his hands were a natural distraction. Those long-fingered white hands attached to his black wrists drew your attention away from the cards automatically, his vitiligo like some kind of peculiar magic in and of itself. This had been less effective when he wore his usual long-sleeved flannel shirts, but after the Magician suggested he take advantage of the natural distraction his skin condition provided, Clay, who had resisted at first, finally started rolling up his sleeves when he performed. After a while, he even took to wearing T-shirts, which was something I'd never seen him wear in all my life.

The double lift was a simple sleight-of-hand maneuver. When holding the deck, you lift the top two cards as if they're one, then you show the outward facing card to the audience. The audience thinks they're seeing the top card, but it's actually the second. When the magician shuffles the top card back into the deck, he retains the second card that he showed the audience, which is then displayed to an eruption of *oohs* and *ahhs*.

The toughest part of the double lift was just that—lifting both cards together so that the audience thinks it's only one card coming off the top. Mia was best at this trick, too, but she was also right about

Clay's recent improvement. We watched him perform it several times, over and over, and even though I knew how the trick was achieved, I could never tell that he was actually plucking two cards simultaneously from the top of the deck.

"What about you, Mr. Warren?" the Magician asked, his lone eye shining like a fleck of topaz. He had his long, greasy black hair tucked behind his ears. After that first day, he'd quit wearing the top hat, cloak, and white gloves, because he'd said it was *time to get down to business*. "Which trick have you mastered?"

I had mastered none, but I had gotten pretty good at the old pick-a-card-any-card routine. I fanned out the deck and had Mia select a card. When I cut the deck for her to return her card to it, I peeked at the underside of the card that would be going on top. When I turned the deck over and thumbed through the stack, I selected the card ahead of the one I'd glimpsed during the cut. A pretty basic trick, really.

"Nice job," Mia said, smiling. "That's really good, Jamie."

"How about showing us the Riffle Force?" the Magician asked me. He was perched on a log outside the entrance of his canvas tent, his long legs stretched out before him so that I could see the scuffed soles of his boots.

"I'm not really good at the Riffle Force," I confessed.

"Go on and show us anyway," the Magician said.

The Riffle Force is basically a trick where the magician appears to have control over the card the mark seemingly selects at random from the deck. The concept is straightforward—it's all about maintaining control over your card—but it requires a deft hand. I attempted the trick for them now, but spilled the cards everywhere on the ground.

"Gather them up and try again," the Magician said, his voice serene.

I gathered the cards off the ground, packed them into a stack, then attempted the trick a second time. This time, only about half the cards fled from my hand, fanning out along the ground at my feet. I tried to snatch a few out of the air as they fell, which made Clay chuckle. It just made me aggravated.

"Shit." I tossed the remainder of the deck on the ground. Clay quit chuckling and Mia rolled her eyes.

"Gather them up and try again," the Magician repeated calmly.

I sulked.

"Go on," he said. "Don't give up."

I collected the cards once more, packed them together in a tight stack in my hands, said a little prayer to myself, then tried the trick again. This time I got it. Ace of diamonds, the desired card, right on top.

Mia cheered and Clay whistled through his fingers. The Magician bolted up off his log and applauded.

"Bravo, Mr. Warren! Take a bow, sir! Always remember to take a bow."

I took a bow.

3

"Show us how you did the trick with the rabbit," Mia said.

The Magician was perched on a large rock my friends and I had rolled over into the clearing, his long legs planted in the ground. His pant legs were frayed and too short, and I could see his black boots went all the way up. I sometimes caught a glimpse of the large knife tucked away in there. The hilt looked like it was made of bone.

"I've already told you kids," he said. "That was no trick. It was *real* magic."

"So then teach us *real* magic," Mia said.

The Magician's lucid blue eye hung on us, and he didn't avert his gaze as he fished out a deck of playing cards from the breast pocket of his dirty white shirt. He shuffled them on one knee.

"Not another card trick," Clay moaned.

"Ms. Mia," the Magician said, unperturbed. "Explain to me how the trick of the Levitating Queen is performed."

"You use an invisible thread that goes through the center of the card and is tied to your ear," Mia said. "It was one of the first tricks you taught us."

"Gold star, Ms. Mia." He stopped shuffling and separated the deck into halves—one half on his knee, the other in his hand held high above his head. A card floated up from the stack on his knee—the queen of hearts—and hovered in the air. "Now come take the queen."

Mia approached, reached out, and plucked the card out of the air. She turned it over, feeling around for the thread. After a moment, she looked up at the Magician, then turned and looked at Clay and me.

"There's no thread." She handed me the card so I could see for myself. The Magician had taught us how to run the thread through a tiny hole in the center of the card, but there was no hole in this card. There was no thread at all. I gave the card to Clay so he could see, too.

"Holy *shit*," Clay said, his toothy grin stretching from ear to ear. He kept turning the card over and over in his hands, about an inch away from his face. "How'd you make it float without a string?"

The Magician rose up from his rock, slapping pencil-yellow pine needles from his pants. He tucked the deck of cards back into the breast pocket of his shirt. We kept waiting for him to say something—to answer Clay's question—but he remained silent as he stepped toward the center of the clearing. His footing struck me as oddly precise, as if he were following a very narrow path that only he could see. Then he turned and faced us.

A breeze funneled down into Black Mouth, stirring the leaves in the trees and causing the pine branches to sway. It smelled of the mountains, but mingled quickly with the vague sulfuric stench of the mineshafts that crisscrossed below us in the earth.

The Magician lifted his arms and held them out like airplane wings. He had his head tilted back the slightest bit, his one good eye focused on something in the distance. I watched as the breeze filtered through his long, tangled hair.

His boots rose off the ground. It was only a few inches, but I could clearly see his shadow on the ground below him, the leaves stirred by the breeze passing unencumbered beneath his feet. He hovered there for a moment, his eye still focused on something far off in the distance, then slowly descended until he was standing on the ground again.

"Holy shit!" Clay cried out again. "Teach us *that* one!"

"Yeah!" Mia squealed.

I looked around at my friends, and then back at the Magician. I felt nearly breathless by what I'd just witnessed.

"Real magic isn't about fooling someone," the Magician said. "It's not about manipulation or misdirection or sleight of hand. It's not a *trick*, in other words. Real magic is *power*. And it's not something you can just teach another person. You can help them *find* it, but you can't *teach* it. It's like going to a well with a bucket—you dip the bucket into the well and carry the water back with you."

"Then how do you learn to do *that*?" Clay asked. "To go to the well and get the water or the power or whatever?"

"You learn that by doing what I tell you to do," the Magician said. "You get there by having trust—in your teacher, in each other, and in yourself. You get there by ultimately taking a leap of faith. Do you kids know what an apprenticeship is?"

Clay and Mia shook their heads. I knew I'd heard the word before—I probably read it in a book somewhere—but I didn't say anything.

"It's when someone takes you under their wing, so to speak, to teach you a trade or a craft. Like how I'm teaching the three of you these magic tricks. But to go any further—to become students of *real* magic—we must share a bond of trust, and in the end, when the time comes, you must all ultimately agree to take a leap of faith."

"I don't really understand," I said. I looked around and could tell that my friends didn't, either.

"You will," the Magician said. "You all will. But that comes later. For now, I just need a commitment from you three—my apprentices— that you will trust me. That you will do as I say without question. Otherwise, this will all just be a waste of time."

"We will," Clay and Mia said at the same time.

"We promise," I added, because it just felt right.

"Very good," the Magician said.

"What does the well look like?" Clay asked.

The Magician appeared to consider his response. "It's difficult to describe, because it is not of this realm. It is an opening that connects this world to the next. A passageway. Much like that hole in the earth over there." He waved a hand in the direction of one of the old mineshafts. "Only it has *teeth*."

"A hole with teeth," Mia said, staring across the clearing at the mineshaft.

"A black mouth," I said.

"Yes, all right," the Magician said, and I watched his eyes take in our wooded surroundings as if for the first time. "A black mouth."

4

My parents had never been the type of folks to care about a curfew, so it was already dark by the time I arrived home that evening, my stomach grumbling with hunger. I came in through the back porch and could already sense something was wrong the moment I entered the house.

My parents were in the kitchen, my father clutching at my mother's neck, pinning her up against the refrigerator. My father was a big man, perhaps six-foot-seven, with a girth worthy of such height. He was shirtless, his jeans slung low enough to reveal the tattered elastic band of his boxers, his longish hair piled in a sweaty, curling heap at his shoulders. He had his face pressed against my mother's temple, forcing her head to one side. I could already see a bruise darkening along the summit of her left cheekbone.

The sounds my father spat at her were not exactly words, but guttural ejaculations of noise dressed up with frothy expulsions of spittle. My mother cried out, cursed, kicked her bare feet at him; I heard the soles of her feet *reet-reet-reet*ing along the kitchen tiles as she struggled to free herself from his grasp. My father just held her in place with one hand clutching her throat, his forehead pinned against her temple, bracing her head.

My mom's eyes ticked in my direction. Her body went limp at the sight of me. A few heartbeats later, my father, whose sensibilities had been anesthetized by booze, twisted his head in my direction. Greasy clumps of hair clung to one sweaty cheek. His face was fire-engine red.

"*You*," he seethed, his speech like something spilled out of a blender. His body was angled just enough for me to see a streamer of blood oozing down the front of his chest. In that same instant, I saw that my mom held a knife, and that her wrist was pinned by my dad's blood-smeared hand to the refrigerator. "You got somethin' to add to this, you little shithead?"

I took two steps back. Suddenly, from my new vantage, I could see Dennis standing in the hallway. He was staring at our parents the way someone might watch a goldfish dart about a fishbowl. That detached, misty look in his eyes. A head filled with smoke. Even though it wasn't very late, he must have been roused from sleep, because he was wearing only his underwear, his bellybutton a yawning bull's-eye within the soft white paunch of his belly.

A moan gurgled up from my mother's constricted throat.

"Then get the fuck *out!*" shouted my father.

I rushed down the hall, grabbed Dennis by the wrist, and dragged him up the stairs. I slammed our bedroom door shut then twisted the lock. Dennis just stood there, his face blank. I heard a liquid pattering on the hardwood floor just as I noticed the crotch of Dennis's underwear grow dark.

Frantic, I glanced around the room until my eyes fell upon an aluminum baseball bat leaning in one corner. I grabbed it, then stood before our bedroom door. I heard glass breaking downstairs.

"Go sit on your bed," I told Dennis. "Get in your turtle shell."

Dennis climbed onto his bed without making a sound. He drew his legs to his chest, his eyes losing focus.

Shouting from below. The crunch of something heavy cracking into pieces. My mother's scream. *Oh please, oh please...*

And then silence. There was more anxiety in that silence than there was in the screaming and breaking of things. I waited, hoping the next sound I heard would be the screen door thwacking against the frame followed by the rev of my dad's Firebird growling to life.

The next sound I heard was footsteps coming up the stairs.

No.

A pause as he reached the landing. A labored gasp of air. My father's heavy, drunken tread staggering about the hallway outside our bedroom door. As if lost in confusion.

Please, no.

I saw the shadow of his feet beneath the door. Could hear his ragged, furious breathing. I waited, waited, waited…

"Jamie…" In his drunkenness, my name sounded like something made of sludge and hair and fingernail clippings, something that might be plunged out of a shower drain. The doorknob jostled but the lock held. "Jamie…" He was wheezing. "You open this door, boy…"

I did not open the door, boy.

"Goddamn it, you little shit, *open the fucking door!*"

I did not open the fucking door.

A fist slammed against the door, rattling the thing in its frame. A kick, too, and I heard the sickening sound of wood splintering. I knew from experience that he could bulldoze that door straight off its hinges if he tried. I only hoped he was too drunk to remember he could do it.

If he comes through the door, I'll hit him with the bat, I told myself, even as my grip on the baseball bat felt too slippery and unreliable to swing it. *I'll hit him one time in the head, just strong enough to knock him out.* I couldn't think beyond that.

"*Jamie, you cocksucking little faggot, you open this goddamn—*"

His words ended abruptly. I heard him stagger down the hall, banging into the walls and cursing under his breath. Then there was a loud bang followed by an almost rhythmic tumbling sound—like clothes whirling around inside an industrial dryer—as he plummeted down the stairs.

Silence pervaded the house. I stood there with the baseball bat cocked over my shoulder, my breath buzzing up my throat. My hands felt made of hot taffy as they clutched the hilt of the bat. On the bed, Dennis was still tucked safely away in his turtle shell.

Once enough time had passed—I wasn't entirely sure how much time—I unlocked the bedroom door and peeked out into the hallway. Plaster dust lay on the hardwood floor, along with slivers of wood from where my father had kicked the doorframe. I went down the hall and peered down the stairwell. I saw my father at the bottom. I knew he wasn't dead—I could see his chest rising and falling with each rattling breath—but he was unconscious. He looked infuriatingly peaceful.

I crept down a few steps, until I was able to survey a section of the kitchen without actually having to go all the way down there. I could see some blood speckled on the floor, jagged bits of glass sparkling along the countertop, and a leg that had been amputated from one of the kitchen chairs.

Two more steps down, and I could make out the spectral form of my mother sitting upright on the sofa in the darkened living room, her knees pressed together, her legs jouncing up and down. I could see the glow of her cigarette floating in the dark.

I hate you, I thought, my whole body trembling. My head felt filled with steam. I wanted to take the baseball bat to the whole house—to smash this terrible place to pieces and be done with it for good. *I hate you both. Fuck you. Fuck you!*

I went back upstairs, cleaned my brother's urine off the floor, then closed and locked the bedroom door.

"Dennis," I said, shaking him gently. "Dennis. Dennis. Dennis. Dennis."

Dennis blinked his eyes. He lifted his head and looked around the room, reorienting himself as he always did when coming out of his shell.

"It's over," I told him. "Are you okay?"

"I am okay," he said in his monotone voice.

"Get up and change your underwear. You're all wet."

He climbed off the bed, dropped his sodden briefs in the hamper, then tugged on a fresh pair. When he crawled back into bed, his pillow made an audible *poof* sound as his head settled into it.

Still dressed and clutching the baseball bat, I climbed into bed beside my brother. Hot tears burned trenches down the sides of my face. I couldn't stop shaking. When I heard a noise somewhere in the room with us, my whole body stiffened. But it was only the box turtle Mia had given to Dennis, stirring about in its wooden chest at the foot of Dennis's bed.

None the wiser.

CHAPTER SEVEN

THE MISDIRECTION OF CLAY WILLIS

1

This is Clay Willis: assured, retrospective, contemplative, a formidable presence when necessary, but mostly a thing that clings to walls and ferments. Ruminates. *Studies.* The best way to observe a situation is to not be part of it—an edict for work, but also a mantra for life. A colleague once told him, "You need to be more assertive with these kids, Clay, and lay down the law when they get too out of hand," to which Clay Willis responded, "It's laying down the law that's fucked them up so good in the first place."

These same colleagues had names for him, though they were only valiant enough to refer to them behind his back. They called him Spook, Ghost, Specter. In the intervening years, Clay's vitiligo—*the vit*—had taken over most of his body, white sleeves running up his black arms straight to the elbows, his face like ground zero of an acid attack, all color stripped from his flesh so that only his dark brown eyes blazed like fiery coals in the otherwise milk-colored pallor of his face. His chest, too—a Jackson Pollock canvas of pallid striations across an otherwise perfectly healthy black torso. He rarely went to the beach, and when he did, he wore long-sleeved Under Armour athletic shirts.

What these colleagues couldn't see was that his feet were much the same—faded slabs with bland, colorless toes at the end, patchy spots of white-pink flesh traversing up his shins to his thighs. The same with his genitals, that permanent embarrassment whenever a relationship with a woman got that far. One girlfriend had referred to his dick as a soft-serve ice-cream twist of vanilla and chocolate. Swirly, she'd called him. His testicles looked no better, like they belonged to someone else, dangling there with all the authority of two blanched peaches in a pouch, someone from a Ripley's Believe It or Not! boardwalk attraction. Once, he had set a mirror on the bathroom floor and straddled it, peering down to see what his undercarriage looked like. Monstrous, really. He could have been a leper, for all his appearance. Fortunately, his response to such an observation was only to laugh himself into hysterics (though he later smashed the mirror).

But there was a cosmic truth about Clay Willis that, in his thirties, he slowly began to realize. He'd been a social worker for the better part of his adult life, and had always had a knack for relating to children, for befriending them and getting down to their core issues. He could lie to himself and say it was a byproduct of his education, his expertise, his clinical prowess. But in reality, it was just another form of misdirection. Children saw him come into a room, and they stared at him as if he was a monster. Invariably, the first thing they talked about was his skin condition. Some kids were timid but curious, and he could interpret from their inquisitive stares that they wanted to know why he looked the way he looked. Other kids were more barefaced, and they'd ask straightaway what the fuck was wrong with his ugly fucking face. Clay took it all in stride, clever enough to understand that no matter the initial approach, it always led down the same path, with the same purpose: getting the kid to *open up* and *talk freely*. To feel comfortable. To know they weren't the only freak in the room.

A seven-year-old girl once told him about a mouse with a scratchy voice living inside her head.

What does he say?

He says hello.

Why does he live in your head?

He's afraid to go out.

Why is he afraid?

He just is.

What does his house look like inside your head?

It's just a mouse hole.

What does he do in there?

He watches mouse news on TV.

What happens on the news?

Nothing much.

What else happens in the mouse hole?

Nothing. Nothing happens. It's safe. It doesn't fill up with water because he covers the hole with boards.

Where does the water come from?

The bathtub.

Who's in the bathtub?

Edward.

Who's Edward?

Mommy's friend.

And so on. The first couple of sessions with this little girl had focused solely on Clay's vitiligo. She'd asked questions about why his skin looked like that and how did it happen, and he'd answer truthfully—that it was an autoimmune disorder, nothing he could control, and of course she didn't know what that was at seven years old, so he said that's when a part of your body doesn't trust another part of that same body, and maybe you sometimes feel that way, too? The little girl had said yes. She sometimes felt that way, too.

(Edward, that fucking pedophile, ultimately went to jail.)

Then there were the older kids—the burgeoning drug addicts and boozers, the cutters, the bulimics, the budding criminals, the physically violent, the suicidal. A thirteen-year-old boy who'd just stolen—and wrecked—his foster parents' car could give two shits about what anyone had to say, but when Clay Willis walked into the room, the tables turned. Uncomfortable with Clay's appearance, the kid laughed. He called Clay names. After a few minutes he said he was done talking with Clay because looking at Clay's skin made him sick. What did Clay do? He nodded, folded his arms, and said the first thing that came to his mind: "I know I look like a monster. Do you want to know why? It's a pretty good story, but it might scare the shit out of you."

This statement caught the boy off guard. There was a *story* here? The kid had to hear it.

Clay told him about Black Mouth—the cursed hole in the ground where he was born. How it sent its poison tentacles straight into Clay's momma while Clay was still in the womb. He couldn't be sure (he told the kid) but his very first memory was of something like an octopus's limb twining around his throat while he was still floating around in amniotic fluid. He had gripped at the tentacle with his hands, which turned them white. It had cut off the circulation to his head, which turned his *face* white, though only in patches at first. And in the end, as a fetus, he'd fought that monster, tore its octopus limb to shreds, and came out kicking and screaming like any normal kid, or almost.

"It just gets worse as I get older," Clay told the kid. "You think it would stop, but it doesn't. It's slowly taking over my whole body. It used to just be my hands, and around my eyes and mouth. But look at me now."

Clay lifted his arms so the boy could see the damage done by the octopus. He always wore short-sleeved button-down shirts in these sessions, because long ago, as a child, he'd learned the power of misdirection. The boy had stared at his arms, looked at his face, then asked how bad it was along the rest of Clay's body. Clay winked at the kid…then bent down, slipped off his shoe, and peeled off his sock. He propped a bone-white foot on the table so the boy could examine it. Specks of black flesh poked through the white, like a photo negative of outer space.

"That's fucking disgusting, dude," said the kid. "Does it hurt?"

"No, but I think I'm fading away," Clay confessed. He put his foot down, pulled on his sock, slipped his foot back into his loafer. "You and me, we're both fading away. Maybe we can help each other."

And sometimes, in the deep recesses of Clay Willis's brain, this statement would be followed by a thought that would bring a chill to the base of his spine. A man's disembodied voice, smooth as a runner of silk, whispering ever so softly: *Do you want to see a magic trick?*

That's me, Clay would think in response. *I'm the magic trick. I'm a walking, talking, social-working magic trick. Now help me help this kid…*

And most of the time, it worked.

2

He had just completed a particularly exhausting workday when he retired to his office in downtown Lansing, Michigan, a bag from McDonald's and a hot coffee in his hands. He dropped in his desk chair behind the outdated computer while he sipped his coffee. Shook a cardboard box containing a Big Mac from the paper bag, ketchup packets scattering. The smell of onions infiltrated his nose. He didn't really like to eat this garbage, truth be told, but he liked cooking for one even less. Anyway, you couldn't beat the convenience.

There were reports to file, emails to send, records to look up. It could all wait until tomorrow, of course, but there was nothing but a disconsolate Sixth Avenue apartment waiting for him at the conclusion of his day, so he didn't mind putting in the extra hours. There was never anything good on Netflix, anyway.

Mostly spam in his inbox. Some notifications for court appearances, a few from police departments throughout Michigan, some other business-related correspondence. But then one email in particular caught his eye. The sender? Goddamn Mia Tomasina. The subject line:

hello from planet childhood

He didn't need a moment to dredge up a memory of her; she'd already been seared into his brain years ago. A girl with a dark ponytail, an oversized white undershirt, and a queer interest in medical textbooks. Some part of him always knew he'd hear from her again. Despite his attempts at repression, the mind possessed an uncanny way of selecting which cards we kept and which cards we shuffled back in the deck. He stared at that line of text for what felt like an eternity, a tumult of emotion swirling around inside him. Thinking, *Mia Tomasina, Mia Tomasina, Mia Tomasina...*

The realization that he could just delete the email unread occurred to him. He even clicked on the little box beside the message then rolled the cursor up to the DELETE icon, preparing to do just that. But then he stopped. Clay's hands were suddenly clammy with sweat.

"Fuck it," he said, and opened the email.

3

For the past several years, Clay had been operating under the belief that nothing truly happens in a vacuum. He'd come to this conclusion through his job. Child abuse, by definition, was never a single occurrence or a solitary incident. That was why they called it a *pattern* of abuse—because it signified something chronic and ongoing. Adults who did heinous things to children did so *repeatedly*.

This understanding prompted him, on rare occasion, to reflect on his *own* childhood—and more specifically, on what had transpired during those weeks in the summer of his eleventh year. An enigmatic man who, now, capered through the fog of Clay's memories, always just out of reach, performing incredible feats of prestidigitation. Coins from empty pockets, sparrows from handkerchiefs, a never-ending tickertape of colorful silk scarves—uncanny wonders, all of them.

Now, in his professional capacity, he recognized all the telltale signs of predatory grooming—the way the man had befriended them all so readily that summer, always repeating their names when he spoke in order to construct a facade of trust. The trust they had so willingly surrendered unto him. How they had stolen food from their houses to earn his gratitude. All of it just another layer of manipulation.

Just seeing Mia's name stirred up those old memories inside him. He read her email, a mounting terror rising up inside him even before he clicked on the attachment. The photo.

"Jesus Christ," he muttered, his voice unsteady. He backed away from the computer, but couldn't pull his eyes from his screen.

4

At home, he poured himself a glass of whiskey, then pulled up the email and its attachment on his personal laptop. Wondering if maybe it might look different now, in his home and on a different screen. Hoping maybe it did. But it didn't. Wishful thinking. That face was still that face.

Only…

How old was he back then? Clay wondered. *Young kids have no true barometer for judging the age of adults. To children, all adults are simply old. Back then, I would have said the Magician was in his thirties, maybe forty at the very most, but he couldn't have been much younger than that, could he?*

The man in the photo looked as though he hadn't aged a day.

Clay got up, refilled his drink, then paced around his small apartment while a headache gradually built up inside his head.

He thought, *Abuse doesn't happen in a vacuum. It isn't a solitary act. What do we find when we find an abuser?*

We find a pattern. We find a history.

He knew where these thoughts were leading him, he was just somewhat disinclined to follow. Not just yet.

Instead, he made a phone call to Nikki Alvarez. He'd known Nikki for several years, since she'd been a troubled teen bouncing from one foster home to another. An extremely bright kid, Nikki had worked long and hard with him despite her problems, enchanted by Clay's promise that there was a light at the end of her very dark tunnel. Clay had not wanted to see her become yet another casualty of a faulty system and a city full of bad elements, so he had worked equally as hard on her behalf. And ultimately, she had come through—a testament to just how bright she actually was. And how determined, too. Now, she had her own apartment in downtown East Lansing, and did IT work for various government contracts. She was a whiz on computers, and Clay had utilized her skills on a few occasions to help track down the identities of children in photographs. He was thinking of this talent now as he dialed her number.

"I'm going to email you a photograph of a man. See if you can run that facial recognition software and get a hit somewhere. I'm looking for maybe a name or an address, but I'll be thrilled with a Facebook page or whatever else you can find."

"Locked and loaded," Nikki said. "This some pedo?"

"Truthfully, Nikki, I don't know *what* this is. But let's keep this one on the DL."

"As per usual, boss," Nikki said. She knew the drill.

Clay asked after her wellbeing (something he always did when he spoke with her), and she said she was "just fine and dandy like a bowlful of candy" (which was what she *always* said), and then they ended the call.

A pattern.

A history.

A chance that son of a bitch was still out there, perpetuating the cycle?

He returned to the computer and started searching for recent news stories involving children in and around Lexington, Kentucky. One news headline jumped out at him right away:

11-YEAR-OLD GIRL FATALLY STABBED BY FRIEND

The victim's name was Charlotte Brown. There was a photograph of her that accompanied the article. Big eyeglasses and an awkward preteen smile. Sandy hair in unkempt ringlets bracketing her delicate face. Something lost in her eyes. Small and thin for her age.

According to the news article, Charlotte Brown had gone with her friend and neighbor, eleven-year-old Molly Broome, into a nameless chamber of woods on the outskirts of Penance, Kentucky, a rural farming community where the two girls lived. Police said there was evidence that the girls had been playing back there for some time; a makeshift little clubhouse of wooden boards lined up against a tree was discovered, as well as some other items that belonged to the girls. By all accounts, the girls were good friends. On that particular morning, however, Molly Broome stabbed Charlotte Brown to death with a knife. Sometime later, when her stepfather, Steve Russell, saw Molly in her bedroom covered in blood, the girl confessed to what she had done. Mr. Russell then called the police. The news story concluded by stating that Molly Broome would be charged as an adult for her crime.

This incident took place a little over a month ago, and the town of Penance, Kentucky—according to MapQuest—was approximately a two-hour drive from Lexington. Clay might have disregarded the story altogether if it hadn't been for a line about Molly's supposed motive for murdering her friend.

Molly Broome claimed she'd killed Charlotte Brown at the behest of a man who had been living in the woods.

Clay leaned back in his chair and stared at the glowing image of Charlotte Brown on his computer screen. A million thoughts shuttled through his mind.

Had he never found this article, Clay Willis would have eventually forgotten about Mia Tomasina's email. Had he not been attuned to the cyclical nature of abuse, he would have never even considered searching for such a thing online in the first place. Even now, a part of him wished he could rewind time and play the ignorant fool. Maybe delete Mia's email after all.

But things were what they were.

Early the next morning, he made a phone call to a colleague in Fayette County, a woman he'd met at a conference a few years back and with whom he'd shared a night in a hotel room. She was happy to hear his voice, and he laid into it, even though there was an unsettled bit of business rattling around inside him by now.

"It was a fatal stabbing last month in some town called Penance—a Molly Broome and Charlotte Brown? Both eleven-year-old girls. Must still be big news down there."

The woman, whose name was Keisha, clacked on a keyboard. She said, "That Molly girl's been in and out of the system for a couple years. You want me to send you the file?"

"That'd be great. The parents' contact info in that file?"

"It's the momma and a stepdaddy, but yeah, it's all right here."

"Perfect," Clay said. "I read in a news article that this girl Molly said a man living in the woods was involved in this somehow?"

"I don't know anything about that," Keisha said. More clacking on a keyboard. "What's your interest in this case, anyway, Clay?"

He closed his eyes, his cell phone burning a hot spot against his cheek. What could he even say to that? "I just came across the story and it sparked something in me." Which wasn't truly a lie.

"Coming your way now, baby. You coming to town anytime soon? Would be nice to catch up. Maybe go out for some drinks."

"Unfortunately not," he said, but then thought, *I could do it. I could drive out there tomorrow. Or today, even. Right now. Is there something here? Is this part of the cycle? Or am I just chasing ghosts?*

He thanked Keisha then disconnected the call.

You coming to town anytime soon?

Fuck it.

He decided to take a road trip.

CHAPTER EIGHT

PENANCE

1

The town of Penance, Kentucky lay flat beneath a hard blue sky, where shiny metal silos raked the bottoms of scudding white clouds. Produce stands were in abundance, just as they'd been for the final hour of Clay Willis's six-hour drive down from Michigan— roadside shacks like puppet theaters, crude approximations of anthropomorphic fruits and vegetables painted on sandwich boards along both sides of the highway. Scarecrows wearing rubber Halloween masks for faces. The town only had one grocery store, one restaurant, one motel, and about a dozen taverns.

Clay met Steve and Jean Russell at one such tavern, a place that stank of cow shit and the weightier odor of human degradation. Jean Russell, Molly Broome's birth mother, had nervous eyes and a twitchiness that might have been the early signs of Parkinson's. According to the file Keisha had emailed him, Jean had been married once before, to Molly's father, who died in some unnamed industrial accident, and then she'd briefly dated a man who had taken an unnatural interest in her daughter. That was how Social Services had gotten involved, but by then, the kid had already been traumatized. At least the son of a bitch who had done the traumatizing was in prison now.

Steve Russell, Molly's stepfather, was the possessor of a quiet, suspicious nature, although Clay wasn't sure how much of that was his normal countenance or how much had to do with the recent murder committed by his stepdaughter. Shit like that tends to make you tight-lipped and uncomfortable, Clay knew.

Steve Russell's first question was: "Good Lord, what happened to your face, son?"

Clay told him it was an autoimmune condition, then explained who he was and what work, for the past eleven years, he had been doing up in Lansing, Michigan. Children with problems were his specialty; he'd always felt a connection to them. He also had a track record of dealing with the courts on a variety of criminal cases. He slid a folder across the table to the Russells, which contained his résumé and a list of references. Steve Russell opened it, thumbed through the loose pages inside, but didn't seem to comprehend much of what he was looking at.

"You got any experience getting kids off on a murder charge?" Steve Russell asked.

Clay admitted that he did not. "But I do understand the system, Mr. Russell. And I've got contacts in the Fayette County Social Services office. Molly's being charged as an adult, is my understanding. The rest of her life is in the balance here. I think I can offer your family some help."

"What kind of help?"

"For starters, I'd like to talk to Molly myself," Clay said.

"She's already got a shrink she talks to up in that detention center."

"I think we should approach this from a different angle," Clay said. "I've had experience talking to children who've been involved in situations where their actions were...let's say *manipulated* by outside influences."

"Outside influences," Steve said. "You talking about drugs, Mr. Willis?"

"No, sir. I'm talking about a person. Often it's an adult who gains a child's trust, then manipulates that child into doing something they wouldn't ordinarily do. I understand Molly mentioned something to the cops about a man living in the woods—a man who may have been involved in what happened somehow?"

"That's right." Steve Russell reached across the table and grasped his wife's hand. "Said there was a homeless man living out there where the girls been playing. She said he talked her into doing what she done."

"Did she describe what this man looked like?"

"Just that he was a homeless fella."

"What about the police?" Clay asked. "Are they looking into who this guy might be?"

"I don't rightly know what the police are doing, Mr. Willis."

"This is my fault." It was the first thing Jean Russell had said since Clay's arrival at the tavern. Her eyes went wide in her slightly tilted, slightly trembling head.

"Jean," Steve said, squeezing her hand. "Please, hon."

Jean Russell slid her hand out from beneath her husband's. "I think I need some fresh air."

It seemed to take an eternity for Jean Russell to lift her frail body from the chair. She trembled like a foal still wet from the womb. Before leaving, she offered Clay a conciliatory smile that never quite touched her eyes, then shuffled across the tavern and out the door into the bright sunshine.

Steve Russell spit a brown globule of tobacco juice into a Gatorade bottle he'd been cradling between his thighs. "This whole thing's been hard on Jean. She blames herself. Couple years back, there was a thing happened with Jean's ex, a thing this fella'd done to Molly that was pretty bad and wound him up in jail."

"I spoke with a woman from Fayette County Social Services," Clay said. "I'm familiar with the incident."

"Jean blames herself for what happened. For letting that fella into their home. I keep telling her it ain't her fault what that fella done, but Jean, she's got the guilt, sir. She knows Molly ain't been right since, and now...well, now this, Mr. Willis."

Clay could see Jean Russell through one of the tavern windows, smoking a cigarette and gazing at the road. Eighteen-wheelers rolled by as if on a conveyor belt. "If there was a man involved in all this, Mr. Russell—a man who coerced your stepdaughter into doing what she did to Charlotte Brown—then that could help Molly's case. It might help ease some of your wife's guilt, too."

Steve Russell leaned forward across the table. "There was no man, Mr. Willis," he said, and there was a grave finality to his voice. "I know what Molly said, but...well. That part was all in Molly's head."

"How do you know that?"

"Because she's a troubled kid. That sumbitch Jean dated, he did a number on her. Ain't her fault. But she ain't right no more."

"Maybe she's right this time," Clay said.

Steve Russell's eyes hung on him. They were weary, troubled eyes. "Look, Mr. Willis," he said. "You think you might be able to help Molly somehow? I'm all for it. But I gotta be upfront with you. Jean and me, we don't got a lot of money. And I been outta work for a spell. What I'm trying to say, sir, is how much is this gonna set us back?"

"It won't cost you a dime," Clay assured him.

2

Since her arrest, Molly Broome had been living in the Fayette Regional Juvenile Detention Center in Lexington. It was a secure facility that housed up to sixty inmates at any given time. Most of its rooms looked like elementary-school classrooms, with maps on the walls and wooden desks in tidy rows. Clay had been to countless facilities no different than this one, and they never failed to instill in him a sense of despair.

He waited for Molly in one of those classroom-styled rooms, the walls an institutionalized pink, the plastic chair beneath his ass just a bit too small and uncomfortable. He'd wanted to bring in his cell phone so he could show Molly the photo Mia had sent him, but it was considered contraband and was not permitted in the facility.

At precisely three o'clock, the door to the classroom opened. The girl who entered the room was tall but overweight—what some people might call a bruiser of a kid. She had a plain round face framed within a mop of uncombed, straw-colored hair, and there were jagged red abrasions down each of her ruddy cheeks. Her upper arms were crusted with pimples that had been scratched to bloody streaks. She moved the way kids do when their bodies grow quicker than their minds.

This was Molly Broome, and she froze in the doorway when she saw him sitting there.

A woman in a brown polo shirt and khaki BDUs came up behind the girl. She nodded curtly at Clay, then instructed Molly to join him at his table, go on now, but Molly wouldn't budge.

"It's all right." Clay smiled at the woman. "I can take it from here."

"I'll check back in fifteen minutes," said the woman, and then the soles of her sneakers were squeaking back down the hall as the door eased shut on a pneumatic hinge.

The girl just stood there, motionless.

"Hi, Molly. My name is Clay Willis. I'm a social worker from Michigan. I heard about what happened and I wanted to come all the way down here to meet with you. Do you mind if we talk for a bit?

You don't have to sit here with me. You can sit at a table over there, if you like."

She just stared at him.

"Your parents wanted me to say hello," he went on. "I met with them yesterday. They're very concerned about you, Molly."

"I know what you are," Molly Broome said. "You don't fool me."

Clay repositioned his chair for better eye contact. "What am I?" She said nothing.

"I'm not trying to fool anyone, Molly. I'm a social worker, just like I said. That's someone who helps kids who're in trouble. I understand you've spoken to social workers in the past, is that right?"

"No," Molly said. "That's not what I mean."

"What do you mean?"

"You're a demon," she said. "I know it. You can't trick me." She pronounced *can't* as *cain't*.

"Why do you say that?"

"My nan told me stories before she died about demons who crawl up outta hell. They look mostly like real people so they can fit in. But because they're demons, they always have to leave a piece of themselves behind. Like you had to leave your face."

"And my hands," he said, and wiggled his fingers.

The girl's head went slowly back on her neck, as though she were trying to create even more distance between them.

Clay considered this for a moment. "I've never heard that demon story before, Molly, but I like it. It's got a sense of logic and history to it. Some style, too. Do you know what I used to tell people when they asked about my skin?"

She twisted her head from side to side, the tendons in her neck crackling. Her eyes never left his.

"I used to tell them that when I was a kid, I woke up one morning to a face and a pair of hands on my ceiling. They looked familiar, and then I realized it was *my* face and *my* hands up there. They'd come off me in the night and gotten stuck up there somehow. I tried all day to get them to come down off the ceiling so I could put them back on, the way you'd put on gloves and a mask, but I couldn't do it. I got scared about that at first, 'specially when my parents and my friends didn't recognize me…but then I realized it was like starting over fresh in a new body. With a new life. And I kind of liked that idea. Anyway, my friends and my family got used to the new me. Things were okay. And so now this is how I look. And I'm good with that."

"But that ain't true," Molly said, and Clay sensed a ridge of distrust in her tone. He imagined her stabbing that little girl in the photo, Charlotte Brown, Molly's clublike hand bringing a large knife down, down, down. He wondered if those scratches he was seeing now on Molly's face were defensive wounds from poor Charlotte's fingernails. "That ain't how it happened."

Clay just shrugged. Then he said, "No, that's not how it happened. It's a skin condition I've had since childhood. Doctors call it vitiligo but I just call it the vit. Kind of boring when you say it like that, huh? I like the story about the face and hands on the ceiling better."

"Is it catching?"

"You mean is it contagious?"

The girl nodded.

"You know, I'm not sure," he said, and looked down at his hands. Then he looked up at her and smiled. "Just kidding. It's not catching."

Molly looked up at the ceiling, perhaps to see if there were any faces or hands up there now. Whole people, even. There was a rind of unwashed flesh in the crease of her neck that Clay could see from all the way across the room. He felt his heart go out to this kid.

"Tell me about the man in the woods, Molly," Clay said.

Something like fear flickered behind Molly's eyes.

"How did you and Charlotte meet him?"

"Charlie," Molly said. "Charlie Brown."

Clay smiled. "Was that her nickname? Like from the *Peanuts* comics?"

"It's just what I called her. Charlie is short for Charlotte. It ain't gotta be a boy's name."

"How long had you and Charlie been friends?"

"Since we was little."

"She was your best friend?"

"She was my only friend."

Clay nodded. "I had a couple of really good friends when I was about your age, too. That's how I know about the man, Molly. The man in the woods. My friends and I met him, too."

Something in the girl's face tightened. Her eyes were turning red and glassy. She looked away from him. Clay listened to the clock on the wall as it counted down the seconds, *snick snick snick*. Finally, when Molly spoke, her voice was just barely above a whisper: "He wasn't no man. He just looked like one."

"Why do you say that?"

"Because his face looked…" She didn't complete the thought.

"What about his face?" Clay prompted.

"There was another face under his face," Molly said. "A demon face. I could see it."

Something about this resonated with Clay, although he couldn't quite figure out why in that moment. Instead, he opted for the logical response: "No, Molly. He was just a man. A very bad man."

Molly's eyes went wide. Her face was so pale her skin looked nearly translucent. "You're wrong. He's not a man. He's still in my head, and he won't let go. I still see Charlie, too. He makes her come to me. At night. Her crying wakes me up."

"That's just…" *In your head*, he was going to say.

"He tricked us."

"How'd he do that, Molly? How'd he trick you?"

"He made a promise. But then he didn't keep it."

"What promise was that?" But Clay already knew.

"He said that if I sent Charlie to the well, he'd bring her back, and then we'd both have special powers. That we'd be full of magic and that no one would ever hurt us again."

There.

There.

Clay felt suddenly out of breath. "The man who made you this promise," he said, and it was like hearing someone else speaking out of his mouth. His voice shook. "What did he look like?"

She turned and studied Clay's face from across the room. Hunting for something behind his eyes, perhaps. A face behind a face.

"What did he look like, Molly?"

"Like you," she said.

"Like me? Why do you say that?"

"Because he was missing a piece of himself, too. Just like a demon would."

"What piece was he missing?"

"His eye," she said. "He was missing his eye."

3

He was sitting behind the wheel of his car in the parking lot of the detention facility when his cell phone rang. It was Nikki Alvarez.

"I'm sorry, boss, but I couldn't get a match on that photo you sent me."

"Shoot. Okay. I appreciate you giving it a try, Nikki."

"There's something else, too."

"What's that?"

"Well, for starters, do you know anything about how the facial recognition software works?"

"Not a clue."

"The program uses biometrics to map facial features from a photograph or video, and then it compares that map to known faces throughout various databases. The software I use has a ninety-nine point five percent success rate."

"So you're saying it's unusual that you couldn't find a match?"

"No, not necessarily. The match would have to already be in a database somewhere. What *is* unusual is that the software was having difficulty mapping the face to begin with. Every time I ran it, the biometrics would calibrate differently."

"Talk to me in plain English, Nikki."

"It's like the dude's face keeps changing," she said.

Clay peered out the windshield of his car and at the detention facility behind its barricade of chain-link fence and concertina wire. For some reason, this comment reminded him of something from his past, much like Molly's comment had, although he still couldn't put his finger on exactly what it was.

"No chance you've got another photo of this guy?" Nikki asked.

"No, I don't. Sorry."

"Anything else I can do for you, boss?"

"I think that's it. Thanks again, Nikki. I appreciate it. You take care."

He hung up, only to have the phone chime a second later in his palm.

"Mr. Willis, this is Ashida Rowe. I'm the attorney appointed to the Molly Broome case, and it's my understanding that you met with my client's parents, Jean and Steve Russell, yesterday afternoon to request a consultation with their daughter—"

"I just left the facility now," Clay said. The palms of his hands were sweating and his shirt collar felt too tight around his neck. "I just saw Molly."

"Can I ask who you are and what your interest in this case is, Mr. Willis?"

What did he look like?

Like you.

Clay told this woman everything.

4

That night, in a shabby motel room off the highway, Clay had a nightmare that faces and hands were turning into people and climbing down from the ceiling. They consorted around his bed, moving with the ungainliness of wooden puppets suddenly spirited to life. A dark figure, more substantial than the ceiling people, rose up from the foot of Clay's bed. Maybe there was the silhouette of a top hat on the figure's head; maybe there was a single eye shining like a beacon in the darkness. The dark figure floated toward him and seemed to hover over the bed, unrestricted by gravity. He reached out and placed a cold hand atop Clay's sweaty chest, which was when he awoke, a scream snared halfway up his constricted throat. He rolled over and switched on the bedside lamp, bracing himself for what he'd find gathered around his bed. Those half-people, those floating facemasks and handprints hovering above him, leering down at him. A swarthy figure swaddled in a black cloak, one solitary eye gleaming. *Do you want to see a magic trick?*

But of course there was nothing there.

He grabbed his phone from the nightstand, pulled up Mia's email, and hammered out a response urging Mia to come out there. Then he switched the lamp back off and lay there in silence, staring at the reflection of traffic lights washing along the ceiling. Feeling jittery and unanchored. Wondering how a grown man with all his shit together could suddenly feel like some frightened and damaged kid.

After a couple more minutes, he turned the lamp back on and looked up. Just to be sure.

Only stains on the ceiling.

III

BLACK MOUTH KIDS

CHAPTER NINE

RED BALL, GOLD COIN

The Apprenticeship, 1998

1

Everything changed the day I brought Dennis down into Black Mouth. The Magician had asked us not to mention his presence to anyone outside our circle, but for some reason I didn't consider Dennis to be included in that. Dennis was just *Dennis*, my strange little brother, often no more attentive than the turtle he kept in our underwear chest back at the house. What harm could it do?

"Well, now," the Magician said, rising up to his full height from behind the vegetable crate as Dennis and I approached through the trees. He had been about to go over a new trick with Mia and Clay, who knelt on the ground in front of him, rapt until they turned their heads in our direction. "I see Mr. Warren has brought a companion."

"This is just Dennis. He's my brother." I gripped Dennis about the shoulders and pushed him forward, like some kind of sacrificial offering. Mia and Clay waved at Dennis, but Dennis was too busy staring at the Magician to wave back.

"Mr. Warren, I did not realize you *had* a brother." The Magician placed his hands flat on the vegetable crate and leaned forward, scrutinizing Dennis. "What's wrong with him?" he asked, eyes narrowing.

"Nothing," I said.

"Then why does he look the way he does?"

"He was just born that way."

"Was he, now?"

"People say it's because we live right next to the Mouth. That he was born all kinds of messed up because some part of Black Mouth got inside him when he was still inside my mom's belly."

"Who says that?"

I shrugged. "My folks, mostly."

"Same thing as my vit," Clay said. He looked down at his own pale pink hands. He was still wearing a T-shirt, and had been ever since the Magician had told him it would help with his misdirection, and I could see a small pattern of tiny white splotches along his black arms, too. "It's like a punishment or something. Black Mouth kids get messed up for being born here."

"Not all of you," the Magician said. He looked first at Mia and then at me.

"Well, I wasn't born here," Mia said. "So I'm pretty much just boring old normal."

"And what's your excuse, Mr. Warren?"

"It's just some old superstition," I said. "Black Mouth is just a stupid old hole in the ground, is all. It's not magic. Not really."

"Maybe Jamie has some strange thing about him, too, only we just don't know what it is yet," Mia suggested.

"Maybe," I said, and smiled at her.

"Fair enough." The Magician swung his one-eyed gaze back toward Dennis. "And you've brought this brother of yours here today for what reason, exactly, Mr. Warren?"

"I didn't want to leave him at home with my dad anymore."

"I *see*," said the Magician.

"Dennis is cool," Clay piped up.

"Oh, yeah, Dennis is the best!" added Mia. She happened to be wearing the macaroni necklace Dennis had made for her, so she tugged it out of her shirt and let the uncooked ziti rattle like shaman bones. "Everybody loves Dennis."

"I *seeeee*," the Magician said again, his single eye narrowing. He began to roll up the tattered cuffs of his white shirt. "Well, I suppose you're both just in time to learn a new bit of magic."

The new trick had to do with a red ball made of sponge and three plastic cups. Red ball goes under one cup, they're all shuffled around, and then you had to guess which cup the ball was under. We watched as he placed the ball beneath one cup, then moved them all around the top of the crate. I swore I knew which cup the ball was under, but when I shouted my answer and the Magician lifted the cup, the ball was not there.

He began the trick again, and my friends and I all gathered around the crate this time to watch his hands more closely. I didn't take my eyes off the cup with the ball beneath it. When he'd finished his shuffle, we all pointed to the same cup, but when the Magician lifted it, the ball was not there. It seemed impossible that we could have all chosen the exact same cup only for each of us to be wrong.

As the Magician performed this trick a third time, I recalled his edict about misdirection. I wondered if there was something in his eye that might give away the trick, so I glanced up at him as he moved those cups around. Only he wasn't looking at the cups; he was peering across the clearing to where I had left Dennis standing in the shade of the tall trees. Dennis's small eyes betrayed no emotion; indeed, it looked as though my brother had just been shaken awake from a deep sleep.

The Magician accidentally knocked over one of the cups. The red spongy ball rolled across the top of the crate and fell to the ground. "Fuck," he said.

My friends and I shared a collective intake of breath. Never once had the Magician fumbled a trick before. Not in front of us, anyway.

Mia picked up the ball off the ground and handed it to him. His one good eye still lingering on my brother (and a fine sheen of sweat appearing along the ridge of his brow), the Magician plucked the ball from Mia's hand, then refocused his attention back to the trio of plastic cups on top of the crate. He placed the ball beneath one, shuffled them around again, but *again* he knocked a cup over. *Again* the ball rolled off the edge of the crate and onto the ground.

The Magician cleared his throat.

"Well," he said, but said no more.

"So what's the secret to this trick?" Clay wanted to know. "Or is this one *real* magic?"

The Magician opened his mouth to speak, but then remained silent. His whole body appeared to stiffen. He was looking past us, so I turned and followed his gaze once more. Dennis had moved closer, from beneath the shade of the trees to the deadfall that lay across the clearing. As I watched, Dennis climbed over the deadfall with his bulky sandals then sat down on it. His knees poked out from his shorts, knobby and callused and red, and his big belly protruded from beneath the too-small hand-me-down polo shirt he wore. My brother always had an unfocused look in his eyes, but something was different now. He seemed to watch the Magician with a sense of calculated scrutiny I would have thought beyond him.

"His name is...*what* did you say his name is, Mr. Warren?" the Magician asked. There was a noticeable crack in his voice as he spoke.

"Dennis," I said.

"Uh, excuse me, Mr. Dennis," the Magician said, raising his voice to a composed falsetto. He withdrew a deck of cards from his pants pocket. "Do you want to see a magic trick?"

Dennis rotated his head to the sound of the Magician's voice, but gave no response.

"Is he deaf, too?" the Magician asked.

"Jamie Warren does magic tricks," Dennis said in his monotone voice before I could respond.

"Yes, Mr. Warren *does* do magic tricks," the Magician agreed, "but *I* am the one who taught him. Would you like to learn how to do magic tricks like Mr. Warren?"

"Jamie. Warren. Does. Magic. Tricks," Dennis repeated.

Embarrassed, I looked at the Magician. He was still staring at my brother, beads of sweat rolling down the sides of his face. His upper lip glistened.

"It's no use having him here. He won't be able to learn," the Magician said. "His mind is not altogether with us."

"That's okay," I said. I had never had any intention of Dennis becoming an apprentice like the rest of us. I just didn't want him home alone with our father anymore. "He can just hang around or whatever."

"Hang around or...whatever," the Magician repeated. Then he blinked his eyes, seeming to snap out of some hypnotic trance. "Why don't you all go on and practice your sleight-of-hand manipulations for the rest of the afternoon?"

"What about the well?" Mia asked. "When do we finally get to go to the well and become *real* magicians?"

The Magician was staring at Dennis again while Dennis watched a pair of squirrels chase each other up and down the trunk of a tree. I saw something constrict in the Magician's throat. His lips went thin and he coughed quietly into one fist. "Soon," he said, and I noted an unsteady quality in his voice. "Very soon."

2

Dennis came down to the Mouth with me for the rest of that week, but it was no longer the same as it had once been. We all sensed the change, although none of us could describe what that change *was*. Dennis was the only thing that had been added to the equation, but his presence couldn't account for the way the Magician kept fumbling his deck of cards, kept knocking over cups, kept sweating through the grimy white fabric of his shirt. There was a clumsy aggression to him now, and my friends and I began to think it was because we weren't learning our magic tricks fast enough. Was he disappointed in our apprenticeship? Did he regret having taken us under his wing?

Yet if he was wrong about us, then he was also wrong about Dennis. *He won't be able to learn*, the Magician had said about my brother on the first day he'd met him. *His mind is not altogether with us*. Much in the way he would watch me practice my card tricks at night in our bedroom, Dennis watched my friends perform theirs down there in Black Mouth. He stared with an intensity that was almost frightening, sometimes losing himself in the complexity of those tricks, other times mumbling some inaudible chant beneath his breath as he watched. On the few occasions the Magician himself deigned to perform—and he did this less and less during these past few days, often dropping the cards and messing up the tricks—Dennis would sit cross-legged on the ground right in front of him, almost too close, his big head tilted all the way back on his neck, moisture glistening in the corners of his open mouth, that laser-focused intensity in his otherwise murky, seawater eyes.

The first time Dennis picked up a deck of cards, he performed the Riffle Force maneuver to perfection. He had seen me do it countless times—clumsily, I'll admit—so he knew how it was done. Yet I would have never imagined him physically capable in a million years. Dennis was the antithesis of dexterous—there was nothing sleek or agile about my younger brother. His hands were oversized mitts, his fingers thick, blunt pegs. I'd once watched him throw a fit because he couldn't pick up a coin off the kitchen floor, but now he could perform the Riffle Force better than the rest of us, and with no practice.

And it didn't stop there: He learned all the shuffles, all the pick-a-card-any-card routines, the double lift that had taken my friends and me days to achieve. While we were at first amazed and then proud of Dennis, the Magician's reaction to my brother's ability was more difficult to read. Like us, the Magician applauded each of Dennis's tricks, even cheered him on…but there was something lifeless and cold in the Magician's stare as he watched my brother perform. His smile no longer tested the boundaries of his narrow face, but merely surfaced on those thin lips for no more than the length of a heartbeat before vanishing again.

And then one afternoon, wholly unprompted, Dennis stumped us all with the red-ball-in-the-cup trick.

Just as he'd seen the Magician himself do it on that first day, Dennis placed the spongy red ball beneath one of the three cups, and then shuffled them around the top of the crate. Only to say that he *shuffled* them was to be generous: He basically just jostled the top of each cup without actually moving them around. It was as if he didn't understand the concept of confusing his audience. He merely placed the red ball beneath the cup in the middle, and the middle cup *stayed* in the middle, just as the other two cups *stayed* on either side of that one. Then he shook each cup around with his large hands, one at a time, making a weird *brrr-brrr* with his big lips, somehow thinking he was fooling us.

"No, Dennis, you gotta move them around fast enough so that we lose track of where the ball is," I tried to explain to him. "You gotta switch all their places so we can't follow where the ball is. See? I know the ball is in the middle cup because you never moved it. You gotta move it around so you—"

He lifted up the middle cup.

There was no ball underneath.

"Holy smokes!" Clay shouted, hurrying over to the front of the crate. He dropped to his knees beside me in the dirt. "We all saw you put it right in there."

"This one," Mia said, coming over and pointing to the cup on the left.

Dennis lifted that cup to reveal nothing beneath it, as well.

"So, okay, it's *here*," I said, tapping the final cup. "But I have no idea how you *got* it under there, because I *saw* you put it under—"

Dennis lifted the last and final cup.

There was no ball beneath it.

"*Bullshiiiiit!*" Clay crooned, laughing and pumping one fist in the air. "Dennis, what the hell, man? How'd you do that?"

"I know how he did it." It was the Magician, having come up behind us to watch this display. For the first time I saw evident displeasure on his face, even though I could tell he was trying to mask it. I thought maybe he was angry at Dennis for figuring out the trick. Or disappointed in us for having been fooled. "That was very good, Mr. Dennis. Excellent, in fact. I'm very impressed. Now what do we do when we've completed our performance?"

Dennis took a bow.

The Magician walked in a wide circle around us, his focus still locked on my brother. He slipped one grimy hand into the pocket of his black pants, then took out a large gold coin. It sparkled when the sun struck it.

"Displacement," he said, holding up the coin. "The relocation of an item from one place to another."

He swallowed the coin in a fist, then brought his hands together. He swiped his palms across each other, then held up both hands, fingers wiggling. The coin had vanished.

"That's a good one," Clay said.

"I'm not finished, Mr. Willis." The Magician pointed at me. "Go on, Mr. Warren. Check your shorts pocket, please."

I stuck my hand in the right-side pocket of my shorts. My fingers touched a flat disc that was cold and solid. I drew it out and saw that it was the very same coin the Magician had been holding just a moment ago.

"No freakin' *way*," Clay marveled. He rushed over to me and snatched the coin from my hand before I could even process what the heck had just happened.

"Let me see, let me see," Mia said, hurrying to Clay's side. She peered down at the coin that shone in the palm of Clay's hand, their sweaty heads pressed together.

I looked up at the Magician, expecting to find him pleased with himself once again for having stumped us with such a wonderful feat of magic. But he was looking at Dennis, who still stood behind the vegetable crate rocking those plastic cups beneath his stubby hands, oblivious to what had just transpired. I noticed the Magician's throat do that strange constricting thing again, like someone was drawing his windpipe closed from the inside. I also noticed that he didn't look so well. Paler than usual. Sickly, almost.

The Magician's eye flicked in my direction. He'd caught me staring at him. For a split second, I saw—or imagined I saw—a look of repulsion ripple across his otherwise stoic features.

He doesn't like Dennis, I realized. *Maybe I shouldn't have brought him down here.*

The Magician strode over to Clay and plucked the coin from his hand.

"Is that some more *real* magic?" Clay wanted to know. "Can you teach us that one or do we need to go to that well place?"

"This one is not for you, Mr. Willis." The Magician's long legs carried him over to the vegetable crate. When his shadow fell over Dennis, my brother looked up at him. "Here you are," the Magician said, and he placed the coin atop the crate. "Try that one on for size."

Dennis's mouth formed a comical *O* of surprise. He loved shiny, glittery things. I watched as he tried to pick up the coin from the crate with his blocky, blunt fingers. It took him a few attempts, but when he finally succeeded, he held it in front of his face and gazed at it with mesmeric intensity.

"Go on, Mr. Dennis…"

Dennis's squinty eyes gazed up at the Magician. That coin sparkled between the wide thumb and forefinger of my brother's hand.

"Go *on*," the Magician insisted.

"Thank. You," Dennis said, and he stuffed the coin in his own pocket.

I thought this might upset the Magician, but when he turned away from my brother and ambled back over to his campsite, I saw what could only be described as smug satisfaction on his face.

3

Later that night, as our father toiled away on his Firebird in the barn and our mom retired early to her bedroom with a box of red wine, Dennis and I made ourselves a dinner of microwavable chicken nuggets and two frosty glasses of chocolate milk. We split an entire Hershey bar that Mom had brought home from the Kroger and kept hidden in her purse by the front door. Because no one was paying any attention to us, we skipped our showers and instead watched TV in the living room. When we heard our father slam the hood of the Firebird, his drunken swearing echoing out across the field, I switched off the TV and we both hurried upstairs to lock our door and go to sleep.

Up in our bedroom, I tugged off my smelly T-shirt and tossed it on the floor. Dennis's warm, moist hand pressed against the small of my back, startling me.

"What, Dennis?"

Dennis held up both hands and wiggled his fingers.

I didn't know what he was doing at first. But then I slipped one hand into the pocket of my shorts, and felt it.

The gold coin.

CHAPTER TEN

THE REUNION

1

We stopped only once on our drive to meet Clay in Kentucky, to pump gas and grab some drinks from a 7-Eleven. We'd returned Mia's rental car back in West Virginia and opted to take my Maverick, but since I had still been a little seasick from the night before and felt about as fragile as a vampire in daylight, Mia had driven up to this point.

I grabbed some sodas, then paused when I spotted a six-pack of Bud Ice behind the frosty glass door of the refrigerator. Had I been traveling alone, I would have tucked that six-pack under my arm and emptied each one down my throat while sitting in my car with the windows down. Had it just been Dennis and me, I still might have done it. But the thought of Mia out there pumping gas into my car—Mia having driven us here because I'd gotten too fucked up the night before, fallen down the stairs, bashed my head—helped curtail that urge. Instead, I carried the bottles of soda to the counter and didn't look back.

There was a DVD bin beside the register, one of the newer Ninja Turtle movies on top. It was only three bucks, so I tossed that onto the counter with the sodas. It was a guilt purchase, no doubt about it, and I could see the headline flashing across my eyes even as I paid for it: ESTRANGED ALCOHOLIC BROTHER MAKES UP FOR YEARS OF ABSENCE WITH DVD PURCHASE!

"Is that everything?" the guy behind the counter asked, as he started to ring up the bottles of soda.

I was about to say yes, but then my eyes fell upon a deck of Bicycle playing cards below the counter. There was only one pack left, and they were tucked away down there among the candy and gum and Slim Jims like someone had picked them up from someplace else then just discarded them there at the last minute.

I picked up the deck, and handed it to the guy. "I'll take these, too."

"Bit of a poker player?" he asked casually.

"Card tricks, actually," I said, and then handed over my money.

2

There was a black man with a white face standing in the parking lot of Gilley's Motor Inn. It was near dusk, the daylight rapidly draining from the sky, but I saw him clear as a billboard lit up on a highway. Crisp pleated chinos and an ugly Hawaiian shirt. He looked like a tourist straight off a cruise ship.

I had taken over driving duties after we'd left the 7-Eleven, and I pulled now into a parking space in the lot of the inn. Both Mia and Dennis were out of the car before I'd even switched it into park.

I got out more haltingly, a queasy knot in my belly. It had been intensifying since we'd left Black Mouth, and I didn't think it just had to do with my hangover. It was a portent, I was certain, of some impending disaster looming on the horizon, something I couldn't see but could feel resonating in the marrow of my bones. I wondered if this reunion with Clay Willis—the fourth and final Black Mouth kid—was that very disaster.

Arms pumping and the buckles of his sandals rattling like castanets, Dennis tore across the parking lot toward Clay. He gathered Clay up in a giant bear hug, lifting him off the ground. Spun him around. Clay's laughter echoed across the blacktop and rose up over the din of highway traffic.

"It! Is! Clay!"

Mia went next, slipping her arms around Clay's waist, drawing him close, kissing the side of his face. I noted an intimacy in the act that made me feel like an interloper for just being there. Mia's eyes lingered on him as she pulled away, studying him, perhaps trying to comprehend the magic in how a boy becomes a man.

There was moisture in Clay's eyes as I approached across the parking lot. We shook hands, hugged, the whole thing surreal.

"This is just unfathomable," Clay said, swiping at his eyes. "You all look really good."

"Lies," Mia countered, laughing. "Nothing but lies."

"It! Is! Clay!" Dennis shouted again. His big belly shook within his too-small T-shirt.

"You're the best, Dennis," Clay said. "Shit, man. You guys—you're *all* the best. Best friends I ever had."

I shrugged. "We were kids. We didn't know any better."

"When Mia messaged me back and said she was with you guys…I mean, it almost felt like a setup, you know? Like I couldn't believe it."

"Like destiny," said Mia. "Everything coming together at the same time for a reason."

"A big reason." Clay's face went somber. "An unbelievable reason."

I felt it, too, but it brought me no peace of mind.

"We're all here now, Clay," Mia said. "What'd you find out? Fill us in."

Clay looked at each of us, his hands on his hips. The tears that hadn't spilled were causing his deep brown eyes to sparkle. "Just let me take a minute and let this all sink in," he said. "I'm sorry. I'm just a bit overwhelmed right now."

Mia hugged him again.

"It! Is! Clay!" Dennis said once more, and somewhere in the distance church bells began to chime.

3

In anticipation of our arrival, Clay had gotten a second motel room right next door to his, where we could open the connecting door and turn the rooms into a suite—albeit a pretty shabby one, as far as suites were concerned. He'd also picked up a case of beer and ordered a few pizzas for dinner. When the food arrived, I set Dennis up in the adjacent room with a few slices of pepperoni and a Dixie cup of room-temperature Pepsi. He'd brought his portable DVD player with him, so I gave him the Ninja Turtles DVD I bought for him back at the 7-Eleven. I expected some sort of excitement at the receipt of the gift, but Dennis just studied the artwork on the DVD cover, holding it so close to his face that his breath fogged up the plastic.

"Let me show you," I said, and took the DVD from him. I loaded it into the player then brought up the menu. An action sequence featuring all four Turtles fighting bad guys played behind the menu screen. Dennis just stared at it with wide eyes. Back at the house, he had only played the same two Ninja Turtle movies on repeat, the ones from the early nineties, so he was only familiar with those rubbery, Muppet-like Turtle costumes.

"Not really there," he said.

"What do you mean? Those are the Ninja Turtles. You love those guys."

"Not really *there*," he said, pointing at the screen.

"You mean the Turtles? They're just CGI, man. Made with computers instead of costumes. Dennis, they look a million times better in this movie than in those other ones you watch."

His head slowly tipped to one side. His eyes never left the screen, but he didn't look happy.

"I was just trying to do a nice thing," I said, then retreated toward the door. I felt aggravated and uncomfortable. A new headline appeared in my head: ESTRANGED ALCOHOLIC BROTHER'S GIFT REJECTED BY UNFORGIVING SIBLING. *Fuck it.* I was thinking about those beers in the next room that Clay had bought. "Eat your dinner," I told Dennis, and went next door.

"Let's do a toast," Clay said just as I came through the doorway. He popped the cap off a bottle of Yuengling and handed it to me. Mia was already halfway through one of her own, a half-eaten slice of pepperoni pizza on a paper plate beside her on the bed. "To the Black Mouth kids," Clay said, and we all clinked our beer bottles together. "I never had friends quite like you guys, you know," he said.

"We were friends because we were outcasts," Mia said. "We shared a commonality in our inability to conform."

"Yeah, well, I never quite conformed like that with any other kids. Or anyone at all, for that matter. And it was tough moving to a new place after we had to leave Black Mouth. Kids can be cruel, and I was a walking target. It only got tougher as I got older, and I had no friends around to back me up."

"I can commiserate," Mia said, and knocked the neck of her beer bottle against Clay's. She gave Clay an abridged version of the story she'd told Dennis and me the night before at the Chinese restaurant—about moving from place to place, Uncle Joe dying, the awful foster homes. The only thing she left out was her attempted suicide.

When she'd finished, Clay leaned over and gave her a one armed hug. Then he looked at me. "Last time I saw you, Jamie, we were getting released from that detention facility. My folks came and picked me up, and I remember the guards letting you stand outside with me. I watched you through the back window of the car as my daddy drove away. My family had already moved by that time, so I never went back to the Mouth. Can't say I missed it, but I sure did miss you."

"I remember," I said, looking down at my beer.

"When I heard about your daddy dying in that accident with his car, I wanted to come see you. But my folks didn't think it was a good idea. They didn't want to go back to the Mouth, either. Not after everything that had happened."

"It's all right," I said. "I don't blame them."

"Where'd you and your family wind up after that?"

I tried to soften my expression. "We just stuck it out in the Mouth."

Clay paused, a slice of pizza halfway to his lips. I saw him fight off the look of surprise that had surfaced on his face. "You never got out?"

"Not until I grew up and split on my own."

"That must have been difficult for you," he said.

"Nothing a six-pack of therapy can't fix."

"So what's this all about, Clay?" Mia cut in. "What'd you find out?"

Clay got up from the table and went over to a leather portfolio that sat on the nightstand between the two twin beds. He unzipped it and took out a manila folder, which he brought back to the table. "First, there's this," he said, opening the folder on the table. There was a stack of pages inside, held together with a binder clip. The page on top was a news article that looked like it had been printed off the internet. The headline read 11-YEAR-OLD GIRL FATALLY

STABBED BY FRIEND and the picture below showed a thin-faced blond girl behind thick eyeglasses. The name beneath the photo was Charlotte Brown.

"For a long time," Clay said, "I considered the possibility that what happened to us that summer may not have been a solitary incident. We didn't realize it at the time, but that man was a predator. And just like how an animal will hunt when it's hungry, predators will continue to seek out prey. It's a cycle. I see it every day in my job.

"So when I got your email, Mia, it started me thinking about all that again. I went online and started looking up news reports, anything that fit the mold that would have happened around the time and the place where you saw him and took that photo. I was thinking that maybe he might have been up to no good while he was out there, just like he was up to no good when he met us in Black Mouth that summer.

"When I found nothing in Lexington during that timeframe, I widened the search parameters. That's when I came across this news story from a month ago. We're ten minutes from downtown Penance right now, and about two hours from Lexington. I thought it was a bit of a stretch at first—the time and distance—but then I came across this one goddamn line in the news story, *and I just knew it was right*."

He handed the news article to Mia. As she scanned it, Clay said, "Eleven-year-old Molly Broome says she murdered her best friend because a man living in the woods told her to do it."

"Oh fuck me," Mia said, and put a hand to her mouth. She handed the article to me.

"Still," Clay said, holding up one finger, "I had to really be sure before I got back with you on this, Mia. So I came out here, to Penance, and met with the girl's parents."

"You did not," Mia said.

"I did. I wanted to confirm this…this hypothesis…that had been bouncing around in my head all these years. I asked them if I could speak with their daughter, who's currently being held in a detention facility in Lexington. They agreed, so I went and talked to the girl."

"Jesus, Clay," I said, setting the newspaper article on the table.

"What'd she say?" Mia asked.

Clay looked at Mia then looked at me. A nerve twitched in one of his eyelids.

"It's him," he said. "The Magician. No doubt about it."

4

Once he finished telling us everything Molly Broome had said, the three of us just sat there in silence. We didn't even look at each other. The story the girl had relayed to Clay had been an almost exact overlay of what we all remembered from our own time with the one-eyed man in Black Mouth—the card tricks, the enticement to send someone to the well, the promise of real magic if the girls did everything he said. Molly had even described the murder weapon she had used on her friend—a large knife with an unusual handle that the man had kept in his boot. A handle that looked made of bone.

"With the exception of that trick with the dead rabbit," Clay said, "everything Molly Broome told me matches what happened to us. She even described him the same way—right down to the eye patch."

"Jesus Christ," Mia said.

A part of me wanted to believe this was some sort of elaborate hoax, but I couldn't convince myself of that. Another part of me wondered if I wasn't actually still in my old house on the cusp of Black Mouth, losing my mind.

"The guy's a predator," Clay said. "We're talking about a sociopath who gets off on having children commit murder. And God knows how many other times he's done it over the years."

Mia shook her head. "I feel sick."

"So, to cut to the chase, here's why I've asked you to come out here," Clay said. "After I met with Molly Broome, I got a call from her public defender, Ashida Rowe. I guess the Russells thought they should clue her in, and I don't really blame them. Ms. Rowe wasn't too thrilled that I went and spoke with Molly behind her back, and she was getting ready to read me the Riot Act, which is when I told her about what happened to us when we were kids. After that, she—"

"Hold on," I said. "You spoke to some attorney about us?"

"I needed to explain the connection."

"I don't believe this, Clay…"

"What's the big deal?" Mia cut in. "It's not like we're fugitives. We did our time when we were kids. It's not some big secret, Jamie; there's a record of what happened back then."

"Yeah, it's a record buried in some filing cabinet in West Virginia. We come out with something like this and it's gonna make the news again. It'll be part of our *lives* again. You think you can still do your job, Clay, if whoever you work for finds out what we did?"

"I need to unburden some of this, man," Clay said. "Trust me, I think about that shit every *day*. I drag it behind me like Jesus drags the *cross*, brother. But you talk about my *job*, Jamie, so let me tell you about my *job*. My *job* is to help children who don't got nobody else to turn to. My job is to be the one hand held out for them to grasp. How do I live with myself now that I know this is happening and still go on about my day? It ain't about a fucking *job*. I can't do that, man. I just can't."

"So what'd this lawyer say?" Mia asked.

"She wants to meet with us tomorrow, along with Molly's parents, to go over all the details of what happened to us that summer. She said the cops don't believe that story about a man in the woods—they found no evidence that anyone was living out there—but that we might be able to change their minds."

"I can't believe you did this behind our backs, Clay." I stood up from my chair. "This wasn't just your dirty laundry to air out. It affects all of us. Jesus Christ, I shouldn't have even come out here, goddamn it."

"Then why did you?"

"Because I was fucking blindsided! I wasn't thinking straight and my head's a mess. Clay, man, my mom just died and I had to go back home for the first time in like a billion years. I spent so much time trying to forget about that place and what happened there, and now here I am, right back in the middle of it. The more I keep dwelling on this shit, it's like some black poison filling my veins."

"It's okay to be angry, Jamie. It's okay to feel used. You're a victim here, too. He manipulated all of us."

Something that sounded like a laugh ruptured from my throat, but there was nothing humorous about it. My eyes were welling with tears. "A victim, huh? I sure as hell didn't feel like a victim after eleven months in juvie. I didn't feel like a victim going back to Black Mouth after that, when everyone was looking at me like some kind of monster. I *felt* like a monster. I know you guys had it bad when you moved away, I get it, but I fucking had to *stay* in that place with fucking *blood on my hands*. It took me a lifetime to crawl out of that nightmare, and now you want me to go back in?"

"You only think you crawled out," Clay said, "but you didn't. You just buried it. If you don't see this thing through to the end, Jamie, then that guy who did this to us, he wins. And you'll be carrying this shit around with you until the day you die. That black poison will only keep pumping through your veins until it kills you."

I shook my head. "I can't go to this meeting with you tomorrow, Clay. I don't want to be a part of this."

"Jamie—"

"I'm not looking to chase after this guy, whatever he is. And I don't need a lecture from you, man. I don't need—"

I watched both Clay and Mia stiffen and go silent. Their eyes told me to turn around, so I did.

Dennis stood in the doorway that connected both rooms. He had pizza sauce on his face, some on his shirt, and a Dixie cup of Pepsi swallowed up in one giant hand. He was staring at me with an intensity uncharacteristic of him.

"Dennis, go back and watch TV."

Instead, Dennis ambled across the room toward us. I suddenly felt sick to my stomach.

"Maybe he should stay," Mia said. "This involves him, too."

"That's not your call, Mia. He's my brother."

"I think we should all just take a breath and calm down," Clay said.

"I'm fucking calm, Clay. I'm fucking calm. I'm just trying to take care of my goddamn brother and not lose my fucking mind in the process."

"She. Is now. Dead." Dennis had come up to the table and was looking down at the newspaper article with Charlotte Brown's picture on it.

"It's okay, Dennis," Clay said, quickly closing the file. "You don't need to worry about that."

"He can't even read it," I said, and Clay looked at me funny. "Dennis can't read."

"She. Is now. Dead. She. Is now. *Dead*." He kept pointing at the folder.

"That's what he was saying when I found him this morning," Mia said. She was staring at my brother now as if he were a puzzle she was trying to piece together.

"Dennis," I said, trying to settle his nerves. Trying to settle my own.

"She. Is now. Dead. *Jamie*." And he turned to me. A chill spilled down my back. For a moment, his eyes were perfectly lucid. He looked like someone else. "In my walking dream."

"What do you mean, Dennis?" Clay asked.

"What's a walking dream?" Mia asked. She was looking at me now, though that same scrutiny was still in her eyes.

I said nothing. My mind was suddenly going a million miles an hour.

Clay reopened the folder and handed it to my brother. "Do you know something about this girl, Dennis?"

"Clay," I said. "Stop."

Dennis brought the folder within an inch of his face, and I watched as his dark, muddy eyes studied Charlotte Brown's photo. His head rocked slowly back and forth on his thick neck. He looked like he was channeling something. "In my walking dream," he said. He kept repeating it with increased urgency: "In my walking dream! She is now dead! Jamie! She! Is now! Dead!"

"What does that *mean*, Dennis?" Clay pushed.

"Give me that," I said, and tore the folder from Dennis's hands. He gasped and staggered backward, as if I'd just struck him. "Enough."

Clay was looking at me hard. "What's going on here, Jamie?"

I said nothing.

"In my walking dream," Dennis said, pointing at the folder in my hands. He sounded calmer now, but there was still an edge to his voice. "In my walking dream. *Jamie*."

"What's that mean?" Mia asked. "What's a walking dream? Why does he keep saying that?"

I exhaled a shuddery breath. "About a week after our mom committed suicide, a police detective from Sutton's Quay found my brother walking along the highway in his underwear. He was sleepwalking."

"Just like how I found him this morning," Mia said. "Was that what it was? He was sleepwalking?"

"I don't know *what* the fuck he was doing," I said. "But that's what he calls his 'walking dream.'"

Dennis's shadow fell over me. "Not *Mom*," he said. "A. Little. Girl. Is now. Dead." He was still pointing at the folder in my hand.

Mia touched my brother's arm. "Her name is Charlotte Brown, Dennis. How do you know about her? Did you see it on the news or something?"

"In my walking dream," Dennis said.

"What's going on here, Jamie?" Clay asked again.

I laughed. Then I rubbed my face and thought about an unopened bottle of Maker's Mark I had purchased back in Sutton's Quay right after Mom's funeral, which was now stashed in the trunk of my car. Right outside the door and less than twenty feet away. "I have no idea, man. Your guess is as good as mine."

Dennis took a step toward me. He reached out and took the folder from my hand. I let him have it. He opened it and stared at the picture of the dead girl for perhaps a full minute as we all stared at him. Then he closed the folder, handed it back to Clay, and sat down on the edge of the bed in silence.

5

I stepped out into a muggy summer night that was hardly any better than that suffocating motel room had been a moment ago. Headlights paraded along the highway in a never-ending circuit. Across the highway stood a gas station, the place lit up against the night sky like a space station.

I went around to the back of my car, popped the trunk, and stripped the bottle of Maker's Mark from its brown paper sleeve. Peeled the wax from the cap and unscrewed it. My hands were shaking with anticipation and the back of my throat seemed to literally *clench* like an angry fist. I lifted the bottle and took a covetous swig, not caring that some spilled down the front of my shirt in the process. I hardly noticed. I felt the booze sear down the quivering channel of my throat then detonate in my gut.

Something had just happened in that motel room, but I was powerless to understand it.

I screwed the cap back on the bottle, not wanting to get too fucked up tonight, but then immediately removed it again. Took another drink. Listened to the booze make its *gluck gluck* sound as it burbled from the bottle and into my mouth. Wiped my mouth on my sleeve then chirped out a pathetic laugh. Funny how a bottle of Maker's Mark is pretty much the same shape as Thor's hammer. Strength and power in liquid form.

When I looked up, I saw Mia standing there in the darkness lighting a joint. Shamefaced, I turned away from her and peered back out across the highway. Jet engines rumbled beyond the cloud cover.

"Don't look all shy on my account. Maybe you've even got the right idea." Gravel crunched beneath her boots as she crossed over to my car. "You up for a trade?" She held the joint out to me. After a slight hesitation, I handed her the bottle of Maker's and took the joint. "That was a little fucked up in there, huh?"

"I don't know *what* that was," I said.

She took a drink then handed me back the bottle. "You didn't tell me your mom committed suicide."

"No? I didn't include that on my annual Christmas card? Must've slipped my mind."

"You don't have to be tough about it."

"I'm nothing about it."

"How'd she do it?"

"Bottle of pills."

"I'm sorry."

I laughed but she must have thought it was a sob or something, because she reached out and squeezed my shoulder. Her fingers were surprisingly strong.

"All this talk about this *man*," I said, and I could hear the tremor in my voice. "What if he's *not* a man, Mia? What if he's really...you know..."

"What?"

I didn't know how to say it. "All those impossible things he did that summer..."

"They were tricks, Jamie. He was manipulating us, just like Clay said."

"Yeah? Then how do you explain him bringing a dead rabbit back to life? Or hovering inches off the ground? What was that, smoke and mirrors?"

"Is that what this is?" she said, and she was looking at me now like someone to be pitied. "You're afraid of this guy because you think he could really do all those things?"

I said nothing, just kept watching the traffic.

"There *was* no real magic," she said. "Whatever we think he did back then, there's a logical explanation for it."

"You don't know that, Mia. You should be careful. You all should be careful. You don't know what you're chasing."

"I'm not sure any of us have a choice. Don't you feel it? It's fate, man. Destiny. It's set the four of us on a course, drawing us all together. All we can do is follow it."

"I don't believe that." Or was it more like I didn't *want* to believe it?

"Think about it. When was the last time you were in Black Mouth before coming back for your mom's funeral?"

"Not since I was a teenager. I got out and never looked back."

"Exactly. Yet you happen to be home again at the same time I see this guy, then show up there looking for you? How do you explain that kind of coincidence?"

"Just like that—a coincidence."

"You're so quick to believe in magic, but you can't entertain the idea that maybe this is fate giving us a chance for some karmic payback? I wanna get the son of a bitch, make him pay for what he did to us." She brought her face very close to mine, her breath scented with a cocktail of bourbon and marijuana, and not wholly unpleasant. "You don't have to be afraid, Jamie. I get where you're coming from, man. When you think back to that summer, you're still a little boy in your head. We all went through something terrible. You most of all, having gone back to Black Mouth after you left that facility. And then your dad died in that accident, and you and your brother and your mother were *stuck*. Right there in the Mouth. Black Mouth kids were pariahs even *before* all the shit that happened that summer. But it's fucked with your head. Your memories aren't what you think they are. And you've forgotten something important."

"Yeah? What's that?"

"That Black Mouth kids are not afraid."

I felt suddenly cold despite the humidity in the air. "I still see them, Mia."

"I see them all the time, too. It's called guilt, Jamie."

"I'm talking *for real*, Mia."

She ran fingers through my hair, eliciting a shiver that ratcheted up my spine. "Can I show you some skin?" she asked.

"What?"

She cuffed the sleeve of her T-shirt to the shoulder. On her upper arm was a tattoo of two bright red hearts—a big one and a little one.

"I carry them both with me, just like you do. It's why I'm driven to do something here. I'm chasing absolution, Jamie. I think you could use some yourself."

I stared at those two hearts, as if they might start beating at any second.

"I think I'm beyond absolution," I told her.

"Bullshit," Mia said. "No one ever is."

CHAPTER ELEVEN

THE FINAL LESSON

The Apprenticeship, 1998

1

There was a spark of something inside my father that, when the spirit struck, impelled him to tender an explanation for his behavior. Maybe he even thought of it as an apology of sorts, but it always struck me more as an excuse. These uncomfortable sermons generally took place a day or two after he'd thundered through the house, banging drunkenly on doors, breaking things, slapping Mom or Dennis or me around. After he'd knocked me down the stairs and broken my arm, I'd had to suffer through an afternoon of fishing at the reservoir with him, listening as he explained that his life was nothing but stress and bullshit, that his wife was a lousy goddamn alcoholic and a pothead and that his one son was a fucking retard and that maybe I'd even grow up to be a faggot because I liked to read books instead of playing sports, and there was always money problems, and the world was shit, and maybe a broken arm is actually a *good* thing because it teaches us that life is just a series of uppercuts to the face, kicks to the groin, tumbles down the stairs. He told me all of this while I jerked the bobber up and down on the surface of the water with my one good arm (the other was in a cast) and he knocked off a six-pack of Michelob. I was six years old.

A few days after he'd pounded on my bedroom door while I stood on the other side ready to brain him with an aluminum baseball bat, he had me drive out to a job with him in his Firebird. As we drove, empty beer cans sliding back and forth in the passenger-side foot well of the car, he groused through a justification of his behavior that night, directing much of the blame toward my mother.

"Thing is, Jamie, I don't get no support from that woman. Not from you kids, neither, but I don't expect that. She's my fucking *wife*, you know what I mean? It's like, she pushes me and pushes me, gets me right to the edge, then blames me for falling over the side. It's like she's setting me up for failure on purpose. You know what I'm getting at, boy?"

"Sure," I said, gazing out the passenger window as we drove. We weren't going into town, I realized, but circumnavigating the forested ridge of Black Mouth. I was antsy because I wanted to join my friends down at the Magician's campsite as usual. Instead, I had sent Dennis off with Mia and told her I'd come down there and join them the very second my dad and I got back. I only hoped that whatever we were doing wasn't going to take all day. I *also* hoped that today wasn't the day the Magician decided to tell us how to get to the well and become *real* magicians. We kept asking him when we would go, and he just kept telling us it would happen *in time.* My luck, it would probably be today, while I was stuck here in this foul-smelling car with my father.

"She's just as to blame for all the shit that happens in that house, you know, but she acts the victim," my father went on. He was wearing a black Harley-Davidson T-shirt with the sleeves cut off, tattoos flexing, oily hair pulled back into a ponytail. There was grease in the creases of his knuckles. "She likes to act the martyr, your mom. But

I'll tell you one thing, boy. She ain't gonna be happy 'til she forces me to break her neck, and then where'll we be? Your mother dead or in a wheelchair, me behind bars? Sound like a good time to you?"

"No, sir."

"Damn right it don't. How old are you, boy?"

"Eleven."

"You think you can raise up your brother at eleven years old? Him being a retard with his head not working right like a regular kid's? You think you can get a job, pay the bills, keep a roof over your goddamn heads without me, Jamie? Bad enough you're gonna have to take care of that little dummy the rest of your life once your momma and me drop dead, you rushing so quick to take on that responsibility now?"

"No, sir."

"I'm working my fuckin' fingers to the fuckin' *bone*, boy, just to keep this family afloat, and I get no fuckin' support from nobody." He spun the wheel and took a dirt road through the trees. The more he talked the faster the Firebird sped down the slope and into the westernmost section of Black Mouth. "It ain't no different in that house than it was over in Shepherd. You think those pricks at the refinery had my back? After all I done for them? *Fuuuuuck* no. No, sir. There's your answer, boy. The answer is *no fucking way*."

We pulled up outside a rundown trailer in a small, wooded clearing down in the Mouth. Lawn furniture was scattered about, and there was a baby's playpen beside an aluminum clothes carousel, the bottom of the playpen dusted with dead leaves.

My father slotted the Firebird up alongside an ugly brown sedan that looked to be mostly made of rust. He shut down the Firebird's engine but didn't get out right away. Instead, he turned to me, his eyes bleary and bloodshot in their sockets, his face crosshatched in old acne scars. Broken blood vessels stretched along the contours of his nose.

"You'll see, boy," he told me, and his breath was rank coming out of his mouth. I imagined something black and poisonous stirring around inside his guts. "You'll be a man someday, just like me, and then you'll see what it's all about."

Then he climbed out of the car, slamming the door behind him.

No, I thought, my entire body trembling. My vision blurred and I struggled not to cry. *No, I will not be like you, I will* never *be like you, I will die before I become like you…*

I watched my father as he knocked on the door of the trailer. Hands on his hips, he glanced around. He even grinned at me when he met my bleary countenance through the windshield, as if we'd just shared some heartfelt moment.

I will not be like you…

A woman came to the door. She was young, just barely out of her teens if I had to guess, and she was cradling a baby to her chest. She gave my father a set of car keys, then she watched as my dad lumbered around the side of the trailer and squeezed himself behind the wheel of the ugly brown sedan. He tried several times to start the car but the engine wouldn't turn over. He got out, popped the hood, and vanished beneath it. After a time, he shouted for me to bring him his tools.

I pulled the toolbox from the Firebird's hatchback trunk. It weighed a ton but I managed to carry it over to him without dropping it. I set it by his feet, then remained by his side, handing him specific tools whenever he asked for them.

At one point, the young woman came around the side of the trailer to watch. She cradled the infant against her chest, the baby's legs impossibly white, one reddened foot extended with its toes spread. The woman was wearing a faded pink tank top, one shoulder strap dangling below her elbow. The infant nursed, and as I watched, she repositioned the child so that I glimpsed the pale swell of a breast, an engorged pink nipple, a delicate smattering of light brown freckles across her bare upper chest.

She met my gaze and I looked away, ashamed.

"That should do 'er," my father said, slamming shut the sedan's hood. He climbed back behind the wheel, cranked the ignition, and the car sputtered to life. A clot of black exhaust belched from the tailpipe, and the woman retreated back toward the front of the trailer with her baby.

I put my father's tools back in the Firebird's hatchback trunk, then slipped into the passenger seat while my father returned the woman's car keys. She was still nursing the baby at her breast, but my father didn't seem to notice or care. They exchanged some dialogue—I couldn't hear any of it—and even though my dad had fixed her car, the young woman did not look very happy. When the baby started to squall in her arms, she repositioned it, then looked like she might cry, too. Then my dad was back in the Firebird and we were cruising back down the wooded passageway in the direction we had come.

I looked in the side-view mirror and watched the woman with the baby standing in her yard. She was cradling the baby's head as it fussed in her arms. I swore that she could see me watching in the reflection of the mirror, so I quickly looked away again. The sight of her bare breast still resonated like the afterimage of a flashbulb in my mind. It had made me feel strange to see it.

My father must have sensed my discomfort. "Caught a peep of that titty, huh?"

I said nothing, just shifted around uncomfortably in my seat.

"She's raising that little bastard out here on her own," he said. "Kid's father pulled a Houdini and disappeared. I cut her a discount on the work. Gotta help your fellow man, Jamie. Do you good to remember that. Gotta help your fellow man."

Fuck you, I thought, and glanced back at the side-view mirror. The young woman and the baby were gone.

2

It was near dusk by the time I got down to the Magician's campsite. I expected to find Dennis, Mia, and Clay gathered around the Magician, listening attentively as he walked them through his latest trick, but when I arrived, I found the campsite empty. All the Magician's stuff was gone, too—the army tent, the pots and pans, the backpack, the bedroll. I looked around at two weeks' worth of empty cereal boxes, soda cans, and candy wrappers, while a column of panic rose up through the core of my body. They had all gone to the well and left me behind. I imagined them basking in some golden spring, their bodies resplendent with a phantasmal light as potent and bright as the sun. They were giddy with laughter, performing impossible feats of prestidigitation one could only dream of, while I was here, left behind, a distant memory. Unworthy. But then I heard some rustling through the trees, and rushed off in that direction.

I saw nothing at first except the irregular entrance of the old mineshaft against the side of the hill, its opening filigreed with tendrils of waxy crimson vines. I caught movement in there—a shadow amongst shadows, shifting furtively about. Daylight was already draining from the sky so it was difficult to see much more beyond that. I crept closer, the crunch of brittle twigs beneath the soles of my sneakers as loud as gunshots.

The Magician stepped out of the mineshaft. He was wearing his black cloak once again, the hem collecting dead leaves as it dragged along the ground. He held his top hat against his chest with both hands. "Ah, Mr. Warren. We've been waiting for you."

I turned and saw Clay and Mia sitting cross-legged on the ground beyond a veil of trees, their backs against a mossy deadfall. A small bonfire burned on the ground in front of them, casting a spiral of slender black smoke up into the trees. Removed from the others, Dennis sat on the deadfall, an emptiness behind his eyes as he stared at the Magician. He had his head craned back on his neck, his big belly stretching the fabric of his striped polo shirt. Even from here I could see that grime had collected in the sweaty creases of my brother's neck.

"Come on over and sit down with us, Mr. Warren."

I followed the Magician across the clearing and sat down on the ground with my friends before the fire. Clay patted my back and Mia leaned forward and smiled at me. I felt something fresh and new lurch about inside my chest, and I didn't know what to make of it.

The Magician sat on a tree stump on the opposite side of the bonfire. His face was pale, his solitary eye recessed into a dark pocket in his skull. The lines around his mouth were overly pronounced. It was as though some sickness had overtaken him in the past several days, ever since I'd brought Dennis down there.

The Magician sprinkled some kind of powder on the fire. The flames grew larger and flashed a bright green. My friends and I stared in awe as a wisp of turquoise smoke corkscrewed up out of the fire and threaded through the air, undisturbed by any breeze that might dare to come by. We watched as it climbed higher and higher until it reached the canopy of curling tree limbs above our heads, then as it disappeared altogether into the deepening twilight.

"Tonight," said the Magician, "will be a night of celebration. Tonight, one of you will be going to the well."

A ripple of excitement traveled through our little group—everyone except Dennis, who had no idea what any of this meant. I glanced over at him and watched as he yawned and leisurely blinked his eyes. He was picking at a grayish callus on his left knee, causing it to bleed.

"Mr. Warren," he said, leveling his one-eyed stare on me. "Place your hand into the fire."

I looked at the fire then looked back at him. "What?"

"Directly into the fire, Mr. Warren. Hold it there until I instruct you to remove it."

"But I'll burn myself…"

The Magician tilted his head back the slightest bit. "Will you, now?"

I looked back at the fire, watched those flames dance. Looked down at my hand, too—the soft pink flesh ripe for burning.

Without thinking, I thrust my hand into the flames. The pain was instantaneous; alarms went off in my brain. I jerked my hand away and clutched it to my chest. It was hot and red and weeping sweat from the palm. It throbbed with its own heartbeat.

The Magician's stare lingered on me for perhaps a second longer before that single eye ticked over to Clay, who sat beside me. "Mr. Willis," he said.

"Wait," I said, still cradling my hand. "That's not fair."

"Mr. *Willis*," he said again, ignoring my plea. "Place your hand into the fire. Hold it there until I instruct you to remove it."

Clay turned to me. There was a look of abject horror on his face. The encroaching darkness coupled with the firelight made the pale patches around his eyes and mouth all the more prominent.

In what seemed like slow motion, Clay extended one ghost-white hand toward the fire. It hovered around the periphery of the flames while Clay gathered his courage. I didn't think he would do it, there was no way he would, but then he lowered his hand until the flames licked his palm. He lowered it still, and I watched as his eyes widened in terror and pain, and the sweat cascaded down his patchy face in glistening rivulets that reflected the firelight.

He pulled his hand back. I couldn't tell whether the hissing sound I heard came from his throat or from his sweat sizzling on the hot stones surrounding the fire pit. Clay's eyes were filling up with tears.

"Ms. Mia," the Magician said. "Place your hand into the fire. Hold it there until I in—"

Mia plunged her hand into the flames. She gasped, in either shock or pain, but did not remove her hand from the fire.

"Mia," I said, leaning forward on my knees, ready to grab her arm and pull her hand out.

Pinpoints of perspiration sparkled across her face; her dark eyes widened until they were two shimmering seabed stones.

"Mia—"

She cried out, then pulled her hand free of the fire.

The Magician surveyed us all from his perch on the stump. Night had come to Black Mouth, but it wasn't enough to mask the dissatisfaction on his face. Much as it had the night I'd met him in our barn, the firelight danced in his solitary eye. I watched as that eye studied each one of us…then ticked to the opposite end of the deadfall, where something had gathered his attention.

A rustling noise behind me. I turned and saw Dennis climbing down off the deadfall. Spongy bits of bark rained to the ground. He approached us with that blank look still in his eyes, his gait eerily steady and controlled. He knelt down in the dirt on the opposite side of the bonfire, close enough to the Magician so that he drew his legs away from my brother, as if fearful he might contract some virulent disease from him. The flames made my brother's face look like a semitransparent mask through which someone was shining a light.

He put his hand in the fire—

"Dennis!"

—and held it there.

I scrambled over to him, but the Magician said, "Mr. Warren, do *not*—"

His voice froze my muscles, though only for the measure of a single heartbeat. I completed a circuit around the bonfire, grasped Dennis around the forearm, and jerked his hand out of the flames. He didn't resist, and his weight sent us sprawling on our backs in the dirt. I sat up quickly, but Dennis remained there, a turtle on its back, staring muddily up at the night sky beyond the treetops. The hand he'd shoved into the fire was extended now in the air in a frozen salute, and I could see it was beet-red and slick with sweat, but it looked otherwise unharmed.

"Oh my God," Mia said. "Is he okay, Jamie?"

I shook my brother's big belly. "Dennis? Are you okay? Are you hurt? Say something."

Dennis's head revolved in my direction until he was staring up at me. His round face was shiny with sweat, his expression serene. I helped him into a seated position while he stared at his hand. He didn't appear to be in pain, although I don't know how that could be possible. Dennis had gotten a splinter in his foot from the porch steps a month earlier and he'd screamed bloody murder.

The Magician rose up from the tree stump. His black cloak swirled around him, and for a moment, it looked as though he'd become part of the night. "A surprising outcome, to be sure," he said. "But it looks like we have made our selection."

My friends and I looked up at him.

"We will send Mr. Dennis to the well," the Magician said.

Mia bolted up from the ground. Her uncle's plain white undershirt was as big as a kite on her small frame. Dennis's macaroni necklace drooped down over her chest. "That's not fair! Dennis just got here. He's not even part of it."

"Mr. Dennis has the faith."

"Just because I didn't want to burn my *hand* off?"

"Either you have faith, Ms. Mia, or you do not. That goes for all of you."

"But we *all* want to be real magicians," Clay said.

The Magician said, "We will send Dennis to the well and he will fill his bucket. Then we will bring him *back* and he will *share* the power with the rest of you. You all drink from the bucket, so to speak. And then you will all become *real* magicians."

"But Dennis can't go *anywhere* by himself," I said.

The Magician withdrew something from beneath his cloak and tossed it on the ground beside the bonfire. I couldn't tell what it was from where I knelt beside my brother, so I crawled over to it for a better look.

It was something wrapped in that filthy blanket the Magician had used as a death shroud for the dead rabbit. Only whatever was wrapped up in the blanket now was smaller, though it had struck the ground with a weightiness that made me uncomfortable.

"Go on, Mr. Warren. Open it up."

I peeled open the blanket to reveal the large bone-handled hunting knife. The one he usually kept in his boot.

"I don't understand," I said, looking up at him. My friends had gathered at my back and were peering down at the knife, too.

"This is your final lesson, Mr. Warren," the Magician said. "This is where you take your leap of faith. This is where you *take control of your destiny.* You can do it quick and painless. And then, just like the rabbit, we'll bring him *back*."

"Whoa…" It was Clay, still peering down at the knife atop that filthy blanket covered in rabbit fur. The awe in his voice was palpable. He took a step backward.

"And not just *bring him back*, Mr. Warren," the Magician went on, "but bring him back *better*. Bring him back so that he'll be like the rest of you. Wouldn't you like that, Mr. Warren? Wouldn't *Mr. Dennis* like that? Wouldn't that be fair to him? To have your brother be…*corrected*?"

It was in that moment that a terrible thing came to me. As I stared down at the knife, the cold steel of its blade winking in the firelight, my father's disembodied voice, textured with his own personal mixture of self-pity and antagonism, returned to me: *Bad enough you're gonna have to take care of that little dummy the rest of your life once your momma and me drop dead, you rushing so quick to take on that responsibility now?*

"When he returns, you will see. You will all gain the power." The Magician took a step toward us, spreading his arms wide. "You will all become the masters of your own destinies. Do you know what that means? It means that *all your problems will be over*."

"You mean *kill*—" Mia began, but the Magician shushed her with a finger to his lips. The look in his eye said: *Come now, Ms. Mia, we do not use that word.*

Clay bent down to get a better look at the knife. "You can bring him back for real, though, right?" he asked. "Just like you did to that rabbit?"

"Of course, Mr. Willis," the Magician said. He had retreated the slightest bit so that he was no longer within the halo of light coming off the bonfire. Just a tall shadow wrapped in a black cloak among the trees. "Just like the rabbit."

Clay looked at me. I could smell the sweat on him, he was so close.

"Anything worth *becoming* requires *sacrifice*. It requires *faith*. There is a power in death, Mr. Willis, that is unparalleled. It's how we open the door. It's the only way to get to the well and bring the magic back for us all to share."

I felt Mia's sweaty hand slip inside my own.

The Magician looked at me. "Do you remember the first magic

trick I ever showed you, Mr. Warren? That night in the barn? Do you still have that card?"

With one trembling hand, I dug the blank playing card from the back pocket of my shorts. I'd kept it with me every day, ever since we'd begun our apprenticeship down here. I looked at the card now, still blank, a flickering orange canvas before the fire.

"What is your destiny, Mr. Warren? What does it tell you?"

An image appeared on the card. A king brandishing a sword. There was blood on the sword and blood on the king's face. Its sudden appearance terrified me, and I accidentally dropped the card in the fire.

"No!"

I tried to snatch it out, but the flames were too high, the fire too hot. Clay yanked me back, and I could only watch through bleary eyes as the edges of the card blackened and curled until there was nothing left of it.

"All the power you will ever need to fix your lives awaits you all. You are on the precipice. It requires only that you *act* on *faith* and follow your *destinies.*"

I looked down at my hands, which were trembling uncontrollably.

...take care of that little dummy the rest of your life...

"Go on," said the Magician.

"Pick it up," said Mia.

I looked over at her. Mia's face was flushed, her brown doe's eyes black in the firelight.

I bent down and picked up the knife. It was heavy, its blade a dark blue steel, its slightly curved bonelike hilt looking like a rib. It looked very old.

My friends' faces hovered above me, eyes ablaze and eager.

I looked over at Dennis. He hadn't moved from where I'd propped him into a sitting position in the dirt. The hand he'd shoved into the fire was still extended away from his body, but he was no longer staring at it.

He was staring at me.

Quick and painless, I thought. *All your problems will be over.*

I knelt beside him, the knife between us. He didn't even look down at the blade; he just kept his dim, senseless eyes on me. Our faces were so close I could feel his exhalations gusting from his lips.

I pressed the tip of the knife against Dennis's big belly.

He looked down then, as casually as you'd please, unsurprised to find his older brother holding a sharpened blade to his stomach. I felt the tautness of his polo shirt all the way up the hilt of the knife. The soft and tender swell of his nine-year-old belly underneath.

I pushed the knife forward. Dennis's shirt dimpled and his eyes went wide. I felt resistance but I kept pushing it forward. Dennis made a *gah* sound at the back of his throat, his hot breath in my face.

A low, moaning susurration filtered through the clearing. It wasn't just my imagination—the others heard it, too—and when I looked beyond my brother to the mouth of that abandoned mineshaft, I saw the curtain of ivy over the entrance billowing out. The sound rolled past me, a physical force that blew the sweaty hair off my forehead. It rustled the nearby trees and caused the fire in the pit to gutter, although it didn't go out.

"I can't," I said, backing away from my brother. I dropped the knife back on the filthy blanket then stood up. "I can't do it."

"I'll do it," Mia said, and she bent down and reached for the knife.

"No," I told her.

She paused, her hand extended to pick up the knife.

"No, Mia. Please." And I began to cry.

She looked at me. Then she glanced down at Dennis, who hadn't moved from his spot on the ground. His swampy gray eyes looked instantly uncertain. There was a hole in the center of his polo shirt.

My legs unsteady, I lowered myself to the deadfall. I sensed the Magician watching me, but I couldn't bring myself to face him. "I'm sorry. I'm sorry. I just can't."

Mia straightened up. Whatever brief spell she'd been under, it seemed to have passed. She came over and sat beside me. Her arm went around my waist, her head on my shoulder. Clay came around to the other side and joined us on the deadfall, too. He patted my back but didn't speak.

Movement in the peripheral darkness—the Magician slinking around the perimeter of trees, his boots nearly soundless along the carpet of dead leaves and pine needles. I looked up just as he advanced into the firelight. His one good eye hung on me as he bent down, folded the blanket back over the knife, and picked it up. I couldn't read his expression—there *was* none. Surely he was disappointed in me. I had failed him. I had failed everyone. I was too weak.

"Our time together has come to an end," he said.

I swiped the tears from my eyes and said, "Please, no. You can't leave."

"The apprenticeship is over, Mr. Warren. There is nothing left for me to teach you."

I hung my head, tears plopping onto my thighs. My face burned. "I just *can't*," I sobbed.

"And I cannot stay," the Magician said. "This place—this *Black Mouth*—has been slowly draining my abilities. Its dark properties have been...well, doing me harm. Perhaps you children have noticed. I was hoping Dennis's journey to the well would replenish whatever this evil place has taken from me, but I can see that is not going to be the case. So to stay here would mean certain death for me, I'm afraid."

"I *hate* Black Mouth," Clay said. His voice sounded thick with tears, too.

"As you should," said the Magician. "As you *all* should. Just look at what it's done to you. Look at what it's done to *all* of you."

I looked over to where Dennis still sat in the dirt. I could see the hole in his shirt from where I poked him with the knife, the fabric darkly stained with blood. The sight of it made me hate myself, though my brother looked largely unfazed.

"Black Mouth has made you weak," the Magician said. And in that instant, I knew he was talking directly to me. "It gives power to the things that hurt and torment you, while it drains you like a vampire. You will die in this place. You will die at the hands of the things that cause you pain. *Unless…*"

The Magician reached out and snapped a pine bough from the nearest fir tree. The tree was dead, its needles sharp orange javelins. He took the bough to the fire and poked it in. The dry pine needles burst into flames. "Unless you take control of your destiny," he said, and extended the burning torch toward us.

It was as if a part of me remained on that deadfall with my friends even as I got up and went to him. He handed me the burning branch, and I took it in one unsteady hand. I looked up at him, my vision blurry, my chest wracked with sobs. His one piercing eye widened almost imperceptibly.

"*Burn it to the ground, Mr. Warren…*"

Sobbing, I crossed over to where the dead pine tree stood and touched the flames to its shaggy, bristling boughs. They caught instantly.

Dennis howled. I glanced over and saw him rocking back and forth on the ground, hands clasped to his ears.

"Come!" the Magician boomed, arms spread toward the stars. "Ms. Mia! Mr. Willis! Rid the evil from this place once and for all!"

Clay rose from the deadfall and broke a branch off another nearby tree. He carried it tentatively to the fire, his eyes on the tree that I had ignited—a tree that was already burning like some medieval pyre.

"Look what this place has done to you, Mr. Willis! That horror show you wear on your face!"

Clay sobbed. He thrust the tree branch into the fire, and a ball of flame roiled out of the pit. Then he stalked over to the dense foliage on the opposite side of the bonfire. His teeth were gritted and tears were streaming from his eyes. As he lit the trees on fire, he screamed into the night.

Mia got up and threw more and more branches onto the bonfire. The flames climbed higher.

I was crying and out of breath by the time I backed up and took in what we had done. The trees were burning, the deadfall was on fire, and Mia had turned the bonfire itself into a great column of flame. Suddenly panicked, I looked around for the Magician, but found that he had gone.

I dashed off through the trees and climbed the wooded embankment that sloped up toward the distant ridge. With the fire behind me, the woods ahead had grown dark. I saw something sleek and fast cutting through the darkness up ahead.

"Wait!" I shouted, racing after him.

He paused in his stride and turned, just as I approached. My breath rattled in my lungs and I felt I might be on the verge of crying again.

"*Are you leaving?*" I shouted. "*Are you leaving?*"

He said nothing, but I could tell what his intentions were.

"Take me with you," I said.

"I cannot do that, Mr. Warren."

"I don't want to live here anymore! I'm *scared* of him! I *hate* him!" And then I *was* crying again—great leaky sobs that seemed to rise up from a wellspring deep inside me. I reached out for the Magician, but he gripped both my wrists and forced my arms down at my sides. In the blink of an eye, he was mere inches from my face.

"*Then do it!*" His fingers tightened painfully around my wrists.

"Take the knife and send your brother to the well, Mr. Warren! All the power in the world will be yours! You could crush that monstrous father of yours, Mr. Warren! All you have to do is *take control of your own destiny*!"

I dropped to my knees, crying harder. I closed my eyes, feeling only the Magician's hot breath on my wet face, his fingers like carpentry nails through my wrists.

"*You. Must. Do. It.*"

I just shook my head and cried.

The Magician backed slowly away, still staring at me. That solitary eye was a black hole devouring any last trace of self-worth and courage I might have still had in me, leaving only a blackened husk of a boy filled with terror, rage, and a deep-seated personal loathing. Then he turned and stalked deeper into the woods.

I was powerless to stop myself: I staggered to my feet and chased after him, crying out to him, begging him to take me with him. When I reached him, I clutched at his cloak, pulling on it.

The thing that whirled around to stare at me was no longer the Magician. It wasn't even human. Its white face contorted and changed shape, its mouth lengthening until I saw a ridge of pointy black teeth. The thing's solitary eye shone with cold fire. The change lasted less than a second, like a ripple passing over his actual face, but there was no pretending I hadn't seen it.

I screamed and fell backward, just as the thing took off through the woods. Before it vanished altogether, I watched it leap into a wall of pine trees, so high—impossibly high—that it might have been taking flight. The sight of what I'd just witnessed rendered me powerless to move, though I kept my eyes locked onto that place where it had vanished high up into the trees. Those pine boughs still shuddered in the wake of its hasty escape.

And then I heard my friends screaming over the roar of the fire.

I looked behind me in the direction I had come to find the ridgeline ablaze. I ran back in that direction, the noose-like hands of panic tightening about my throat.

What have we done?

As I reached the clearing, a tree came down with a *whoomp!* A ball of fire rolled up into the night. Clay and Mia were standing just outside a ring of flames, sheer terror on their faces. Dennis was curled on his side, his legs drawn up to his chest, his eyes staring off into some other realm. His turtle shell.

I ran over to him, dropped down into the dirt at his side, and began vigorously shaking him while shouting his name. When he came out of it, it was with a violent shudder. He cried out, seeing everything on fire all around us. My friends were screaming, too.

"Get up, Dennis! Come on!"

I somehow managed to drag him to his feet. Clasping his hand in mine, I pulled him toward the section of woods that was still unburned, his stocky legs and sandaled feet pumping furiously to keep up with me. Clay and Mia followed us, running with us now, galloping through the trees, *gazelling* through the foliage.

A scream trapped halfway up my throat.

3

A police officer found me hiding in our barn later that night. Dennis was right there beside me, curled up in his turtle shell, his unblinking eyes staring sightlessly off into nothingness. The policeman asked me if I was okay, but he was focused on Dennis. Our father materialized in the darkness behind the officer, shirtless and with his long hair hanging in his face.

Then the officer was scooping Dennis up off the ground. My

father extended a trembling hand in my direction; he snatched me about the wrist and tugged me aggressively to my feet. Even through the smoke that was filtering into the barn, I could smell the alcohol on him.

He slapped me across the face then dragged me out into the night.

Black Mouth was on fire.

The *world* was on fire.

There were police cars and fire engines parked along the ridge. Helicopters whirred in the sky above, their spotlights like the spiteful gaze of God. Sirens blared and the air was dense with smoke.

Dennis came out of his turtle shell in the police officer's arms. He began to flail his arms and legs so the officer set him down on the ground. I pulled free of my father's grasp and went over to Dennis, put my arms around him. Despite the impossible heat, I felt cold. The air was hard to breathe.

A pair of EMTs were heading in our direction, but our mother shoved them aside and rushed over to us. Dropping to the ground at our feet, she grabbed Dennis and pulled him close, kissed his face, his hair, his neck. She groped for me as well, and I suppose I went with it, too stupefied to resist. I took in a deep breath then went into a coughing fit.

We weren't allowed back in the house. The fire was too close and the air was too thick with smoke. My father argued with the police, his drunken rants competing with the sirens and helicopters. When he took a swing at one of the cops, he was unceremoniously thrown to the ground and handcuffed.

My mother refused to have us go with the EMTs. Instead, she drove Dennis and me to the elementary school in Sutton's Quay, where volunteers were handing out coffee and water bottles and blankets in the gymnasium to the collection of people who had been displaced by the fire. I looked around through the crowd, searching for Clay or Mia, but I saw neither of them.

We stayed there for hours, the three of us camped out in one corner of the gymnasium. Each time I closed my eyes, my head would rock forward, jarring me awake again. I kept seeing the Magician's face change before my eyes, twisting into something not of this world. I must have vacillated between restless sleep and wakefulness straight until morning, because when I finally looked up at the windows of the gym, I could see daylight bleeding across the sky.

Someone rolled a TV into the gymnasium. The image on the television was of a smoldering pit in the earth, the video footage taken from a news helicopter high in the sky. A surreal detachment came over me; it was as if I was watching this all unfold from outside of myself.

A photograph of a woman's face appeared on the screen. Young, pretty. I recognized her immediately as the young woman with the baby my father and I had visited the day before. The chyron at the bottom of the screen read:

WOMAN AND CHILD KILLED IN FIRE

My mom's hand tightened painfully on my shoulder. Something like a whimper rose out of her.

Their names appeared on the screen next—Sarah and Milo Patchin. The scrolling text at the bottom of the screen said Milo had been only four months old.

My whole body began to shudder. I couldn't stop my hands from shaking. My vision blurred until I could no longer read any of the text on the TV screen.

Sarah Patchin.

Milo Patchin.

"She. Is now. Dead," said Dennis, and he pointed to the image of Sarah Patchin on TV.

The next thing I knew, I was being taken to a room in the school by two police officers, where I confessed everything we had done.

CHAPTER TWELVE

MOUTH-SHAPED MOUTH

1

In a conference room at Halcyon Elder Care in downtown Evansville, Indiana, a man named Wayne Lee Stull sat across a table from two men in neckties. Early morning sunlight poked through the slatted window blinds, jabbing Stull in the eyes; he kept repositioning himself in his chair in an attempt to avoid it, but he wasn't having much luck.

The man directly across from him was Tom Hewson, manager of custodial and environmental services for all three of the Halcyon facilities in and around the city. He was also Stull's supervisor. Hewson was a tall, humorless man who wore a pair of glasses on a cord around his neck. Maybe in his late forties, if Stull had to guess. The man next to Hewson was from Human Resources, and Stull didn't know his name.

Stull had an inkling what this meeting was about—there'd been rumblings throughout the custodial department for the past several weeks now—but he sat quietly and let Hewson go through what sounded like a rehearsed monologue without interrupting. Times were tough, sacrifices needed to be made, and the Halcyon facilities were facing unprecedented budget cuts. Surely Stull could appreciate Hewson's position, and the difficult decisions that had to be made.

This monologue segued seamlessly into a detailed explanation of the severance package Halcyon Elder Care was willing to offer. The man from Human Resources opened a folder and began sliding papers in front of Stull. Hewson explained that there was no room for negotiations, but that he was certain Stull would find the package more than generous.

"Are you saying I'm fired?" Stull asked.

"Your *position* is being *terminated*," Hewson clarified, "so unfortunately you're being laid off, Wayne. Not fired. I'm happy to write you a letter for reference. You've been a stellar employee."

Human Resources Man started to go over the paperwork he'd placed in front of Stull, but Stull wasn't paying any attention to him.

"Is it because of my face?"

Human Resources Man went silent, and Tom Hewson looked like someone had just sucker punched him in the stomach.

"Of course not, Wayne," Hewson said, cracking his knuckles—a nervous tic. "Don't be silly. We've got to make a ten percent reduction in force across the board. You're not the only one who's having their position terminated."

Human Resources Man cleared his throat and began his spiel again, less confident this time, but Stull cut him off.

"If you were blind," he said to Hewson, "would I still be losing my job?"

Hewson looked over at Human Resources Man. The guy seemed more than just uncomfortable; Stull thought he looked apprehensive. Hewson's face was turning red, but Stull thought he looked more aggravated than nervous.

"Wayne, I don't really see—"

"You *do* see. Is *that* the problem? Meaning, if you were *blind*,"

Stull continued, "and you *couldn't see my face*, would I still be losing my job?"

"That has nothing to do with—"

Human Resources Man cleared his throat again—much more purposefully this time—and Tom Hewson went quiet.

"Is it because my face frightens you?" Stull said. "Do you have nightmares about it? Or does it just make you uncomfortable?"

"This has nothing to do with your face, Wayne. These are strict budget cuts. My hands are—"

"It's not like you eat with me at lunch in the cafeteria—no one does, in fact—so it isn't like my face can make you lose your appetite. And it's not like I haven't been wearing a facemask when I'm working. Not that most of these moldy oldies would know my face—or even your face, for that matter—from a kumquat."

Tom Hewson pushed his chair back from the table. "Maybe we should discuss this at a later time," he said.

"Like when?" Stull asked. "When I have a mouth-shaped mouth? Because that'll never happen."

"If you'd like to file a grievance, Wayne, Mr. Laghari here will walk you through the process. But I won't sit here and listen to this." Hewson had both hands on the armrests of his chair, prepared to lever himself up and out of the office. But he didn't move right away, perhaps waiting for Stull to come to his senses.

Stull just folded his hands across his abdomen and stared at him.

"Uh," Human Resources Man said, his dark eyes volleying between the two of them. "Should we maybe reconvene after lunch?"

Tom Hewson said, "Wayne?"

Stull kept staring at him. Didn't say a word. After about a full thirty seconds of this, Human Resources Man gathered up his papers and said, "Yeah, I think that might be a good idea. We'll reconvene after lunch." Papers tucked in their folder and the folder tucked under his arm, Human Resources Man got up and went to the door. When Hewson didn't follow, Human Resources Man cleared his throat for a third and final time, and said, "Tom?"

Hewson got up from his chair. The cell phone clipped to his belt was as big as a paperback novel and looked ridiculous.

Wayne Lee Stull watched them leave.

2

He skipped lunch that day, and instead went into the supply closet in the maintenance corridor of the hospital to browse the shelves of industrial cleaners. After some deliberation, he selected a gallon jug of bleach. Bibby showed up and asked what he was doing, but Stull ignored him.

Five minutes later, Stull was pulling his car out of the facility's parking garage, the jug of industrial bleach strapped into the passenger seat right next to his uneaten brown-bagged lunch. He waved to Mike in the attendant's booth as he waited for the arm to go up. Then he drove toward home in the glare of the midday sun.

In the bedroom of his quaint but well-maintained duplex, Stull opened what looked like an ordinary brown leather briefcase. The items inside were anything but ordinary, and after some consideration, Stull selected what he felt was the appropriate face. He took it into the bathroom where he applied the liquid adhesive then pressed it over his actual face. It took less than forty-five seconds to dry completely, so while he waited, he meticulously combed his hair.

Sometime later, he turned onto Pine Hill Terrace, a well-manicured residential street in a well-manicured residential neighborhood. He slowed his car to a jogger's pace as he studied the houses along this street. He knew which house belonged to Tom Hewson, but he wanted a good look at the neighboring homes, just to see if anyone was out watering their lawn or standing on the curb waiting for the mailman. Long ago, Stull had made it a point to learn many of his coworkers' and supervisors' home addresses, because sometimes it was just good planning to have such knowledge at your fingertips.

Tom Hewson's house was a modest two-story affair in a cul-de-sac of similarly modest two-story affairs. There were potted geraniums on the columned porch and an oil stain as prominent as a melanoma in the driveway. It was midday of a work week, of course, and all the houses looked quiet and temporarily unoccupied. Stull parked several houses away from the Hewson home, unbuckled the seatbelt from the jug of bleach, grabbed his lunch, then got out of the car.

Tom Hewson was a big fat liar. Sure, there were budget cuts, but Stull could think of at least three other custodians at Halcyon Elder Care that should have gotten the boot over him. One guy in particular, Dave Sloman, liked to wipe boogers in the hair of some of the facility's dementia patients. That shitheel should've been bounced ages ago.

Well, that booger-hooking slime ball Dave Sloman has a mouth-shaped mouth. Can't compete with that. No, sir.

As he walked to the Hewson house, the handle of a jug of bleach in one hand and his lunch bag in the other, he considered how nice it would be if he could pucker his lips and whistle. No one who whistled was ever up to no good, was Wayne Lee Stull's assessment.

Tom Hewson had a wife and two grade-school children—Stull had seen them on a few occasions when he'd driven by the Hewson house, usually through their dining-room window while they all sat gathered around the table for dinner—but he figured the wife was at work and the kids were at school. There were no cars in the driveway.

The Hewsons had a dog, too, Stull knew. It was a Labrador, its pelt rich as chocolate. As Stull went around to the side of the house and approached the Hewsons' privacy fence, he heard the jangle of the dog's collar as it bolted across the yard in his direction. It started barking when it reached the fence, but Stull already had his lunch bag open. He tossed half of his liverwurst sandwich over the fence, and the dog went instantly quiet as it gobbled it up.

Stull went to the gate, opened it, and entered the yard.

The Lab looked up at him. It had devoured that section of sandwich in no time, and it was still licking its chops. It barked at Stull, then moved at a quick clip in his direction. Stull already had the other piece of liverwurst sandwich in his hand (and the jug of bleach on the ground at his feet), and when the dog approached, he held it out to the beast.

The dog sniffed it, then ate it right out of Stull's hand. Stull upended the lunch bag, and a hunk of homemade cornbread, a Snickers bar, and a can of Coke rolled out onto the lawn. The dog turned its attention to the other items, and decided on the cornbread. Stull could hardly blame the beast; he made good cornbread.

While the dog ate, Stull unscrewed the cap on the jug of bleach. He peeled the foil seal off the nozzle, then reached down and took the dog by its collar. Kneeling down beside the animal, he said, "Good boy, good boy," through his latex mask.

Then he poured the bleach into the dog's eyes.

The Lab whined and jerked its head away, but Stull held fast to its collar. He only let go once the dog started snapping at him, but by then, he had emptied nearly the entire contents of the jug onto the dog's face and into its eyes.

Free from Stull's grasp, the dog bolted across the yard and began racing along the perimeter of the fence. The sound it made as it ran was like steam shrilling from a kettle. Stull collected what remained of his lunch and dumped it back in the brown paper bag, then screwed the cap back on the bottle of bleach. By the time he exited the yard, pulling the gate closed behind him, the dog was still running frantically around the lawn and screaming like a person.

CHAPTER THIRTEEN

A DISCOVERY

1

Penance, Kentucky was the type of small town where a murder like the one committed by Molly Broome would be talked about for generations. It would become a thing of myth and legend, and many decades from now, young children growing up among the cornfields and sunflowers and shiny steel grain silos of this remote little farming community would wonder if such a thing had, in fact, ever actually happened at all.

Her parents, Jean and Steve Russell, lived in a farmhouse along a quiet residential street. There was a chicken coop in the front yard and a sweeping expanse of woods beyond. A weathervane on the peaked roof squealed as it rotated in the breeze.

Jean Russell answered the door. She was a woman of middle age who gazed out at us with the medicated stare of a psych-ward inmate. She wore an open denim shirt with a turtleneck underneath despite the late summer heat. She recognized Clay, who smiled and reintroduced himself. Her bleary eyes bounced from Clay to Mia to me, then finally to Dennis. She appeared too anesthetized to be flustered by my brother's appearance.

The house was gloomy and still. Jean Russell led us down a hallway and into a small dining room where a man in a tank top sat at a table before a cup of coffee. This was Steve Russell, and his demeanor was only slightly less sedate than his wife's. He lifted a slack, beard-stippled face in our direction but offered no greeting beyond a thinning of his lips as we all filed into the cramped little room.

Seated at the head of the table was a young woman in an inexpensive-looking taupe pantsuit, a notebook and an open file bristling with papers spread out on the table in front of her. She rose as we all gathered around the table and she introduced herself as Ashida Rowe, Molly Broome's legal aid attorney.

I had popped an Ativan prior to going there, but it no longer seemed to be working; I felt jittery and on edge as I sat down with Clay and Mia at the table. There weren't enough chairs, so I told Dennis to sit in an armchair in the corner of the room. He sat in it without comment. Both Jean and Steve Russell stared at him, uncertain what to make of him.

"These are the friends I told you about on the phone," Clay said.

Ashida Rowe looked up from her yellow legal pad, which had nothing written on it but the date at this point. "Who took the photo?"

"That'd be me," Mia said.

"When was it taken?"

"About two weeks ago, in Lexington. It was at a carnival."

I saw Clay turn to Mia. "You didn't say this was at a carnival."

Mia shrugged. "Does it matter?"

Clay appeared to stew on this, then ultimately shook his head. "I guess not." He looked at Ashida. "Did you show the photo to Molly?"

"I *did*," said Ashida Rowe. "She agrees it looks like the same man..."

"But?" Clay said. "Is there something else?"

"Well, she wasn't one hundred percent sure. She thought his face looked a little different than the guy in the photo. Longer, she said."

I stiffened in my seat. The image of the Magician fleeing through the woods on that last night flashed across my brain. The way his face had appeared to ripple and change…

"But I don't put much stock in a single photo ID," Ashida went on. "People look different in photos. That's why police prefer to do in-person lineups. And Molly's suffered a great trauma."

Across the table from me, Jean Russell made the sign of the cross.

"What bugs me a little," Ashida continued, "is how old you said this man was back when you were kids."

"I said he was probably in his thirties," Clay said, and Mia nodded her head in agreement.

"And that was almost twenty-five years ago," Ashida said. It wasn't a question. There was an official-looking document on the table among her papers, and I could see the words SUTTON'S QUAY POLICE DEPARTMENT printed at the top. She glanced down at it now.

"It was in 1998, yeah," Clay said.

"In that case, your guy should be in his fifties by now," Ashida said. "The man in the photo doesn't look that old."

"It's not a great photo," Mia conceded. "I mean, it's a little blurry. He looked older in person."

"Like I said, photographs can be deceiving," Ashida agreed, "although Molly also said the guy was probably in his thirties, too. But eleven-year-old kids aren't really a good barometer for judging the age of an adult. When I was eleven, anyone over thirty looked as old as my grandfather."

"I guess he could've been younger when we met him back then, too," Mia said. She looked around at the rest of us for corroboration. "In his twenties, even."

I didn't believe this was true, but I kept my mouth shut.

"I've got the police report here, which has your statements about the fire," Ashida said, and I felt something tighten in my stomach as I watched her turn the pages. "Three of the four of you gave statements to police."

"That's right," Clay said. He looked at me, then over at my brother. "Dennis didn't give a statement, did he, Jamie?"

I just shook my head.

"Two of you gave pretty similar accounts of what happened," Ashida continued. "That'd be Mr. Willis and Ms. Tomasina. You both talked about a man living in the woods who convinced you to light that fire. There's no description of the man in the police report—no mention of an eye patch or anything like that—which is probably just shoddy police work. But everything you've already told me, Clay, lines up eerily close to Molly's story. Almost too close."

"So what do we do about that?" Mia asked.

"I'll get to that." Ashida looked up from the report and across the table at me. "Mr. Warren, I found your statement the most interesting. Do you remember what you told the police back then?"

I remembered, of course, but I wasn't going to talk about it here. "I guess so," I said, my voice hollow.

"Something about a man who turned into a monster," Ashida said. She was looking at me the way someone might humor a child. Clay and Mia turned to look at me, too, as did the Russells. Only Dennis seemed to not be paying attention; he was too occupied with staring out the window that looked onto the Russells' wooded backyard. "You mentioned that his face seemed to…well, to change."

I needed a drink so bad I could scream.

"It goes to show what trauma can do to our recollections," Ashida said. "Particularly when we're children. It also goes to show how easily children can be led to believe in the unbelievable, and that they can be manipulated. I think that's the biggest takeaway in all of this.

"Back in 2014, in Wisconsin, two girls the same age as Molly lured another girl into the woods and stabbed her nineteen times. The girl miraculously survived after crawling to the highway and spending about a week in the hospital. When her two assailants were asked why they had attacked this girl, they both said they wanted to become proxies to a fictional character called Slender Man."

"I've heard of that story," Mia said. "I thought it was just some urban legend."

"Oh, it's a true story, you can look it up," Ashida said. "In Molly's case, the police conducted a search of the woods for evidence of someone living out there based on Molly's initial statement, but they found nothing. Not even a footprint. When Molly started referring to this man as some kind of literal monster—similar to what you said in your statement when you were a child, Mr. Warren—the police stopped taking this claim seriously. And it certainly didn't help matters that Molly started talking about how Charlie's been visiting her in her dreams, either."

I stiffened at this, but said nothing.

"Our defense at this point was to present Molly as not criminally responsible due to temporary insanity brought on by a history of trauma and abuse. As I'm sure you're aware, Mr. Willis, given your profession, that's a tough sell to a jury. But until you folks came forward, that was all we had."

"So you're saying this information will help her case," Clay said.

"I'm saying that if we can build a case around this man-in-the-woods theory—even if it's just to plant the seed of possibility in a jury's mind—then we can leverage it to Molly's benefit. We don't have to prove this man existed at all; we just have to suggest it's a *possibility*. Even if it's not the same man whom you all met twenty-four years ago, which would also be a tough sell, your story could serve as expert witness testimony that things like this do actually happen."

"Of course it's the same man," Clay said. "When I spoke to Molly, she described the exact same guy. She brought up the eye patch, not me. She even described the same *knife* he gave her to use, which, I understand, still hasn't been recovered."

Ashida Rowe smiled thinly at us. "It doesn't really matter," she said. "That brings me back around to your question, Mia. What the four of you are proposing is quite a story. A man befriends children only to manipulate them into killing one of their friends. A man with an eye patch who does…well, magic tricks. That in itself is unusual enough, but add to it the suggestion that he's been doing this over a period of two or more decades, and the story becomes…well, it becomes almost unbelievable."

Clay sat forward in his chair. "I know how it sounds. But it's all true."

"Like I said, we don't have to prove that this was the same man, or if there was really a man at all. We just have to plant the seed of doubt to make a jury wonder if such a thing could be a possibility. I'm going to continue as if this *is* the same man, and that Molly is just another victim here, but in reality and as far as Molly's defense is concerned, we don't even need him to be."

"Because it's all about doubt," Clay said, leaning back in his chair. "I get it."

Ashida smiled. "That's right."

"So what else do you need from us?" Mia asked.

"For starters, I'd like to send your photo of this man to the media as soon as possible, see if we can even get it on the evening news tonight. Let's see if anyone else can identify him. Maybe we get lucky and find out who he is. If not, we're at least frontloading our defense to show we believe this story."

"That sounds great," Mia said. "Let's do that."

"I'd also like to have you folks come in and speak with the detectives on this case. I'd like to schedule that as soon as possible. Today, if I can, because I know you folks are from out of town. There's a chance this could throw a big enough wrench into the mix that we might get a plea deal and avoid going to trial altogether, although I'm not counting on anything at this point. I assume you folks have no problem meeting with the police?"

"Of course not," Clay said.

"Absolutely," Mia said.

Ashida looked at me. "Mr. Warren," she began, but I cut her off.

"I should probably keep out of it, and hang back with my brother."

Ashida was quick to sense my apprehension. "I wasn't going to ask you to join us. Clay's and Mia's stories are a perfect overlay of each other's. Yours varied a little too much, and it's best we don't confuse things this early in the game."

She means my story makes me sound like a lunatic, and she doesn't want me telling it to the police. And that's just fine by me.

"You might all be asked to provide a sworn statement in the future, however, so that's something to start thinking about." She was still looking at me.

"All right," I muttered, and averted my eyes.

"Wonderful." Ashida closed her notebook. "In the meantime, there's a decent diner in town. Why don't you folks get something to eat, and I'll make some phone calls. With any luck, I may be able to set something up within the hour."

"That'd be great," Clay said, and he leaned over the table and shook Ashida Rowe's hand.

I was about to stand up when one of Jean Russell's arthritic claws sprung out and clamped down on my own. Startled, I looked up at the woman.

"Thank you," she said. "Thank you for coming all this way to help my baby girl. You are good people."

Her hand was cold.

2

All the storefronts in downtown Penance looked like theater props. We ate lunch at a diner that resembled an old boxcar someone had cut loose from the nearby train tracks. Clay, Mia, and I sat in a booth while Dennis—too big for the booth—straddled a chair at the head of our table.

Clay rushed through his meal, ready at a moment's notice in case his cell phone happened to ring with Ashida Rowe on the other end of the line. Mia was a bit more even-keeled; as she worked her way through a salad, she kept gazing up at the wall of windows that looked out onto the sidewalk like someone contemplating a riddle.

I didn't think I could eat, so I worked my way through two gin and tonics, sucking the booze from the lime wedges when the drinks were done. Dennis was devouring his second plate of chocolate-chip pancakes with a tuft of whipped cream on top, and he had already gone through an entire regiment of chocolate milk.

Clay must have sensed something in Mia. He asked her what was wrong.

"Just something that attorney said. Bonus points if she finds the guy, sure, but she said she didn't need to. I mean, I wanna help this kid's case, sure, but I also wanna find the son of a bitch. Track him down, you know?"

"I'm sure Ashida will do everything she can," Clay said.

"Maybe we should do more."

"Like what?"

"I don't know. Find him ourselves."

"How?" Clay asked. "I get where you're coming from, Mia, but that's over our heads."

"Yeah," I said. "We're not the fucking Hardy Boys, Mia."

"Maybe *you're* not," she said, glaring at me, "but I'm the hardiest fucking boy there is."

An elderly couple in the next booth glanced over at us disapprovingly.

"We're doing all we can," Clay reiterated. "Let's just see how this meeting goes with the detectives before we start kicking the tires."

"*If* it goes," Mia said, and just as the words came out of her mouth, Clay's cell phone chirped.

It was Ashida Rowe, all right, and she had good news. The two detectives working the case were anxious to meet with them. They could do it in an hour at the police station. Could Mia and Clay meet up with Ashida beforehand to go over a few things?

"You bet," Clay said into his phone. "We're on our way." He disconnected the call, then practically jumped out of the booth.

"Dennis and I will meet you back at the motel," I told them.

Clay clapped me on the back, then snagged the check off our table. "Lunch is on me," he said.

Mia and I protested, but Clay wouldn't hear it. "Listen," he said. "I appreciate you guys coming out here. You didn't have to. But I threw out the Bat Signal and you guys came running, no questions asked. You're all good people. I'm proud to call you my friends. So just let me show my gratitude and buy you all lunch, okay?"

Mia laughed, then actually began applauding. Dennis looked up, and the elderly couple in the next booth swiveled around to see what all the fuss was about. "Is that your Academy Award speech?" Mia said. "Holy shit."

Clay just grinned, shook his head, then strode over to the register.

Mia stood and stretched, exposing a panel of tattooed flesh at her navel. "Come outside with me for a sec," she said to me.

I told Dennis to stay put, then followed Mia out onto the sidewalk where she was already poking a cigarette between her lips.

"I never knew you said that shit to the cops back then," she said. "What exactly did you see the night of the fire?"

"Mia, it was a long time ago..."

"Don't bullshit me, Jamie. I saw your face when that lawyer brought it up. What'd you see?"

What *had* I seen? The memory seemed impossible now, over twenty years later, and in the bright light of a new day. As impossible as those old ghosts who still lingered in Black Mouth.

"I don't know. His face changed. I mean, I think it did. Like there was someone else inside him trying to get out." I sighed and felt instantly ridiculous. "That's what I remember thinking at the time, anyway. I don't know. There was so much shit going on that night, maybe I just..." I couldn't complete the thought.

"Is that why you're so spooked by him?"

"I don't know anymore," I confessed. What I meant was, *I don't know what's real anymore.*

"He was just a man, Jamie, and those were just tricks, just like I said. Nothing more. Don't be fooled by what you think you remember from that summer. Don't be scared."

Before I could say anything, Clay was out the door and hurrying around to the driver's side of his Toyota. Mia got in, too, and a moment later they were rolling down the street, the sun reflecting on the rear windshield like a giant cigarette burn. A honk, and their hands waved from their respective windows. I stood there on the curb and watched them leave. When they took a turn toward the highway, I stood there a moment longer, eager to untangle the knot of complicated emotions that had unexpectedly arisen inside me.

My cell phone vibrated in my pocket. As if to compound my guilt, I saw I had several unread text messages and missed calls from Emily Pearson. I felt a pang of remorse, but I couldn't bring myself to deal with it at the moment. The gin and tonic I'd had for lunch was still fresh in my bloodstream, guilty as a conscience.

Back inside the air conditioned luncheonette, I watched Dennis from across the room as he scraped the last remaining bits of pancake off his plate and into his mouth. There was a gumball machine standing beneath a bulletin board loaded with local business cards, flyers for car washes and haircuts, that sort of thing. I dug a quarter from my pocket, plugged it into the gumball machine, and twisted the crank. A gumball as red as a clown's nose rolled down the spiral chute and spat out into my hand.

There were unused coffee cups on the empty tables. As I walked back over to Dennis, I snatched three of these cups from their place settings and then set them down—upside down—on the table in front of my brother. Having just finished his meal, he shoved the syrup-sticky plate aside and appraised them with his foggy, nickel-colored eyes.

I slid into the booth. Held up the red gumball, pinched between my thumb and index finger. Then I set the gumball on the table between us, right there next to the lineup of coffee cups. "Okay, go on," I told him. "Trick me."

The last time I had witnessed my brother perform this trick, he had been nine years old. Yet as if no time had passed, Dennis picked up the gumball, placed it under one of the coffee cups—the one in the center—then moved all three cups around. Just as he'd done when he was nine, this was less a shuffle to confuse his audience and more of a jostling of each cup in its place. He never actually repositioned any of them, so that the middle cup—the one with the gumball beneath it—never stopped being the middle one.

When he was done, Dennis settled back in his seat, his hands dropped down into his lap.

I reached out and lifted the middle cup.

There was no gumball beneath it.

My eyes ticked up, connecting with my brother's vacuous stare.

I picked up the other two cups, but there was no gumball beneath them, either.

"Okay," I said. "It's just a trick, right? Then show me how you did it."

A proud smile stretched across my brother's round face. There was a streak of whipped cream on his chin, exclamatory as a punctuation mark, but he didn't seem to notice. He lifted one big hand and showed me the gumball he cradled in his palm.

"But I saw you put it under that cup. The one in the middle."

Dennis reached out and lifted the middle cup, placed the gumball beneath it…and then, much more slowly than he had done the first time, he tipped the coffee cup toward me so that its repositioning momentarily blocked the gumball from my sight. As this happened, I saw him palm the gumball and then use the index finger and thumb of that hand to bring the base of the cup down on the table. Done quickly, it would have looked as though the gumball was still underneath. But done more slowly for my benefit, I was able to follow my brother's sleight-of-hand maneuver. He opened his palm now to reveal the gumball in it.

"So you never put it in the cup in the first place. Son of a bitch." Such a simple trick, yet as a kid, I had been completely bewildered. "Did you really dream about that dead girl, Dennis?"

"Walking dream," Dennis said.

"You ever have walking dreams about any other kids?"

"Ye-e-es."

"How many?"

He didn't say.

"Where do you go when you walk in your dreams?"

"I am trying to find it."

"Find what? The kids?"

"The way in," he said.

"The way in to what?"

"To the well," Dennis said. His fork went *skreet* across his plate, and the elderly couple in the next booth glared at us again.

"You don't want to go to the well, Dennis. The well means death."

He smiled at me again, then popped the gumball in his mouth. I took a deep, shuddery breath. My anxiety was back, making me restless and agitated. Something felt out of joint. I glanced around the diner, searching for a glimpse of Sarah and Milo Patchin. Could they reach me all the way out here, so far from Black Mouth? What about my father? Was he still waiting for me in the barn?

Don't be fooled by what you think you remember from that summer.

Don't be scared.

When the waitress came by to collect Dennis's plates, I ordered another gin and tonic.

3

An inexplicable thing happened back at the motel.

After returning from lunch, we entered the room and Dennis went straight for his DVD player. I had the bottle of Maker's with me, its contents hot from an afternoon spent rolling around in the trunk of my car. I set the bottle on the nightstand then grabbed the ice bucket from the bathroom. I told Dennis I'd be right back, then headed outside.

There was an ice machine out here, tucked in an alcove between two rooms and next to a vending machine. I held the bucket beneath the nozzle, my head already swimmy from the drinks I'd had at lunch, and listened to the ice cubes detonate like mortars as they tumbled into the pail. My head craned back on my neck, I closed my eyes and took in a deep breath.

I smelled smoke, and immediately opened my eyes.

The flattened palm of a hand slapped against the motel window to my right. I jumped, and dropped the bucket of ice at my feet. There were no lights on in that room, and the window itself was nothing more than a black panel of glass, except for that fleshy starfish of a hand upon it. The creases in the palm were black with soot and there was black ash on the tips of the fingers.

As I stared at it, one finger began to move in an arc along the glass, carving through a film of ashy gray-black sediment that clung to the pane. A circle, I thought…but no. A *half*-circle. A word. That finger—

COM

Beyond the scrawl, in the murky depths of that motel room, I could see Sarah Patchin standing on the other side of that glass, baby Milo motionless against her chest. One bare breast hung over the downed section of her faded pink tank top, the flesh a pale, livery white, the twisted gray nipple like a knot in the bole of an oak tree.

E HO

Sarah Patchin's eyes flared like lamps, cutting through the rising smog inside that room and shining straight through the grimy window. Straight through the letters she was carving in the soot with one finger.

ME

No.

The doorknob shook in its casing. She was trying to turn it from the other side of the door. I reached out and grasped it, held it firm, refusing to let her open it.

No.

Held it, held it, held it, held it, the metal growing hot inside my hands, my eyes locked on the phrase she'd printed in the soot on the windowpane—

COME HOME

—until the knob stopped turning.

I snapped from my paralysis and bolted out into the parking lot.

4

The next thing I knew, I was being jostled awake on the bathroom floor of our motel room by Mia's boot. My head felt like a car crash and my stomach was sick.

"Jamie, where's Dennis?"

I rolled across the cold tiles until I was able to prop myself up in a seated position against the bathroom wall. I saw vomit on the side of the toilet and a collection of tiny white tablets scattered about the floor. For some reason I was naked from the waist up.

Mia bent down, picked up one of the tablets. "You shouldn't take these with alcohol." She tossed it back on the floor, then crouched down beside me. "Jamie, where's your brother? Where's Dennis?"

I had a fuzzy memory of returning to the room after witnessing something terrible and quickly getting shitfaced. I had a pull from Thor's hammer—the bottle of Maker's that was still hot from the trunk of my car—while Dennis sat watching cartoons on TV. I wasn't sure how I'd wound up in here on the floor with what was clearly my puke on the side of the toilet, my Ativan spilled everywhere, my shirt missing, but I'd be lying if I said this was the first time something like that had happened.

"He's not watching TV?" My mouth felt cottony. I suddenly remembered what had frightened me so badly out by the ice machine, and every muscle in my body tightened at the thought of it. Had that been real? Was it possible?

"He's not *here*, Jamie."

Clay appeared behind her in the bathroom doorway. "I walked around the whole motel but didn't see him," he said, and then he looked around at the mess I'd made in there. The mess I'd made of myself.

"Dennis!" I clambered to my feet, brushing off Mia's attempts to steady me as I kept shouting my brother's name. "Hey, Dennis! Quit fucking around!"

Mia gripped me high up on the arm. Hard. "He's not fucking *here*, Jamie."

I shook her hand off me then shoved past Clay, who was still standing in the bathroom doorway. The motel room Dennis and I shared was empty, Dennis's portable DVD player still on. I went through the adjoining door and into the room Clay and Mia shared, still shouting Dennis's name as I pulled open the closet doors, checked the bathroom, swept the shower curtain aside.

"Listen to me," Mia said as I came out of the bathroom. She was standing there with her arms folded across her chest. Clay stood behind her, looking uncertain and helpless. Scared, even. "Your door was open when we got here. He must have walked off somewhere."

"*Fuck!*" I kicked a hole in the wall.

"Oh, real nice," Clay said, running his hands over his head and turning away from me. "Real fucking nice."

"You need to chill out," Mia said, gripping me by the shoulders.

Her face was inches from mine. "You hear me? Get your shit under control so we can go find your brother."

I shoved her aside. Hard.

Mia backed away from me, clutching her wrist to her chest as if I'd injured her. I wasn't sure; maybe I had. An instant later, I felt myself deflate. I leaned back against the wall, my whole body trembling.

A grim reflection stared out at me from the bathroom mirror. I recognized the figure's sad posture. I knew that pathetic slouch against the wall, those red eyes wet and bleary in their sockets. Somehow this dismal creature was even worse than the ghost of my dead father who still haunted the barn back in Black Mouth. Because this thing was *me*.

"I'm sorry," I said, tearing my eyes from that wretched thing in the bathroom mirror.

Mia waved me off. She kept blinking, like there was something in her eyes. Clay just watched from across the room.

No, no, no…

I could feel that thing in the mirror still staring at me. I'd turned away, but my reflection refused to cooperate. It wanted me to know it was watching me. That it wouldn't grant me the satisfaction of looking away.

Something started ringing. It was Clay's phone. He dug it out of his pocket and stared at the screen. "It's Steve Russell," he said, sounding perplexed, and then he answered the call.

5

Steve Russell was standing in his front yard when Clay pulled his Toyota to the curb. I nearly fell to the pavement as I climbed out of the back seat. Mia came up beside me, gripped me once more high up on the arm. Drew me closer to her. "Why don't you wait in the car?" she said into my ear.

"I am *fine*," I emphasized, speaking directly into her face.

"You're a mess, but I'm not going to argue with you right now," she said, and released me.

Steve Russell met us halfway across the front yard. "That big friend of yours was standing out back when I called you, Mr. Willis. I saw him through the kitchen windows and figured something was up. Recognized him right away from this morning, a'course."

"Where is he now?" Clay asked.

"He went up through the woods."

We followed Steve Russell to the back of the house, where a wall of dense trees butted up against the Russells' property. There was a footpath worn in the soil that cut through a fence line of white birch. Steve waved a hand toward the footpath. "He went up along this path here. Almost like he knew where to go. I tried to talk to the big fella, but he wasn't in no frame of mind for it. Looked to me a little strange, to speak frankly. Something wasn't right with him."

I was already passing through the trees along that path when Mia called after me. I ignored her. She hurried after me and Clay came up to join us while Steve Russell stood back there in his yard, watching us go.

"Slow down or you're gonna break your neck, Jamie," Mia said, coming up beside me.

"I'm okay."

"You're not," she said. "You're fucked up."

"Dennis!" I shouted, my hands cupped around my mouth. My voice echoed through the trees.

"Why does he keep doing this?" Mia asked.

"He says he's trying to find the well," I told her, and Mia paused in her stride.

I kept moving. The path advanced up an incline, toward what I determined was a rocky ridge in the hillside. I could see the sky beyond the trees, a steely platinum color. My head was throbbing and my legs weren't one hundred percent sturdy, but I pushed on.

"These were the woods where Charlotte Brown was killed," Clay said from somewhere behind me.

"The mailbox on the house next door said 'Brown,'" Mia said. "I just noticed when we pulled up out front."

"That newspaper article said they were neighbors," Clay said.

Which meant this path had probably been worn into the earth by the two girls who played in these woods, I realized. I also recalled how intently Dennis had been staring at these woods from the Russells' dining-room window during this morning's meeting with them and Ashida Rowe. That had actually happened, right? It wasn't just a false memory in my faulty brain, was it? It was getting difficult for me to tell the difference.

Not a false memory, I convinced myself. *He's hooked into something.*

"There he is!" Mia shouted. "Dennis! Hey, Dennis!"

I looked up in time to see Dennis's cumbersome body climbing over the ridge at the crest of the wooded hill. I picked up my pace and chugged after him, though it felt like I had about a hundred ball bearings rolling around in my stomach. My head and my lungs ached, too.

Once I climbed over the ridge, I saw Dennis standing in a shallow clearing surrounded by trees. This wasn't the summit of the hill after all, just a niche carved into the hillside. The hill continued to climb at a steep grade, the tree-lined slope replaced by a wall of smooth brown rock. Dennis was looking at the wall as if deciding whether he should climb it.

"Hey," I managed once I'd reached him. I was wheezing and out of breath.

Dennis didn't turn to look at me. He didn't acknowledge me in the least. He kept staring at that wall of rock as if mesmerized by it. His eyes had that unfocused, dreamlike quality they used to have when, as a child, he'd retreat into his turtle shell. Only unlike back then, he wasn't just curled up in a ball on his bed, knees drawn to his chest; he'd walked a considerable distance from the motel and then climbed this ridge just to get here.

My condition caught up with me, and I leaned over and vomited a pungent brown rattail of whiskey onto the dirt. I kept heaving until everything was exorcised from me, and there were hot tears leaking from my eyes.

Mia came up over the ridge, then paused to look around. Clay was a few paces behind her, wincing and clutching at a stitch in his side. "She was killed right here, wasn't she," Mia said, and her voice was paper thin. It did not sound like a question. "Charlotte Brown..." She looked at Dennis. "What's he doing?"

I just shook my head. I was still bent over at the waist, waiting to see if my traitorous stomach was finished revolting. My mouth tasted like an acid bath.

"Dennis," Mia said, going over to him. "You okay?" She looked back at me. "He's not responding. Just like yesterday morning."

I righted myself and took a deep, foul-tasting breath. I went over to Dennis, reached out and touched his arm, but he didn't snap from his trance. I turned and followed his muddy gaze to the rocky hillside. Vandals had spray-painted most of the exposed rock, and there was garbage snared in the underbrush. A place for local kids of all ages to hang out, it seemed.

"Look." Mia pointed across the clearing where a pennant of yellow police tape flapped loosely in the breeze. One end was tied around the trunk of a tree. "They don't take that shit down when they're done here?"

Clay came up beside me. He was winded, and there was a mustache of perspiration shining on his upper lip. "You okay?"

"Fine, fine," I wheezed.

"How'd he know to find this place? How'd he know to come here?"

"I can't explain it."

"It's just like how he knew Charlotte Brown from her photo in that news article," he said. His brow was furrowed and there was a slightly pained expression on his face. I could see he was trying to work things out in his head. So was I. "It's like he's plugged into something the rest of us can't see or feel."

That comment was so much like what I had thought myself only a moment ago as I climbed the hill—that Dennis was *hooked into something*—that hearing it spoken aloud gave me a chill.

Mia was rubbing Dennis's shoulder. "Sweetheart? Hey? Snap out of it, love." She looked at me, then at the outcrop of rock in the hillside. "What's he staring at? Is it the graffiti?"

It wasn't the graffiti.

There was a vertical opening in the rock, no more than a fissure, that looked to be the opening of a narrow passageway. It was this opening in the hillside that my brother, in his trancelike state, was staring at.

It reminded me of those barn doors standing open back home…

"Dennis, sweetheart," Mia kept saying, thumping him tentatively on one shoulder now.

"He'll be okay," I told her, then dug my cell phone from my pocket. I fumbled it, dropped it on the ground, and felt my stomach threaten to revolt again as I bent forward to pick it up.

"Jamie," Clay said.

"I'm fine, goddamn it." I switched on the flashlight app on my phone, then crept over to that slender opening in the rock.

"What are you doing?" Clay called after me.

"Just give me a minute."

I reached the opening and held my phone up in front of it. The meager beam of light coming from my phone barely penetrated that Stygian darkness. I poked my head inside, then slipped my body in after. It was a snug little chamber but it was wide enough where I didn't feel I ran the risk of getting stuck. Not this close to the entrance, anyway.

"Jamie—"

"I'm all right, Clay," I called back, though I didn't pull my eyes from the darkness ahead of me. The temperature in there was about fifteen degrees cooler than outside, and there was an earthy smell to the air. At least it felt good on my clammy skin.

I ducked and crept farther into the chamber. My shaking hand caused the light from my phone to jounce around the stone walls. The walls themselves brushed against my shoulders on both sides. Another step, and I began to feel the initial stirrings of claustrophobia settling quietly over me. Just as I started thinking this was pretty stupid and that I might get stuck in here after all, I reached the end.

It was only a small cave, a handful of yards into the hillside. Kids probably did all kinds of weird shit in here, I realized, and this notion was confirmed as my eyes grew acclimated to the gloom. I saw more graffiti on the rock walls. Garbage on the ground, too, that had either been left in here or blown in by the wind—paper cups, crushed soda cans, flattened cigarette packets.

One particular item on the ground caught my eye. It sat against the rear wall of the cave, half buried in a pile of dead leaves. I held the beam of light on it, steady as I could, as I approached.

It was a cheap plush rabbit in bright pink suspenders. It looked like one of those stuffed animals you'd spend too many quarters trying to pull out of a claw machine in a video arcade.

I picked it up. It smelled moldy but didn't look old.

Underneath it was a crinkled piece of indigo paper. A flyer or advertisement. I shined the light on it so I could read what it said:

PRESENTING

THE HAPPY HORACE TRAVELING CIRCUS & CARNIVAL!

FOOD ✳ RIDES ✳ GAMES ✳ FUN

COME ONE, COME ALL...

...FOR THE YOUNG, FOR THE OLD...

...AND SING THE SONG OF THE PURPLE HIPPO!

JULY 1–12
4 PM–12 AM!
PENANCE, KY FAIRGROUNDS

$10 all-you-can-ride wristbands available!

At the bottom of the flyer was a cartoon hippopotamus clutching a squadron of balloons.

Something cold and hard turned over in my stomach. I thought I might be sick again.

"Hey." It was Clay, his silhouette blocking out the daylight at the entrance of the cave. His voice had startled me. "The hell are you doing in there?"

I tucked the stuffed rabbit under one arm, picked up the flyer, then backed out of the cave. The top of my head thumped against the craggy ceiling the entire way, which didn't help my headache any.

And despite the cooler temperatures in there, by the time I was back outside, my shirt was soaked with perspiration.

Dennis was sitting cross-legged on the ground in a spangle of sunlight. His broad shoulders were dusted with leaves. Mia stood by his side, her fingers raking back his mop of curly black hair. When my brother saw me, he broke into an easy smile. *Returned to the Land of the Living*, I thought.

"He came out of it just as you went in there," Mia said.

"You okay, bud?" I asked him.

Dennis gave me a thumbs up.

"Mia, you said you saw the Magician at a carnival in Lexington."

"That's right."

"Was it this carnival?" I handed her the flyer.

She studied it, looked up at me, then looked back down at the flyer again. "Jesus Christ, it might be. I don't know." She shook her head, still staring at the carnival flyer. "I mean, all carnivals look the same, don't they?"

"What is it?" Clay went over to her, peered down at the crinkled sheet of paper in Mia's hand.

"Yeah," I said. "All carnivals pretty much look the same. But I'd remember that purple hippopotamus motherfucker anywhere."

"Me too." Clay's eyes turned in my direction, and I was taken aback by the stark look of fear I saw in them. He suddenly looked the way I felt. "I remember that stupid Happy Horace jingle playing as Tony Tillman kept hitting me in the face. You guys remember that? It's seared into my memory. I'll never forget it."

"Wait a minute," Mia said. "You're saying this was also the same carnival that came to the Quay that summer?"

I looked back at Clay's haunted eyes and knew he was thinking the exact same thing as me.

"He travels with the carnival," we both said at the same time.

6

Steve Russell was still waiting for us in his backyard, smoking a cigarette and pouring birdseed into a plastic feeder. He seemed relieved when he saw Dennis come marching out of the woods with us.

"The big fella okay?"

"He's just fine," Clay said. "He gets a little turned around and confused from time to time, and I guess we kinda lost track of him. We're sorry if he scared you."

"Didn't scare me. Just thought he might need some help or something."

"Mr. Russell, do you happen to know if your stepdaughter went to a local carnival out here last month?"

Steve Russell didn't even have to think about it. "Sure did. There was one come in at the fairgrounds. Jean and I took both girls. Why do you ask?"

"Both girls?" Mia said.

With something like sad resignation, Steve Russell nodded toward the neighboring property. "Charlie came with us," he said.

Back up on the hill, Clay had taken the stuffed rabbit from me. He held it out now toward Steve Russell. "We found this in the woods. Thought it might belong to one of the girls. Your daughter, maybe."

Something in the man's eyes went dead. "Keep it," he said. "I don't want it."

7

An air of disquiet followed us back to the motel. I couldn't speak for the others, but I was wrestling with a series of questions that felt layered like an onion in my brain. The discovery of that flyer and all of its implications was unsettling enough, but became downright inexplicable when I considered how it had been found. Or, more accurately, how Dennis had led us there to find it. Add to this how he'd somehow recognized Charlotte Brown's photo as a murder victim he had allegedly dreamed about, and I felt like I was courting madness just trying to unravel what all that meant.

I stared at him for nearly the entire drive back from the Russells' house, he and I crammed in the back seat of Clay's Toyota. Clay and Mia were caught up in some discussion in the front, so they paid me no attention when I leaned over to Dennis and, in his ear, whispered, "Why did you go to that cave?"

He gave no answer. That was my brother's typical response when he either didn't understand the question or didn't know how to explain the answer.

"Did that cave have something to do with the well?" I asked. Then more directly: "Was *it* the well?"

Dennis looked at me from the side of his eye. I kept waiting for him to answer my question—to say anything at all—but he didn't. A moment later, I watched that eyeball snick back into position as he stared straight ahead through the windshield. My head was still a mess from the pills and Maker's Mark, and my stomach felt no better, but in that moment I suddenly felt stone fucking sober and scared beyond comprehension.

Earlier, in our haste to leave the motel to retrieve my brother, Mia had left her cell phone in the room she and Clay had shared. The first thing she did when we returned was to swipe it off the bed and pull up the Happy Horace Traveling Circus and Carnival website. That horrible jingle—one that immediately shuttled me back to the summer of 1998—chimed out of her phone as the website loaded. Clay was packing up his things; at the sound of the jingle, he stopped what he was doing and looked up at Mia from across the room. Dennis appeared to freeze as well, the stuffed rabbit I'd found back in the cave pinned beneath one of his thick, hairless arms. He looked as if someone had just delivered an electric shock to his backside.

Happy Horace,
The Purple-Purple Hippo!
The Purple-Purple Hippo!
The Purple-Purple Hippo!

"I don't like that song," Dennis said.

Mia quickly switched off the volume on her phone. "I don't like it either, man," she said.

"What are you doing?" I asked her.

"Looking to see if there's a calendar or schedule of where this carnival stops." She scrolled through the website on her phone. "Okay, here we are. Yeah, Happy Horace was in Penance, Kentucky last month, just like the flyer said. And it was out in Lexington where I saw him less than two weeks ago." Something in her face changed. Out of nowhere, she looked about as nauseated as I felt. "Oh. Oh. Fuck *me*."

"What?" I said.

"Where is it now?" Clay asked.

She looked up at me, then over at Clay. "Jesus Christ, fellas. It's in Sutton's Quay."

Clay still seemed frozen on the other side of the room. It was like someone had turned him to stone.

"What do you mean?" I asked. My head still felt like someone had stuffed it full of dirty laundry, and I wasn't too quick in putting the pieces together. "You're saying the goddamn carnival is in—"

"Sutton's Quay," Mia finished. "Yes. Right now. According to their website. That's what I'm saying. We're out here and it's back home."

"I don't believe it," Clay said. The words nearly creaked out of him.

"It's fate stepping in," Mia said. "Bringing us all back together. Telling us all to go back home."

"It's not fate," I said. "It's not even a coincidence. That carnival came through town every year back in the Quay."

"But the symmetry of it all happening *right now*…I mean, I think we should go there," Mia said. She was becoming re-energized again, I could tell. "It feels like the right thing to do. We need to see what's going on for ourselves."

"See if *he's* there, you mean," Clay said.

"He was in Lexington and he was here in Penance. Both places where the carnival had been. And he was in the Quay, too, when we were kids, the same time that carnival was in town, *and now it's right back there again*. Full fucking circle, man."

Clay was staring at me from across the room for some reason. His stare made me uncomfortable.

"So maybe he works for the carnival," Mia went on. She sounded now like she was talking more to herself than to us. Working things over in her head. "Maybe he's their goddamn *magician*." Her laugh was dry and humorless, underscoring just how preposterous this entire scenario really was.

"What about the detectives you guys met with earlier today?" I asked. "What happened with that? Why don't we just call them, tell them what we found out?"

Mia made a bitter face. "Forget those dickheads. That meeting was a waste of time. They think Molly's making shit up and that we rolled in here to confuse the issue on her behalf, like we've got some kind of agenda. They didn't like Clay doing his social-work voodoo in a state where he wasn't licensed, and they didn't like Molly's lawyer showing her the photo I took."

"Why?"

"It's complicated," Clay interjected. "Ashida acknowledged showing Molly the photo was a mistake. It taints the police's ability to do an official lineup if they ever catch the guy. Molly was shown one photo, asked if it was the guy, so she says yes. It's tainted."

"She said *maybe*," Mia corrected. "The girl wasn't a hundred percent sure, remember? Whatever the case, it makes us look like a pair of assholes."

"Well, then let's call that lawyer, tell her what we know," I said.

Mia was shaking her head. "Fuck that, Jamie. I don't wanna just hand this off to someone else. I want us to *find* this guy. This is what we've all been brought back together to do—get fucking payback on the son of a bitch."

"It's not payback," Clay corrected. "It's to stop him from doing this again, and hopefully help Molly in the process."

"Yeah, right," Mia said. "All that good stuff. Whatever it is, the four of us have been brought back together to *do* this."

"You gotta stop with the destiny bullshit," I said. The room was starting to spin and I felt like my blood was boiling inside the too-tight sack of my flesh.

"It's not bullshit, man. Can't you *feel* it? It's like we're all being directed toward some inevitable conclusion."

"Please." I pressed the heels of my hands to my eyes. "Just please stop for a second."

"Jamie Warren is scared," Dennis said.

"I'm not scared. I'm just trying to wrap my head around all this."

"Jamie Warren is scared."

"I'm not fucking *scared*, Dennis!"

"Ashida's still on board," Clay interrupted, "but we tell her that we've connected this guy with a traveling carnival—after following Dennis's little sleepwalking routine, no less—and even she's gonna think we're crazy. We need a little bit more proof that we're right about this before we take it to her."

"So then what?" I said.

Clay leaned against a wall, rubbed his face. "Maybe Mia's right. Maybe we head out for the Quay and just have a look around. We might get lucky and see him in the crowd, just like Mia did in Lexington. At least then we'll know for sure that we're right. And if we *do* see him, we can call Ashida and she can phone in the cavalry."

"You want us to go back to Sutton's Quay? Back to Black Mouth?"

"Listen," Clay said, holding up one hand. "No one said anything about going to the Mouth, okay? We don't have to do that. Just the Quay. The fairgrounds behind the church is where it used to set up, right? We go there and no place else."

"We're not staying at my fucking house, Clay." My voice was shaking so badly I wasn't sure he understood what I was saying. I wasn't sure I fully understood it, either. "My fucking house is haunted, man."

"We don't gotta stay at your house," he said.

"Jamie Warren is home." Dennis was staring at me.

"I'm *not*! I'm *not* home, Dennis! Goddamn it!"

"Shhh," Clay said. "Let's everybody just be cool for a minute."

I peeled myself off the wall and sat down on the edge of one of the twin beds. I couldn't seem to catch my breath. Something was wrong with me.

Mia walked over to Dennis. She rested her head against his arm. Still staring at her phone, she said, "If we leave right now, we can make it there before the carnival closes for the night."

I looked at Mia, then over to Clay. Neither was looking at me. I turned to Dennis then, and saw that he was staring right at me.

Like he was gazing into my soul.

8

Before we left for Sutton's Quay, I went into the bathroom where I'd puked my guts out earlier, and cleaned the place up a bit. I scooped up the Ativan off the floor and tossed all those tiny white pentagonal pills into the wastebasket, along with the prescription bottle. I washed my face and hands beneath an icy stream of water from the tap. I ran a cool, wet hand along the nape of my neck. With my eyes closed, I could almost trick myself into relaxing.

There's always the patented Jamie Warren Disappearing Act, said a small, cowardly voice lurking near the deep end of my consciousness. *You were good at it once. Maybe it's time to resurrect that old magic trick?*

I could do it.

I could drive right the hell out of here and never look back.

In the mirror, I saw the bottle of Maker's Mark on the edge of the tub. It was partially hidden by a mold-speckled shower curtain, but I could still see it. Thor's hammer.

I'm bigger than you, the bottle said.

And I thought: *One more minute, one more minute, one more minute...*

Someone knocked on the bathroom door. Clay's muffled voice: "Ready when you are, Jamie. We'll be outside."

"I'll be out in a minute," I said, then reached out and locked the door.

I grabbed Thor's hammer, realized there wasn't even a cap for me to contend with, and let the amber fluid spill down my eager, quivering throat. Then, when I was done, I dug all of those tiny white pills out of the wastebasket, dumped them back into the prescription bottle, and tucked the bottle in my pocket.

That terrible wraith stared out at me from the other side of the mirror.

"Fuck you," I told it, and fled that place.

IV

SUTTON'S QUAY

CHAPTER FOURTEEN

A MAN OF FACES

1

Wayne Lee Stull was just finishing up a Hungry-Man Double Meat Bowl in front of the television when the image of a man wearing an eye patch appeared on the evening news.

"Police are seeking any information on *this man* as a possible eyewitness in last month's fatal stabbing of eleven-year-old Charlotte Brown of Fayette County, Kentucky," a newscaster's voice spoke up over the photo while a phone number appeared below the image. "Molly Broome, a neighbor and classmate of Brown's, was taken into custody last month by Fayette County Police, but Broome's attorney is seeking any information on the whereabouts of this potential eyewitness to—"

The rest of the broadcast disappeared under the sound of Stull's Double Meat Bowl striking the wall beside the TV. The trumpeting that wrenched out of him might have been mistaken for a cry of anguish or even pain by anyone within earshot, but in reality, it was *elation*.

Wayne Lee Stull was laughing hysterically.

2

He showered, brushed his teeth with meticulous precision, applied a stick of deodorant to his underarms, then dressed himself in a pair of navy-blue slacks, a dark brown polo shirt, and startlingly white tennis shoes. He was fastidious about the part in his hair, so he spent an inordinate amount of time before the bathroom mirror combing it, readjusting, combing it again. Afterward, he cleaned up the remnants of the Double Meat Bowl from his living-room wall, dumped the microwavable container and the coagulated gruel into the trash, then thoroughly washed his hands under the hot tap until his fingers ached and his palms throbbed with their own metronomic heartbeats.

In the bedroom, he packed some clothes into a suitcase. Ordinarily, he would have to call Halcyon's automated employee leave-schedule line and submit sick leave before leaving town this abruptly for an unknown number of days, but he hadn't returned to work after the incident with Tom Hewson's dog, and he had no interest in finishing out the month just to be laid off anyway, so that was a non-issue. Maybe things were working out in his favor after all. Would be nice for a change.

The last thing he did before hopping into his Kia and heading southeast out of Evansville was to pack a selection of his favorite faces in what looked like an ordinary brown leather briefcase.

3

No more than forty minutes later, he drove past a rustic roadside tavern with a smattering of cars in the gravel parking lot. When traveling, he preferred to stick to the secondary roads, which was why he was on this unencumbered ribbon of asphalt this evening instead of the interstate. Had he taken the interstate, he never would have seen the woman in the luminescent white halter top standing in the gravel lot on her cell phone and smoking a cigarette.

Stull, who never went even a single mile over the speed limit, slowed to five below it as his pre-owned Kia Rio rolled past the tavern. The place was called Shirley's, as evidenced by the neon pink sign on the roof. Shirley was a good, solid, reliable name. Stull's mother's name had been Shirley.

He drove about a quarter of a mile down the road before executing a casual U-turn. He rarely did maneuvers like this in his car—he was a rule-follower by nature, and he shuddered at the idea of a police officer pulling him over, berating him, handing him a ticket—but he hadn't seen another vehicle on this stretch of road in the past ten minutes, and anyway, there was nothing else around here but trees and telephone poles.

He returned to Shirley's and pulled into the lot. The car rocked along the gravel like a small ship on turbulent waters.

The woman was still out there on her phone, tucked between a white SUV and a red pickup truck with its tailgate down. He got a better look at her as he drove to the far end of the lot. She was older than he'd originally thought when he'd glimpsed her from the road—maybe in her fifties—but that didn't matter. He could hear her voice even with the windows up and the A/C running. Whoever was on the other end of her cell phone was taking a beating.

He parked in a space farthest from the tavern door, where the gravel lot gave way to a tangle of dark, jungle-like trees. He rolled down his window and could hear country music playing inside the tavern. He could hear the woman's shrill voice, too. Someone named Eddie was being read the Riot Act, all right.

Normally, he would wear a face for this. He even considered it—

the leather briefcase was right there in the trunk of the car—but in the end he found he was too wound up to take the time to painstakingly select the appropriate face, apply the glue, wait the forty-five seconds for it to adhere. Besides, this wasn't part of his formal process; this was just an impromptu detour to expel some pent-up excitement. So there'd be no face tonight.

He got out of his car and headed across the parking lot, hands in his pockets.

"Fuck you, Eddie, you're an asshole," the woman said into her phone. She was wearing heels and kept wobbling along the gravel as she paced back and forth. She sounded drunk, and looked it, too.

There was a drainpipe running down the side of the building, a thin tributary of water trickling from its opening near the ground. The water pattered on a flat hunk of gray slate about the size of a dinner plate that was half sunk into the earth. Stull dug it out of the wet soil then went over to the woman.

"You know I love you, Eddie," the woman whined into her phone.

Stull smashed the hunk of slate against the side of the woman's face. It was a good, solid, reliable strike, and she went down face-first into the gravel without incident. Her cell phone skittered away, and Stull could hear Eddie on the other end still talking, oblivious, but Stull didn't care. He bent down, rolled the woman over, and marveled at the majesty of all that blood in her hair and running in delicate streaks along the side of her face. Her mouth was partially open and there was gravel in her teeth.

He removed a single tube sock from the back pocket of his slacks, balled it up, and stuffed it in the unconscious woman's mouth. Better safe than sorry on that score. Then he bent down, grabbed hold of her ankles, and dragged her toward the line of trees at the far end of the parking lot. Wayne Lee Stull was by no means a tall man, and to be honest, the majority of his bulk was in his belly, but he operated like some compact little machine built just for this very task. He wasn't even winded by the time he'd dragged her into the trees.

Maybe it was dragging the back of her wounded head over the gravel or maybe he just hadn't struck her hard enough; whatever the case, she regained some semblance of consciousness as he pulled her the final few yards into those trees. Her eyelids fluttered. A soft moan vibrated against the tube sock stuffed in her mouth, but that was about it. Her halter top had ridden up as he'd dragged her, exposing one flat, ugly tit with a nipple like an acorn. He released her ankles, her heels wedging in the loose soil as her feet came down.

Stull looked around, suddenly realizing he'd left the bloody wedge of slate in the parking lot. He smiled—what passed for a smile on his face, anyway—then jogged back out into the lot. He retrieved the slate, and carried it back into the woods.

The woman was still on the ground, but she was moaning louder around the sock now and rocking back and forth on her back. She was apparently too dazed to realize she could have pulled the sock out herself, and that made Stull smile to himself once more.

Bibby was suddenly there, breathing down the back of Stull's neck. Sometimes Bibby showed up near the end to watch, other times Bibby just stayed gone. It used to bug Stull whenever Bibby showed up near the end—always there for the fun, never around for all the prep work—but he'd stopped caring a long time ago. It was what it was.

Stull knelt down in the dirt beside the woman, where he gave that bulbous acorn a righteous twist. The woman bucked her hips and shook her head. Stull heard a scream building up behind that tube sock. Another two seconds like this and she'd start struggling to her feet and clawing at the air with her fingernails, Stull knew.

He slammed the hunk of slate down on the woman's face. He felt the ethmoid bone surrender and the front of her face collapse.

He lifted the slate to examine his handiwork, and was pleased to find that his practice had paid off. She was still alive, but there'd be no screaming coming from her now. Her flailing had stopped, too. He peeled the tube sock from her mouth—it was soaked with blood and gritty with gravel—and tossed it aside.

The woman moaned.

Stull thought he felt Bibby's erection pressing into the small of his back.

He spread the woman's lips apart, seeing the blood on her busted teeth, the pathetic squirm of her tongue beyond. Her upper palate had cracked down the middle by the force of his blow, her two front teeth separated by a good inch, inch and a half now, with a raw, bloody chasm running between them.

The chunk of slate, while big as a plate, was shaped suspiciously like the great state of Texas—all corners and sharp, geometric edges. Stull proceeded to knock the woman's teeth out with one of those pointed edges, all the while wondering what Texas must be like. He'd never been, and thought it might be fun to own a cowboy hat and call everybody partner.

The woman was still alive when he brought the slate down one final time, splitting her head open down the middle.

The spark of her entered Wayne Lee Stull, as dim and fleeting as a firefly. He sat in the dirt with his back against a tree, soaking it all up. He was out of breath; this, he supposed, was a young man's game, and Wayne Lee Stull hadn't been a young man in some time now. Bibby, that cowardly little bitch, had vamoosed again. Always here for the party, never to help clean up.

Before leaving the woods, Stull gathered up the bloody sock and the hunk of slate, took them back to his car, and stashed them in a plastic bag in his trunk. (He kept a whole roll of plastic bags in the Kia's trunk.) Then he cleaned his hands with sanitizer, changed his shirt—he couldn't abide wearing a messy shirt, and there was shit all over this one now, thanks very much—and got back into his car.

The parking lot was deserted, so he drove slowly around before leaving, his window down and the A/C off, listening. Nothing at first, but then he heard it—a cell phone ringing from somewhere under a car. No doubt Eddie the Asshole, ringing back his best gal. Good, solid, reliable Eddie the Asshole.

Feeling pretty good about himself, Wayne Lee Stull exited the parking lot, hit the road, and continued heading southeast toward Kentucky.

CHAPTER FIFTEEN

THE CARNIVAL
(FIRST NIGHT)

1

Dennis Warren stood on a bluff overlooking a dazzle of flashing lights and a cacophony of sound. Even from this distance his senses were attuned to the spectacle of the carnival—the smell of corndogs, popcorn, cooked peppers and onions, sawdust, and the odor of the bristling brown logs excreted by the ponies in their pen next to the Porta-Johns. He could smell the grease that lubricated the rides, too—the Tilt-A-Whirl, the Scrambler, the solitary rollercoaster shuddering uphill on its rotating conveyor belt. He heard the screams and shouts of the people on rides, the triumphant cheers of those winning at the game booths, the boos of the losers, the distempered caterwauling of countless children, each of their cries united in one plangent column of mounting distress. He heard, too, the *pop-pop-pop*s echoing from the shooting galleries, the tinny shouts of the barkers in their booths conniving passersby out of their money, the melodious music-box serenade from the merry-go-round, and the jolting *zzzt zzzt* of the bumper cars. All of that beneath the boom of hair metal over a fuzzed-out PA system.

I was perched on the hood of the Maverick, peering across the roadway at the carnival pulsing in the night. My brother's formidable silhouette was the only obstruction to a clear view. Given my condition, Mia had driven me down in the Maverick, with Clay and Dennis following us in Clay's Toyota. This, of course, had prevented me from performing the patented Jamie Warren Disappearing Act and driving off into the night. That wouldn't have worked, anyway; five minutes in the car with Mia behind the wheel and I had fallen asleep. I'd stayed that way for much of the drive, and when I'd awoken, it was to a monster truck rally in the center of my skull.

We had deliberately avoided going through town, and instead took an exit off the highway that was safely past Sutton's Quay, having then only to backtrack a few miles along an old mining road to arrive here on the hill overlooking the fairgrounds. This way, we didn't have to see downtown Sutton's Quay and all the memories that might stir up. What it *didn't* do was keep us a safe distance from Black Mouth. As it had done when we were kids, the Happy Horace Traveling Circus and Carnival had set up in the field behind St. Joseph's, which meant the carnival grounds were cradled snugly between the church and the southernmost rim of Black Mouth. Even now, beyond the spectacle of carnival lights, I could see the Mouth's craggy, fire-scarred ridge with its crown of trees as jagged as lightning bolts in the distance. My childhood home was somewhere on the far side of that giant ash-filled crater. There were so many stories about Black Mouth, and they all seemed to fight for real estate inside my head at that moment.

Sometimes, when my father was only a beer or two in and in what passed for one of his good moods, he would tell stories of growing up in Black Mouth. He told these stories with the same sense of commiseration you might find among ex-cons who learned they had served time in the same prison years apart. The story my brother and I heard most frequently was of the night he and some buddies had chased a group of Quay boys down into the Mouth. The reason for chasing these boys varied depending on his mood (and how much alcohol he had consumed). In some versions of the story, he and his friends were just goofing around with those Quay boys, wanting to give them a good scare, whatever that entailed. In the more sinister versions, he and his friends were bent on breaking bones and smashing faces. Whatever the reason, my father and his friends—as well as those Quay boys—had the shit scared out of them that night by something in the woods. Not a man, but a *thing*. Something that rushed out of one of those old mineshafts in a bluster, with glowing white orbs for eyes and a body that was part corporeal, part smoke. The thing had emitted a siren's wail, which had reverberated straight down to the marrow of my father's bones.

Whatever it was, it had *touched* him—or, more accurately, *ghosted through him*—leaving behind a block of ice in the center of his body and, once he'd hit puberty, a curious hairless patch in the center of his chest. One of his friends fell backward over a log and split his head open; another boy—one of the Quay boys, as the story went—screamed until he bled from his mouth. Another was stricken blind, if you can believe such a thing. The creature that had come whirlwinding out of the mineshaft circled them like a twister, gathering up a flurry of sticks and dirt and dead leaves into the air. The kids who still had their wits about them—my father was included in this group—bolted for the ridge. They had no inclination to see what else that Black Mouth thing was capable of.

Dennis and I had heard this story countless times, and I never once questioned the validity of it. These things happened in Black Mouth. Simple as that.

A year or so after the mine collapsed—this would have been in the early fifties, I believe—there were several reports of strange lights down there in the Mouth. Gaslights, people called them. Gaseous runoff seeping up from the soil. Peculiar, but not necessarily supernatural, or even dangerous for that matter. But then people living near the rim began to report seeing *people* in those lights. Superstition dictated that these were the souls of the dead miners, forever trapped in that spectral light the same way their earthly bodies were forever entombed beneath the town of Sutton's Quay.

That story itself was unnerving enough, and it certainly helped perpetuate the myth of Black Mouth for decades, but the creepiest part was that one woman claimed that her husband, who'd died in the mine collapse a year or so earlier, had returned home to her. She'd been asleep with a summer cold when she heard a noise downstairs. She crept down the stairs and turned on the hall lights, which was when she claimed to have witnessed her deceased husband standing in the kitchen. He was wearing his coveralls and miner's helmet, which were both caked in mud, the light on the front of the helmet flickering like Morse code. He was standing at the counter making a ham and cheese sandwich. When the woman turned on the light, the man looked up at her, blinking his eyes in a daze. Then, as if realizing he was supposed to be dead and buried under the ground, he turned and, with a perceptible look of disappointment on his mud-streaked face, sauntered out of the house. After recovering from the shock, this woman called her neighbor—a woman who had also lost her husband in the collapse—and when this neighbor arrived, they both marveled at the muddy boot prints on the kitchen floor.

But those were just stories. Scary fairytales passed down from generation to generation. Who could really vouch for the authenticity of them?

Kids at my elementary school had told stories about the snake-headed boy—born along the rim of the Mouth a seemingly normal child, though as he matured, his flesh had toughened into reptilian scales. His eyelids became translucent, nictitating membranes, and the prow of his nose flattened to the plane of his face until it was nothing more than two constricting slits beneath the widening sockets of his yellow eyes. His tongue, of course, became forked. As is always the way with stories like these, no one actually knew this boy firsthand, but everyone seemed to know something about him. When asked what had become of him, the response invariably was that his parents had grown afraid of him, and so he had slithered his way down into the Mouth, where he lived to this day in one of those abandoned tunnels deep in the earth.

There were stories, too, of the Wicker Witch. A decrepit old hag who lived in the Mouth, she had the power to turn children into stunted, arthritic trees that never blossomed, never grew. You could tell what trees had once been children because their faces were hinted at in the crenulations along the bark. If you touched these trees— either on purpose or accidentally—your hand would stiffen, your fingers transforming into twigs, until that morning when your mother came into your room to wake you for school, only to find an uprooted dogwood in your bed.

Then came the fire that claimed the lives of Sarah and Milo Patchin. It reignited old tales of Black Mouth, and some old-timers even blamed those old spectral lights. Others suggested it was the Wicker Witch, setting fire to all her charges deep in the heart of the Mouth. No one actually believed these theories, of course, but that didn't matter. Soon, however, the truth about the fire came out, and it was worse than any urban legend or ghost story. My friends and I were to blame; we were the real monsters behind the masks.

Two nights after the fire, Black Mouth saw it fit to send my sins back to me. Terrified, I'd held my breath and stared at the thing standing at the foot of my bed, my eyes finding its black silhouette against the less black backdrop of my open bedroom closet. A woman. A woman holding an infant child, sucking at her breast. *Thhhk-thhhk-thhhk.* Sarah and Milo Patchin. The two of them reeked of charred flesh and ash. As I stared at them, Sarah Patchin retreated into the closet until she and her baby lost all form against the night. They left behind the smell of smoke in their wake.

Thinking of all this now, I found I was trembling again, and that my eyes were wet. I'd spent the remainder of my childhood seeing Sarah and Milo Patchin in that house, but they'd never followed me until recently. They'd never touched me until Sarah's hand had gripped my ankle. I wondered if Mia wasn't right, and that there were things being set into motion—things beyond our mortal abilities to fully comprehend.

After talking quietly together for a while out of earshot, Clay and Mia came up to me in the darkness. They said nothing, only leaned against the front of the car and stared at the lights of the carnival on the horizon along with me. Or maybe they were staring at Dennis. He looked like something from another world against all that Day-Glo illumination.

"So I've been thinking about this whole scenario on the drive out here," Clay said eventually. "I considered whether we should just go straight to whoever runs this thing, show him the photo, ask who the guy is. But then I thought, no, that's not a good idea."

Mia lit a joint, took a drag, then extended it to Clay. He shook his head. She didn't offer it to me.

"So what I *think* we should do," Clay continued, "is keep as low a profile as possible. We don't know who this guy is friends with, who might tip him off that there are people walking around asking questions about him. I think it's best just to get in there, walk around, and hope we see him. Same way Mia saw him back in Lexington."

"What if he's off somewhere right now, hiding in the woods?" Mia said. She turned away from the carnival lights and peered due west, where the landscape was a wooded curtain of blackness as far as I could see. "Back down there in Black Mouth, like when we were kids."

"We can't help that," Clay said. "But I don't think he is. He's dealing with kids, so he's gotta work their hours. He dealt with us in the daytime."

"Except on that last night," Mia reminded him.

"Yeah, okay. Except for that. Still, I think the best plan is to just walk around and see what we can see."

"I'm game," Mia said. She turned to me. "You okay?"

I swallowed what felt like a mouthful of sawdust. "I think so."

"You wanna wait in the car?"

I thought about this. Actually considered it. But then I heard Mia's voice coming back to me in my head: *He was just a man, Jamie. Don't be fooled by what you think you remember from that summer. Don't be scared.*

I pulled in a lungful of air. "I'll go down there with you guys," I said.

Mia nodded, her face stony. I caught her glance at Clay before turning away from the both of us altogether.

"It feels so weird to be back home," Clay said.

"We're not exactly home," I informed him, then pointed clear across the road to the ridge of black, twisted trees rising up against the night sky. "Home is on the other side of *that.*"

A silence fell down upon us. We let it simmer, each one of us lost in thought. In memories.

As if suddenly alerted to our presence, Dennis turned around and waved at us. He was grinning like a fool.

2

A sense of déjà vu came over me as the four of us entered the carnival. I remembered the excitement, the all-you-can-ride wristbands from the summer of '98. I also remembered the way Dirk the Jerk had strutted around with Clay's hat on his head, and how Tony Tillman, when wearing the hat, kept punching Clay in the face every time he tried to take it back. I looked at Clay now, watching the carnival lights detonate across his blotchy face. I thought about the boy he'd once been, and how he'd cried silent tears as Tillman kept hitting him and knocking him down in the dirt. How I hadn't done a damn thing to stop it.

Dennis was standing to my left, his big round head on a swivel. His eyes were wide and reflecting the flashing colored lights all around us. When a buzzer went off nearby, he clapped his big paws over his ears and winced, but he didn't stop looking around. In fact, as we walked along the midway, he seemed eager to take everything in—the sounds, the sights, the smells. He paused to watch a group of teenagers chuck baseballs at ceramic bottles stacked into pyramids. When one of the pyramids went down, the teenagers cheered and Dennis went wild. He started clapping his hands and stomping his feet, cheering right along with the teenagers. They turned and stared at him, stupefied at first by his appearance. But then they pointed and laughed, which made Dennis point and laugh right back, like it was some kind of game.

"Come on, Dennis." Mia slipped an arm through his and tried to pull him away.

"Look at that fat monster!" one of the teenagers shouted. "Holy shit! What's *wrong* with him?"

Dennis kept laughing and pointing right along with them. When the kids stuck their tongues out at him, Dennis did the same. This encouraged them to make more faces to see if they could get my brother to copy them.

"Why don't you cocksuckers go fuck yourselves," Mia said to them. She kept tugging on Dennis's big arm. "Come on, sweetheart."

Dennis's head tilted to one side, as if he was forcing all these stimuli to slide from his ear directly into the center of his brain. His smile faltered and his eyes went foggy. Perhaps the reality of the situation was beginning to dawn on him.

I still had a decent amount of chemicals barreling through my system, so I was feeling particularly self-righteous at that moment. I made a move toward those assholes, but Clay gripped me high up on the arm, his fingers digging painfully into my bicep. The teenagers flipped me off, then strutted away in the opposite direction. One or two of them looked at us over their shoulder as they fled, their gremlin laughter shrill over the din of the gaming booths and carnival rides.

Her arm still looped through Dennis's, Mia came up beside me. "Is there any reason your brother can't enjoy himself tonight?"

"What are you talking about?"

She pointed to a custard stand. "I mean, it's a fucking *carnival*, for Christ's sake."

"Sure. Go for it."

"Come on, big guy. I know you've got a sweet tooth." Mia led Dennis toward the custard stand. For whatever reason, Dennis began cackling with laughter.

I watched them slip away together in the crowd. A memory returned to me then, and I was suddenly remembering Dennis and our mother coming to visit me in a place that was politely referred to as a "young offender institution" soon after the fire that had killed Sarah and Milo Patchin. My mother had come up with excuses why my father couldn't be there, each excuse a lie to cover the truth—that he was drunk and furious at me. I remembered Dennis bringing me a whole stack of crayon drawings, pages and pages of drawings, but it was all the same picture, over and over and over again, like some lunatic's nightmare: a large black circle in the middle of each page. Why I thought of this now, I had no idea.

Suddenly weak, I leaned against a nearby trashcan.

"Hey." Clay came around in front of me. "You okay?"

"I'm fine. Just a little woozy."

He rested a hand on my shoulder. "You wanna talk about what happened earlier?"

"You mean my brother doing his *Twilight Zone* hike through the woods? I don't know what to say about that, man."

"I'm not talking about that. I'm talking about finding you passed out on the floor of that bathroom."

I turned away from him. "Shit, come on…"

"It's cool, Jamie. You don't gotta be ashamed in front of me." He gave my shoulder a little squeeze. "We've all been through some shit. I had a problem with the bottle for a while myself. Question is, are you doing anything about it?"

"Yeah, man, I'm in AA, can't you tell?" I laughed.

"I'm being serious here."

"So am I." But then I thought of all those missed calls and unanswered texts from Emily Pearson, and it sobered me up. "Look, I was going to AA back home. I was only a week in, but I was doing good. Before that, I did ninety days in rehab. Stone fucking sober the whole time, swear to Christ." I had to laugh at that—a pathetic, birdlike squawk, unlike my previous eruption. That time in rehab seemed like a snapshot from someone else's life now, and it made me feel funny to think back on it. "But then my mom died and I had to drop everything and get back to the Mouth. For Dennis."

"Was it your mom's death that made you slip? Or the idea that now you're responsible for your brother because she's gone?"

I looked up at him, my vision blurry. "It's Black Mouth," I told him. "It marches all those old ghosts right out in front of me, same as it did when I was a kid, and it's to the point where it's getting harder and harder to tell what's real and what's not."

"That isn't Black Mouth, Jamie. It ain't even this one-eyed man we once called the Magician. You got a lot of shit to deal with from when you were a kid. If I had to guess, I'd say highest on that list is your dad."

I felt something ugly and sharp twist inside me. I looked around, expecting to find the jeering, accusatory faces of the dead among the crowd. My father there, too.

"I didn't know what it was back then," Clay said, "but I see it every day now on my job, Jamie. I'm sorry I couldn't help you. I'm sorry you had to live like that."

"I don't wanna talk about my dad…"

"You *face* it, you *deal* with it. You learn something about yourself so you can learn to get *through* it."

"I don't wanna learn something about myself…"

Clay laughed. His hand was still on my shoulder. "That's an old AA mantra right there, my brother. Most alcoholics would rather die than learn anything about themselves. And as a matter of fact, they do."

"Clay, man, this isn't about drinking. I got the same rottenness inside me that he had."

"That's just your excuse, Jamie."

"It's not," I said. "It's the truth. I'm all fucked up inside. I grew up to be just like the son of a bitch. I swore I never would, *cried* about never being like him, but look at me now, Clay. Look at me now." I pointed through the crowd, in the direction Mia and Dennis had gone to get custard. "All that destiny and fate talk Mia's been spouting? Well, this is *my* destiny. This is *my* fate. There's a history in my blood, man. I don't drink because my father was an abusive piece of shit, and I don't drink because we killed a woman and her baby when we were kids. I don't even drink to keep their ghosts away—that's just a bonus, man.

"I *drink* because it's my sad fucking *nature* to drink. That I find comfort in a half-inch of alcohol sitting there in a bottle. That I bring a drink to my lips and it's like someone wrapping their arms around me, telling me it's all gonna be all right. That I keep getting tricked by a bottle of fucking poison, thinking I can put life on pause the moment I take a drink, buying some time to figure my shit out.

That's it. That's all it is. I'm my father's son, man. There's no great secret here. I was just born bad."

His hand still on my shoulder, Clay Willis leaned down so he could put his face close to mine. There was suddenly something hard and resolute behind his eyes. "No children are born bad, Jamie," he told me. "No children are born bad."

I stared at him. My voice a grating whisper, I said, "Back when we were kids, locked up in that institution, I told you what I saw that night in Black Mouth. The night of the fire. Do you remember?"

"I do," he said. "It all came back to me this morning, when Ashida was talking about your statement to the police. I remember we were having lunch one afternoon in that institution. It was soon after your mom and your brother came to visit, I think. I remember Dennis bringing you a whole stack of really strange drawings. Wheels, I think."

I laughed, and a tear spilled from my eye. "Circles," I said. "They were circles. I was just fucking thinking about that."

"Circle is a wheel; wheel is a circle. Or maybe they were just big fucking holes. Who knows?" Clay smiled, then lowered his voice. "I remember you saying the Magician was not a man, but some kind of monster. Just like that statement you gave the police that Ashida mentioned. That when you chased after him that night, his face changed. You said he'd scared you so bad."

"That's right," I said. "It was true."

"Maybe it was true then. You still believe that's what you saw now? That this guy we're out here looking for is some kind of devil or demon or whatever?"

"I don't know what I saw. I don't know what's real anymore." I pushed myself off the trashcan, and Clay's hand fell away from my shoulder. "Clay, I think I'm gonna puke."

I hurried past him and nearly collided with a guy trying to win a goldfish for his girlfriend by tossing ping pong balls into a fishbowl.

There were no Porta-Johns in the vicinity, so I darted into the shadowed passageway between two of the game booths. A second later, I was spilling my guts onto a braid of industrial extension cords on the ground.

When I was done puking, I leaned against the side of one of the booths to catch my breath. It felt like someone had taken an auger to my stomach. The stink of my vomit simmering at my feet didn't help any.

I was in a dark, narrow cavity where the backs of two rows of gaming booths came together. As my vision realigned, I saw an amorphous figure standing a distance away from me down that narrow channel, staring in my direction. Crazily, I thought this silhouette was dressed in a top hat and cloak, although I didn't quite trust my eyes at this point. As I stared at it, the figure pivoted to the right and vanished into the dark.

I squeezed between the booths in pursuit, but my feet got tripped up in the cables, sending me crashing to the ground. My stomach made another lurch, but thankfully nothing came out this time.

I climbed to my feet, my right arm aching something fierce now, and continued down the gap between the booths. When I reached the end, I came out to where great flashing lights turned everyone on that side of the midway into shadow puppets. I was standing in front of the Ferris wheel, the wheel's neon lights blinking along its towering spokes. The hairs on the nape of my neck stiffened. I turned around and looked back toward the passageway between the gaming booths, but could see nothing.

Had the figure vanished into the crowd?

Had there even *been* a figure?

I got caught up in a wave of people that swept me around to the far side of the Ferris wheel. There were kids there getting rides on a few morose-looking ponies in a pen. The air stank of horseshit, which did little to help my unsettled stomach.

Set off from all the other rides and attractions, dark in the shadows against a backdrop of desiccated trees, stood the facade of a house that, at first glance, looked remarkably like my childhood home. Except this one had a pair of swinging saloon doors on the front and a neon sign above the entranceway:

HOUSE OF FEAR

There was a chain draped across the front of those saloon doors, and a sign hanging from it which said OUT OF ORDER. Beyond the sign and on the other side of those double doors stood my father. Not as he looked in death, but as he looked in life—hulking, massive, angry. A slab of a man who, just like me, was broken and poisonous inside. As I stared at him, he receded into the darkness of that house.

Before I realized what I was doing, I was going after him. I ducked beneath the chain and shoved open those swinging doors. Laid out before me was a dark, unforgiving corridor with only the dimmest sense of light shining at the opposite end. Occluding that light was my dad, standing midway down the corridor, staring back out at me.

I went to call to him, but I couldn't formulate words. Something vital had broken inside me. Instead, I staggered forward, but only managed a single step before I tripped over something and fell crashing to the floor.

I was lying on a set of cold metal tracks. What a cart might roll on when this attraction was in operation. For a second, I became confused, and thought I was in an old mining tunnel in the heart of Black Mouth, but then I heard a man shouting at me, and I snapped out of my reverie.

"You can't go in there," the man was yelling at me. He was a big guy in a reflective vest, like a construction worker, only he wore a bowler hat cocked on his head. "Come on, buddy."

I glanced up and saw that my father was no longer there, if he ever had been. So I climbed to my feet, apologized to the guy in the vest and bowler hat, then skirted back toward the flashing lights of the midway.

I found myself in the center of an aisle, bookended on either side by red-and-white striped tents. Barkers spotted me, grinned clownishly, beckoned me into various tent flaps. A belly dancer twirling a snake above her head locked eyes with me. The grin she summoned to the surface of her lips was chillingly lupine in nature. She stood beside a person whose face had been cosmetically transformed into a leopard's face, with his flattened nose, cleft lip, and cat's-eye contact lenses. Nylon whiskers bristled from this person's swollen, spotted jowls.

I felt like I had inadvertently passed through a portal to an alternate plane of existence. *Must I travel back between the game booths to return to my own space and time?*

That was when I saw it. There, facing me from the opposite end of the midway like two gunfighters in a standoff, stood a solitary tent slightly removed from all the others. Its striped red-and-white canvas aflutter with multicolored flags, pointed as vampire teeth. There was a placard set up on an easel right outside the tent flap:

PATCH THE PRESTIDIGITATORI
Great Feats of Magic for an Unsuspecting Populace!
Only $4 for the THRILL of a LIFETIME!

And then below that:

Tonight's performances have been cancelled
(no refunds)

A hand fell on my shoulder, and I nearly leapt out of my sneakers.

I spun around to find Clay, Mia, and Dennis standing there. Dennis was going to town on a chocolate-and-vanilla soft-serve ice-cream cone. The sight of it caused my stomach to turn over. I thought I might puke again.

Without saying a word, I pointed to the magician's tent at the opposite end of the midway.

"Patch the Prestidigitator," Mia said. "Patch..." She looked at me. "Holy fucking shit. Did you see him?"

I shook my head.

"It's him," she said, and there was no room for uncertainty in her voice. "Patch the Prestidigitator. Son of a bitch."

"All shows cancelled for tonight," Clay said, reading the fine print on the bottom of the placard. "I wonder what that's all about."

"The son of a bitch is probably off in the woods somewhere coercing children to murder their friends," Mia said. "You never can tell these days."

Clay checked his watch. "And this place closes in about forty-five minutes."

Mia took out her cell phone and snapped some photos of the magician's tent.

"I'm gonna go sit down on that bench over there," I said, and shambled through the crowd to where a wooden bench sat beneath the blinking neon of the Ferris wheel. Dennis ambled over and sat beside me. He craned his neck around to watch the Ferris wheel pull its slow rotations against the night sky. He wore an ice-cream goatee.

Clay and Mia had their heads together in discussion. They kept looking over at me. Then Clay walked off and Mia came and sat on the bench beside me. She patted my thigh.

I leaned closer to her. Whispered, "I'm sorry for being a dick earlier. Not going to talk to the police with you guys and everything."

"Dude, your breath is *rank*." She dug a pack of cinnamon Dentyne from her pocket and handed it to me. "Anyway, forget it. We've all gotta deal with this in our own way. There's no right or wrong. Nobody needs to apologize."

We sat in silence until Clay returned. He handed me a bottle of water and told me to drink it. I unscrewed the cap, took a sip, then waited to see if I'd puke it all up. Fortunately, I didn't.

"What do we do?" I asked. I was staring at the ground between my feet. The whole world was spinning.

"We're gonna hang here until the carnival closes," Mia said. "See if he shows up at the end of the night."

"And if not," Clay said, "then we'll come back tomorrow. Someone's gotta be here to man this tent."

Mia patted my thigh again. "I want this motherfucker, Jamie."

The ground was swimming between my feet. After a time, I looked up and stared, hypnotized by the flutter of those colored vinyl flags on the magician's tent.

"Pretty lights," Dennis said. He had one eye closed and was tracing the outline of the Ferris wheel with one finger.

For whatever reason, I burst into tears. People turned and stared at me. Mia and Clay, too. When I saw them looking, I hid my face in my hands.

3

There was only one motel in the vicinity of Sutton's Quay, a squalid roach-infested breadbox out along the highway. The billboard in the parking lot said STAY AT THE QUAY, though I didn't know if this was the name of the place or just a simple command. Unlike Gilley's Motor Inn back in Kentucky, this place was practically deserted, yet we all agreed to share a single room to conserve funds.

Mia steered my car into a parking space outside the motel while

Clay and Dennis pulled up beside us in Clay's Toyota. Before getting out, Mia turned to me. "Can I make a suggestion?"

"What?"

"How about you lay off all the shit for a while?"

I looked down at my lap. My hands were vibrating on my knees.

"You wanna stay in this motel tonight instead of at your house, that's fine by me. But there are no ghosts waiting for you there, Jamie. It's not haunted. There's no dark magic in Black Mouth, and the Magician was just a man. All that horror inside your head? It's just your conscience speaking to you. Will you listen to it? Will you listen to *me*?" She shook her head, as if I'd disappointed her somehow. "All of those things are true. If you'd just let yourself have a moment of clarity, you'd realize that."

"I don't know if that's true," I told her. I was thinking about my dad, about Sarah and Milo Patchin, about everything. I felt on the cusp of some breakdown.

"I wouldn't lie to you," Mia said. "I love you, Jamie. I always have."

I looked at her. "Why don't you just let Clay turn this all over to that lawyer and be done with it?"

She leaned over and kissed the side of my face.

"Because maybe I want to kill the son of a bitch," she said, and got out of the car.

4

"I've seen subway restrooms that looked cleaner than this," Clay commented, hesitating in the doorway of the motel room.

"Don't be a pussy," Mia said, shoving past him. "Dibs on the shower."

Clay looked at me, quite visibly unhappy. "Tell me again why we can't stay at your place?"

"Because it's haunted," Mia said before I could answer, and I noted an edge of exasperation in her tone.

"Yeah, but does it have roaches that might mug you at gunpoint?"

I offered up a weak laugh. I was feeling a little better than I had been back at the carnival. My head was clearing up and my stomach didn't feel like someone had lit a bonfire in it anymore.

"You're such a big baby, Clay," Mia said. She carried her duffel bag into the bathroom and closed the door. A second later, I heard the water come on.

"What are you gonna do with that old place, anyway?" he asked. He set his bag down on one of the two twin beds.

"Hire an arsonist." I tossed my own bag on the other bed. "We should call the lobby, ask if they've got a couple of cots we can use."

"That kid working the front desk didn't seem to know he was even awake, let alone where a couple of spare cots might be."

Dennis sat on one of the beds and turned the TV on with the remote. He surfed through the channels until he found a Ninja Turtles cartoon.

"Aren't you Turtled out, buddy?" I asked him.

"Ninja Turtles fight the Foot," he said, and how the fuck could I argue with that?

My cell phone began vibrating in my pocket. I took it out and saw it was Emily Pearson calling. I didn't decline the call, but I didn't answer it, either. I just let it go to voicemail, feeling shitty the whole time.

Clay took his laptop from his bag and climbed onto the bed with it. "How many people do you think it takes to set up those carnival tents?" he asked, leaning his head against the headboard.

"What do I look like, the carnival strong man?"

"No, that's Dennis. You look more like..."

He's going to say drunk, I look like the carnival drunk...

"...like the guy in the paper hat who sells you cotton candy."

"What? Really?"

"Hey, it's a respectable gig. People gotta eat."

"What about Mia?"

"Shit. Mia's the fortune teller. Didn't you know that? All her talk about destiny and fate and looking for the secrets of the universe in the shape of her cornflakes."

"I thought she was the painted lady." I ran a finger up and down my arm. "All those tattoos."

"She's more than one thing. She's always been more than one thing."

I smiled. "Fair enough. So what about you? Who're you?"

"The freak show attraction, of course."

"Come on, Clay."

"Nah, it's cool." He waved a hand at me.

"Isn't there anything they can do for your condition? Medication or treatments or whatever?"

He tapped on his laptop, disinterested in the topic. Or feigning disinterest. "There's creams and there's laser treatments, but no one can say that they actually work. But it's okay. It doesn't bother me anymore." His fingers paused on the keys. He looked up at me. "I've got the Magician to thank for that, you know. Despite all his twisted games that summer, he actually gave me some confidence. Can you imagine that? Something good coming from a monster like him?"

"I think you look great." I nodded toward the bathroom door. "I think Mia thinks you look great, too."

"Yeah?"

"I saw how she hugged you outside that motel in Kentucky. When all this is over, you should ask her out."

Clay laughed. Dennis turned away from the television and laughed, too, even though I was sure he had no clue what was going on.

"Why's that funny?" I asked Clay.

"I don't think I'm Mia's type," he said.

"She doesn't date black guys?"

"She doesn't date *guys*," he said, still laughing.

"Oh. I didn't know that. She told you that?"

"You guys were just in a car together for like a billion hours. You didn't talk?"

I didn't want to admit that I'd been passed out for much of the drive. "I guess I'm not as observant as you. Hey, I'm gonna go outside and make a phone call. Keep an eye on Dennis?"

"I am watching the Turtles," Dennis said, not pulling his eyes from the TV.

Clay just winked at me: *No worries, I got him.*

Outside, the smell of the mountains hung heavy in the air. Across the highway was a shopping center. I saw a liquor store there.

I took a deep breath then called Emily Pearson. This was a woman I'd only known for a handful of days. Kind but demon-haunted. I had amassed quite a collection of unanswered texts and voicemails from her since I'd stopped showing up at AA meetings, but could no longer ignore her in good conscience. I had enough weighing me down as it was.

She answered breathlessly, as if she was in the middle of running a marathon. "Oh my God, Jamie! Oh, thank the Lord! Bless Him! Where have you been? I've been calling nonstop."

I told her I was okay and that my mom had died. I told her I'd had go back home to West Virginia to take care of some things, and that I was currently dealing with my brother, who'd been living with my mom.

"I didn't know you had a brother. You never talk about him."

"Listen, I just wanted to call you so you didn't worry. I'm sorry for not getting in touch with you sooner."

"Jamie, tell me—are you sober?"

I closed my eyes. Those neon lights from the liquor store across the highway were somehow capable of searing through my eyelids, though, because I could still see them.

"I am right now."

"A death in the family can be a triggering event. Your *mother*, no less. Jamie, what can I do for you?"

"Nothing. There's nothing you can do. I just wanted to put your mind at ease."

"If you feel the urge, you call me, Jamie. Will you do that?"

My eyes still closed, I said, "Yes. I'll do that. Thank you. Have you been doing okay?"

"No. I had a setback. I had to start over. It was terrible."

"I'm sorry, Emily." Sorrier still because I was the one she was supposed to call if she was feeling tempted. If she was feeling weak. And I hadn't been answering my phone.

"Ghosts," she said. "So many ghosts. You'd think that'd be enough to keep me sober, scared to death of the ghosts that come when I drink, but it's not. They scare the shit out of me and I scream about it at the time, but it's not enough to keep me away from the drink. You know about those ghosts, don't you, Jamie?"

"Yes," I said.

"They're just *terrible*."

"Are you drinking right now, Emily?"

"No…"

"Where are you?"

"I'm at home. Snug as a bug."

"Are you alone?"

"Do you want to hear the name of my autobiography? *Alone with Cats*. Isn't that clever? I'm going to write it."

"You don't sound good, Emily."

"Oh," she said, then made a sound that could have been a sob, a laugh, a sigh.

"Do you have the number of anyone else from those AA meetings?" I asked her.

"George Epperson keeps in touch. Do you know George? He's a retired proctologist! Ha!"

"Do you have his number in your phone?"

"I do!"

"Can you look it up and tell it to me while we're on the line?"

"What's the matter? You need a proctology exam?" She brayed with laughter.

"Can you get me his number, Emily? Please?"

"Hold on." She said this in a sing-song voice. Then she prattled off a phone number, which I scrawled in the dust on the hood of my car.

"Emily, sit tight for a sec, and I'll call you right back, okay?"

"I was just so *worried* about you, Jamie…"

"I know. Thank you for that. You hold tight, okay, Emily?"

"Okay!"

I disconnected with her, then called the number she had given me. I didn't know George Epperson, but he sounded more like a grizzled army colonel than a retired proctologist when he answered the phone.

"Mr. Epperson, my name is Jamie Warren. I'm in recovery with Emily Pearson. She just phoned me now and she sounds pretty bad. Drunk, I think. I'm out of town so I can't—"

"I know where she lives," Epperson said. "I'm grabbing my car keys now."

I called Emily back and sat on the phone with her until Epperson knocked on her door. She giggled when she saw him, then accused me of orchestrating this little surprise party to make up for my recent absence. "You're just so *thoughtful*, Jamie!"

"I just want you to be okay, Emily."

"You're a good man, Jamie. Thoughtful and good."

"Can you put George on the line?"

I heard the phone fumble through some gyrations before Epperson's gruff baritone came on the line. "You were right, she's plastered. There's an empty bottle of Everclear right here on the coffee table. I mean, Christ, if you're gonna fall off the wagon, *Everclear*? I'd do a nice bottle of Laphroaig myself."

"Take care of her, George. Thanks for getting out there so quickly."

"God bless," he said, and ended the call.

I stood there in the dark, a symphony of cicadas in the surrounding trees, and stared at the lights of the liquor store across the road. I still felt like shit, having puked my guts up at the Happy Horace Carnival less than two hours ago. I had that loaded, cruddy feeling in my stomach that I knew would linger for a good day or so after tonight...yet I still had to pry my eyes away from that liquor store across the road.

To keep my mind off drinking, I went down to the lobby and roused the twenty-something night clerk from his phone. They only had one cot, and the kid charged me a five-dollar rental fee. It was folded in half and on casters, so I wheeled it back to the room. It was easy enough, but when I got to our door, a bone-deep pain was radiating up my right arm. I massaged my elbow and flexed my arm as a wave of nausea passed over me. I remembered injuring it when I'd fallen down the stairs back at the farmhouse. It was the same arm I'd broken as a kid when my father had shoved me down the stairs.

In the room, Clay was still reclining on the bed, hammering away at his laptop, and Dennis was still sitting on the edge of the other bed watching cartoons. Mia came out of the bathroom amidst a profusion of steam, wearing a plain white undershirt that hung nearly to her knees. She had her arms up and was fiddling with her hair; as I set up the cot, I glanced at the tattoos on her legs. Swirling dragons and fire-breathing rabbits and Chinese symbols and what looked like an anthropomorphic mushroom with blazing red eyes and vampire fangs. I also happened to notice, by the impressions left in the thin fabric of her shirt, that her nipples were pierced.

She caught me staring, and I quickly averted my eyes. Busied myself putting a sheet on the cot.

"Patch the Prestidigitator doesn't have his own website," Clay said from his bed.

"Shitty marketing," Mia said. She turned down the corner of the bed where Dennis was sitting, watching his cartoon.

"He's listed on the Happy Horace Carnival site as a vendor, but that's it."

"Any photos?" Mia asked.

"None."

"So what's our game plan from here on out?"

"We go back to the carnival tomorrow," Clay said. "Stake it out. See if he actually shows up. He's gotta be in the area."

I finished making up the cot, then took the remote from Dennis's hand. I switched off the television—

"That. Is. The. Ninja. Turtles."

—then ushered him into the bathroom, where I cranked on the shower and handed him some fresh clothes, a toothbrush, and a brand-new bar of motel soap.

"Dennis is home. Jamie Warren is home."

"No, buddy, we are *not* home." I watched him peel off his clothing, his pink, hairless body like something out of a scientific journal. "Hey," I said to him. "Did you feel anything strange at the carnival tonight?"

"Pretty lights," he said.

"You remember the Magician, don't you?"

His movements slowed. His lower jaw protruded and his eyes took on a distant look—more distant than usual. "He is not really there."

"The Magician's not at the carnival?"

Something tightened behind my brother's face. *What magic must transpire back there to turn those thoughts into words*, I wondered.

"He Is. *Not*. Really *there*."

It was the same thing he'd said about the CGI Ninja Turtles in the movie I'd bought for him. *Not really there.* He didn't like that version of the Turtles because they weren't *real*, only computer generated.

Dennis extended one hand and traced a rough circle in the steam Mia had left behind on the mirror.

"What's that?" I asked him.

"The well." He looked at me, and for the first time I saw a flicker of fear in his dull, seawater eyes. "I have to find it."

"Where is it?"

"I have to *find* it," he repeated. "There is. *Something*…" His tongue pushed out from between his thick lips.

"What something?" I asked.

"*Some. Thing.*" He looked up at the single light bulb in the center of the bathroom ceiling. Steam from the shower still swirled in the air.

"Dennis," I said, my throat suddenly feeling tight. "Do you ever see Dad at the house? Or a woman with a baby?"

He looked at me, his face a blank canvas. "Dad is dead."

I hated that I was suddenly thinking about that liquor store across the road. I could hear those bottles' voices rising in one collective chorus, calling out to me in the night: *We are bigger than you…*

"Soap," I reminded him, and slipped out of the bathroom.

5

Dennis was too big to share one of the twin beds, so he got the cot. I had planned on sharing the bed with Clay, but he was a night owl, still propped up against the headboard in the dark, a spectral being in the electric glow of his laptop screen.

Mia peeled away a corner of her bedspread and batted her eyes at me. "You can share my cozy love den, Jamie Warren," she said, and Clay laughed.

I slid beneath the cool sheets, feeling Mia's body heat radiating from her side of the narrow little bed. I took a breath and smelled her there—cheap motel soap and freshly shampooed hair. Something deeper, too. She rolled over in my direction, her face inches from mine. The room was dark now, except for the soft glow radiating from Clay's laptop screen, and Dennis was already snoring on the cot at the foot of our bed. In the darkness, she could have been that eleven-year-old girl again, the first girl I'd ever had a crush on. The first girl I'd ever truly loved.

"You've got a boner, don't you?" she said.

Clay laughed and I told her I absolutely did not, even though I did.

"This Happy Horace Carnival has been around since 1972," Clay said. In the darkness, his profile was silvered in the light from his laptop screen. "Travels as far west as the Mississippi, and operates nine months out of the year. Basically, they take the winter off. Ownership's changed hands a ton of times, from what I can tell. And...hey, tell me this isn't creepy as hell."

He held up his laptop so Mia and I could see the image on the screen. It was a vintage photo of a man in a purple clown suit. His greasepaint made his face look more like a jack-o'-lantern's leering countenance rather than a clown's.

"The hell is that?" Mia asked.

"That's Happy Horace," Clay said, turning his laptop back around. "The carnival's mascot used to be a clown before they had the good sense to change it to a cartoon hippopotamus."

"Excellent decision," Mia said. She settled into her pillow, gazing at me in the darkness.

"I'm sorry I didn't realize all the shit you went through when you were a kid." She'd lowered her voice now, so that Clay wouldn't hear. "I didn't understand what was actually happening until I was older and I thought back on it."

"It's okay."

She leaned forward and kissed me on the corner of my mouth. Then she rolled over, her back toward me. Loud enough for Clay to hear, she said, "I bet you've got a boner *now*, buddy."

Clay chuckled, then kept on tapping away at his laptop.

CHAPTER SIXTEEN

BABY IN A MINESHAFT

1

I woke up early the next morning. The motel room was dark, and the heavy drapes were drawn across the window beside Clay's bed. The A/C unit whirred, falling in synch with Dennis's sonorous respiration.

I crawled out of Mia's bed, then winced as a bolt of pain raced up my right arm. My elbow still ached from my fall down the stairs back at the farmhouse. I rubbed it as I went over to the window and peeked beyond the drapes, expecting to find the sun poking through the trees on the other side of the highway. Instead, I saw a sky terminal with storm clouds, and a gray mist creeping out from the trees on the opposite side of the road and rolling like some sentient being across the asphalt toward the motel.

It looked like smoke from a fire.

2

After a night spent sleeping in his car, Wayne Lee Stull arrived at the Department of Public Advocacy in downtown Lexington, Kentucky, at precisely 9 a.m. Two hours earlier, he'd located a

YMCA, where he'd showered, dressed himself in clean clothes, and spent an irrational amount of time combing his hair in front of a cracked and spotty mirror. Now, fully refreshed and sipping a chai tea latte through a straw, he entered the building and requested to speak with the person who took the photo of the one-eyed man that he'd seen last night on the TV news. He had some information for them, he told the woman behind the reception desk.

By 9:07, he was led to a small conference room filled with bookshelves and a single window that looked out on the street below. He finished his latte, then placed the empty plastic cup (and straw) in a wastebasket that sat on the floor beneath a painting of a cow standing in a field.

Two minutes after that, the door opened and a slim black woman in an ugly olive pantsuit entered the room. She introduced herself as Ashida Rowe, DPA attorney, and shook Stull's hand. If she'd been caught off-guard by his facial disfigurement, she did a good job hiding it. Or perhaps the woman he spoke with in the reception area had forewarned her.

"What can I do for you, Mr. Stull?" she asked after he'd introduced himself and they were both seated at opposite ends of a wobbly metal table.

"Are you the one who took that photo of the man wearing an eye patch? The one I saw on the news?"

"I didn't take it, but I sent it out to the media outlets."

"I know who he is," Stull said. "I met him when I was ten years old." He took a handkerchief from his pocket and blotted at the trickle that seeped through the ruin of his mouth. "He killed my brother."

3

"I think we should go to Black Mouth," Clay said.

The four of us were in my car, parked on the hill across from the carnival set up in St. Joseph's field. The carnival didn't open until 4 p.m., but Clay had wanted to stake the place out until evening. Without a pair of binoculars, however, we couldn't see shit. We'd tried going down there earlier, thinking we might be able to walk around unnoticed among the throng of carnival workers setting up the games, testing the rides, stockpiling supplies into the many kiosks and booths and food stands throughout the grounds, but we were quickly dismissed by a man in a trilby hat who told us the carnival was currently closed and to come back later that night.

Clay was seated in the passenger seat beside me, Mia and Dennis in the back. I turned to Clay now. His right eye looked puffier than the left for some reason. "Why do you want to do that?" I asked.

"It's not that I want to," he said, "but I think that we should." He turned around so he could address us all. "Think about it. When we met him, it wasn't at the carnival in the middle of the day. It was down in the Mouth."

"You think he's there now?" Mia said.

"I think we should *look*," Clay said. Then he turned to me. "You and Dennis don't have to go with us."

"I. Am. Going," Dennis said. He was wearing another tight-fitting Ninja Turtles T-shirt, the front of which was already darkened with sweat.

"There's nothing *in* the Mouth anymore," I told Clay. "It's just a big fuckin' ashtray."

But Clay had already made up his mind; I could tell from the steadfast look on his face. It was the same look on Mia's face, I realized. And as if I needed confirmation from my brother once again, he repeated, "I. Am. *Going*."

"Fuck it," I said, and cranked over the ignition. "It's pointless sitting here, anyway."

4

I drove us out to the section of Black Mouth where Clay was born—to where his childhood home had once teetered along the precipice of the Mouth until the night the fire had claimed it. There was nothing left of it now.

Clay stood for a time looking at the empty place in the land where he'd been born, and the rest of us stayed back and let him have this moment. I thought of Tony Tillman and all the bullies Clay had had to contend with when he'd lived there, and of the fights he'd gotten into during our incarceration in that institution. It would be nice to think things had eased up for him once he'd gotten out and left all that bad shit behind, but I knew that wasn't the case. The fact that he wasn't a drunken, insufferable mess like me was nothing short of a miracle.

He went over to the ridge and peered down into Black Mouth, and at what we'd done all those years ago. What trees remained were nothing but charred black stakes poking up from the earth, as far as the eye could see. It was like an optical illusion. The ground down there was white with ash. It had been over twenty years ago, yet still nothing had grown there.

Clay crossed over the ridge and descended the slope into Black Mouth.

Mia followed him, and Dennis followed Mia. I watched as they sank down below the ash-white rim of the earth, powerless to move. Everything came at me at once—the magic tricks, the fire, the way the Magician's face had changed before he'd flown up into those trees. The deaths of Sarah and Milo Patchin. Eleven months in that nightmare institution. And then the ghosts that awaited my return to this place, needling into my brain and turning me into a trembling, paranoid mess.

I felt like I wanted to scream. Instead, I went after them, climbing down that sooty embankment for the first time in twenty-four years.

I could still smell the smoke in the air, could taste it at the back of my throat. Up ahead, Mia and Clay meandered through the sparse, blackened tree trunks, their feet stirring up clouds of white powder. As kids, we'd known this place like the backs of our hands, but the damage caused by the fire had rendered it unrecognizable. I tried to tell myself it was because it'd been so long since we'd been down here, but I knew that wasn't the truth of it.

"Touch the Wicker Witch tree, touch the Wicker Witch tree," Mia intoned, though without any real conviction. She ran her fingers along a charred black stave of wood leaning crookedly from the ground. One good shove and she sent it toppling on its side, its twisted black roots crumbling to dust as they were wrenched from the earth.

"All those stories about this place," Clay said. I could see that his eye had gone from puffy to swollen, as if he was allergic to something down here. What was going on with him? "All that old dark magic. We killed all of that with the fire."

"*He* killed it," Mia said. "The Magician. He made us do it."

"He didn't like it down here," I said. "This place made him uneasy." Dennis had made him uneasy, too, although I didn't say so now. I watched Dennis as he carved a passage through the ashy soil with his chunky sandals, his eyes fixed on the overcast sky directly above Black Mouth. The sweat stain on the back of his shirt looked like angel wings.

"She lived somewhere nearby," Clay said, pausing to look around.

He was right. I knew exactly where Sarah and Milo Patchin had lived. I'd been to their home the day of the fire. I'd seen them hours before their deaths. I'd watched that baby suckling hungrily at his mother's breast while she gazed emptily, almost accusingly, at me.

"Milo Patchin was my brother." The words came out of me before I realized what I was saying.

Mia turned and looked at me.

"I mean, my half-brother, I guess. Mine and Dennis's. It was something my father said when I came home from the institution. I think it just slipped out of him because he was upset, and that he didn't realize he'd said it at first. But even before that, I think I knew."

Mia and Clay were both staring at me. Dennis stood beyond them, bits of gray ash sticking to the sweat on his shins, his mind lost somewhere in the clouds above.

"The Magician wanted us to kill my brother," I said, "and we did. We didn't realize it at the time, but we did. He had us do exactly what he wanted all along."

Mia shook her head. "No. What happened to that woman and her baby, that was an accident. We didn't mean to do it. But what he wanted us to do to *Dennis* was something completely different…"

"Dennis," Dennis said, staring off now into the deeper parts of Black Mouth. "Jamie Warren is home."

I suddenly wanted a drink very badly.

Mia came over and hugged me. Clay just stood there, uncertain what to do or say.

"There," Dennis said, his voice clear as day. He pointed toward a shallow ravine. At the bottom was a hole bored into the side of the embankment. The mineshaft. We had inadvertently wandered back to the Magician's old campsite.

"Jesus Christ on a trampoline," Clay said.

We went down the ravine and stood around the clearing. Remembering where he'd hung his coat, his hat, his cloak on a tree that was no longer there. Where the army-green nylon tent had been. Where he'd set the bonfire in front of the mossy deadfall. The deadfall was gone now, too, reduced to nothingness in the fire, but the opening to that mineshaft was still there. Looking at it, I wondered if forest fires could burn *down*, or if the interior of that tunnel had been left untouched by the inferno.

How far into the soil does blood seep? That old question, back at me again. *Does it go on forever? Does it continue to pollute and corrupt the land indefinitely?*

"Doesn't look like he's been here," Clay said.

"Doesn't look like *anybody's* been here," Mia said. She cupped her hands around her mouth and shouted into the opening of the mineshaft: "Hello!"

...lo...lo...lo...

Dennis clapped his hands over his ears. Gritted his teeth.

"Oh, *fuck*, what is *this*?" Mia said. She was looking at her left arm, at her wrist, and I could see blood trickling down her tattooed forearm. "What the hell..."

I went over to her, took her arm in my hands. The scar at her wrist had opened up, and there was blood oozing down her forearm to the crook of her elbow. "How'd that happen? What'd you do?"

"I don't know. I didn't do anything. I just felt it start bleeding."

"Does it hurt?"

"Well, kinda."

Clay came over, pulling a handkerchief out of his pocket. He examined the wound on Mia's wrist, then tied the handkerchief around it like a makeshift tourniquet.

"Your eye looks pretty bad, too," I told him.

"It just itches," he said, rubbing at it once he'd finished tying up Mia's wrist.

"It's swollen."

"Maybe we should get out of here," Mia suggested. "I don't like it. I feel funny."

"So do I," I said. I looked around. "Dennis?"

"He was standing right there a minute ago." Mia nodded toward the entrance of the mineshaft.

"Goddamn it." I hurried over to the mineshaft, but it was pitch black in there. I couldn't see a thing. "Dennis? What are you doing? Get out of there!"

…ere…ere…ere…

I went in after him, hurrying along that black passageway until the sunlight disappeared behind me and I was suddenly standing in a cavernous chamber as lightless as a black hole. I spoke Dennis's name again, though my voice was robbed of its strength. Probably a good thing, because I didn't know how much   or how little—vibration might cause the roof of this tunnel to collapse upon me.

I heard him moving about somewhere ahead of me in the dark.

"Do you see him?" Mia said, coming up beside me. I heard the flywheel of her Zippo spin, and a tongue of flame cast an orange glow along the walls of the tunnel. Clay was a few paces behind me, coughing. The air in here was not only musty, but smelled foul. Toxic, almost.

I took out my cell phone and activated the flashlight app, just as I'd done in the cave back in Kentucky. The pencil-thin beam of light bored through the darkness up ahead while Mia's lighter plastered our wavering shadows along the uneven earthen walls. There were wooden struts every few feet, braced against the ceiling of the tunnel. The deeper we went, the more roots descended from the ceiling and tickled our faces and shoulders. I crouched lower, shivering against those wispy tendrils, and imagined Dennis getting stuck down here.

I glimpsed him up ahead, a blur in the shadows, his broad shoulders carving trenches in the dirt walls. I saw clumps of earth fall from the ceiling and heard the wooden struts creaking and groaning. This whole tunnel could come down on our heads at any moment.

"Dennis, stop," I hissed at him.

The channel constricted all around us. Farther ahead, I watched Dennis lower himself to his hands and knees and begin crawling through a smaller aperture in the tunnel.

"Dennis!"

Clay stopped following us, and instead braced himself against the wall. I glanced over my shoulder and saw him staring at the beams crisscrossing the ceiling of the mineshaft as dust and bits of dirt rained down between them.

Mia was still at my side, and I could smell the lighter fluid burning in her Zippo. I absently wondered if there were any pockets of flammable gas down here that her Zippo might inadvertently ignite. "Maybe you should wait with Clay," I suggested, but she shook her head and kept pace with me.

Another step forward, and something snared my foot and sent me crashing to the ground. I rolled over and saw that I'd gotten caught up on a rung of track that the mining carts had used back when this shaft had been operational. A sense of déjà vu washed over me—I was thinking of myself back at the fairgrounds, tripping over the track at the entrance to the House of Fear. The guy chastising me, *You can't go in there*, as I scrambled to my feet and got the hell out...

I stood, brushing the dirt from my body. Mia asked if I was okay and I made a sound that suggested I was, even though I felt like the world was about to come crashing down on my head.

The collapse of the mine was evident here. The brackets and beams, each one as thick as a railroad tie, lay scattered about. Roots as formidable as telephone lines bisected the tunnel. Dennis was grunting on his hands and knees, trying to shove himself through that system of roots and into a constricted opening at the far end of the tunnel. He gripped one of the roots, shook it like an ape in a cage, and I watched as a shower of dirt rained down upon him.

I crawled the rest of the way and knelt down beside him. "Stop. Stop, Dennis. What are you doing?"

He looked at me. In the glow of Mia's lighter's flame, his dirt-streaked face was an alternating mask of shadow and light. His dark eyes gleamed.

"Baby," he said.

And as if his voice had summoned it, I heard the unmistakable cry of an infant echo straight up the throat of that tunnel. The sound of it nearly turned me to stone.

"It's not a baby," Mia was saying. She was kneeling down, too, a few paces behind me. The flame from her Zippo shook and jittered in her hand, causing her shadow to dance along the walls and the collection of broken beams. "It's just the wind blowing through the tunnels, Dennis."

I heard it again…and although I knew Mia was one hundred percent correct, I couldn't help but believe that there was a baby at the bottom of this mineshaft. Right there with us.

Milo Patchin.

"Jamie—" Mia said, and it was her voice that alerted me to the fact that I had crept around Dennis and was crawling deeper down the throat of the tunnel. "Are you fucking crazy? Let's get *out* of here."

Sarah Patchin, quiet your child, I thought, tears running down my cheeks. *Sarah Patchin, quiet my brother…*

The top of my head struck something solid. Dirt fell in a cold clump along the nape of my neck and crumbled down the collar of my shirt. I reached out and felt a jumble of wooden planks in front of my face. I remembered I had my cell phone in one hand, so I brought the light up and shined it on whatever was impeding my progress through this tunnel.

The mine had collapsed here, the shaft concluding in a clot of old wooden ties, massive screws, and a snake's nest of twisted iron bars.

I could see small gaps between the wooden ties where cold air filtered through, but there would be no passage beyond here.

I listened for that baby's cry, but heard nothing.

Dennis gripped my ankle, startling me. I shined the phone's light on his face, and was surprised to find tears had carved channels through the dirt on his cheeks, too.

"Are you okay?" I whispered to him.

"Baby," he said.

"No baby," I whispered back.

"No baby," he repeated. His bleary eyes hung on me a moment longer. Then he began to retreat backward through the tunnel. I did the same, following him out, my breath ragged in my throat, the smell of that terrible place clinging to me like a poison.

5

We all returned to the motel to shower and change our clothes. When I was done, I went outside to the parking lot, where Clay was talking to someone on his cell phone. The sky still looked angry, although it hadn't yet rained. The carnival would no doubt shut down for the night if it stormed, and what did that mean for us? One more night holed up here in Sutton's Quay? One more night drawn into the haunting, magnetic orbit of Black Mouth?

I gazed like some slack-jawed imbecile at the liquor store across the highway.

Mia came out, glanced warily at the sky, then lit a joint. I quickly averted my gaze from the liquor store, and instead pretended that I had been observing the storm clouds, too. A quick glance in Mia's direction told me I hadn't fooled her.

"How's your arm?" I asked her.

She still had Clay's handkerchief tied around her wrist. The blood had soaked through. "It's stopped bleeding but it hurts." She exhaled pot smoke into the air. "I still don't know what the hell happened."

I know, I thought, but didn't say. *We're reverting to the children we once were. Me with my broken elbow, you with your sliced wrist, and Clay with his swollen right eye from catching one of Tony Tillman's fists that summer. Somehow, as impossible as it may seem, it's all coming back to us.*

For the first time, I wondered if Mia wasn't right about destiny playing a role in all this.

Clay ended his call, then looked over at us. I couldn't read the expression on his face. "That was Ashida Rowe," he said.

"The attorney from Kentucky?" Mia said.

Clay nodded. "You won't believe what she just told me."

I wasn't sure I really wanted to know.

"A guy showed up at her office this morning, said he saw the photo of the Magician on the news last night. He said he *recognized* the guy from when he was a kid. Said he was the same guy who was living in the woods behind his house when his brother was killed twenty-five years ago."

"Holy shit," Mia said.

"Guy's name is Wayne Stull. Ashida said she looked up the case, and it corroborated this guy's story. Police never found the guy and the brother's murder is still unsolved."

"Son of a bitch," Mia said. "Son of a fucking *bitch*. We're bringing them out of the woodwork now." She actually laughed.

"Ashida said the guy wanted to meet with us, but she didn't want to give him my information," Clay said. "Instead, she gave me his number, said I could call him and talk to him if we wanted. What do you guys think?"

"I think destiny is conspiring to fuck this Magician bastard up the ass," Mia said. "Call this Stull guy, see if he'll come out here. I want to hear his story."

Clay turned to me. The flesh around his right eye looked painfully swollen and red. "What do you think, Jamie?"

I think I heard a baby crying in that tunnel. I think it smelled like blood down there.

"I guess it's up to you," I said, then looked toward the sky as thunder sounded in protest.

CHAPTER SEVENTEEN

STULL ON THE OUTSKIRTS

1

A light rain pattered on the windshield of Stull's Kia as he crossed into West Virginia. He had spoken with a man named Clay Willis earlier that day, and when Willis agreed to meet with him, Stull had struggled to hide his enthusiasm over the phone. He told Willis he was only a few hours away, and he could get there before suppertime. Then he'd hopped in his car and headed east. It was all he could do to keep himself restrained and not bump up even a mile over the speed limit.

When he saw the road sign informing him that Sutton's Quay was only ten miles down the road, an eagerness like indigestion curdled inside his stomach. It occurred to him that he hadn't eaten all day. Someone else might have pulled into a drive-thru at some point along the way, eaten greasy burgers in their car while they drove, but Stull never ate in his car. He kept his car clean. Just like his clothes, and his entire duplex back home in Evansville.

When he passed a shopping center, he saw among the storefronts a building that looked like a hunting lodge. According to the sign, they sold hunting, fishing, and camping gear.

Bibby was suddenly leaning over from the back seat, whispering in his ear.

"You be quiet," Stull said, because he'd already been thinking about what Bibby had just whispered to him. Sometimes Bibby thought he was so goddamn smart, but he really wasn't.

Stull pulled into the parking lot of the hunting and fishing retailer. The outside of the place really did look like a hunting cabin, albeit an enormous one. Stull had never been hunting—as a child, he'd had no father to take him hunting or fishing or camping—but he could imagine why men did things like that. There was a sense of empowerment in taking a life.

As Stull walked through the mechanical doors, the interior of the place took his breath away. No ordinary retail store, this place had massive fish tanks among its racks of camouflaged nylon coats, and an actual waterfall spilling down a rock wall toward the rear of the store. Stull went up to one of the tanks and gazed at the fish inside. The fish were shiny silver with red bellies, and their lower jaws protruded like someone with an underbite.

"Those are South American piranha," said a man with a beard as dense as a Nordic pine. Stull caught his reflection in the fish tank's glass.

"Those are the fish that eat whole cows?" Stull asked. He was bent over and peering at the fish flitting about in the tank.

"That's kind of a myth. We feed them mostly smaller fish and worms. I'm Jack, by the way. Can I help you find anything today?"

Stull straightened up and turned toward the man. Jack, in his khaki shirt and bright orange vest, recoiled at the sight of Stull's face. But then he quickly regrouped and said, "We're having a special on fishing rods today."

"I'm looking for a knife," said Stull.

"Sure. Got plenty of knives. Come with me to the counter."

There was a glass display case near the waterfall, dozens of large knives inside it. Stull peered down into the case, studying each one.

Some pretty nasty items in there, to be sure, but nothing that jumped out at him right away.

"Any type of knife in particular?" the man asked.

"A really good one."

"These here are all very good." Jack ran a hand along the glass case. Stull studied the knives. "Are some of those handles made of bone?"

"Sure are. These buck knives over here have handles made of wood with heavy-gauge brass bolsters, but you can see they've got some nice bone inlay around the edges. Elk, I think."

"Do you have any made entirely of bone?"

Jack with the Nordic pine beard grinned. He was nodding his head as if he and Stull had just shared a secret. "I know what you're looking for," he said, and went farther down the case. There were shelves below, hidden cubbies that Stull couldn't see. He imagined a whole chamber of secret goodies down there in a bunker below the store, so many knives with intricate bone handles hanging from hooks in the ceiling and pegboards on the wall, people down there polishing those gleaming blades and wearing special cotton gloves so that they didn't leave fingerprints on the steel. Stull felt a bolt of anticipation fire through him. The man returned with something wrapped in a green velvet cloth. He set it on the glass case and unfolded the cloth.

The sight of the thing caused the crack down the center of Wayne Lee Stull's face to leak. He fumbled a handkerchief from his back pocket and hastily wiped the slobber from his lips. On the other side of the display case, a look of distaste briefly washed across Jack the salesman's face, but Stull no longer cared.

"What *is* it?" Stull said, that *S* hissing out of him as if he were really a serpent in a man's skin.

"That is a fifteen-inch Damascus steel fixed-blade hunting knife with a camel bone firm-grip handle," said Jack. "This baby's the real deal, here. Imported from southern India."

The blade itself was detailed with what looked like intricate scrollwork, and the bone handle actually looked like a femur. The base of its hilt concluded in what appeared to be a knuckle joint, the sight of which set Stull's mouth to watering again.

"How much?" he asked, once more patting his leaking face with the handkerchief.

"Six hundred," Jack said.

"*Dollars?*"

"Hey, I know it sounds steep, but this is the real deal, my friend. See those patterns in the blade? Those aren't surface etched. The pattern-welding comes from melding and hammering various types of steel at high temperatures to form a welded—"

"I'll take it," said Stull.

Back in the car, Bibby asked to see the knife. Stull took it out of the box that Jack the salesman had fitted it into, and held it up so that Bibby, sitting in the Kia's back seat, could see it. The knife had a decent weight to it. Good, solid, reliable.

Bibby made some comment about the handle. Criticized Stull for spending six hundred dollars on something he was just going to dismantle anyway. Stull knew Bibby was right, but it annoyed him to hear his dead brother say it nonetheless.

"Does this look like the one that opened up your belly all those years ago?" Stull asked. When no response came, Stull craned his head around to peer in the back seat. But Bibby, that little momma's boy, was already gone.

2

He avoided the town, as he so often did when he traveled from place to place. Like a mouse traversing the baseboards, he preferred to stick to the outskirts and not tempt fate by inadvertently making a spectacle of himself. He preferred to remain anonymous.

He pulled into the parking lot of a roadside motel just as the afternoon light began to drain from the sky. The lighted words on the sign out front, STAY AT THE QUAY, reflected in reverse across the Kia's windshield.

In the glove compartment, Stull kept a collection of paper masks, which he'd worn whenever he worked at Halcyon. Those days were over, of course, but the masks would still come in handy. He strapped one on now, then went into the motel lobby and got himself a room.

There was something decidedly momentous about his arrival; he felt it like a surety in the cosmic design of his bones the second he stepped through the motel room door. Even Bibby had returned, stirring about behind him as Stull entered the room, then turned and bolted the door. He carried his briefcase in one hand, a small metal toolbox in the other, and a powder-blue grease-stained sleeping bag rolled up under one arm. He set both the briefcase and the sleeping bag on the lumpy bed, then went directly into the bathroom to study the parting in his hair. Its imperfection grated on him, so he slipped a plastic comb from his pocket and went to work getting it all back into place. He could hear the bedsprings in the lumpy mattress creak as Bibby jumped up and down on it.

Bibby lost interest in jumping on the bed, however, once Stull returned and went over to the sleeping bag. It was rolled into a tube and held closed by bungee cords. Stull undid the bungee cords and unrolled it across the mattress.

A jumble of pale bones lay inside.

Behind him, Bibby grew excited. He asked the question that he always asked whenever Stull unrolled the sleeping bag and those bones tumbled loose: *Is that what's left of her?*

Stull hated the question. Bibby *knew* the answer, so Stull refused to humor the little bastard. Instead, he ignored Bibby and studied the bones splayed out before him. He'd cleaned them pretty well already, but there was still some residual costal cartilage attached to the "true ribs," which were the first seven sets of ribs found on the human sternum. They were good, solid, reliable ribs. Stull selected two ribs that appeared to be the same approximate length and width.

The next thirty minutes was spent removing the camel-bone handle from the Damascus knife he'd purchased and fashioning a new hilt made from a composite of the two ribs. He used the small battery-powered drill from the toolbox, as well as a few screws he found in there. A bit of sanding with some fine-grade sandpaper over the bathroom sink as a final touch, just to make it all clean and perfect. He'd become rather skilled at doing this over the years— it had become a compulsion of his to fashion a new knife for each performance—yet the excitement and satisfaction he felt whenever he built a new knife never waned.

Is that what's left of her? Bibby wanted to know again.

"Go fuck yourself, Bibby," Stull told him. He turned around, jabbing at the air with the gleaming blue steel of the blade, but Bibby— of course—had already vanished.

CHAPTER EIGHTEEN

A STORM (SO TO SPEAK) GATHERS

1

Something was off with Dennis. He hadn't been the same since we'd come climbing out of that old mineshaft down in the Mouth, dusted in soot and feathered with ash. Neither Clay nor Mia could tell the difference in his demeanor, but I could.

I got him an early dinner, hoping some food in his belly might bring him back around. But he barely touched his fast food burgers and only picked at the fries. He seemed preoccupied—even more so than usual. I waited for Clay and Mia to leave the motel to go meet the man from Indiana, Wayne Stull, before pulling the drapes closed over the motel room window. I caught a glimpse of that sky as I did so, and thought it looked pretty goddamn angry. If Mia was right about destiny intervening here, why did I suddenly feel like something was pushing back against us?

Dennis was lying on his cot, the cartoons on the television screen reflecting in his big gray eyes. I went around to one of the beds, sat on the edge. Stared at the back of my brother's woolly head.

"What's wrong, Dennis?"

He had his head in his hand, propped up on an elbow on the cot.

At the sound of my voice, he lowered his head to the pillow. I couldn't see his face.

"Dennis?"

"Hole," Dennis said. "Into. The. Hole."

"What?" I asked. And when he didn't respond, I said, "Help me understand what the hell is going on here."

"Go. *Deeper.*"

"Go deeper *where*?"

But that was all. He stayed like that for a long time, not saying anything more about it. I kept quiet, too, gazing blankly at the back of his head. When I finally got up and turned the TV off, I saw that he had fallen asleep.

2

Before pulling into the parking lot of the Chinese restaurant along the highway where they were supposed to meet Wayne Stull, Clay parked outside a gas station convenience store.

"What are we doing here?" Mia asked.

"You need something for that arm," he said, meaning the scar that had opened up on her wrist. He left the car running as he got out.

There was a bottle of peroxide and a box of gauze bandages on a shelf down one of the convenience store aisles. Clay took it to the counter, tugging his wallet from the rear pocket of his jeans.

The man behind the counter rang up the items and groused a total at him. He had his long black hair pulled into a ponytail, strands of hair swinging in front of his face. When he looked up, Clay saw he was sporting a shiner under one eye. He had the bloodshot gaze and gin-blossomed nose of a career alcoholic.

Clay looked at the man's nametag—TONY.

"You're Tony Tillman." It wasn't a question. Clay's voice was composed, steady. He could have been talking to a child in his office back in Michigan.

The man looked shocked at first, but then looked away as he bagged Clay's items. Clay placed a twenty on the counter.

"You don't remember me, Tony? Your old pal Skullface?"

Tony Tillman made no acknowledgement that he recognized him, or that he even heard him. He had a vape pen in the pocket of his shirt, just below his nametag, and a tattoo of a spider web on his neck.

"You don't remember my face, Tony?" Clay smiled at him. "Yeah, you do. Of course you do."

Without a word, Tony slid Clay's change across the counter.

"Keep it," Clay said. Still smiling, he took his items off the counter and left.

3

A man and a woman entered the Chinese restaurant together, looking around for someone. Wayne Lee Stull raised a hand over his head, and when they both turned in his direction, he could see by their expressions that the attorney down in Lexington—the one in the ugly olive pantsuit—hadn't warned them about his face.

Clay Willis was a man dealing with his own cosmetic condition, Stull was surprised to see. A black man whose face looked like someone had splashed him with milk, had let it run in all directions, had let it dry there permanently. Willis's hands were just as remarkable. Less white and more pink than his face, his hands looked as if he'd dipped them into some kind of solution that had siphoned all the pigment from his flesh.

The woman was attractive, but there was something butch about her that caused Stull to wonder if she wasn't a carpet muncher. She wore a Twisted Sister T-shirt with a low collar, and Stull could see she had a giant bat or bird or something with splayed wings tattooed across her upper chest. When she sat down across from him in the booth, he caught a whiff of marijuana coming off her. There was a gauze bandage wrapped around her left wrist.

They exchanged some pleasantries, and when the waitress came by, Stull told them to please order, his treat, even though he wasn't hungry himself. Both the man and the woman declined food—Stull assumed they found his face too off-putting to eat while seated across from him—but the man ordered an ice water and the woman ordered a beer. Stull asked for a refill of the hot tea he'd been drinking (through a straw), and the waitress smiled and executed a little bow in his direction.

"What's your story, Wayne?" the black man with the white face asked. "I'm eager to hear it."

Stull tugged his handkerchief from his pocket and soaked up the leakage from the crack in his skull. Over the years, he had learned to speak well despite his deformity, but when he got nervous or excited—and he was both right now—he had difficulty pronouncing *s*-words, *th*-words, or making *o* sounds. He had to concentrate now so that they could understand him.

"When I was ten years old, there was a homeless drifter who stayed for a time in the woods behind our house in Indiana," Stull said. It was the same opening he'd given Ashida Rowe back in Lexington. "My brother Robert and I used to play in those woods, and we would see him sometimes. I wanted nothing to do with him—there was something strange about him, something that made me uncomfortable—but Robert became friendly with him. He would bring him food and hang out in the woods with him. In exchange, this man would teach my brother card tricks."

The black man with the white face nodded in commiseration; the lesbian remained stoic and emotionless, her eyes hanging on him like lead weights.

"After a while," Stull continued, "I stopped going to the woods altogether, but Bibby—I'm sorry, *Robert*—kept going." Giving them what passed for an apologetic grin, Stull said, "Bibby was Robert's nickname. I couldn't pronounce 'Bobby' when I was younger because of the...well, my condition..."

He tipped his head back and opened his mouth wide, presenting this man and this woman with a full view of the open crab claw that was his upper palate. He didn't actually do this to make them uncomfortable or to turn their stomachs; it was just his way of explaining the severity of his condition in one simple visual.

It was at that moment the waitress came by with the man's water and the woman's beer. She saw Stull with his head tipped back and his mouth open, those stalactite teeth jutting from the split chasm of his upper palate, and actually uttered, "Oh, no," at the sight of him. Then she scurried away, a little slant-eyed cockroach, Stull thought, clamping shut his mouth with an audible clack.

"We'd kept the fact that the man was living back in those woods a secret. But when Robert never came home one night, I told our mother about him, and all the time Robert had been spending there. The food he had brought him, and the sneaking out in the middle of the night to see him. We walked into the woods together, my mother and I, and that's where we found him. Robert. His belly had been opened up and there was blood everywhere. He'd been dead for hours."

"Jesus Christ, I'm sorry," the black man with the white face said. "That's just awful, Wayne."

"Were there any other children involved?" the woman asked. "Kids from the neighborhood who would also go see this man with your brother?"

"We lived on a cow and chicken farm that was owned by an abattoir in town. About two hundred acres of property. There were no other children. There was no neighborhood."

"So you think the man *himself* killed your brother?" she said.

"Who else would have done it?" Stull said.

"We thought his M.O. was to coerce others to do it for him," she said. "Something about…about the ceremony of the act."

"Did you see a knife?" the man—Willis—asked him. "Did this man ever show it to you?"

"There was a knife made of bone," Stull said. *It was so beautiful*, he wanted to add, but didn't. "I remember seeing it once. I believe that was the knife he used on my brother."

"He never tried to get you to do something to your brother?" the woman asked. "Or your brother to do something to you?"

"Not that I recall," Stull said. "But like I said, there was something about him that troubled me, and I didn't spend a lot of time around him, the way Robert did."

"And the police never found out anything about this man?" Willis asked.

"Nothing whatsoever. And I'm sorry to say that the stress of the whole thing really ruined my poor mother. She'd always been such a…a good, solid, reliable woman…but after Robert's murder, well, she was never quite the same again. Each day that went by with nothing to show for it—that man having disappeared in the night leaving no trace behind, like some sort of phantom—and poor Mother's condition only worsened. It got to where she could barely take care of herself, let alone take care of me, and she was unfortunately institutionalized for a while."

Willis's face looked compassionate, but the woman was still eyeing him from the other side of that booth like she could see the zippers in his costume, the strings on the marionette.

Stull made a *guh* sound way back in his throat, then said, "Is that a terrible thing to tell you people? I don't know. I'm not one to ordinarily volunteer such personal information, but I feel like we three share some…some *unity* in all this. Like we're all part of a wheel." That wheel line had just come to him now out of the ether; everything else he had rehearsed on the drive here. "I guess it's just comforting to know my brother and I weren't the only ones, as selfish and horrible as that may sound. There's camaraderie in misery, isn't there?"

"When did this happen?" the woman asked, ignoring him.

"Robert was killed in 1997."

The man called Willis leaned back in his seat. He looked at the woman, who was still staring at Stull. The man said, "We met him in 1998. How long could he possibly have been out there doing this?"

"And still is to this day, judging by the incident that occurred in Kentucky," Stull said. "That little girl being stabbed to death? Just awful. I read all about it after I saw the picture of him on the news. Incidentally, which one of you took it?"

"That'd be me," said the woman.

"How is it you happened to come across him? Had you been tracking him down somehow?"

"It was just dumb luck," she said. Then, like an afterthought: "Or fate."

Yes, fate, Stull thought. *I suppose that's something…*

"And you're sure it's the same guy you and your brother dealt with back then?" the woman—Mia somebody—said. "Eye patch and everything?"

"Oh, it's him," Stull said. "No doubt. I'll never forget his face." Which was true.

"How old do you think he was when you knew him in '97?"

"Oh, I can't really say…"

"You don't think he should look a lot older than he does in that photo?"

Stull thought about this. "You know, I hadn't considered that," he said, truthfully.

"You said he looked older in real life, when you saw him," Willis said to the woman.

"Maybe," she said. "I don't know. I just said that to Ashida so she wouldn't think we were nuts."

"Photos," Stull interjected, "can be misleading. I'm a bit of a novice photographer myself. Things behind the lens aren't always what they are in front of it." And for some reason, he felt compelled to trace a circle in the air with his finger.

The woman named Mia was studying him hard from across the table. Stull didn't like that. He didn't like *her*. Maybe he'd shared too much with these people. Maybe he'd gone a little overboard here.

"I agree," she said after a time. "That's pretty astute, Mr. Stull. You've got a pretty good memory, too, to remember what this guy looked like from 1997."

Stull felt himself nodding in response, even though what she'd said hadn't actually been a question. She was a dyke, all right, this cunt; Stull could sense her queerness coming off her in fetid waves. It made him angry for some reason.

"You said you were only ten years old at the time?" she continued.

"That's right."

"And how old was your brother?"

"He was ten also. We were identical twins. Except he wasn't... he didn't have my facial deformity. The purer, better version of me, you might say." He tried to grin, then blotted more spittle with his handkerchief. "You must have a pretty decent memory, too," he added, "to glimpse him in a crowd all these years later and snap that photo of him. Tell me—what did he do to you poor folks when you were children? Did he hurt one of you?"

"He wanted us to murder one of our friends," Willis said. "When we wouldn't do that, he convinced us to burn down a section of woods behind our homes. Two people ultimately died in the fire."

"Oh no." Stull sat back in the booth. He wanted to make sure they were aware of how much space he was putting between them and him. "That's pretty awful," he said. "I'm sorry to hear it. The two of you must feel terrible about that. Was it…just the two of you?"

The moment those words were out of his mouth, he worried that he'd overdone it, and immediately regretted having said it. He didn't want to make them feel guilty, nor did he want to sound too inquisitive; he wanted to earn their trust. He opened his mouth to soften the comment with some other blather, but the woman—*Mia, Mia, Mia* – said, "There were four of us. And yeah, it fucking sucks, dude. That's why we want to find this guy."

"As do I," Stull said. He folded his hands on the table and leaned closer to them. *Four of them*, he kept thinking, or maybe it was Bibby shrieking inside his head. *Four of them!* "How do you think we go about doing that?"

"It's not up to us," Willis said. "We've told Ms. Rowe everything we know. It's up to her and the police to figure things out from here."

Liar, Stull thought. *You, my white-faced friend, are a motherfucking, cocksucking liar.*

"You know," Stull said, "my mother died a few years back. Ovarian cancer that ultimately worked its way throughout the entirety of her body. She wasn't altogether with it by the end, and she kept getting me confused with my brother. Even with my deformity. She kept asking, 'Who did that to you, Robert? Who cut you up so bad?' I know it was that man. I'd like to see him finally brought to justice."

"Then you should do what we're doing," Willis said. "Keep in touch with Ms. Rowe, provide her any statements that you can. Tell her anything else you might remember over time. It's not just about bringing him to justice, but about helping other kids who have…"

"Fallen under his spell?" Stull said. It would have been the perfect interjection had he not fumbled the *S* in *spell*, and launched a gobbet of spittle onto the tabletop. Everyone seemed to notice.

"That's right," Willis agreed. "And I don't mean to take away the pain you and your mother have suffered, or what happened to your brother, but this thing is bigger than what happened to each of us individually. It's a pattern. It's ongoing. This guy is a predator and he's still out there doing his thing."

The woman named Mia took a chug of her beer, then set the bottle down on the table. Hard. "What was his name?" she asked him.

"I never knew him by any name," Stull said.

"What did you call him?"

"I called him nothing," Stull said. He let a moment pass between them, mainly because he did not like this cunting bitch. He wanted her to sweat for it. "But my brother Robert called him the Magic Man."

4

I didn't realize I had fallen asleep until a dull *thump* wrenched me from a nightmare. I sat up in bed. The motel room was mostly dark now with the drapes drawn; outside, those storm clouds still held steady in the deepening sky over Sutton's Quay.

Dennis was standing beside my bed, staring straight at the wall.

"Dennis?"

He placed both hands on the wall. I could hear his taxed breathing, engine-like, a rattle somewhere in his lungs.

"Den—"

He slammed his head into the wall.

"*Dennis!*"

Unfazed, he peered into the hole he'd punched into the drywall, as if searching for something in there. He even reached in with one hand and began feeling around, rummaging through the broken hunks of plaster and moldy tufts of insulation.

Afraid he might slam his head into the wall a second time, I bolted out of bed and gripped him about his wide shoulders. Had he wanted to fight me, he could have done so without difficulty. Thankfully, he came away from the wall without protest, extracting his arm from the hole and dropping his considerable weight onto the bed.

He looked up gloomily at me in the dim light of the motel room.

"Jamie Warren," he said. His throat sounded choked with tears. I switched on the lamp beside the bed and saw that, yes, he was crying.

I sat beside him on the bed. "Dennis, what's wrong? Was it another walking dream?"

He brought his face close to mine. There was drywall powder stuck to his sweaty forehead. "We have to go *deeper*," he said.

"How do we do that?" I asked him. "Tell me how we do that, Dennis."

"Find. The. Well."

"*Where?*"

"I do not know." He dropped a big, clublike hand on my shoulder. "*Jamie Warren* do not know."

"That's right," I said. "I don't."

I put an arm around him. Hugged him.

Then I looked at the hole he'd made in the motel room wall.

A perfect circle.

5

Clay and Mia were grateful once the meeting with Wayne Stull was over. They got back in Clay's Toyota, cranked the A/C, then looked at each other.

"We're in agreement that there was something decidedly *off* about that guy, right?" Mia said.

"I thought about telling him the carnival connection, but by the end of that conversation, I'd decided against it," Clay agreed.

"You think he's making it all up?"

Clay knew Stull hadn't made it up; he had googled the incident after he'd gotten off the phone with Ashida Rowe earlier that day. The story Stull had just told them matched the story Clay had found online. His brother, Robert Stull, had been murdered and the murderer had never been brought to justice. Moreover, Wayne Stull's account to the police back then when he'd been a child matched the story he'd told them tonight. He told Mia this now. "But, yeah," he added, "I agree. Guy was giving me the creeps. And it had nothing to do with—"

"I know, I know," she said, and she reached out and patted his knee.

"I mean, I'm the last person to judge someone by the way they look. It wasn't that."

"No," Mia agreed, "it wasn't. There was just something...I don't know..." It was on the tip of her tongue, just out of her grasp. She couldn't focus.

It wouldn't be until later that night, as she entered Patch the Prestidigitator's red-and-white striped tent, that it would come to her. A filmmaker with a half-dozen indie horror flicks to her credit, and years of experience dealing with actors, Mia Tomasina would realize what had made her so uneasy about their meeting with Wayne Lee Stull: While he might have been telling them the truth, he had sounded as though he was reciting lines from a script.

CHAPTER NINETEEN

BIBBY AND THE
MAGIC MAN

1

Across the parking lot of the Chinese restaurant, Stull sat in his Kia and waited for Willis and the woman named Mia to pull onto the highway. They seemed to be taking their sweet time, discussing something behind the steamed-up windshield of the car. Stull wondered if they might start necking, lesbian or not.

Bibby stirred in the back seat.

Stull glanced up at his dead brother's reflection in the rearview mirror. Robert "Bibby" Stull, forever ten years old. Forever lurking about in the margins of his twin brother Wayne's consciousness.

In theory, they had been born identical twins. But Stull had seen those early baby photos—the few that Mother kept loose in a highboy drawer in the foyer of the old house on Slaughterhouse Row—and he always knew which infant child was him, which infant child was Bibby. There was never any question.

Stull's baby face was bisected down the middle, a double cleft lip hoisted like a theater curtain toward each flattened, twisted nostril. An upper gum line like an open clamshell. In the few photos where baby Wayne was laughing, you could see straight through that chasm to the back of his throat. When his baby teeth came in, they protruded forward through the gum line instead of straight down. When his adult teeth came in, they were even worse. He looked like something dropped to the pavement from a great height.

"Bibby," he'd say, when the twins were learning to talk. Not *Bobby*, not *Robert*, but that bastardized, tongue-injected version of his twin brother's name. *Bibby, Bibby, Bibby.* And Mother would grow frustrated and grasp at his jaw, her pincer-like thumb and forefinger manipulating young Wayne's mouth, hard enough so he could feel the palate constrict, the jawbones bending, the jagged kernels of teeth scissoring into one another.

When his tongue would come through the crevasse in his face, Mother would strike him open-handed across the jaw. "No one wants your spittle in their apple pie," she'd chastise him. "No one wants to see the pink worm poking through that broken hole." So he worked on his speech, concentrating on the *s*-words, the *th*-words, the long and short *o* sounds that caused him such difficulty and grief.

Robert had no difficulty. Robert had no grief. Robert was a handsome, well-adjusted boy. "He's the kind of son a father would be proud to have," Mother had said on more than one occasion to Wayne. "Do you see how Robert *articulates*? Do you see how he keeps his *tongue* in his *mouth* when he *speaks*?"

Young Wayne saw all of that. The pink worm stayed in its hole. He tried to mimic Robert's way of speaking, but he just couldn't. There was a crack in his face, and there was nothing he could do about that.

He's the kind of son a father would be proud of. Yet there had never been a father in that cold echo chamber of a house on Slaughterhouse Row. As he got older, Wayne Stull grew up to believe that he and Robert had been sired by one of the hulking, blood-streaked slaughterers who worked the killing floors at the abattoir down the road, although he never had any real proof of that. So from birth to age ten, it had just been the three of them in the creaky, rambling ranch house.

Mother had homeschooled them both to a certain point. But then, around the age of eight or nine, Robert had wanted to go to the public school in town. At first, Mother appeared offended that her favorite son would deign to abandon his family for strangers in a classroom. But in the end, Mother had acquiesced.

Robert got new shoes, a backpack, a pencil box with cartoon action heroes on the lid. When young Wayne asked to go along with his brother to that very same school, Mother laughed at him, then shook her head in great pity. "You have a difficulty speaking and your aptitude for following instructions is wanting, Wayne," she had replied. Then, rather more succinctly: "Besides, you'd scare the other children."

Every morning Robert filed onto the big yellow school bus, and every afternoon it dropped him off at the end of their long driveway. Young Wayne sat by the window for much of the afternoon, after completing his own schoolwork, waiting for his twin brother to return. At first, Robert would regale him with all sorts of interesting and impossible stories of what it was like to attend an actual *school*. But then, after a while, Robert got tired of filling young Wayne in on all of these details. They were *Robert's* stories, *Robert's* experiences, not Wayne's. Robert stopped wanting to share them with him.

Still, Wayne waited by the window for Robert to come off that big yellow school bus. Robert always came, though he sometimes kicked the chickens out of his way when he headed down the driveway, and he sometimes brought a friend home with him. Robert never brought his friends in the house, though, and Wayne knew it was because Robert was ashamed of Wayne's face. They stuck to the yard, the cowshed, or chucked rocks at the chickens. Sometimes Robert and his friends played in the woods beyond the farm.

At the end of fourth grade, Robert received school photos. He brought them home on a shiny bit of cardstock, columns of tiny rectangular pictures of Robert grinning for the camera. Mother did not keep these photos hidden away in the highboy like she did Wayne's baby pictures; she cut them out and mailed them to distant relatives, and even had one framed for over the fireplace. A similarly framed photo found a place on the nightstand beside Mother's bed. Sometimes, when Wayne was feeling audacious, he would pretend the boy in the photos was him.

The boys had shared a room for as long as Wayne Stull could remember, but after a year of public school, Robert relocated to the spare bedroom at the end of the hall. Mother bought him brand-new bed sheets and pillows and decorations for the room. When Wayne asked if he, too, could have new bed sheets, Mother shook her head and gave him that pitying look that, by now, Wayne found all too familiar. "You'll gum them all up in the night," was Mother's response, which meant he'd drool uncontrollably on them until they grew crusty and stank like old dinner plates.

It wasn't on purpose, but he started wetting the bed. He started suffering terrible nightmares, where Robert—*Bibby*—would pick pieces of Wayne's face apart, and use the pieces as he saw fit on his own face. An eyeball here, a cheekbone there. *My handsome, handsome boy.* Sometimes in these nightmares, men from the slaughterhouse would arrive and collect whatever was left of poor Wayne in a cattle wagon, and drive him straight out to the abattoir. They'd show him the killing floor, which looked like an ice rink of shiny red blood, and they'd show him the giant sledgehammers they used to open bovine skulls. They'd whisper to him, *One good, solid, reliable whack, Wayne Lee, and I can wipe that horrible face clean off you, once and for all.*

When he started getting erections in the bath at the age of nine, Mother would reprimand him for his impure thoughts. Robert never got *maladjusted*, as Mother would call it, so why should his twin brother Wayne get *maladjusted*? Was this just more evidence that Wayne was a broken child? Wayne couldn't help it; Wayne didn't know.

After several occasions of this ridicule, Mother brought out the elastrator. It was a thick and unforgiving rubber band that she used to castrate bulls on the farm. She tied it around young Wayne's testicles until his *maladjustment* corrected itself. It was painful and it made Wayne cry, though he learned to take this punishment without argument. Sometimes he even went to bed with that merciless band of rubber wrapped around his scrotum.

"We do this *now* so we don't have to do this *later*," Mother explained. "It's a teaching lesson, just like they do at Robert's school in town." And she looked him up and down as he squirmed uncomfortably in the tub and tried not to cry. "They're a couple of pert grapes at the moment, but it will hurt much more once you grow up and they become hangdowns."

And he went to bed every night, thinking, *This is all because of my face. She thinks I'm the devil and Bibby's the angel. She hates me.*

Not until Wayne Lee Stull was an adult did he come to find out that something could have been done about his cranial condition back when he was still an infant. A rather simple cosmetic procedure, actually. It was too late for that now, of course—by adulthood, the window for fixing his face had closed—but that didn't stop him from asking Mother why she had neglected to correct his appearance when he was a child.

"That's how God sent you to me, Wayne, and I'm not one to suggest God's ever made a mistake." She had told him this one afternoon as he came by the old house on Slaughterhouse Row for a visit. They'd been sitting in the kitchen, each enjoying a plate of his mother's homemade cherry cobbler. Mother sat in a block of sunlight that shone through the window over the sink, casting her in a golden halo of light. "Child comes to you with black eyes, you praise God," she said. She sounded like she was quoting scripture, although it was none Wayne had ever heard before. "Child comes to you with black skin, you praise God. Child comes to you with black mouth—"

"Enough." He'd said this quietly but firmly, a fist on the tabletop beside his half-eaten cherry cobbler.

Mother leaned back in her chair, her chin cocked loftily in the glow of sunlight coming through the window. "Have you lost your faith, Wayne? Is that what you're telling me?"

Wayne Stull was twenty-two years old at the time of this conversation. He had already killed four people—the first of whom was Bibby, back when they were both ten years old—and there was very little left in this world that gave him pause. Mother, however, was the exception.

Still, he felt something overtake him in that moment. Some power that he believed came to him after this most recent murder, only just a few weeks back and still fresh in his mind, in his body—a prostitute he'd picked up in Carmel, a woman whose face he'd taken great pleasure in demolishing with a hammer. He still had her teeth in his apartment, in a plastic cup on his bathroom sink next to his collection of plastic combs and hairbrushes.

Wayne stood up from the table, undid his pants, and let them drop to the kitchen floor. Mother balked in horror, and held her hands up in front of her face to block out this violation. Very calmly, Wayne said, "No, Mother. I want you to look."

She would not look.

"You'll look or I'll pick up my fork and dig both of your eyes out of your skull." Still very calm.

Trembling, his mother lowered her hands. She stared first at his face—the nightmare that was his face—but then she looked down to his mangled, castrated groin.

"Child comes to you with testicles," he said to her. "Where's the praise God in that?"

She did not give him the satisfaction of weeping. Instead, she extended some explanatory platitudes about how things were done for Wayne's own good back then. Everything had always been with good intention. She was only human, and prone to foibles. She had been a single parent and had worked hard. She had lost a *son*, for the love of God. Couldn't he forgive her?

"What good have you done here, to me, Mother?"

She straightened up in her chair. When she spoke, her voice was membrane-thin and shaky, and Wayne could tell she struggled to remain prideful. "So's you'd never sire a child with your same face. *That's* what I've done for you here, son."

Still very calm, Wayne pulled his pants up, buttoned the fly, fastened his belt. "Mother," he said. "Three nights ago, I picked up a prostitute. I drove her in my car to a back alley then beat her to death with a hammer. When I was done, I found a tidy place to dispose of her— *most* of her. I did this, Mother, because even in the weakest, most pitiful dregs of society, there is some power to be siphoned from them in the act of taking their lives. It's like breathing in a certain *magic*."

He planted both hands on the table, one on either side of his unfinished plate of cherry cobbler, and leaned closer toward his mother. She was trembling quite visibly now and sitting about as far back in her chair from him as she could get.

"Except for you, Mother," he said. "There's nothing good I could ever siphon from you. In that regard, consider yourself lucky."

And then, much to his own surprise, a curious thing happened: Wayne Lee Stull began to cry. He went over to where his mother sat shaking in her chair. He sat on the floor at her feet, resting his disfigured face in her lap, and wept. She cursed him, told him to get out, but he didn't move. He just stayed that way for a long time.

"Comfort me," he said at one point, and she ran a shaky hand through his hair. He sat bolt upright and quickly pulled a plastic comb from the breast pocket of his shirt, fixing his hair. Making that part perfect. Always perfect. When he'd finished, he laid his head back in her lap and said, "Rub my shoulder, Mother."

Mother massaged his shoulder with one hand. Her fingers felt like lug nuts poking into his flesh. Her lap smelled dirty, her housedress tacky with old cooking grease.

"Call me a good boy, Mother."

She called him a good boy.

"Say I'm your favorite."

She said he was her favorite.

"Tell me you're sorry."

She told him she was sorry.

After a while, all was forgiven.

When he left the house later that afternoon, there was peace between them once more. She came out onto the porch to hug him goodbye, and their embrace lasted longer than it ever had. When they pulled away from each other, Wayne caressed Mother's cheek. There was a tear in his eye and, arguably, a smile on his face.

"You ever speak a word of what I've told you today," he said to her, "and I'll come back here and open you up from throat to cunt."

Then he kissed her cheek, leaving a glister of spittle behind.

He did not get in his car right away, but instead walked around to the rear of the property, past the barn and the empty cowshed, the chicken coops where the feed had rotted and the feathers on the ground had turned gray, the farming equipment that had fossilized in the fields. A special thing had happened back here, deep in the woods, back when he and his brother had been ten years old. A bit of magic had come into their lives, you might say. Wayne crept through the overgrown forest, searching for the exact spot where he and Robert had met the Magic Man all those years ago. At some point during the trek, Wayne noticed that Robert—*Bibby*—was in step right alongside him. Still ten years old, and still as handsome as ever. Even in death.

He eventually found the clearing where he and Robert had met the Magic Man. It was also the clearing where Robert's body had been found after his murder. It wasn't much of a clearing anymore, what with the dense foliage having encroached on this previously bald patch of forest, but Wayne could sense the power in the soil and so he knew it was the right spot. Wayne sat on a rock and absently traced a circle in the dirt as he fell backward into his memories.

The Magic Man had come into their lives in the fall of his and Robert's tenth year. Truth be told, he had come into *Wayne's* life first, but really, that was splitting hairs. The Magic Man was just there one day in the woods behind the ranch on Slaughterhouse Row, his long arms folded across his chest as he leaned against a tree, his filthy red suspenders hanging in loops straight down to his knees. Wayne had been playing back there by himself and didn't see the man at first, so when the man spoke to him, Wayne froze and looked around, startled by the sound of his voice.

"Where's your mask, my young friend?" the man said. Wayne saw that he was wearing an eye patch and a black top hat cocked jauntily to one side of his head.

"What mask?" Wayne asked, confused.

"The grinning pumpkin head," said the man, and just like that, Wayne understood.

There had been a carnival in town all week, and Mother had taken both boys one afternoon to play the games and ride the rides. She'd made Wayne wear a cheap dime-store Halloween mask—a sneering orange jack-o'-lantern face—to hide his disfigurement. When the mask blew off on the whirling teacups, the other children stared at him in shocked horror, and a few of the younger children began to cry. Mother found the mask in the dirt and quickly strapped it over his face, but the damage was already done. He stood wearing that mask by Mother's side for the rest of the afternoon, while Robert whirled on the teacups, cheered on the Scrambler, hooted and hollered as the rollercoaster jounced across its rickety tracks.

This man must have seen him that day at the carnival.

"What's your name, son?"

"Wayne Lee Stull."

"Where's your brother, Mr. Stull? The one who was with you that day at the carnival?"

"Playing with his friends."

"Don't you have friends?"

Wayne shook his head. He felt a trickle of saliva spilling down the crack in his upper jaw, and he dug around in his pockets for a Kleenex or a napkin.

"Let me help you there, Mr. Stull." The man raised one arm—he was wearing what looked like a fancy white shirt, but some of the buttons were missing and there were streaks of grime across it—and reached into his sleeve. What came out was a never-ending parade of colored silk scarves, each one more beautiful than the last.

Wayne Lee Stull laughed, and the Magic Man took a bow.

"If you like that trick," the Magic Man said, "then I've got many more to show you…"

The next day, Robert came down to the woods with him. The Magic Man spoke of grand and magical things, including a mystical well where *real* magic could be siphoned and carried back; Robert was only mildly intrigued, but Wayne was downright *ravenous* to learn more. When Wayne asked the Magic Man where he had come from, the man had said, "Everywhere," and then he'd sketched a rough circle in the dirt at his feet. It made Wayne think of a hole in the ground. "Now tell me, Brothers Stull—do you want to see a magic trick?"

In reality, it was *Wayne* who had become infatuated with the Magic Man. It was *Wayne* who had ferried him food and learned his magic tricks and promised to do everything the Magic Man told him to do. Robert was curious at first, but he had school friends and was playing sports and had many other interests, so he soon stopped coming around the woods to learn simple card tricks and palming coins from the Magic Man. At first, it upset Wayne that Robert no longer found the Magic Man interesting, but soon thereafter, Wayne found he was happy that Robert had stopped coming down to the woods. Wayne didn't want to share the Magic Man with anyone, he realized. Particularly Robert.

"He hasn't told anyone about me, has he?" the Magic Man would sometimes ask, and Wayne would assure him that Robert hadn't said a word.

The Magic Man promised to fix Wayne's face if Wayne brought Robert down to the woods one last time. Wayne wanted nothing more than to have his face fixed, but he was struck with disappointment at the Magic Man's insistence that Robert return. When he asked the Magic Man what was so special about Robert, the Magic Man had laughed…and had actually rubbed a hand through Wayne's hair, messing it up.

"Do you know what an apprenticeship is, Wayne?"

Wayne admitted that he did not.

So the Magic Man told him how both Wayne and Robert had started out as apprentices, but that Robert had gone astray. The Magic Man needed reassurance that Robert wouldn't speak of him to anyone. And then he told Wayne what he wanted him to do.

It was a cool autumn evening, and there were storm clouds rolling in from the north, when Wayne convinced Robert to come back down to the woods with him. Robert hadn't wanted to go, but Wayne assured him he'd want to see the Magic Man's latest trick. It was not to be believed.

So Robert followed Wayne into the woods, smoking a cigarette that he'd found on the street. The Magic Man wasn't there, and Robert became angry. Wayne just said, "Wait, wait, wait—*I'll* show you the trick myself!" To which Robert laughed and called him an ugly fucktard.

The Magic Man had left his bone-handled hunting knife planted blade-first into the trunk of a tree. Wayne pried it out, then carried it over to Robert.

Robert's eyes gleamed with greed. "That's some knife," he said. "I want it."

"You can have it," said Wayne, and then he plunged the steel blade of the bone-handled knife into Robert's belly.

Sometime later, after Wayne had not only unzipped Robert's belly, but had bashed his brother's skull—

(my handsome, handsome boy)

—to smithereens with a large rock, the Magic Man returned. Wayne hadn't seen him approach, and he assumed he had materialized there by magic.

"Well done," the Magic Man said, and then he extended his hand. Wayne placed the bloodied knife in the man's open palm, then watched as his impossibly long, impossibly pale fingers closed around it. Swallowing it up. "Do you feel all that magic inside you now, Mr. Stull?"

He *did*. Whatever power that had, moments ago, resided in his brother was now in *him*. The confidence, the charm, the intelligence. The *handsomeness*.

All of it.

"You can fix my face now," Wayne said. He'd already thought it all out—that he'd return home with his face fixed pretending to be Robert so that Mother wouldn't think anything unusual had taken place. Later, if anyone ever discovered Robert's body back here in these woods, they would assume it was *Wayne*. It would all work out.

"That magic is up to you, Mr. Stull," the Magic Man explained. "That power you felt leave your brother's body and enter yours after you'd taken his life? That's the magic that will fix you. Even now, in this very moment, I can see the gap in your face has shrunk just the slightest bit."

Wayne shook his head. "But...but you *thed...said...*you would fuh-fix me if I...if I..." The words were gushing out of him, sloppy and wet and uncontrollable. He felt his hair was in disarray and furiously combed it back into place with his bloodstained fingers.

The Magic Man knelt down before him. For a split second, his singular eye flickered with an unnatural firelight. "Only you can fix your face, Mr. Stull. Only you can harvest *real magic* and make it work for you."

And with that, the Magic Man tucked the bone-handled knife— bloody blade and all—into his boot. Slipping his hands into his pockets, he turned and began wandering deeper into the woods. He even began whistling a song that Wayne recognized as the Happy Horace jingle from the carnival.

He thought about chasing after the man, but in the end, he didn't. He just stood there, trembling and sweating despite the autumn chill in the air, and watched him go.

The rest had played out pretty much exactly as he'd relayed to Willis and his lesbian girlfriend back at the restaurant. When Robert never returned home that evening, their mother called the police. Robert's mutilated body was soon discovered in the woods behind their house. When the police questioned Wayne, he told them how Robert had been hanging around with a one-eyed homeless man living among the trees. A manhunt commenced, but it never amounted to anything, and all these years later, Robert "Bibby" Stull's murder was still *officially* unsolved.

There was a power that had come from killing Bibby. The Magic

Man had been right about that. Stull had literally felt the magic come swirling out of the opening he'd carved in Bibby's belly—a magic that had transferred straight into ten-year-old Wayne Lee Stull himself. And had he felt the cleft in his face stitch together just the slightest bit? Almost imperceptibly, but yes, he had. In the years that followed, he attempted to recreate that transfer of power by taking the lives of others—prostitutes, mostly, because those were the easiest to dispatch. Yet while there was certainly a *spark* of something that would transmit from them to him as he slashed their throats, opened their bellies, demolished and removed their faces, it was never quite the same as it had been with Bibby. Was this because Bibby had been his brother—his *twin*, no less—and there was an inherent magic that ran through their blood? He assumed this was the case, but then Bibby came to him one evening and explained the real reason to him.

The difference, Bibby said, was that those prostitutes hadn't been *apprentices*. The magic in them hadn't been cultivated; it was weak and pitiful. Moreover, Wayne had stripped them of their lives *himself*, a crude act to say the least, while the Magic Man had allowed for one apprentice to take the life of the other. It was ceremonial, Bibby explained. The power was in the coercion of another, not in the act itself. Much like how Mother had always said the devil will tempt, so Wayne Lee Stull was told that the strongest power came from that very act of temptation. The symbolic *ceremony* of it. After all, the Magic Man never actually took anyone's life, and he was without a doubt the most powerful person Stull had ever met.

"How do you know this?" he asked Bibby.

The Magic Man told me so, said Bibby. I live in the well with him now.

Which was curious, because for a moment during their conversation, Wayne felt as though he'd actually been talking to the Magic Man himself.

Regardless of who had actually been speaking out of dead Bibby's throat, Wayne Lee Stull now understood what he was supposed to do.

Tonight would be different, however. These people were no mere children; there would be no coercing them. Crass as it was, he would just have to accomplish the deed himself. His only hope was that his knife was powerful enough and that they themselves were powerful enough for him to take from them whatever he could.

The four of them.

When the Toyota's headlights came on and the car pulled out of the parking lot and onto the highway, Stull followed.

2

He tailed them all the way back from the Chinese restaurant to the very same shithole motel out by the highway where he himself was staying. Not so much a coincidence than it was the only motel in proximity to the town, but it gave Stull a satisfied sense of symmetry nonetheless. He liked it when things felt nice and pat. STAY AT THE QUAY the big billboard read, but Stull drove right past it as the Toyota turned into the motel's parking lot. There was a deserted strip mall across the highway, so Stull drove there and parked with the Kia's headlights off right beside a liquor store. He had a perfect view of the motel and of Willis's car parked out front. Were all four of them holed up like rats in that dump?

Stull felt hot and itchy. He opened the Kia's glove compartment and was comforted by the sight of the hunting knife. The one made of true ribs. He could feel Bibby's hot breath coursing down the nape of his neck as he, too, stared at the knife from over Stull's shoulder.

Sometime later, Willis and the lesbian came out of the room, followed by two other men. One guy looked just like your average schlub, but the fellow bringing up the rear looked like a walking cement truck. There was a bland, lackluster look to his face, too, that Stull could see from clear across the roadway.

They all piled into Willis's Toyota, then pulled onto the highway.

Stull waited a couple of seconds, then followed. When they took an exit, he took an exit. The road was dark and seemed to cut through an expanse of dense black forest.

Then, out of nowhere, the lights of the carnival filled his windshield.

This unsettled Stull. He wondered briefly if this was a setup—if Willis and that lesbian had lured him here as some sort of trap—but then he wondered how that could be. Trap him *how*? Trap him for *what*? Could it all just be an amazing coincidence?

In the back seat, Bibby whispered that there were no coincidences, and that these people had also figured out that the Magic Man traveled with the carnival, just as Stull had all those years ago, when the Magic Man had asked him where his pumpkin-head mask was. These people must have figured it out along the way, too. Were they actually *here* looking for *him*?

Bibby began jabbering nonsensically. The little bastard was either excited or frightened; Stull didn't have the patience to figure out which.

"Shut the fuck up," Stull told him, and parked several cars away from theirs.

He watched them all get out of the Toyota and walk down the slope toward the carnival entrance. Stull rolled down his window, and he could hear the cheering and laughter coming from the carnival, the game booths buzzing and the heavy metal music echoing across the roadway.

There was a Members Only jacket folded on the passenger seat. Stull undid his seatbelt then crawled into the jacket. Fortunately, the night had cooled in anticipation of the storm, so maybe he wouldn't stand out as much wearing this jacket as he'd initially feared.

Next, he reached into the back seat, trying desperately to ignore Bibby, and grasped the handle of his briefcase. He set the briefcase on the passenger seat, thumbed the combination, then popped the clasps.

The faces were arranged on plastic panels inside the briefcase, two to a panel, five panels and ten faces in all. They were all fairly similar—he rarely strayed from his favorite latex mould, once he'd perfected it—but some were in better condition than others.

He selected face six on panel three. Good, solid, reliable. There was a tub of liquid adhesive and a brush in the case as well, and he removed them now, and unscrewed the adhesive's cap. The chemical aroma caused his eyes to water, but it wasn't altogether unpleasant. In fact, that smell was the closest thing to arousal that Wayne Lee Stull could achieve.

He applied the adhesive to the interior of the mask, then placed the mask over his own face. Forty-five seconds was all it took for the glue to adhere, and then he was in business.

The next part rankled him immensely, but it was a necessary evil. He dug a baseball cap from the glove compartment and slipped it over his head, no doubt mussing up his painstakingly combed hair. Without the hat, the mask looked too much like a mask; the hat was an indispensable subterfuge.

The last thing he did was strip the bone-handled hunting knife from the glove compartment and slip it into the inner pocket of his Members Only jacket before heading down into the spectacle of the carnival.

CHAPTER TWENTY

THE CARNIVAL
(SECOND NIGHT)

1

It was fully dark by the time we arrived at the carnival for the second night in a row. Clay and I walked a few paces behind Mia and Dennis, who strolled ahead of us holding hands like a couple of teenage crushes. I'd been zonked out of my mind the night before, but everything was loud and shiny and clear right now. I tried to keep my apprehension under control.

Clay filled me in on their uncomfortable meeting with Wayne Lee Stull, and then I told him what Dennis had done in the motel room. "He just pushed his head right through the wall, Clay. I don't understand what's going on, man. He's acting weird even for Dennis."

"Maybe we're not supposed to understand it. Maybe we just muddle through to the end, whatever that is. Fulfill our destinies, as Mia would say."

"She wants to kill him, you know," I told Clay.

"The Magician? Yeah, I know. But she won't."

"Don't be so sure."

"I won't let her do anything stupid."

"I think this whole thing might be stupid," I said, and Clay looked at me. "I've felt funny ever since we came back here. Dennis has been acting even stranger than usual, and I'm not just talking just about that whole motel room scene. And you and Mia…"

"What about us?"

"Mia's wrist? Your swollen eye? Even my arm's been aching, where I broke it when I was a kid. And that crying baby that Dennis said he heard in that mineshaft? I heard it, too, man. It wasn't just the wind."

"Then what was it? Ghosts? Black Mouth getting inside our heads? Or the Magician, casting his spells?" He laughed at this last part, but I could tell it was forced and nervous.

"Is it really that impossible to believe?" I asked. "What if this has nothing to do with fate? Or what if this sense of destiny Mia keeps talking about is actually just warning signs that we're being set up. Like it's too fucking perfect how the four of us found ourselves back here chasing this…this guy." I swallowed what felt like a brick of chalk, and said, "What if it's Black Mouth controlling this whole thing and we're the fools walking blindly into its trap?"

"You're talking about a hole in the ground, Jamie."

"I don't know, Clay. Is that all it is? Things feel weird. I don't know what to think anymore."

Clay's expression was firm. "I think we got a job to do tonight," he said. "That's what *I* think. When it's all said and done, you never have to think about this shit again. How's that sound?"

I just shook my head. "I don't think it'll be that easy, Clay."

We walked past a woman in a belly dancer's bedlah with a snake twisted around her body; a clown juggling bowling pins; a cadre of female dancers in tasseled tops writhing in unison to an otherworldly current. We walked past—

"Wait wait wait, my big friend!" crooned one of the barkers. He was a tall fellow in what looked like a striped pirate's shirt, his dreadlocked hair fashioned into moose antlers along the sides of his head. He leaned against the shaft of an immense mallet. Behind him was the Test Your Strength tower. I'd seen modern versions of this game where the whole thing was digitized, but this was an old one, constructed of wood and with an actual bell at the top. Grinning devil faces were painted along the shaft of the tower. "That's right, my big friend!" the barker bellowed, pointing at Dennis. "I'm talking to you!"

His eyes wide and hungry, Dennis shuffled toward him while Clay, Mia, and I watched.

"You look like a man of brute strength!" shouted the barker. He was talking loudly and energetically enough to attract a small crowd of onlookers. "What's your name, my herculean acquaintance?"

"I am Dennis Warren," said Dennis.

"Well, Dennis Warren, five bucks will get you three chances to ring the bell. What do you say?"

"What's the prize if he rings it?" Mia asked.

"Take your pick," said the man, and he motioned toward a kiosk where countless stuffed rabbits hung upside down from cables.

"Jesus," Mia said under her breath, staring at the rabbits.

"You can do it, Dennis!" Clay said, abruptly clapping his hands. He dug out a five-spot from his pocket and handed it to the barker, who speedily tucked it away in a fanny pack at his hip.

"Go on, sweetie." Mia urged Dennis forward with a hand between his massive shoulders. "You got this."

Dennis went, dragging his sandals through the dirt. The barker handed the mallet to him, but in doing so, got a better look at my brother. The barker glanced over at us, as if to calibrate whether or not we were a group of weirdos or possibly even circus performers ourselves, then decided that five bucks was worth whatever hassle might come of this.

Dennis lifted the mallet off the ground then just stood there.

"My tremendous friend," the barker spoke up, back in character. A decent crowd had formed to watch now, and he was reeling them in. "Three chances to swing the hammer and ring the bell. Do you understand?" He looked at the rest of us. "Does he understand?"

"Hit this with the hammer," I instructed him, pointing at the spring-loaded plate at the base of the tower.

Dennis nodded, but handed me the mallet.

"No, Dennis, you do it—"

From the pocket of his shorts, Dennis removed a long red bandana. He tied it around his head, then slipped it over his eyes. Two eyeholes were cut into it. The crowd of onlookers cheered and applauded.

"That's showmanship for you, folks!" cried the barker.

Dennis brought his face close to mine. In what passed for a whisper, he said, "Go. Ninja. Go."

"You know it," I said, and fitted the mallet's long handle against my brother's big palm.

Dennis dragged the mallet over to the tower. Head craned back, he stared up at the tall red structure with its pitted metal bell at the top and its cackling devil faces along its sides. Then he picked up the mallet with both hands...but then casually dropped it on the platform. The dinger popped up maybe a foot then dropped back down.

The crowd booed. The barker held up one finger high above his moose antlers. "That's one, folks!"

"He doesn't understand," I told the barker. "Can I show him how to do it?"

The barker waved me over to the tower.

"Dennis, watch me." I picked up the hammer, swung it down as hard as I could. The mallet struck the plate, the dinger shot up a few feet, then plummeted back down.

"That's two!" the barker said, holding up two fingers.

"Hey! That's not fair. I was just showing him how to do it."

The barker's grin widened, those two fingers pivoting above his head. "The game is the game is the game, my man," he said.

"Knock the top off this thing," I told Dennis, and handed him back the mallet.

Dennis chocked up his grip on the mallet, lifted it over his head, and brought it down on the plate. The dinger blasted to the top of the tower. The sound of the bell was oddly muted, and the dinger did not come back down. I peered up there and saw that the dinger had somehow become wedged beneath the bell.

The crowd went nuts, but the barker did not look happy.

Dennis tugged the red bandana off his eyes. He looked around at his cheering audience in awe, perhaps unable to comprehend any of this at first. But then he smiled his classic Dennis Warren smile, and with one hand leaning on the hilt of the mallet—

"Holy shit," Mia said, laughing.

—he took a bow.

Clay was laughing, too, and clapping his hands. Mia skipped over to the kiosk and examined the dangling bundles of stuffed rabbits. Dennis dropped the mallet then shuffled over to her, staring up at the rabbits, too. He didn't say anything, but somehow Mia was able to interpret his gestures. He was asking her which rabbit she wanted.

The barker scowled at me. "Guy broke my shit."

"The game is the game is the game, my man," I told him. Beside me, Clay was rolling with laughter.

"I want that one!" Mia shouted, pointing at one of the stuffed rabbits.

The barker retrieved a large hook, detached the rabbit from the bunch, and handed it to Mia. She squealed like a schoolgirl, really putting on a show, then jumped up and kissed the side of Dennis's face. Dennis laughed. He pressed a hand to his cheek. His eyes were shiny with tears of joy.

2

As Stull entered the carnival, he tugged the brim of his hat down lower over his false face, and peered out through the eyeholes of his latex mask.

It wasn't long before he caught sight of the four of them again, at the center of a growing crowd of people in front of some wooden tower with a bell at the top. The big freakshow was having a difficult time comprehending what he should do with the mallet. Stull sidestepped through the crowd, his head down, and slipped around the opposite side of a cart that said FUNNEL CAKE FUN on the side in doughy beige font.

In his ear, Bibby reminded him that *all four of them* were apprentices, not just the black man with the white face and the pussy-eater with the tattoos. *All four of them.* He didn't need Bibby's insight, however, and he resented Bibby for thinking his comment was informative in the least. The comment did, however, remind him to be careful. They could be dangerous. There was a power that radiated from the four of them that Stull could sense, even back here behind a funnel-cake cart. Could it possibly be a power even stronger than his own? They were, after all, apprentices just as he had been. The four of them together while Stull was only one man…

But then he checked himself. *Keep a cool head, don't get overzealous.*

He watched the big guy swing the mallet one last time, striking the bell, and winning a stuffed rabbit for the lesbian. Something curdled in Stull's stomach at the sight of that woman kissing that freakshow on the cheek.

Then they moved on, and Stull followed.

A huddle by the carousel, while the four of them discussed something Stull was not privy to. Stull turned away from them, feigning interest in the sights. He watched the merry-go-round go round.

3

"Let's split up and go wide," Clay suggested. "We'll ultimately meet up at that magician's tent, but I think we should take the long way getting there, see if we spot him in the crowd. That's how Mia saw him back in Lexington."

"Good idea," Mia said.

I nodded, but I felt like something was slowly crushing my ribs. I needed a drink.

When I looked over at Dennis, I saw him staring off into the crowd. Not with his standard lights-are-on-but-nobody's-home look, but with something akin to scrutiny. I put a hand on his shoulder, gave him a gentle shake. "You okay, buddy?"

A rapid blinking of his eyes, and then he turned to face me. I could still see confusion clouding his features, but as I stared at him, I saw it slowly begin to dissipate. After a moment, he gave me one of his wide grins, though he wasn't fooling anyone.

4

It had seemed for a moment that the big freakshow with the sandals on his feet had spotted Stull through the crowd. And not just spotted him, but *recognized* him. Which, of course, was impossible because they had never met, not to mention that Stull was wearing a mask below the tugged-down brim of a ball cap. He even had the collar of his Members Only jacket up, for Christ's sake. Still, he couldn't ignore the sensation that, for just a few seconds, the big bastard's gaze had zeroed right in on him. *Target acquired.*

Stull crept around the side of a game booth where a giant wheel *tck-tck-tck*'d, and peered at them through a mélange of hanging plush toys. The freakshow in the sandals was no longer staring at him; they all seemed involved in some serious conversation now. *What the hell can they be talking about so seriously, the state of the Middle East?* Then Willis and the lesbian went off in one direction, and the big freakshow and the schlub went in another direction. Stull followed Willis and the lesbian.

A child shrieked. A Mylar balloon launched itself into the night sky. Oblivious assholes slammed their shoulders into Stull's chest, chattering on in a language Stull knew to be English but was as alien to his ears as a foreign tongue. At one point, something wet dripped into the left eyehole of Stull's mask; he cast his gaze heavenward and realized that a storm was building directly overhead.

It was a dangerous game, but he managed to inch his way through the crowd until he was directly upon them both. The urge to slip the newly fashioned bone-handled knife out of his jacket and plant its gleaming blade into the small of Willis's back was nearly overwhelming, but Stull knew that would be foolish. This was no place for such a performance; he needed only to follow them and make sure they didn't get away until the time was right. He'd choose the time and place carefully.

Leaning over so that the brim of his ball cap nearly grazed the back of Willis's neck, Stull inhaled the man's sweat, which he could smell even over the chemical odor of the liquid adhesive. Willis smelled briny but not necessarily off-putting. Absently, he wondered what Willis looked like nude, given his bleachy face and ghost-white hands. A leopard man? Stripes like a zebra? Maybe he'd get to find out.

The lesbian stuck close to Willis. Stull was discomfited by the look of determination on her face, because it didn't seem to fit the atmosphere. It was as out of place as the secretive little conversations she and her friends kept having, thinking no one was watching them. Had this crazy bitch come to this carnival just to burn it to the ground? Was she a suicide bomber, a hunk of C-4 hidden beneath her sleeveless Twisted Sister T-shirt? Whatever it was, something was decidedly *off* about her.

Is this some ruse? he wondered. *Have they lured me here to this carnival on purpose? Is there a SWAT team waiting for me on the other side of the midway?*

As he'd done with Willis, he found an opportunity to creep up behind her, sniff her skin, and graze the delicate white hair follicles along her upper arm with one surreptitious, trembling hand. Her neck smelled of cigarettes and hairspray. Her upper arms were tanned and tattooed, and they glistened with pinpricks of sweat. He felt himself salivating behind his mask, unexpectedly aroused—or what passed for his arousal—by the thought of his tongue running up and down her arm, ingesting that shimmery sheen of saltwater.

There were enough people squeezing in and out of the crowd that he chanced bumping his crotch against her thigh. A tingle of excitement shivered up his spine. But this chick was more perceptive than most, and she spun around to seek out who had given her the old how-do-you-do.

Stull quickly turned tail in the opposite direction and cut a beeline through the crowd. He supposed that made him a bit more suspicious, had she focused in on his retreat, but he thought it better to get away than to linger and have her look too closely at his mask.

Bibby followed him through the crowd, weaving around children his own age. Stull tried to will him away, which sometimes worked, but it didn't seem to have any effect on Bibby tonight. Maybe he just liked the sights and sounds of the carnival too much to leave.

Through the crowd, Willis and the lesbian were engaged in serious conversation again. Their faces were very close. Willis looked like he was trying to placate her. She just looked determined. And angry.

Stull was content watching them until they continued down the midway. He headed once more in their direction, head down and with a single-minded purpose, sensing Bibby's presence close at his heels.

5

And then Dennis and I were there, staring at Patch the Prestidigitator's tent at the opposite end of the midway. Once more, it seemed removed from all the other attractions, set apart like something contagious. As we stared at it, a young woman—no more than a teenager, really—came out from the tent wearing what looked like a sequined bathing suit and tuxedo tails. Her face was painted like a harlot's. She caught the attention of a group of young men passing by. They were apparently charmed enough by her to fork over some money and enter the tent.

I looked up and saw Mia and Clay weaving their way toward us through the crowd. Clay looked contemplative; Mia looked invigorated and volatile, like she might launch herself into space at any moment.

"Looks like he's performing tonight," I said, and jerked a thumb over to where the girl in the sequined outfit was collecting money for the magic show.

"Four bucks per person," Mia said. "You think I can write this off on my taxes?"

Clay was intently watching the girl in the sequined suit. "I don't think we should all go in," he said.

Mia looked at him. "Really?"

"Look, it's not like I think this guy will recognize us all these years later, but I *do* think my man Dennis and I bear some pretty unique characteristics. No sense in us going in there and making him suspicious. Dennis and I can wait out here."

"Okay. Maybe you're right." Mia looked at me. "You okay to go in with me?"

I looked over at the tent. Festive, with its multicolored flags. Harmless, almost.

Mia touched my arm. "Jamie?"

"Yeah, okay. I'm good. I'll go in with you."

"Remember," Clay said. "You're just going in to confirm that it's him. Don't talk to him, don't even try to snap a picture with your phone." He shot a look at Mia. "Point is, don't do nothing that might arouse his suspicion. Once you make the ID, we can call Ashida and see how she wants to handle this."

"Roger that," Mia said. She handed her stuffed rabbit to Dennis. "Take care of him for me until I get back, okay, big guy?"

"I will do that for you," Dennis said.

Mia grabbed my hand. "Let's go."

"And be careful!" Clay shouted after us.

Mia pulled me toward the tent. She turned toward me as she ran, her face alight, her eyes blazing with a maniacal glee.

I tried to share her enthusiasm, but found I wasn't up to the task.

6

The inside of the tent was set up like a religious revival meeting, with a floor of straw, a wooden pallet serving as a stage toward the front, and rows of folding chairs set up beneath a network of halogen lights. There were only a few other people in there besides us—mostly young kids and their parents, plus those young men who had been so charmed by the ticket-taker out front—but Mia and I still sat near the back, where the lighting was poorest. Maybe she had forgotten to let go of my hand, because she was still clutching it as we took our seats.

"His story sounded rehearsed," Mia said, her voice just barely above a whisper.

"Whose story?"

"The guy Clay and I met earlier tonight. Stull. I don't know why, but it just occurred to me now what was bothering me about it. The story about his dead brother might be real—Clay looked it up and said it was—but the way he told it sounded phony."

Before I could say anything, the house lights went dark. I felt something cold ripple through my body. Suddenly, I was eleven years old again, chasing the Magician through Black Mouth, begging him to take me with him, groping pathetically at his cloak as his face changed and the world burned…

He was just a man, nothing more.

Don't be scared.

A spotlight winked on, framing one section of the warped wooden stage. Prerecorded calliope music trilled from a single PA speaker up high in one corner of the tent. I realized I was holding my breath.

The kids cheered and the young men toward the front clapped lackadaisically. They probably would have preferred a performance from the girl in the sequined bathing suit.

"*There*," Mia whispered close to my face.

A black shape flitted across the front wall of the tent. I squeezed Mia's hand, my erratic pulse transmitting from my palm to hers.

And then he was there, his cloak aflutter, a flourish of his arms as he swept the top hat from his head and extended himself forward in an exaggerated bow.

It wasn't him.

The man on stage was maybe in his fifties, with a pronounced belly beneath the bright red tuxedo shirt he wore. He had a trim black mustache and salt-and-pepper sideburns that hooked nearly down to the line of his jaw. The pièce de résistance of his entire ensemble was the multicolored patchwork jacket he wore.

Patch, I thought, and I felt my body relax. *Motherfucker.*

Beside me, Mia uttered a clearly audible "*Oh*," and then slipped her hand out from mine.

The man on stage put one hand to his forehead in a facsimile of a salute. He made a show of peering around the darkened tent, though I doubted he could see anyone beyond the first row of chairs with all those lights shining in his face. "Looks like we've got a packed house tonight, ladies and gentlemen!" Which was a strange thing to say, seeing how much of the tent was empty. "All of you, hungry for magic!"

He waved his hands and a flash-bang of smoke exploded in the air in front of him.

I shifted uncomfortably in my seat, then asked Mia if we should leave.

"Not just yet," she said.

"Speaking of *hunger*," the magician continued, still surveying the crowd. My body tensed as his gaze leveled on me. He pointed at me. "Sir! Please stand!"

Mia gave me a nudge. "He's talking to you."

"Sir! Rise from your seat, sir!"

Reluctantly, I rose from my seat. The palms of my hands were perspiring.

"Ah, yes! My good man! Check your pocket, good sir!" the magician commanded.

I put my hand in my right pocket, which was empty.

"The other pocket, sir!"

I put my hand in my left pocket, and felt a large metal coin in there. I froze, unable to move. Unable to breathe.

"Good sir!" the magician beckoned.

Just as I pulled the coin out of my pocket, the spotlight that was on the magician swiveled over in my direction, blinding me. I shied away from it, cringing.

"Behold!" shouted the magician on stage.

I opened one eye and saw the coin was actually a token for a free corndog.

"Valid at all participating Calliope Corndog stands," the magician said, "and cannot be exchanged for cash."

The spotlight swished back toward the stage, where the magician folded forward in an exaggerated bow.

7

Stull watched the lesbian and the schlub enter a red-and-white striped tent together, while Willis and the freakshow lingered outside. There was something *calculating* about what they were doing that set Stull on edge. There had been a rapid discussion between the four of them before the lesbian and the schlub went inside the tent, and Stull thought they were behaving like people about to rob a bank now. No one else noticed, of course, because no one else was watching them as intently as he was. But Stull could see it, and it was making him uncomfortable. What were they all *doing* here?

And then it dawned on him, and it was all he could do to stifle a hysterical laugh.

They were here looking for *him*. The actual *Magic Man*.

He did laugh, a sound like a small engine backfiring. The glue held the latex fast to his face, but any further outbursts like that and he might jostle it loose.

My God, they're a quartet of lost sheep…

The freakshow looked across the midway and appeared to make eye contact with him once again. Stull blinked his eyes in disbelief, then quickly looked away. As he did so, he caught the gaze of a young girl being led by her father through the crowd, a wand of cotton candy clasped in one of her sticky hands. She saw the mask he was wearing beneath the brim of the baseball hat and her eyes went wide. Something akin to a tremble affected her lower lip. Stull attempted a smile, but the mask restricted it.

When he looked back up at the red-and-white tent, he saw the big freakshow fellow was still staring at him. Willis wasn't paying attention—he was gazing at the bimbo in the sequined bathing suit standing outside the tent taking people's money—but this big monster was shooting daggers at him from across the midway.

What in the name of Moses are you staring at, you big ugly bastard?

Bibby got nervous. He whispered some pointless nonsense into Stull's ear, then scurried off into the crowd. Good fucking riddance.

Still staring.

Still staring.

Mind your own fucking business, you overgrown mongoloid. Cut those eyes away or I'll cut 'em out for you. How'd you like that, you cocksucking son of a bitch?

Still staring.

Still—

The freakshow began moving through the crowd in Stull's direction.

8

Clay looked up and around, searching the crowd, while trying to quell the sense of trepidation that had been slowly stewing inside his guts for the better part of an hour. He kept rubbing at his swollen eye, too. The bright carnival lights were causing the vision in it to blur.

He glanced up at the Ferris wheel, and at those glowing spokes pulling impossible rotations against the cloud-filled night sky. The sight of it gave him vertigo, and he stared up at it as if the great wheel might come down on his head at any second. He even closed one eye—his swollen eye—and traced the great wheel with one finger. He felt compelled to do it, even though he had no clue why.

"Your brother was right. Something's weird about all this, Dennis," he said, still staring with one eye closed at the Ferris wheel as it went round and round and round. But he hadn't actually meant *weird*. What he'd meant was *familiar*. A sense of déjà vu, only stronger. Something driven deep into the bone. *Predestined?* For some reason, he thought about those drawings Dennis had brought with him on a visit to the institution all those years ago—nothing but a solitary black circle on every page. Like a single staring eye.

He turned around to find Dennis moving away from him through the crowd.

9

Stull attempted to convince himself that he was mistaken, that this giant moron had set his sights on something or someone else, but he couldn't deny that as the freakshow drew closer, eyes still laser focused, the son of a bitch was coming straight for him.

Stull backed up and nearly toppled over a trash barrel. A group of teenagers laughed and pointed at him, but they shut up pretty quickly when they realized something was wrong with his face. He regained his composure, then cut swiftly to the left, weaving between strolling lovers and rambunctious kids.

To his dismay, the freakshow recalibrated. He pivoted in Stull's direction once again.

No fucking way, Stull thought. He could feel a tremulous panic tightening around his windpipe.

Then there was Bibby, materializing through the crowd and beckoning Stull to follow him.

Stull whirled in Bibby's direction, cutting a wide berth around the base of the Ferris wheel. Lights flashed, casting a moving fan of people-shaped shadows across the grass. Stull barreled through the crowd, then ditched around the far side of the Ferris wheel. He scanned the horde of people, momentarily relieved that he was no longer being pursued…but then he saw the freakshow's head above all the others, chugging stealthily in Stull's direction. He caught a glimpse of the man's dull eyes, and knew he was staring straight at him.

10

"Dennis!"

Clay reached him, groped for one of Dennis's big arms. But Dennis was too big to stop. Where the hell was he *going*?

Nonsense creaked out of Dennis's mouth: "A…*liiiiiittle*…"

Clay said, "Please, Dennis. Calm down. Stop."

Yet even as he said this, a counterargument surfaced in his head: *Let him go and see what happens…*

11

Bibby ran toward a darkened section of the carnival grounds, where a forgotten attraction lay half hidden in shadow behind a wall of gas-powered generator exhaust. The carnival's haunted house, with its sign above a sloping arcade in startling neon font:

A mannequin in a rubber mask leaned against the front of the house with a sandwich board over its chest that read CLOSED FOR MAINTENANCE, and there was one hanging from a chain that read OUT OF ORDER. But Bibby paid the signs no mind; he flitted in through the saloon-style doors.

Stull slipped under the chain, scuttled up to those same doors, and vanished into the funhouse as soundless as a spirit.

12

As Patch the Prestidigitator lifted a startled white dove from a hat, I leaned over to Mia and said, "Do you feel okay?"

She looked at me, studied my face. I knew what she was thinking. "I haven't had a drink all day," I told her.

"Then what is it?"

I couldn't put it into words. "I don't know. It's like my heart's going a mile a minute. Also, I think..." I paused, catching my breath. "I think I smell smoke."

As I scanned the interior of the tent for signs of Sarah and Milo Patchin, Mia slipped her hand into mine and squeezed it.

13

Clay chased Dennis into the House of Fear, and down a warren of tunnels, blind and groping in the darkness, Dennis shrieking ahead of him, a stampede of footfalls, an echo chamber of sound all of this at a frantic pace, though even in that heightened state, Clay could sense they were in pursuit of *something*, that those footfalls held ownership elsewhere, and that a figure, barely glimpsed, frantic and skittish and elusive as smoke, kept evading them at every turn, every time they rounded some darkened, horror house corner—

14

—Until Dennis shoved his way out of a fire exit and they both stumbled out into the night.

Clay struck the ground hard, body surfing across the grass while stars exploded in front of his eyes. Once he'd caught his breath, he propped himself up on his hands and knees and saw Dennis a few feet away, lying on his back, not moving.

Clay scrambled over to him. He saw that Dennis's eyes were open, but the sightlessness behind them triggered a panic in him that he hadn't felt since he was eleven years old. He slapped Dennis's face lightly, repeating his name over and over again.

"Dennis? Dennis? Please, buddy…"

Clarity filtered back into Dennis's eyes. He looked at Clay, the confusion evident on his face. His mouth started moving, his tongue working, but no sounds came out.

"Just take it easy, Dennis. You're okay."

Clay helped him sit up. They had come out of a rear exit of the House of Fear, and were in a darkened patch of grass now beyond the lights and commotion of the carnival. Thunder shifted about in the low clouds, and Clay cast a wary glance skyward.

"A. Little. Boy," Dennis said.

"What boy?"

Dennis scrunched up his face, as if it caused him physical pain to work out whatever equation was jumbled about in his head.

"It's okay, pal," Clay said, and slung an arm around Dennis's shoulder. In a flash of lightning, Clay thought he saw a dark figure running toward the woods in the distance, though he didn't quite trust his eyes at the moment. "It's okay. We'll just sit here for a while."

Dennis nodded. He was staring at the distant tree line, too. Black Mouth, of course, was beyond there.

Dennis mumbled something else, which Clay didn't quite catch.

"What'd you just say, Dennis?" Clay asked, but Dennis did not repeat it. And maybe Clay had misheard, but he could have sworn Dennis had mumbled something that sounded oddly like *Bibby*.

CHAPTER TWENTY-ONE

PATCH THE PRESTIDIGITATOR

1

At the conclusion of the show, the magician took his final bow, that circus music began pumping from the PA speaker again, and the spotlight went dark. When the lights strung up across the ceiling came on, the stage was already empty, and Patch the Prestidigitator was gone. The young woman in the sequined outfit slipped into the tent and bid everyone departing a good night.

"I think we should talk to that guy," Mia said.

"Why?"

But she was already moving through the row of folding chairs toward the woman in the sequins.

Mia told her that she was a filmmaker shooting a documentary on carnival magicians, and she'd love to speak with Patch the Prestidigitator for a few minutes. The young woman peered over Mia's shoulder at me. "He's with me," Mia said.

"Yeah, okay," said the woman. "Follow me."

She led us toward the rear of the tent, where a doorway was cut into the fabric. We crossed out into the night, which was cool after the stuffiness of that tent. Storm clouds argued directly above our heads.

I looked up and saw a luxury motor home parked beside a rank of noisy generators. The girl in the sequined outfit knocked on the motor home's door then slipped inside while Mia and I waited in the grass.

I tugged on Mia's arm. "Clay's gonna flip out when he doesn't see us come out of the tent."

"Relax. We'll just be a couple minutes."

"Why are we even doing this?"

"I'm following my gut, man."

The motor home's door opened and the young woman came out. She waved us inside.

2

The interior of the motor home looked like a Vegas suite. It wasn't at all what I had expected. Patch the Prestidigitator had stripped off his multicolored patchwork jacket and unbuttoned his blood-red tuxedo shirt down to his navel. He was smoking a cigarette and pouring whiskey into a rocks glass.

"So, Becky says you folks are in the movie biz, huh? That's stellar. I did an on-camera interview for a Netflix show a year or so ago, but they left my segment on the cutting-room floor. Maybe I wasn't cinematic enough. Who knows? I guess that's showbiz for ya."

"Well, maybe we'll get you some screen time this go round," Mia said. She handed him a business card for authenticity's sake. "I'm Mia Tomasina, director, producer, writer, and all-around ass-kicker. This is Jamie Warren, my producing partner. We loved your show."

"Ah, you guys are great. Thank you. It's mostly geared toward the kids, but I throw in a little over-their-heads humor for the parents." He shook both our hands. "Patch the Prestidigitator, of course." He did a little flourish with one hand. There was a large sapphire on his pinky. "My real name's Roger Kowalski, but do me a favor and use the stage name for your TV show."

There was a square tabletop screwed into the center of the motor home's floor, a few chairs around it. He motioned for us to have a seat, and Mia and I did. I stared at him as he took a long pull from his glass of whiskey. Up close, he looked older than he had on stage; I could see that he was wearing makeup, and there were silver threads in his black, slicked-back hair, and deep grooves around the corners of his eyes.

"How long have you been doing magic?" Mia asked.

"I been doing magic my whole life. I was born on the circuit, and never left."

"The circuit?"

"The carnival. My old man started as a ride jock when he was twenty-two. That was like a million years ago. Didn't have a pot to piss in when he got the job. He ran the rides for a while before he realized that's a lousy gig, then went over to the games because there was more money in it. He was a bit of a hustler, my old man—what they'd call a 'confidence man' back then. Those were the days when the games weren't regulated by the state, and you could pretty much get away with murder.

"When he married my ma, they got a concession stand and started making real money. And then when I was just a little rat, my old man gave me a buck a day to walk around holding a stuffed gorilla. It was advertising for my old man's joint. Marks see the prizes in the crowd, they think they can win 'em, too. That's how you reel 'em in."

"Was it at this carnival? Happy Horace?"

"That's right. I mean, they were hired on as independent contractors, my folks. They turn a profit, give a cut to the operator. There weren't no written contracts back then, it was all done on a handshake, which meant sometimes they'd rob you, sometimes they wouldn't. But I was smart and picked up a few things. I bought into the company a few years back. Me and about a half-dozen other guys. I do this magician bit as a goof. It's fun, I always liked magic, and Becky gets to wear her spangly costumes."

"The Happy Horace Carnival used to come through my hometown when I was a kid," Mia said. "Back then—"

"That purple hippo sure gets around," he said.

"Right. He sure does." Mia crossed her legs, banging her knee against the bottom of the tiny table. Kowalski held tight to his rocks glass. "Back then, there was a magician who wore an eye patch. I don't remember what he called himself, but..."

Mia's voice trailed off when she saw the look that came over Roger Kowalski's face. It was as if he suddenly smelled something offensive.

"I take it you know who I'm talking about," Mia said.

Roger Kowalski exhaled a boozy breath in my face. "Christ, yeah. I know who you're talking about." He knocked back some whiskey, then stared at us from across the table. "Is that why you're here? To hear that guy's story?"

Mia glanced at me, then back at Kowalski. "What's his story? We're not familiar."

"Come on." It was clear Kowalski thought we were putting him on. "You're asking about the guy, doing a TV show on carnival magicians, but you don't *know*?"

"He's just somebody I remember from when I was a kid," Mia said.

Kowalski arched his eyebrows and shook his head just enough to send the loose skin beneath his neck to shaking. "Well, I won't lie, lady—it would be nice to get on one of them Netflix shows. So I'll tell you the story, if you wanna hear it, but don't blame me for ruining any fond childhood memories..."

3

"I never knew his name. Everyone just called him the Magician," said Roger Kowalski. "This was back in the nineties, and things were a little looser back then. I was maybe thirteen, fourteen years old at the time. I remember my old man had hernia surgery, and he was laid up for a while recovering, so I was running his joint while Ma worked the concession stand. It was the balloon dart throw that year. My old man's darts were as blunt as broom handles. He used to dull them on a large rock he kept on top of the cashbox. But the real trick is to underinflate the balloons. People think it's the darts, making 'em dull like that, but it's really the balloons, or at least a combo of the two. I mean, with those dull darts and those underinflated balloons, you really gotta nail 'em just perfect to get that *pop*.

"By that time, the Magician had already been around for a while. He had a little tent he'd set up, charge a quarter or a buck or whatever it was back then, and he'd do his thing. Like I said, I was always big into magic, so I gravitated toward the guy. And I mean, he pulled out all the stops—the black tuxedo, the top hat, that bizarre Dracula cape he wore. Even his whole attitude, like he'd never break character, you know what I mean? Had a real stage actor's pageantry, is what I'm saying. Guy knew how to put on a show."

Whatever discomfort I had felt back in the tent while watching this guy perform returned to me tenfold now. I kept picturing the Magician's face in the glow of the blazing trees that last night, and how it had changed before my eyes—or had *seemed* to. I realized I no longer knew what I believed.

"He was always a little weird," Kowalski went on, "but that's nothing new on the circuit. Everyone's weird around here. But the kids loved him, and even I became a little infatuated with him, too, if I'm honest. If I was on a break, maybe around lunchtime, I'd pop over to his tent. If he wasn't doing a show, he'd teach me some card tricks, or how to pull a coin from your ear. Beginner's stuff, but it was cool. And if he *was* doing a show, I'd poke my head in and watch for a few minutes. The parents would sometimes get bored sitting in that tent—his tricks were more geared for a younger audience, kinda like mine—but, man, those kids just went wild. He was *good*, is what I'm saying, which is why what happened to him was a damn shame."

"What happened to him?" Mia asked.

Roger Kowalski had been gazing into his whiskey for much of this conversation, but he stared up at us from across the small table now. He suddenly looked about as sober as a judge. "Tent pole took his eye out. Damnedest thing. I was there, I saw it happen, you know. Scared the shit out of me. These tent poles, they're like goddamn spears, some of 'em. I just remember there being a lot of blood, and then he's on the ground, holding his hands over his eye socket.

"But that wasn't the worst of it. As he's lying there bleeding with his eye poked out, the poor son of a bitch goes into cardiac arrest. That's right—a goddamn heart attack. He starts clutching his arm, clutching at his chest, and all I'm doing is staring at that bloody eye socket and setting myself up for a week's worth of nightmares.

"Some guy runs over and starts giving the poor bastard CPR, but by the time the paramedics get there, the son of a bitch looks about as dead as Elvis. The paramedics keep working on him, doing those chest compressions even though it's clearly a lost cause, and then they're *still* doing 'em as they load him up in an ambulance and take him away.

"I mean, I was upset. My ma was, too. It was a pretty traumatic thing. I remember I finished setting up his tent later that day, set up all his folding chairs, lined his decks of cards out on the old podium he kept beside the stage, the whole nine yards. I figured he'd need all his stuff up and running for when he came back. But even then, I mean, I knew I was just fooling myself. I saw what he looked like when they hauled him outta there. I was just kidding myself."

Once again, Mia glanced in my direction. "So then…?" she began.

"So then the son of a bitch comes back two days later!" Kowalski guffawed, slapping a hairy-knuckled hand on the tabletop. "His eye's all bandaged up and he's a little paler than he was before the hokey pokey, but he's otherwise right as fuckin' rain. I couldn't believe it." Kowalski's eyes shifted to Mia. "Sorry for the language, lady."

"No fuckin' problem," Mia said.

Kowalski grabbed two empty rocks glasses and the bottle of whiskey from a shelf behind him, and set them down on the table. He offered Mia a drink, which she declined. "What about you, fella?" he asked, looking at me.

"Maybe a pinch," I said. Then: "Wait, no. Never mind. I'm good. Thanks."

"Right." Kowalski gave me an intuitive grin. "Been there, my friend." He refilled his own drink and took a sip. His sapphire ring chimed against the glass.

"So then what?" Mia said. "He just went back to work?"

"Well, he tried, anyway," Kowalski said. "You two know anything about card tricks?"

Speaking for the both of us, Mia said, "Yeah, we know a little bit about card tricks."

"See, you got one eye, your depth perception is off," Kowalski said. "He couldn't do the sleight-of-hand manipulations no more. He kept fumbling the cards, dropping them on the floor. It was really pathetic to watch, to be honest with you. I felt bad for the guy. And he just kept practicing to get it down again, but it was no use. It's like trying to watch a man learn to walk all over again. It's lousy."

Kowalski downed his drink and refilled it a third time. I felt like a man stranded on a desert island watching someone on a cruise ship devouring an all-you-can-eat buffet.

"So what'd he do?" Mia asked.

"What else could he do?" Kowalski said. "He lost his mind."

4

"The first thing he did was change his show," Kowalski said. "He really had to simplify the tricks, dumb 'em down, which meant no one over the age of ten was gonna be interested. So he made his shows for children only. Literally put a sign out front—'No Adults Allowed.' The kids thought this was a hoot, and even the parents laughed about it at first. Junior sits in the tent watching the show, and mom and dad can hit the beer garden. Everyone's happy.

"It went okay like that for a while, I guess, but then some people started noticing kids coming out of the tent at the end of the show crying. His tent was set up directly across from my dad's joint, so I always got a good look at them going in and coming out, and I noticed it, too. None of these kids' parents ever thought much of it, far as I know—you give me a buck for every kid you see crying at the carnival, and I'll never have to work another day in my life—but I started to think it was a little strange. I figured maybe they got spooked by his eye patch or something.

"One day I'm on my lunch break and I figure I'll poke my head in, see what the new routine is all about. So I do that, and there he is, on the little raised platform that he used for his stage. He's holding up what I thought was one of the prizes from the game booths at first—a stuffed animal or whatever—but then I realize it's not a stuffed animal at all. It's a cat. A dead cat.

"So I'm just staring at him, and he stops whatever he was doing and smiles at me. 'This is a private performance, Mr. Kowalski,' he tells me—I remember it perfectly; he always called me by my last name, all formal like that—and then he asks me to leave. That was something he'd never done before, asking me to leave like that, and I thought he was joking at first. But he just stood there, holding up that dead cat, waiting for me to leave. So that's what I did. I left."

Kowalski lifted his glass, examined it, but didn't take a drink. He was lost in reverie now, perhaps thinking about things he hadn't thought of in ages. "You know what I remember most about that? It wasn't the dead cat, although that was crazy enough. No, man. What I remember most was that none of the little kids in that audience—*not a single one*—ever turned to look at me. They just stayed focused on the Magician. It was like he'd hypnotized them."

"What the hell was he doing with the cat?" Mia asked.

Bringing it back to life, I thought. *What else?*

"I'll get to the cats in a minute," Kowalski said. He was invested now, I could tell; reliving the story as he told it.

"Cats?" Mia interjected. "Plural?"

"Yeah, that's right." Kowalski nodded. "There were a lot of cats. But before I learned about that, I went back to his tent later that night. Before the accident, we used to sometimes play cards at night, or he'd show me his latest and greatest trick. We hadn't done it since he'd lost his eye, but I thought I'd see if he was up for some company. I didn't like how he'd told me to take a hike earlier that day and I wanted to make sure things were still good between us.

"I went into the tent, and it was all dark, no lights on in the place. I thought maybe he'd unplugged the generator, but then I remembered hearing an electric fan buzzing from someplace. It sounded like a thousand flies. I looked around, thought the tent was empty, but then he called out to me. 'Mr. Kowalski,' same as he always called me.

"My eyes adjusted to the dark, and that's when I saw him. He was sitting on the ground beside the raised platform of his stage. Only not just on the ground—he'd actually dug a hole in the dirt floor, and he was sitting in *that*. I was just a dumb teenager at the time, and admittedly a bit of a stoner by then, but I knew right away something was messed up here. I asked him if he was okay, and he just looked up and smiled at me. I remember thinking he looked so old all of a sudden. Christ, he was probably younger than I am now, but I remember thinking he looked fuckin' *ancient*.

"'I died, Mr. Kowalski.' That's what he told me. I've never forgotten it because it spooked me pretty bad. I can still hear him saying it now, in my head, and it gives me chills. 'I died, but I came back. An agreement was made. And now I got a job to do.' And then he said he wanted to show me something.

"He climbed out of that hole and went over to the podium that was on the edge of the stage. I remember he was barefooted, his feet black with dirt from that hole. He took out something wrapped in a filthy red towel, set it on the podium, and asked me to open it. I hesitated—this whole scene was starting to bug me out, not to mention I'd probably smoked some dope before popping in there, so I was getting kinda paranoid—but then I peeled open that filthy towel.

"I knew it was some kind of bone right away. I thought maybe from the cat, but realized pretty quick it was too big for a cat's bone. I asked him where it came from, and he lifted his shirt and showed me a real nasty fuckin' scar running along his side…"

Kowalski traced a finger down his own ample flank to illustrate where the scar had been, but I was hardly seeing him now. Instead, I was seeing a nude and shimmering man crouched before a bonfire in a barn, a jagged wound at his side. I remembered asking him about it, and his reply: *This? This is a dark bit of business. Maybe I'll tell you about it some other time.*

"The scar still looked fresh. I thought maybe they'd had to cut him open at the hospital to fix his heart or whatever, and that's where he'd gotten it. But then I kept looking at that curled bit of bone on that towel, and goddamn if it didn't look like a rib."

"Are you…" Mia began, but then paused to collect her thoughts. She tried again: "Are you saying it was—"

"I don't know what it was," Kowalski said, holding up his hands, "and he never explained it to me. I guess I didn't wanna know. I just wanted to get the hell out of that tent. I turned to go, but he reached out and he grabbed me high up on the arm. Hard. I remember thinking his face didn't look right anymore. I thought it was because of the eye patch, but I wasn't sure. Even now, all these years later, and I'm not really sure."

"What was wrong with his face?" I asked. I kept replaying in my head what had happened the night of the fire. My final glimpse of him as he fled through the trees.

"I don't know," Kowalski said. "I can't explain it. It's just, it was *him*, only it didn't look *exactly* like him. Like there was someone or something else trying to poke through."

"What happened then?" Mia asked.

"He told me about the cats," said Kowalski. "He knew I saw the dead cat from earlier, of course. He said they were a part of his show now, and he needed more. He asked if I'd bring him some."

Mia was shaking her head. "I don't understand. Cats? Where were they coming from?"

"There's always a million stray cats hanging around carnivals. You come back tonight, after everything shuts down, and you'll see 'em, their little yellow eyes poking out of the darkness between the rides and the game booths. The cats rule this place at night."

"He wanted you to bring him these cats for his act," Mia said. "What was he doing with them?"

"Bringing them back to life," Kowalski said. "That was the trick, anyway. He never showed me how he did it, but I guess he needed the dead cats to swap out for the live ones so that it looked like he was resurrecting them. I'd seen him do it a few times. He'd wrap the dead cat in a blanket, waggle his fingers over it, then when he whipped that blanket off…well, presto chango. The thing would hop down and shoot like a bullet right out of that tent. To this day, I don't know how the hell he did it."

"The dead cats," Mia said. "Did he kill them himself?"

Kowalski leaned back in his seat, far enough so that his unbuttoned shirt opened even wider. "Look, this part's not gonna sound too nice." He paused, presumably waiting for us to tell him we'd heard enough. But when we said nothing, he leaned forward again, and said, "No, he didn't kill 'em. I did."

"Oh," Mia said. She sounded like someone had knocked the wind out of her.

"Listen, I'm not proud of it, but I was a dumb kid, like I said. He gave me a few bucks, and I'd get him the cats. I did what I had to do—break their necks mostly, because I couldn't do anything that would leave visible marks—then brought them to him."

"Why did he need you to kill them?" I asked. "Why didn't he just do it himself?"

"After a while, I asked him that same thing. He told me he *couldn't*. He couldn't take a life. But others could on his behalf. Said he was bound by some…"

"Ceremony," Mia said.

Roger Kowalski's eyebrows arched straight toward his hairline. "Yeah. That's exactly right. He was bound by ceremony. How'd you know that?"

"Lucky guess," Mia said.

"Well, I didn't know what the fuck that meant, but I was beginning to see this guy's head wasn't screwed on so tight. So I told him I was done bringing him cats. I didn't wanna do it no more."

"What'd he say to that?"

"He didn't seem to mind. He wasn't upset or nothing. He had some other kids fetching him cats, too, and I think he was even paying 'em less than what he was paying me. But by then, he was up to…well, other things."

"What other things?" Mia asked.

"I don't know, exactly, because by that time I'd stopped hanging around him. And I certainly never went back into that tent at night. But I remember some of the younger kids—carnie kids, living with their folks on the circuit—they started acting real funny. They became violent and angry. They got into fights with each other, and they got into fights with kids coming with their families to visit the carnival. They…well, they hurt people. Broke things. Set fires."

"Fires," I heard myself say. Under the table, Mia put a steadying hand on my leg.

"In the beginning, I think he was paying these kids to do these things, but after he ran out of money, he'd teach them magic tricks in return for whatever bad business he wanted them to do. And not just the carnie kids, but some of the other kids who came to the carnival. You show up in a small town where there's nothing much to do, some kids come with their friends every day. He seemed to have a soft spot for the runts—the nerdy, picked-on kids—because he talked to them the most. Maybe it was because he felt sorry for them, or maybe it was because he could get them to do crazy shit more than the other kids. I don't know. And now, when I look back on all this, I can't begin to think what he was doing all this *for*. Like, had he just lost his mind after that accident? If you're clinically dead for a few minutes, does that just scramble the fuck outta your brains? I don't know.

"The carnival operators spoke to him, told him to change up his act and quit being so weird. I mean, for a *carnie* to say that to you?" Kowalski laughed, but there wasn't much humor in it. "Maybe he thought it best to lay low from time to time, because he started disappearing for a while, sometimes weeks at a time. Sometimes we'd even leave one town without him, set up someplace else, only to find his tent there across from my dad's joint a few days later. As if he'd arrived and set it up in the night. I was real curious what the hell was going on with him by this point, but I was too spooked by him to ask. Anyway, my dad told me to keep my distance, so I did.

"The Magician never changed up his act and he never quit doing weird shit. Those kids kept coming out of his tent crying, and cats kept disappearing. Eventually, the carnival operators told him to pack up his shit and never come back."

"And that's what he did?" Mia said. "He just left? Just like that?"

"No," Kowalski said. "What he did was he held one last performance. All ages. Come one, come all, that sort of thing. People flooded into the tent, but they were mostly the vendors and the carnies, people who'd watched this poor bastard slowly lose his mind after that accident. They wanted to see what crazy shit he'd do for his grand finale.

"I wanted to see it, too. I was there toward the back, stuffed into that tent with what felt like a hundred other people. No chairs were set up—this was standing room only. He'd taken down all the lights, shut down the generator, so the tent was hot and dark and airless, and it smelled like a barn. I remember some guy making a joke, saying, 'For his final performance, he's going to make us all disappear,' and then some other guy said, 'Yeah, he's gonna set the tent on fire with us in it.' I remember that got some nervous laughter, but holy shit, I could *see* it happening, and I suddenly wanted to get the hell out of there. I think I even turned to squeeze through the crowd toward the exit, when everyone went silent.

"A single flame flickered in the center of the stage. This made me panic all the more—I was suddenly certain the guy was right, and we were all about to be cooked alive in there—but then I saw the flame was flickering atop a small candle that sat on the warped floorboards of the makeshift stage.

"I don't know how long he kept us all in there, watching that candle burn. In my mind, looking back on it, it felt like hours, but clearly that wasn't the case. Maybe two minutes? I don't really remember. What I *do* remember is that at some point, we all heard his boot heels on the wooden planks. He just sort of appeared in that candlelight, and he was wearing his full costume—right down to the white gloves, the top hat, and the red flower in his tuxedo jacket's lapel."

"I remember the flower," I heard Mia say, her voice a hoarse whisper.

I remembered it, too.

"He thanked us all for coming. He wished us all farewell. He specifically thanked the children—I remember that—and that earned him some angered catcalls from some of their parents. People started cursing at him, throwing stuff. It's like they wanted to lynch him. The Magician just stood up there, arms spread wide, grinning at the audience. I remember how his one eye kept moving all around, taking us all in. And for one terrible second, I thought he was going to single *me* out, maybe even call me up on stage. But he didn't.

"As we watched, he took what looked like a long hunting knife from his boot. He held it over his head, the blade shining in the candlelight. I recognized the hilt of that knife, even from where I stood toward the back of that tent. It was the rib bone he had shown me, no doubt about it.

"He said something then that I've never forgotten. He said, 'Now it's time for transcendence.' And then he lifted his shirt and plunged the blade of that knife right into his side. Right where that scar was."

"My God," Mia said.

"He died right there in front of us, on the floor of that stage."

Mia shook her head. "He *died*?" She looked at me then looked back at Kowalski. "That can't be…"

"Saw it with my own two eyes, lady," Kowalski said. "Most people turned and ran the hell out of that tent the second it happened. It was like a goddamn stampede. But a few folks went to the front, right up to the stage. I guess maybe they wanted to see if they could save him, even if they hated him by this point. I went to the stage, too. I needed to see him. Maybe it sounds strange to you guys, after all I've told you about him, but there was a time when I actually *liked* this guy. I'd even say we were friends. And there he was, laid out on those wooden boards, surrounded by a puddle of blood, that handle made out of bone sticking right out of his side. I remember looking at his one good eye, searching to see if there was any life left in him. But there wasn't. He was dead."

I looked down and saw that I was pressing my hands against the tabletop so hard, my fingertips had turned white. Beside me, Mia looked as if she'd just climbed, dazed and disoriented, from a car crash.

"That can't *be*," she insisted. She took her cell phone out, pulled up the photo of the Magician, and then showed it to Kowalski. "I've *seen* him," she said. "That's him in the photo, isn't it?"

Kowalski studied the image on the screen. I watched his eyebrows knit together and a series of creases appear across his large forehead. After what seemed like an eternity, he settled back in his seat. "My God. Sure looks like him," he said.

"So then explain this to me," Mia said.

Kowalski shook his head. "I can't, lady. All I can tell you is what I know. The guy committed suicide. I watched it happen. He's dead."

Mia sat there staring at the photo of the man on her cell phone. Eye patch, head tilted slightly back, a single eye refracting some distant light. It was him, wasn't it?

"There is one other thing," Kowalski said, and Mia looked up at him. "I might be a part-time carnival magician, but I don't put much stock in supernatural hocus pocus, okay? I just want to make that clear upfront."

"All right," Mia said.

"There's been a few times over the years when I've seen him in the crowd," Kowalski said. "I finish a performance, go out back for a smoke, or maybe I'm just walking the midway with Becky, eating chili dogs. I look up, and there he is. Another face in the crowd. Eye patch and everything. It's only just a passing glance—there one second, gone the next—but his face always seems so clear to me. I know it's just my mind playing tricks on me. But in that moment, it seems so real. Like it's him, back from the dead. And now you're showing me that photo, and I don't know what the hell to think."

"Neither do I," Mia said. She looked at me, and said it again: "Neither do I."

5

We found Clay and Dennis sitting in a dark patch of grass behind the House of Fear. They were far enough away from the clamor of the carnival, where they could listen to the rolling sound of thunder while staring at the ridgeline of trees in the distance. Without uttering a word, Mia and I sat down on the grass with them. We stayed like that for a while, not speaking, hardly thinking. Just being there in the moment. The four of us.

When a light rain began to fall, Mia said, "The Magician is dead."

Dennis remained staring off into the distance, but Clay turned and looked at her. He looked at me, too.

She told him everything Kowalski had told us. When she'd finished, Clay looked down at his hands, which were draped limply over his knees. White hands, nearly luminescent beneath the glow of the three-quarter moon.

"If he's dead," Clay said, "then who's in that photo you took?"

"I don't know," Mia said.

"If he's dead, then who's the guy in the eye patch who coerced Molly to kill Charlotte Brown last month?"

"I don't know, Clay."

Clay just shook his head. "That Kowalski guy had to be lying."

"He sounded believable," I said. "Anyway, why would he lie to us?"

"I'm sure there's a record of what happened, too," Mia said. She was talking to Clay, but looking past him and at me. As if my face held the answer to this puzzle. "There's always a record, isn't there?"

I nodded, feeling suddenly ill.

"I guess there are just some things you can't explain," Clay said. He looked at me. "Your brother was out here chasing a ghost earlier tonight."

Dennis's big head swiveled in my direction. "A. Little. Boy," he said.

"What boy?" I asked.

"I don't believe in ghosts," Clay said. "But if I did, I'd say it was the brother of the man Mia and I met earlier tonight. Another one of the Magician's victims."

"How do you know that?"

Clay thought about it before answering. "I guess I don't. Maybe I just misheard something Dennis said. It doesn't matter now." Clay rose to his feet, and Dennis followed him. Mia and I did, too. The rain was starting to come down harder now, and it was a bit of a hike back to the car. "Tomorrow I'll call Ashida and tell her everything we know."

"It's gonna make us sound crazy," Mia said.

"It's not about us anymore," he said.

6

We said our goodbyes in the parking lot of the Stay at the Quay motel, taking turns hugging each other in the rain. Mia and Clay were going to spend the night here, then call Ashida Rowe in the morning. Mia had already booked a flight back to L.A. for tomorrow afternoon, and Clay promised to drive her to the airport.

As for me, I had decided to take Mia's advice and go back home to the farmhouse and face whatever ghosts waited for me there. Sober, this time. I'd take Dennis with me, of course. If indeed there were ghosts there, we could confront them together.

"Are you sure you're ready for this?" she said into my ear as we embraced in the rain.

"Don't talk me out of it now," I warned her.

"My flight doesn't leave until noon tomorrow. You call me if you need some support."

"I think it's something I need to do on my own." I looked over at Dennis, who was clapping Clay on the back, a huge smile stretched across the highway of his face. "Me and Dennis, anyway."

She touched the side of my face. "You're stronger than you think you are."

"I hope you're right." I tugged on her macaroni necklace. "Better get inside before these things turn soggy."

She and Clay crossed beneath the motel awning as Dennis climbed into the passenger seat of the Maverick. I opened the trunk, dumped our bags inside. I heard a solid *clang* as the bottle of Maker's Mark, buried deep inside my duffel bag, knocked against the spare tire. I'd hidden it in my luggage back in Kentucky.

I unzipped my bag and took out the bottle. Stared at it.

I'm bigger than you, it said.

"No, you're not." I carried it over to where Clay and Mia stood beneath the awning. "Here, take this." I handed the bottle to Mia. "Drink it, flush it down the toilet, whatever. I don't care."

"You got this," she said.

"She's right," Clay said. "You do."

"I wish I had your confidence," I told them. "Now get inside before I rip that bottle right back out of your hands."

Neither of them said another word. They didn't need to. They understood. I watched them retreat back inside the motel room and close the door.

Listen, I won't lie—a bolt of panic rocketed through me. I wanted to drink and I wanted to never set foot in that farmhouse again. Yet here I was. So I just closed my eyes, took a breath, and counted backwards from ten. Then I backed out into the parking lot, letting the rain wash clean what sins it could reach.

Lightning cracked the sky above the motel. I hurried around to the driver's side of the Maverick, but before I got in, I noticed a man in a vehicle a few parking spaces away, staring at me through the foggy window of his car. The car was parked at an angle beneath the STAY AT THE QUAY sign, clouds of exhaust pumping from its tailpipe. It could have been the poor lighting or the fog on the glass or a combination of the two, but I swore something was terribly wrong with the driver's face.

Another bolt of lightning, and Dennis laid on the car horn, startling me.

I climbed in, turned the ignition, then looked at my brother.

"Do not be scared, Jamie Warren," Dennis said.

"I'm trying, buddy," I told him. "I'm really trying."

V

IN THE HOUSE
OF FEAR

CHAPTER TWENTY-TWO

HOME

1

The farmhouse had committed to self-destruction in our absence. It had been just a handful of days since we were last here, but in that time, the porch steps had collapsed, and there was a subtle yet undeniable concavity to the roof that hadn't been there before. Window shutters lay strewn about the lawn, like so many dead things having dropped out of the sky. One corner of the gutter and drain spout had come unhinged; the whole contraption lay now at a forty-five-degree angle across the front of the house. It almost looked like it was barring our entry and warning us to turn back.

I felt like the house looked: a thing falling apart. Ravaged not by time or the elements, but my own predilection toward self-destruction. I was getting that old familiar twitch again, the itchiness of my too-tight skin. The opening salvo of the Detox Boogie. Yet I had come too far to blow it all now. A part of me even wondered if this was the destiny Mia had felt unfolding.

Hands shaking and my body leaking sweat, I steered the Maverick up the long driveway, feeling every cell in my body begin to quiver. As I spun the wheel, the Maverick's headlights washed across Mom's old Econoline van, the front of which now appeared sunken into the earth up to the bumper. The ground was in the process of swallowing it whole.

"Jamie Warren is home," Dennis commented, peering up at the house through the windshield.

"Well, what's left of it, anyway," I said.

I pulled the car around to the side of the house and parked it where my father once kept his Firebird, the car that had killed him. In a manner of speaking.

We got out of the Mav, and I stood there for a moment in the cooling night, rubbing the mysterious ache in my right arm while searching the dark pools that served as windows for any movement, any shapes lurking about in there. The rain had tapered to a misty haze, where the raindrops hung in midair, unaffected by gravity. Despite my discomfort at having returned once again to this place— and despite the tremors from withdrawal gaining potency throughout my body—I couldn't deny that it somehow felt *right*.

Come home, Sarah Patchin had scrawled on that motel room window. *Come home.*

Here I am.

I turned and saw that Dennis had wandered into the overgrown field behind the house. He had his back toward me, his big shoulders slumped, his head gently cocked to one side. Raindrops in his hair caused it to shimmer like candy floss. It was dark enough out there that I hadn't even seen him at first, but now he was all I could see.

My teeth rattling in my head and my body feeling like it was about to confront a fever, I went over to him, then followed his gaze out across the field. The old barn looked tired and wilting in the dark, the barn doors shut tight. Beyond, a white mist slithered over the ridgeline of Black Mouth. It wove around the blackened husks of trees and cast smoky tentacles across the field toward both the barn and the farmhouse. Toward *us*.

"It's not smoke, it's just some fog," I told Dennis, and hoped I was right.

2

Cloistered in darkness and shrouded by black trees, Stull turned off the car and listened to the engine go silent. He leaned his head back on the Kia's headrest and closed his eyes. He had calmed considerably since the queer little foot chase back at the carnival, and his careful pursuit of them all the way out here, but his nervous breath still kept fogging up the windows.

That big son of a bitch sensed me in the crowd. I don't know how that's possible, but I know it's right. No doubt he's the most powerful among the four of them. No doubt he's the most dangerous, too.

Beside him on the passenger seat, the leather briefcase lay open. The faces in all their glory stared up at him. He had considered going faceless for tonight's performances, but decided it might be more fun to give them a good scare in the final fleeting seconds of their lives.

He selected the Magic Man's mask, applied the adhesive, then pressed it to his own face. He switched on the car radio and listened to a Hall & Oates number while he waited for the glue to dry.

3

"I found it," Clay said. He was at the table in the motel room, staring at his laptop. "There's no photo and no name. He's a John Doe in the news story. But your guy Kowalski was right. Fatal, self-inflicted knife wound to the abdomen, right there on the carnival grounds. There were about forty witnesses."

Mia, who lay reclining on the bed and staring at the muted television, said, "What's the date?"

"October 1998," Clay said. "About three months after we'd met him in the Mouth."

She looked at him.

She looks frightened, Clay thought.

He looks lost, Mia thought.

"For a minute there," she said, "I thought you were gonna tell me he'd committed suicide *before* we met him. Ha ha."

Clay tried to smile, but it came off as a grimace. Like he was tasting something awful. "I was worried that's what I'd find, too," he confessed. "So at least we know he was a man and not some ghost."

"Is that supposed to be a joke? Because I'm feeling really unsettled here."

"No joke, just a fact." He drummed a set of fingers on the table. Studied his computer screen. "It still doesn't explain who the man in your photo is."

"Do you think it was smart to let Jamie and Dennis go back home alone?"

Clay's fingers tap danced on the keyboard. He wasn't listening to her. "It doesn't explain the man Molly Broome and Charlotte Brown saw in the woods in Kentucky."

Mia got off the bed, snatching her phone and Clay's car keys from the nightstand. "I can't think about this anymore. I'm going out for some food. What do you want?"

"Just get double of whatever you get," he said, not looking up from his laptop.

When Mia stepped outside, it was as if time had stopped. Droplets of rain hung suspended in the atmosphere, and an unsettling white mist lay motionless across the highway like a—

(death shroud)

—stark white sheet.

Something's wrong, Mia thought. *Are Jamie and Dennis in danger back at that house? Was it a mistake to tell them to go back? To let them go alone?*

But in danger from *what*? There were no ghosts waiting for them there. There wasn't even the Magician.

Whatever it is, I don't like it, she thought as she climbed into Clay's Toyota and started the engine.

4

The house was dead. No power. I stood in the middle of the hallway, breathing deeply, trying not to lose my shit while Dennis went around frantically flipping light switches that didn't work.

"It's okay, buddy," I told him. I was desperate to keep my voice calm in the face of my brother's rising panic, but in truth, there was a vein of apprehension pulsing through me as well. "There's candles in the kitchen. Give me a hand?"

We set the short, fat candles on saucers and the tall, skinny ones upright in glasses, then I lit them all, one by one. Dennis followed my match flame from candle to candle with his eyes, seemingly mesmerized by the way my hand shook. The flame kept going out whenever I trembled too badly, and it took me several attempts to get them all lighted. Together, Dennis and I placed them around the house—the kitchen, the living room, on the floor in the hallway.

When we were done, I cut through the living room and went out onto the back porch. I needed fresh air, but the air out there tasted like motor oil. The mist was still creeping across the field, but above it, the night was clear. The rain had stopped, and the clouds had mostly moved on, except for a particularly nasty snarl of them directly over the barn at the edge of the property. I could see flashes of muted lights behind those clouds. A storm building.

The barn doors were still closed.

Okay, I thought. *Okay okay okay okay okay.*

Back in the kitchen, I asked Dennis to take down all the liquor bottles out of the cupboard, open them up, and pour them directly down the sink. Dennis did so without question, laughing as each bottle chugged and belched and emptied itself down the drain, as if this was some kind of new game.

Sure is, I thought. *The Sober Stooge. Everyone's a winner, as long as you don't lap that shit up out of the sink!*

I'd done worse in the past.

"There's a bottle of mouthwash in the bathroom," I told Dennis. "Pour that out, too, please."

He did so. And when he was done, I had him rinse out all the bottles and then the sink, and take the empty bottles out to the trash.

While he did all this, I kept pacing between the hallway, the living room, and the back porch. This place was a poison stronger than booze; I could feel it shuttling through my veins, weakening my constitution, corrupting my thoughts. My mounting anxiety from not having a drink all day wasn't helping matters.

At some point, I realized I had been counting the holes in the living-room wall. Good-sized holes, about the height of Dennis's head. I went out in the hall and examined the broken plaster there, arriving at the same conclusion. The same with the hallway upstairs.

I came back down and found Dennis sitting in the dark on the couch in the living room.

"Did you make all these holes?"

"Ye-e-es."

"Did you make them with your head? Like you did at the motel?"

"Ye-e-es."

"Why?"

"I am looking. For the well."

"Is the well in the house?"

He didn't answer right away. Then: "I do not know where the well is." His dark eyes met mine. "Jamie Warren will find it."

"Buddy, I have no idea—"

A floorboard creaked behind me. I spun around, saw nothing at the far end of that pitch-black hallway...but then I looked up the stairwell, just in time to see something drift out of the reach of our candlelight. Or so I thought.

"Who's up there?"

Behind me, Dennis began moaning.

Another creaking floorboard, and something pale and amorphous drifted along the upper landing. In the center of my brain, like a record skipping in a groove: *thhhk-thhhk-thhhk.*

Mia's voice, reverberating inside the echo chamber of my skull: *There's no dark magic in Black Mouth, and the Magician was just a man. All that horror inside your head? It's just your conscience speaking to you.*

Sarah Patchin's dirty finger on glass: *Come home...*

I climbed the stairs, slow as some fool in a dream. The upstairs hallway was dark and empty. I looked into the bedrooms, under the beds, the closets, up and down the hall a second time. I felt the residue of something simmering in the atmosphere, but I couldn't say for sure if it was all in my head or in reality.

When I came back downstairs, Dennis was still sitting on the couch. He was watching me, as if to decipher some secret code I didn't know I had in me.

"What?" I said.

"Someone. Is. Here," he said.

5

Stull tugged the baseball cap down over his latex mask as he stepped out of the car. He did this not to hide the mask this time, but because it was still drizzling a little and the latex tended to lose some of its integrity whenever it got wet. When he stepped beneath the awning and out of the rain, he peeled the hat off his head and tossed it into some nearby hedges. From the pocket of his Members Only jacket, he pulled out a black satin eye patch, and strapped it on over the mask.

Bibby came up behind him. Stull could sense his brother's excitement. He would have normally told him to back off, to chill out, to take a fucking hike. But Stull felt that tonight was different. Tonight was *special*. Bibby was here to watch his twin brother take in the magic of these other apprentices. Just as he had with Bibby himself.

"Don't fuck this up for me," Stull said, and even he couldn't say if he was speaking to Bibby or to himself.

He pulled the bone-handled hunting knife from the inner pocket of his jacket.

And knocked on the door.

6

Less than a mile from the motel, Mia saw a billboard advertising rental property in Ocean City, Maryland. Above the phalanx of ocean-side condos was a cartoon sun wearing sunglasses. She stared at it, then actually stomped on the brakes in the middle of the highway. There were no other drivers around to lay on their horns, so she just idled there in the middle of the road, staring at that cartoon sun on the billboard.

Something's coming, and it's gonna cross your path. Whatever you been running from, it's about to catch up to you. So keep an eye open so you don't miss it. You get me, sis?

Not only was the cartoon sun wearing sunglasses, but it had hands—white-gloved Mickey Mouse hands. The sun wasn't pointing at the condos, but back in the direction Mia had just come.

Mia Tomasina spun the steering wheel, hopped the median, and headed back to the motel.

7

Clay Willis answered a knock on his motel room door, certain it must be Mia having forgotten something.

A man in an eye patch stood on the other side of the door. Clay froze at the sight of that eye patch, and he even had time to register that there was something *not quite right* with this man's face, but before he could consider things further, the man inserted a rather large hunting knife into Clay Willis's belly.

The pain wasn't instantaneous. What Clay felt first was the *insinuation* of this man's hand pressed so intimately against his stomach, then driving him backward into the motel room. The man barreled his way in, slamming the door behind him. His hand remained at Clay's belly. Clay still felt no pain—only a dull and distant sense of *what the fuck?* and *this is just a really bad joke.*

But then the pain came, and it was like a fire at the center of his body. Clay screamed and staggered backward. The man did not relent; he kept pushing against Clay's belly, and Clay couldn't tell what he'd been stuck with, except some part of him *had* seen a knife, so was that it? Had he actually been impaled by a *knife*? A bit much for a joke—

He uttered a breathless cry as the man withdrew the knife from his abdomen. Clay saw the blade was red with his blood, and that streamers of it pattered on the carpet. He looked down and saw a crimson stain spreading across the front of his Hawaiian shirt.

The man came at him again, and there was nothing Clay could do to deflect the blow. His body accepted the blade again. There was that eerie sense of intimacy as the man's hand pushed against Clay's body.

Clay reached up and gripped the man around the shoulders, pressing his fingers into his shoulder blades as if that might accomplish something. The room tilted, and Clay realized he was going down, down, down to the floor, the man riding on top of him the entire way.

He reached up and clawed at the man's face. Something *fell away*, and Clay glimpsed a face behind the face, a blazing black eye hiding beneath the eye patch. A mouth like a busted bear trap.

The man pulled the knife out of Clay's stomach, lifted it over his head, and brought it back down again.

8

Mia pulled back into the motel parking lot, and noticed a car door standing open several spots away, beneath the STAY AT THE QUAY sign. She jumped out of Clay's Toyota and went to the motel door, already pulling the keycard from the pocket of her jeans. She ran the card through the censor, then shoved open the door.

Had she not been bracing herself for some inevitable calamity for the past several months, things might have ended differently in that motel room. As it happened, she hardly paused when she came in and saw the man straddling Clay on the motel room floor, a spreading pool of blood leaking from Clay's side.

She kicked the man in the back of the head. He went forward, splayed out on top of Clay. His knife—some aggressive-looking monstrosity—spun along the carpet and wedged itself beneath the TV credenza.

The man rolled off of Clay, and she saw that half of his face had been ripped away to reveal a hideous, broken-mouthed countenance beneath. She simultaneously recognized the man yet, in her panic, couldn't place him.

The man was trying to scramble to his feet, but Mia didn't let him: She rushed at him, driving him clear across the room and slamming him against the far wall. He was stronger, and he struck her across the face, then groped for her throat. His fingers felt like machine parts, and he might have wrapped them around her neck except he got tangled in the macaroni necklace she wore, buying her just enough time to peel away and roll across the bed. The necklace snapped and uncooked ziti scattered like buckshot.

The man grabbed her ankle, pulled her back toward him. She fell off the bed, her chin colliding with the fire-retardant carpet. Pain fired through her skull and flash-bangs detonated behind her eyes.

The man drove a knee into her spine, his fingers searching for purchase around her neck again. She bucked her hips, freeing herself, and scuttled in a half-crawl, half-run away from him. The man didn't try to stop her; in fact, he shoved her hard enough to send her flying into the television, which crashed against the wall then slid down behind the dresser it was on.

Dizzy and bleeding from her forehead now, Mia shoved herself off the dresser just as her assailant collided with it. She backed against a wall, the door to the motel room seeming like a million miles away. She bolted for it, but the man kicked her sharply in the upper thigh, knocking her back down onto the bed.

It was the bottle of Maker's Mark on the nightstand that she grabbed, wielding it like Thor's hammer, swinging for the cheap seats.

It connected with the side of the man's head—she felt the solidity of the strike all the way up to her elbows—and he went down like a heap of laundry.

Mia didn't stop. She'd been making low-budget horror movies the majority of her adult life, and her one criticism of the genre she loved was that once you incapacitate the bad guy, you didn't run, you didn't relent, you didn't crawl to the nearest phone and dial 911. No, motherfucker—what you did was you *finished the fucking job.*

Mia got down on the floor, straddled the son of a bitch, then proceeded to bash apart his face with the bottle of whiskey.

9

Weeping, shaking, her vision blurred, Mia dropped the bottle of Maker's onto the carpet. There was blood and bits of hair stuck to it, and a few loose teeth scattered about the carpet, but Mia hardly noticed.

She rolled off the shattered mess of the man that she'd been straddling, and crawled across the blood-soaked carpet. Clay was staring up at the ceiling, motionless. His teeth were gritted and his hands were pressed to his stomach. Blood pumped out of the lacerations in his ugly Hawaiian shirt.

Mia gently gripped his face, a hand on each cheek, and said, "You're gonna be okay," then she looked around the motel room for a phone. (She had her cell phone in her pocket, but she wasn't thinking, and forgot all about it.) She went for the phone on the nightstand, dialed 911, then returned to Clay's side while his respiration became wet and labored and shallow.

"No, baby," she said, as Clay's eyelids fluttered and his eyes rolled back in their sockets. "No, Clay."

She touched his face, and left bloody fingerprints on his beautifully white cheeks.

10

I awoke from some disremembered nightmare to find myself curled up on the living-room floor, shaking and cold. Somehow, at some point, I had fallen asleep. I looked around and saw the candles in their saucers had shrunk a good couple of inches, and the light outside the windows seemed darker.

Dennis was no longer in the room with me. I called his name, but my voice fell flat, and I didn't like hearing it. My whole body ached, and I could sense that old marching band warming up once more in the practice room of my cerebral cortex. I got up and went to the staircase, thinking Dennis might have gone upstairs to bed, but then paused when I heard something that didn't sound like Dennis shifting about up there.

I stared up into that black pit at the top of the landing. Held my breath.

Sarah Patchin appeared at the top of the stairs. She was cradling her baby—my half-brother, Dennis's half-brother—and little Milo Patchin was making his suckling sounds, *thhhk-thhhk-thhhk*, as his mother glided with him slowly down the staircase.

A smell of smoke came with them. They say our olfactory sense is the one linked closest to memory, and in that instant, I knew that to be true. The smell of them coming down those stairs brought me right back to that night twenty-four years ago, as Black Mouth burned and the man who wasn't really a man at all bared his true face to me and took off into the trees.

She passed within inches of me, turning her head to watch me as she drifted by. She looked the same as I remembered her on that day so long ago, one strap hanging off her shoulder, baby Milo nursing at her breast. She was younger than me now—I had aged while she, in death, had not—and I felt some twinge of paternal or at least familial compassion toward her. There was no expression on her face—no accusation, no anger, no sadness—and somehow that was the worst thing of all.

I backed up against the far wall as she crossed the living-room carpet toward the open door that led on to the back porch. In her wake, all the candles in the house flickered, guttered, went dark. Sarah and Milo Patchin drifted out into the night, the *thhhk-thhhk* sound of Milo's feeding fading as they vanished into that cool mist that had come right up to the house now, and disappeared from my sight.

Mia's voice rushed back to me then: *All that horror inside your head? It's just your conscience speaking to you. Will you listen to it?*

Would I listen to it?

I walked out onto the porch. Sarah and Milo Patchin were gone, but as I peered through the swirling mist and across the field, I could see Dennis standing among the alfalfa, gazing at the barn at the edge of the property.

The barn doors were now open.

I knew what was in there, waiting for me, of course. I'd always known. I could see it in my mind's eye, as clear as the day it happened...

The Firebird jacked up off the ground, him working beneath it. Cans of beer in an Igloo cooler full of ice within arm's reach. Tools scattered about the dirt floor of the barn.

I'd been back just a few days from the institution. Those eleven months spent in that horrible place had broken something inside me. It had broken something inside all of us, I think. Yet there was little relief in coming home, because this was the place where all those terrible things had happened. The place where my father waited for me...

He'd spent the afternoon getting drunk and taking swings at Dennis and me. He'd knocked Dennis down, and Dennis had bloodied his head on the table in the living room. When Mom tried to intervene, my father had smacked her across the face then slugged her in the stomach. She'd collapsed on the living-room floor beside my brother, sobbing, while Dennis watched everything with his bleary, unfocused, confused eyes.

I'd tried to intervene, too—I'd foolishly shoved my dad to keep him from pursuing my mother, so he'd grabbed my right wrist and twisted my arm behind my back until I felt something snap. I screamed as pain radiated up my ulna from my elbow. An old break made new again.

I came into the barn that afternoon, after the so-called dust had settled, clutching my arm to my chest. The pain was great, and I was still crying, but I wasn't making any noise. I felt like a coward enough already. I'd been seeing ghosts since the fire—that dead woman and her baby. They'd granted me a reprieve for the eleven months I'd been incarcerated, but they had been right here, waiting for me to return. I didn't want to be a coward anymore.

"D-D-Dad," I stuttered.

He grunted, still buried beneath his car.

"I think my a-arm's broken, Dad…"

"Don't be a little bitch," he grumbled. When I didn't say anything more, he dragged himself out from beneath the Firebird. The front of his shirt was lathered in grease. "Lemme see it."

I didn't move; I just kept my aching arm clutched to my chest.

He grabbed my wrist and tugged my arm down to a ninety-degree angle. Pain as sharp as knife blades shot through the bone. I cried out, and he slapped me across the face.

"You and your retard brother killed two fuckin' people, and now *you're* gonna cry? Maybe they didn't put your faggot ass in jail for the rest of your life, but I'm still gonna get sued. I'm still the one who's gonna have to pay. Same as always. Same as fucking always!"

He slapped me again.

I refused to cry out this time, but the tears spilled freely.

"Only good thing to come outta this is I don't gotta worry 'bout that whore askin' for money for her little bastard no more. Did me a solid on that one. Now get outta my sight." He dismissed me with a wave of his hand, then got back down on the floor of the barn. A swig from an open can of Natural Ice, then he was back under that Firebird, wrenches clanking.

My face burned. My arm screamed. My eyes were welling uncontrollably with tears.

I didn't even think about it.

I saw the jack right there, propping up the car.

I took three steps toward it, pulled my leg back, and kicked it out from under the car. I gave it everything I had.

The Firebird collapsed on my father, crushing him from the middle of his chest on up. The sound of it would chase me into my nightmares for years to come.

My father's legs bucked, then went still. There was blood on the dirt floor of the barn. There was blood on his blue and white Igloo cooler. There was blood on my sneakers, too, and along the legs of my pants. In the blink of an eye, it had sprayed everywhere.

I stared at what I had done for a very long time. Tears continued to burn tracts down my cheeks. My arm continued to scream. There was something screaming deep within me, too—some part that, in truth, has never *stopped* screaming.

After a time, I went back to the house, cleaned my father's blood off my sneakers, stripped out of my clothes, and crawled into bed. It was the middle of the afternoon, but I wanted to fade from the world as quickly as possible. Please, God, let me fade.

At some point, Dennis curled up behind me in bed, spooning me, his big sweaty arm over my body, his sour-sweet breath against my cheek. He pulled me into his turtle shell, where we floated together in a sea of peace, where the real world was just a dream and the inside of my brother's head was as vast and as hopeful as an archangel's dreams. We stayed that way until we were roused by the screams of our mother coming from the barn.

11

I came up beside Dennis in the field. That eerie white mist eddied all around us. He was staring at those open barn doors as if in a trance. I placed a shaking hand against one of his big shoulders. "Stay here," I told him.

The mist was waist-high, and I trod through it. Overhead, lightning pulsed from cloud to cloud, but there was no thunder. Midway through the field, I started receiving transmissions from my childhood—flashes of brutality that had weakened and destroyed me. Things that had turned me into some shambling, ruined husk. A scarecrow with phobias. I'll admit—I paused halfway through the field, and considered getting the fuck out of there.

But I didn't.

Not this time.

As I approached, a soft firelight came to life in the black space between the two open barn doors. I reached the threshold and peered inside, but all I could see was darkness. I couldn't tell where the light was coming from.

"Let me see you," I said.

Nothing.

I bladed my body and slid in through the open doors. The soil beneath my feet felt spongy. For the millionth time, I thought, *How far does the blood seep? How deep into the earth have I sent that man? Does my father's blood continue to trickle down to this day? Straight to the core of the planet? Does it burn as fumes when it reaches that magma center? Have I been inhaling his lifeblood ever since his death? His murder?*

My foot struck something on the ground. I looked down and saw it was my old aluminum baseball bat. Right where I'd dropped it the last time I was in here.

I gathered it up now, choking up on the handle. Remembering what my dad had looked like that night, unconscious at the bottom of the stairs. How I'd wanted to crack his skull open with this very bat...

"Let me see you..."

Not a sound. The barn was silent. That firelight seemed to be coming from all the places I wasn't currently looking. There was no source to it.

"I said, *let me see you.*"

A sudden whip crack of thunder. Rain began tapping on the tin roof.

I tried to imagine him just as I had whenever I'd come in here as a kid, after his death—a shape ambling along the far wall of the barn, progressing around the side of the hay bales until he was silhouetted against the perforations in the barn wall. Chambray work shirt, filthy cargo pants, his long hair and raven-black beard dusty from working in the barn. A drunken swagger that, I'll admit, looked very much like my own.

"Come," I said, "out."

But he wouldn't give me the satisfaction of showing himself to me now.

I turned instead to the Firebird beneath that crinkly blue sea of tarp. The sound of that engine growling up the driveway each night had instilled in me a Pavlovian sense of dread that echoed to this day throughout my DNA. I remembered driving to Sarah Patchin's trailer with him on the morning of the fire, and how his empties rolled around in the footwell, and how the whole car stank of sweat and booze and anger.

I pulled the sacks of mulch and seed off the car's roof, swiped with one arm the farming implements from the hood. With a theatrical flourish, I whipped the tarp off the car, revealing a dusty black time machine that transported me all the way back to my childhood.

I ran a palm along the passenger window, clearing an arc in the grime. But the reflection in the glass was not my own. That bristling black beard clotted with dust and bits of straw, and the mad, roving eyes—

I smashed the window to pieces with the bat. Hair hanging in my face, my pulse racing, I glimpsed my father's reflection in the dust-coated surface of the passenger door. I swung the bat, driving a dent the size of a softball into the door. I swung again, again, again. His reflection mocked me, gliding along the warped and dusty black exterior of the vehicle. I hammered the rear quarter panel, busted up the rear windshield, knocked out the taillights. I was laughing maniacally as I reduced the shitty plastic spoiler on the hatchback trunk to smithereens.

Once I'd suitably destroyed that side of the car, I went around to the driver's side and gave a repeat performance. I smashed those sneering, slatted headlights, the bird-beak grille, banged away at my father's reflection in those cheap chrome-plated hubcaps.

When I'd finished, exhausted and broken, I dropped to my knees and pressed my throbbing forehead against the car door. There were cubes of safety glass in my hair and the palms of my hands pulsated from swinging the bat.

I turned and saw my father's reflection in the side-view mirror. It was me, but it was him, too. Back from the grave to let me know that

I couldn't escape his DNA, couldn't redesign that familial blueprint in my blood.

I shoved myself to my feet, swung the bat, and knocked the side-view mirror clear across the barn. It clattered on the wooden pallets, the mirror somehow unbroken, reflecting the otherwise unseen firelight. My father's reflection continued to leer at me from the glass.

A cyclone of black flies whirling inside my head, I climbed onto the pallet, raised the bat over my head, and smashed the fucking mirror into a million pieces. When it was nothing but broken glass and shards of plastic, I continued to bring the bat down.

Again.

Again.

Again.

I felt every strike, my body aching, my right arm a cavalcade of agony. I kept bringing the bat down, down, down, until I'd busted apart the rotted boards at my feet, yet I kept swinging, my chest aching, my eyes spilling tears. And then I collapsed out of a mixture of exhaustion and anguish. The cries of pain and terror and fear I'd imagined coming from my father's battered and cracked reflection had only been my own.

12

A noise behind me.

I turned and saw Dennis standing between the open barn doors. The storm had returned, and he was soaked from trudging through the field. Rainwater spilled through the cracks and crevices in the roof and made muddy puddles on the dirt floor of the barn.

Dennis's thick-soled sandals left imprints in the dirt as he advanced toward me. Bits of rotted alfalfa clung to his damp body.

I was on my hands and knees on the pallets, sobbing. The baseball bat had rolled away, and the aggression that had fueled me just moments ago had rolled away with it. I felt hollowed out, emptied, spent.

"Jamie Warren is a good man," Dennis said, coming up behind me. "Jamie Warren is a good brother."

This caused me to cry harder. I felt like all the bolts holding my bones together had come loose. After a while, I wiped the tears from my eyes, and struggled to clear my throat. "Thank you, Dennis. You don't know what the fuck you're talking about, but thank you."

He stepped up onto the pallet, the tips of his sandals coming within inches of the hole I'd busted through the dry-rotted wooden slats. I told him to be careful, and that these boards weren't sturdy, but he wasn't listening to me. He was staring down into the hole I'd smashed in the wood.

Lightning detonated through the cracks in the ceiling.

Dennis got down on his knees and began wrenching the boards loose from the pallet's frame, widening the opening I had made with the baseball bat. I just watched, too defeated to stop him or even ask what the hell he was doing.

When he was done, he planted both hands on the pallet and gazed down. I leaned forward and peered into the hole, too. There should have been a dirt floor down there, but there wasn't. What I saw was a pitch-black chasm just below the pallet that tunneled deep down into the earth. It went so far that I couldn't see the bottom.

"I don't believe this…" The words rasped out of my throat. I was thinking of—

(circles black circles)

—crayon drawings, so many of them, given to me by Dennis when I was in the institution all those years ago. When we were both just children.

"This is the way," said Dennis. "To the well." He lifted a leg over the side of the hole.

"No, Dennis." I groped at his Ninja Turtles T-shirt. "That's not the well. It's one of the old mineshafts from the Mouth. This whole place is sinking into the ground."

As if my words held magic, the entire barn suddenly pitched to one side. The beams creaked and splintered, bolts broke free and rained down from the rafters, and a sound like a deep-throated moan emanated from all around us. It was why the farmhouse was falling apart, too, and why Mom's Econoline was sunk down to its bumper in the front yard. Black Mouth was finally gobbling this place up.

"*No.*" Dennis's voice was firm. He shook his head, then placed one large hand over my own—the one that was still clutching at the front of his T-shirt. Gently, he pried my hand off. "It is the way to the well. We go *deeper.*" And then he slung his other leg over the side of the hole and started to climb down.

"You'll break your goddamn neck!" I shouted after him. "Dennis! Dennis!"

The barn pitched to the opposite side now, and a collection of rakes, shovels, and tools fell from one wall and into the rotten bales of hay. A shower of carpentry nails rained down upon me.

"Dennis!"

Whatever mist had been creeping stealthily across our property had made its way into the barn now; it circled around me like a whirlpool until it spilled down into the hole. I watched Dennis sink farther down into the darkness, until I couldn't see him anymore, and he was swallowed up completely.

"*Dennis!*"

...*nis...nis...nis...*

A wooden beam came crashing down, splitting in two as it struck what remained of my father's demolished Firebird.

Every fiber in my body wanted me to turn and run, but that's not what I did.

...*nis...nis...nis...*

I climbed down into that hole after my brother.

CHAPTER TWENTY-THREE

INTO THE WELL

1

I was blind beneath the earth. Somewhere in the darkness ahead of me, Dennis moved swiftly through the tunnel. The sounds of his exertions echoed back to me in a confused jumble of noise. I called out to him just once, but the vibrations of my voice caused clumps of dirt to patter across my face and slip down into the collar of my shirt. Too much noise—too much vibration—and this dank, intestinal chamber might collapse on our heads.

I went after him, flailing blindly through the darkness, patting the earthen walls with my hands, testing the solidity of the ground before taking each step. Dennis, not so cautious, was putting a distance between us; I could tell by how faint his heavy breathing had become.

The tunnel had started as a vertical drop, but it soon leveled out so that I was walking on a fairly graduated slope downward. I estimated that I was moving in the direction of Black Mouth, so perhaps this tunnel connected with one of the mineshaft openings down there. If so, I'd need only to keep going until I breached the surface down in the Mouth.

A light flickered on up ahead. It looked like a single bulb jutting straight out of the tunnel wall, as impossible as that seemed. As I stared at it, a second light came on a few feet from that one, and then a third, each one farther down the tunnel, until there were a series of lights guiding my way.

I stood there for a moment, not moving. I could no longer hear my brother; he had gotten too far ahead of me. All I could hear now was my own ragged breath, and the faint electrical *zzzzt* of those glowing yellow lights up ahead.

I crept toward them, the implausibility of what I was seeing causing me to wonder if I wasn't actually passed out drunk somewhere and dreaming all this. When I reached the lights, I saw they were indeed small circular lamps poking through the dirt walls of the tunnel. Each one was fitted into what at first appeared to be a curved bit of stone protruding from the wall, but on closer inspection I realized what these things actually *were*, and my breath caught in my throat.

They were miners' helmets. And beneath the helmets—*wearing* the helmets—were the fossilized countenances of the dead coalminers, mummified and decomposed. Their faces were veiled behind a meshwork of cobwebs, and the exposed bits of their skulls looked more like stone than bone.

This wasn't real.

This was an hallucination.

A conga line of dead faces, each one with a pair of empty eye sockets gazing out at me...

Those headlamps in the helmets flickered but held.

2

I followed the glowing lamps to the end of the tunnel, where a disc of moonlight revealed itself. *The way out*, I knew, but I was too frightened to bolt for that opening. Instead, I picked my way slowly toward it.

Tendrils of ivy covered the opening; I swept them aside, then stepped out into a sunken, wooded landscape, where the trees bowed and grew horizontally from the rims and ridges, and where the moonlight reflected in soft puddles and winding, threadlike tributaries that meandered deeper into the trees. It wasn't raining here, and the sky far above the trees was perfectly clear and embroidered with innumerable stars.

"It's Black Mouth," I said, looking around in awe. It *was* Black Mouth, only as it had been in my youth, before the fire. Lush, deep, haunted. Otherworldly. Yet the more I looked around, the more I realized that wasn't exactly true. This place was different. Unlike the Black Mouth of my youth there was something feral about this place. The trees were much bigger than they'd ever been when I was a kid, the circumference of some of their trunks like ones I'd seen in photographs of the redwood forests in California. The foliage looked almost prehistoric—immense ferns, arrowhead palm fronds, banana leaf plants that surged weightily in the cool breeze.

"No," Dennis said.

His voice startled me, and I spun around to see him standing beside the opening of the tunnel. I must have staggered right past him in my fascination at having set foot in this strange place.

Dennis was looking around, too, but with a mark of skepticism on his face. He seemed to be searching for something beyond the trees. "This is the well."

I heard movement somewhere behind me. I turned around just as something shifted beyond a snarl of thick, thorn-studded vines and dense vegetation. Something large. I held my breath, my eyes trained on the spot, waiting for whatever it was to move again. It didn't.

"There." Dennis pointed to a cavity between the trees, where the land sloped downward. It was dark down there, a channel carved through the center of this prehistoric jungle-land version of Black Mouth. It seemed to go on forever. "We go there."

"We need to go *back*," I told him. "We can't be in this place." What I meant was: *This place can't exist.*

"We have to go." He was still pointing toward that dark channel that ran straight through the center of the woods.

I went to move, but found my feet tangled in vines. I lifted one foot off the ground, and felt the vines constrict around my ankle. I looked down at my other foot and watched as one of those vines—pale pink and thick as a drinking straw—twined around my inner thigh.

Panic caused me to bolt forward, but the vines snared around my ankles were strong, and I was sent crashing to the ground. I quickly propped myself up on my hands and knees just as more vines twisted about my wrists. These were the same pale, fleshy pink as the others, but they had tiny serrated leaves of a blood-red hue sprouting from them. They gave off an acrid, chemical smell that made my eyes water.

Dennis lurched over and tore the vines from the ground, then stripped them from my wrists. He helped me up, then ripped apart the vines that had been constricting around my ankles, shins, and thighs. They'd been trying to crawl up the trunk of my body.

"We shouldn't *be* here." It was hard enough to get the words out through the rising panic that was strangling my throat. "We need to get back. I don't even know how this place can…" *Exist* was the word I was going to use, but I suddenly didn't have the strength to use it. I felt on the brink of madness.

Dennis pushed forward through the underbrush, swatting away those prehistoric plants and stomping down kudzu with his sandals. I looked back toward the mouth of the mineshaft—the mineshaft that had brought us here—and saw, with mounting horror, that the individual strands of ivy that hung over the entrance had threaded together to create an impenetrable tapestry. As I stared at it, small blue flowers budded along the curtain of ivy and began to open up.

I want to get out of here.

I hurried after my brother, ducking beneath the arched trunks of trees and climbing over exposed root systems breaching out of the earth. After a time, I became aware that something large and furtive was pursuing us, cloaked behind dense foliage and masked by darkness. It was the same thing I'd nearly glimpsed as I stepped out of the tunnel. At one point in its pursuit of us, it had come so close, I could hear its bellows-like respiration, and I thought I could smell it, too—a swampy, malodorous combination of stagnant water and fetid decay.

I turned around, my eyes scanning the dark spaces between the trees. Nothing at first…but then I caught movement in the corner of my eye. Something blackly iridescent, like a beetle's carapace, shimmered behind a fan of palm leaves. Whatever it was, its exhalations were strong enough to make the leaves billow out.

"Something's following us," I said.

"It will not hurt us," Dennis said.

"What is it?"

"Do not look at it."

But his warning came too late: The thing rose up on its hind legs, its size uprooting the palms around it, wrenching their roots from the ground in a spray of rocks and dirt. It was vaguely anthropomorphic, in that it had a bulging central torso studded with three pairs of suppurating black teats. Its arms and legs were stunted and barrel-like, and it had a head like a VW Bug.

As it moved, the moonlight sparkled along its flank. Its hide was coated in the shifting purple iridescence of an oil spill, and a pair of snarled black tusks curled from a protruding lower jaw. It had eyes recessed into deep black pockets that glowed with a dim, idiot sensibility.

I knew what this thing was, yet the impossible nature of it—the sheer *preposterousness* of it—refused to allow me to make the connection in my brain.

It dropped forward onto all four of its massive, stocky legs, and I felt the ground quake beneath me. Its giant head swiveled with a creaking twist of leather in my direction. In that same moment, the thing's lunatic theme song burst from seemingly everywhere all at once, from PA speakers suspended high up in the trees that I was only just now noticing. The jingle played too slowly, like a record at the wrong speed:

> Haaaappeee Horrrrace,
> The Purrrrple-Purrrrple Hiiiippohh…
> The Purrrrple-Purrrrple Hiiiippohh…
> The Purrrrple-Purrrrple Hiiiippohh…

I clamped my hands to my ears and screamed.

Dennis wrapped an arm around me, pulled me tight against his broad chest. He pressed his nose to my cheek. Said, "It. Will not. Hurt. Us. *Do not move.*"

To prove my brother wrong, the thing lowered its head and snorted. It took a formidable step in our direction, steam billowing from its gaping nostrils and smoldering from the corners of its tremendous mouth. It was getting ready to charge us.

"*Dennissss…*"

"*Do not move—*"

I peeled away from Dennis's grasp and ran for cover behind the trunk of a massive redwood.

The thing whipped its head in my direction and charged.

I rolled behind the tree, tumbling down a slight dip in the ground. Hooked, talon-like thorns sprouting from the foliage sliced me across my arms and cheeks and snagged into the fabric of my pants.

Before I could catch my breath, the thing bulldozed into the trunk of the redwood. The tree halted its progress, but I could hear the wood stressing. Large branches and acorns the size of grenades rained down all around me. One of the PA speakers tumbled down until it hung suspended in the air from its cable mere inches from my face. That terrible jingle droned out of it—

...Haaaappeee Horrrrrrrr...

—before it died altogether.

The thing moved around the side of the tree, tearing through a tangle of shrubbery. It squeezed between the tree I was hiding behind and the one next to it, moving at a quick clip. I curled up in a ball, arms over my head, and felt its passage, the way you'd feel a large vehicle whizzing by your face as you crossed a particularly busy intersection. I could smell its musky aroma, could sense the body heat radiating from it.

I glanced up and saw it turning in a wide circle, twisting its monstrous purple head back and forth. It was searching for me, trying to catch my scent in the air. I peered around the side of the tree and saw that Dennis hadn't moved from where he'd been standing when I'd first spotted this thing. He wasn't looking at the beast; he was looking at me.

The thing grunted, expelled dual clouds of steam from its wet, constricting nostrils, then charged at me again.

I scrambled to my feet and sprinted around the side of the redwood. I hoped to hear the thing strike the trunk of the tree again, but it wasn't that easily fooled a second time; I heard the bark crumbling and limbs snapping as the thing bolted between the tree trunks, gathering speed as it gained on me.

There was a large deadfall up ahead, blanketed in moss and studded with enormous white conical mushrooms. I half-vaulted, half-tripped over it, then crashed to the earth on the opposite side. The great beast's footfalls thundered along the ground toward me. I rolled to my right, not stopping until I heard the beast explode through the deadfall. Shrapnel showered down all around me.

I sat up and saw the thing's tail whipping back and forth, the black excrement cemented to its massive hindquarters, the hairs as thick as porcupine quills rising along its razorback spine. It trudged in a semicircle through the underbrush, its body like a tanker truck, until its unwieldy head was once again leveraged in my direction. Its eyes pulsed with a light that didn't look fully charged.

I groped for purchase on a nearby tree limb and hoisted myself to my feet. I was about to run again, but caught sight of Dennis still standing there, a sedate and almost sleepy look on his face.

Do not move, Dennis had said.

I turned around and stared at the thing as it gathered speed in my direction. Its forelegs tore through the soil, its lumpy head bent forward so that its luminescent white eyes could hold me in their sights.

Suddenly, I remembered being eleven years old, and watching Clay Willis get his face pummeled by Tony Tillman that afternoon at the carnival. After it was all over, I had looked around and—

—saw someone in a plush Happy Horace costume seemingly staring in our direction from across the midway, certain this person would come over, but perhaps challenged by my stare, whoever was in that purple hippo suit only turned away, dancing off in the opposite direction until they were swallowed up by the crowd—

The thing that had been charging in my direction came to a skidding halt. A carpet of dirt rolled up in front of its massive forelegs. Waves of heat radiated off its shining purple flanks.

I just stared at it.

Stared it down.

My whole body shook atop a pair of quaking knees.

The thing returned my stare, perhaps contemplating—in whatever fashion passed for contemplation inside its dim-witted brain—whether I was a fool or if I possessed some secret magic up my sleeve. Steam roiled in ribbons from its glistening nostrils. I caught a whiff of it again—that musky animal stench that spoke of degradation and the unstoppable, lustful need to *feed*.

I didn't move. I held my ground.

I stared it down.

Those luminous eye sockets pulsed with their own heartbeat.

Then the thing labored a retreat back through the underbrush. Its feet left behind massive craters in the dirt that were quickly filled with mud. Its final exhalation blew a clot of small black gnats into the air. A moment later, the beast was gone, with only the gentle swaying of disturbed palm fronds to indicate that it had ever been there at all.

I waited for my own heartbeat to regulate itself, then crossed over to where Dennis stood. I asked him if he was okay, but in truth, *I* was the one who felt like he was about to fall apart. Dennis's cool gray eyes shifted in my direction. One corner of his mouth edged upward in the approximation of a smile.

Then he turned around and walked deeper into the woods.

3

It only got worse from there.

As we followed the wooded channel toward the heart of the well, the sense that we were still being watched was all-encompassing. I kept glancing over my shoulder and at the perimeter of the forest, waiting to see if that oversized purple hippopotamus might come barreling back through the underbrush. But I could see nothing.

An arching neon sign covered in black vines and writhing with snakes stretched above a bleak, lightless clearing. Several of the letters were missing, but I could still make out what it said:

THE HA PY ORA E RAVELING IRCUS & ARNIV L!

We crossed beneath it, waiting for the next surprise to spring out at us. But there were no sudden attacks, no Hollywood jump scares. We weren't alone, however; I could see the shapes of things around the perimeter of the clearing—immobile, discarded relics of some post-apocalyptic wasteland. As we crossed to the center of the clearing, the things became more clearly defined beneath the pearlescent glow of the moon.

A carousel, its canvas rooftop shredded to ribbons, was partially sunken into the earth. Thick vines secured it in place the way you'd stake a hot-air balloon to the ground; they spooled around the wooden horses, with their fiery manes and ruby-red eyes and amputated limbs, and spread like a cancer across the carousel's central post.

There was a section of rollercoaster track arcing crookedly from the earth, a scatter of busted black cars snared in the nearby trees.

The whirling teacups lay in pieces across the clearing, each one like a giant broken skull beneath the moonlight.

Moldy stuffed toys hung from skeletal tree limbs. They were crawling with beetles and centipedes, the toys' plush bodies squirming as if alive. I peered closely at one—a stuffed rabbit, no less—and saw that it had actually *grown* from the tree; there was a membranous web of tissue that connected the rabbit to the branch. I could see some vaguely bloodlike fluid pumping through the semitransparent stalk of the tree branch.

Reigning over all of this chaos was the Ferris wheel. It stood at the far end of the clearing, a thing that looked like it had been there since the beginning of time. Small trees had graduated into massive, stately oaks, weaving themselves as they grew through the spokes of the great wheel. Those sentient, fleshy vines had wrapped themselves around the ride's steel girders and corkscrewed their way along the support beams. The Ferris wheel's base had sunk so far into the loam that if it ever conjured the temerity to rotate, its gondolas would carve a trench deep into the earth.

The rides weren't completely unoccupied. Small, pale figures lay draped over the carousel horses; they leaned against each other in the rollercoaster carts snared in the treetops; they lay sprawled on the ground amidst the broken shells of the whirling teacups. I peered up at the Ferris wheel and saw slight figures slouched over the sides of the gondolas, a pale blue arm dangling here, a lock of mossy hair fluttering there.

They were children, all of them. Dead. I didn't need to get any closer to them to know this.

Very slowly, Dennis said, "This…is where…he keeps them…"

Something stirred off to my left. I looked toward the carousel and didn't see anything at first…but then I saw one of the dead children raise its head off the flank of a wooden horse. It moved with the clunky, disjointed gracelessness of a wooden puppet, its head unnaturally askew on the bluish, moldy stalk of its neck. Its eyes were two black sockets in its skull, but as it twisted its reluctant head in our direction, pale lights flickered to life inside them.

Before my mind had a chance to reconcile what I was seeing, a second child, suspended like a marionette by those fleshy pink vines beneath the tattered canvas rooftop of the carousel, began to twitch. This child's eyes opened, shining like fireflies. I watched as the vines lowered them to the ground and they clambered down off the carousel.

On the ground in front of us, the bodies of dead children strewn about the shattered teacups began to writhe and rise. They moved with a somnambulist's lassitude, their bodies uncooperative at first, but gaining a slow understanding. A conspiracy. A collusion.

"Dennis," I said, and took a step closer to him.

Dead children began climbing out of the Ferris wheel gondolas. The ones closest to the ground simply spilled out over the gondolas' sides, struck the ground, then shuddered to their feet. The ones higher up attempted to scale down the spokes of the great wheel. They all twisted their heads around to study us on the ground below, their eyes yellow pinpoints of light so far back in their skulls that the distance seemed unimaginable.

In the trees, those firefly eyes stared down at us from behind the safety bars of the rollercoaster cars. The children began climbing over the front of the cars and dropping like lead weights out of the trees. They struck the ground with enough force to break bones, but that didn't seem to have any effect on them; they shivered and shook as they ratcheted to their feet, and stared at us with those flickering yellow eyes.

We were being surrounded, the dead children's ashen, shuffling bodies forming a circle around us in the clearing. More descended from the Ferris wheel and a few even fell several stories to the ground; they struck and bounced, then lay motionless until whatever dark magic that flowed through their bones saw fit to revive them. They clambered slowly to unsteady feet and drifted closer to knit themselves in among the circle formed by their brethren.

"What do we do?" I asked, as the children drew closer. The firelight deep in their eye sockets danced.

"Do magic," Dennis said.

I just shook my head. "I don't *know* magic…"

"Jamie Warren does magic," Dennis said. He pointed down at my pants pocket, just as he had done when we were children changing our clothes in our bedroom. Back then, I had fished out a shiny gold coin. I reached in now, and took out a brand-new deck of Bicycle playing cards.

It was the same deck I'd purchased at the 7-Eleven somewhere between West Virginia and Kentucky, on the afternoon we drove to meet with Clay. How they had gotten in my pocket now, I couldn't fathom.

"What am I supposed to do?"

"Jamie Warren does magic."

Something large knocked over a tree near the carousel; I jerked my head in that direction and watched the tree come crashing down, pulling a network of vines down with it. When the dust settled, I caught a glimpse of that iridescent purple hide chugging behind a blind of ferns.

I peeled away the cellophane wrapper then shook the cards out in my hand. They were cool and stiff—a fresh pack. I tossed the box aside, then did a simple overhand shuffle. But I was nervous, and half the cards fluttered out of my hands and onto the ground.

I cursed, dropped quickly to my knees, and swept them up. The children's sneakers, furry with moss, inched closer toward us. I glanced up and, for the first time, saw the wounds they'd suffered in life—black slashes across their throats and bellies, where the blood shined like fresh tar. Among them was one child whose face had been pulverized, leaving only a dark crater in the center of its skull where those twin flames for eyes still glowed. Another child—this one with a pair of oversized eyeglasses cocked at an angle across her narrow face—possessed the dimmest resemblance to Charlotte Brown; the front of her blouse was shredded and oozing with blood.

I rose to my feet, took a breath, and reshuffled the deck.

"Step right up, step right up," I said, my voice shaking. "Can you follow the queen of hearts?"

I lifted the queen from the deck, showed it to the children, then seemingly placed it back on top of the deck. But in reality, I had palmed it, and made it reappear a moment later as if from thin air.

An invisible shockwave sent the dead children staggering backward, widening their circle. The flames in their pumpkin-headed eye sockets nearly blew out.

I reshuffled the deck, my hands shaking so badly I feared I might drop the cards again. *Don't look at them*, I told myself. *Focus on the cards and don't look at them.* I did a one-handed "Charlier" cut. It was clumsy, but I managed to keep the cards in my hand.

The children stopped advancing on us. They stood wavering on cockeyed feet, their heads rolling from side to side on their necks.

They're mesmerized by the tricks, I thought, and a maniacal giddiness bubbled up inside me.

I split the deck, showed them the ace of spades on the bottom of one, then made it magically reappear on the top of the other. I then performed a variation of the Four Burglars, slipping all four jacks into various positions throughout the deck, only to reveal that all four had somehow made it to the top of the deck to "escape" capture.

Escape capture, I thought. *Escape capture, escape—*

"The Riffle Force," I announced, and I had already begun the trick before I remembered that I had never been very good at it. I force-pulled the two cards off the top of the deck, but one went fluttering to the ground.

The children's eyes burned brighter as their heads straightened up. A few of them managed a step in my direction. I felt the heat from Dennis's back against my own. Sweat rolled down the sides of my face.

I quickly picked up the dropped card, reinserted it in the deck, and attempted the trick again. This time, in my panic, I dumped half the stack onto the ground. The cards scattered about my feet and I dropped to my knees to collect them in a fever. My heart was crashing against my chest, and I could no longer control my fingers.

"Dennis!"

But Dennis only stood there, staring out at those children and then down at me. Casual as you could please.

"Dennis, *help* me!"

The children crept closer. I could smell the death on them, the blackness of their wounds. One rotting sneaker stepped on the five of diamonds. My hand froze midway to grabbing it. Looking up, I was mere inches from those dancing flames in their otherwise hollow eye sockets. One half of the child's nose was missing, exposing a triangular gorge rimmed with cartilage.

I plucked the card from beneath the sneaker, poked it back into the deck, and stood up just as a set of eerie green hands reached out for me. More than one pair of hands—they were all reaching, all close enough now to grope at my clothes. A wisp of smoke spiraled up from the place where one of them touched my shirt. Dennis whined and bumped against me. They were pawing at him, too.

"The Riffle Force!" I shouted.

I held the cards above my head so the children couldn't grab at them. Closed my eyes as I felt their hard fingers start poking between my ribs. I could smell acrid smoke coming off my shirt from the places they poked and prodded at me. A small hand the color of seawater reached out and clutched at my left arm. I felt nothing but cold, dead flesh at first...but then my own skin began to burn beneath that hand, and flakes of gray ash billowed out from between the child's fingers. I tore my arm free, glimpsing a series of burn marks along my flesh where the child's fingers had been. I could smell the acrid stink of scorched flesh in my nose.

My hands, shaking uncontrollably now, went through the motions, the *manipulations*, the children groping and touching, burning holes in my clothes and scorching my bare flesh, Dennis's high-pitched keening rising to a zenith behind me, until I lifted the top two cards to reveal the one I'd selected, completing the trick, *completing the trick—*

Calliope music suddenly burst through the silence. I turned back to the carousel and saw its rounding board suddenly aglow with tiny white lights. It began to rotate as the music played, fighting against the vines that kept it immobile. The vines went taut, and the sound of a metal gear being stripped rang out across the clearing. The vines were too strong for the carousel; they held fast against its desire to keep rotating. The horses went up a notch then ground to a standstill, too. The tiny white lights on the rounding board blinked and a few went out.

The children's hands withdrew from me, and the burning sensation fled with them. They were all staring at the carousel now. Mesmerized by it.

Dennis's hot breath against the side of my face: "*Take a bow.*"

My heart still galloping, my breath hissing from my throat, I took a bow.

The carousel lights blazed brighter. It started to rotate again, a few vines snapping, and then a few more, until the whole tangle of them ripped free from the ground.

I watched as a handful of children detached themselves from the others. The flames in their eye sockets had gone out, and they no longer appeared interested in coming after me. They wandered in a confused circle for a few seconds before filing in the direction of the carousel. It was fully rotating now, the music—discordant and minor-keyed, yet echoing loudly across the clearing—drawing the group of children closer. When they arrived, they climbed onto the carousel and groped their way onto the saddles of their wooden horses. The horses began cranking up and down along their pitted brass posts.

The Ferris wheel lit up next. The bars of light along each enormous spoke flashed an alternating red, white, red, white. Impossibly, the great wheel began to churn. I watched as the first gondola dug a trench through the earth, then broke free from its spindle.

The rollercoaster track shuddered up from the dirt, revealing a concentric series of loops and curves. The carts strung up in the trees fell onto the track and rolled until they arrived at a metal platform covered in odd purple flowers.

The dead children, who still surrounded us in a ring-around-the-rosie circle, backed up. As the dancing flames extinguished from each of their eye sockets, they retreated toward their respective carnival rides; a few others swayed on their feet, unsure of where to go or what to do.

I stood there, shaking. I had dropped the cards again—they lay scattered about the ground at my feet—and was caught in a trance, watching these dead children climb onto their rides as the carnival music played and that enormous Ferris wheel kept digging up the earth with each rotation.

Dennis stepped in front of me. He meticulously picked up each card, one at a time, stopping to blow bits of dirt off some of them. He filed them all back into a tidy stack, which he cradled in one immense hand. When he stood up again, I leaned momentarily against him until I felt some semblance of strength return to my deflated body.

"Jamie Warren does magic."

A hot tear burned down the side of my face.

"They will not hurt us now," Dennis said, watching the dead children on the rides.

"Okay," I managed, desperate to believe him.

"*He* will hurt us." And he pointed beyond the Ferris wheel, to where the opening of a cave stared back at us with all the gravitational pull of a black hole. It had surely been there all along, but somehow I had missed it.

There was a set of saloon-style doors over the cave entrance. In neon letters above the doors, a sign said:

HOUSE OF FEAR

Something small and luminously white cartwheeled along the ground. I saw it was another playing card—one that Dennis had missed—so I went to it and picked it up.

It was blank.

When I looked back up, Dennis was already passing through the double doors and into the cave.

CHAPTER TWENTY-FOUR

DESTINY

1

There was a figure sitting in a hole in the ground inside the cave. A small fire burned nearby; it was the only source of light. The figure was nothing but a shadow at first, but as Dennis and I drew closer, he transitioned into a familiar silhouette. I felt something grow cold and hard inside me at the sight of him. In a top hat and cloak, the Magician's silhouette suddenly reminded me less of a circus performer and more of the thing Dr. Jekyll turns into.

"The Brothers Warren," the Magician said, looking up at us. His voice was silken and seductive. His single eye shone in the firelight. "I sensed your arrival in this place and knew instantly that it was the two of you. It has been a long, long time."

I glanced around and saw that the interior of the cave was vast, its high, vaulted ceiling networked with a series of beams and rafters. There were blocks of hay stacked in precarious towers, the tops of which disappeared into the darkness among those rafters. There was also something else back there—something alive and crouched in hiding, watching us from some hidden warren in the darkness. I sensed it more than saw it.

"We're in the barn," I said.

"Good observation, Mr. Warren, though not precisely accurate." He stood up in his hole, sweeping his hat from his head and casting it into the darkness. "Things here only appear the way you perceive them. This is, of course, the well. The place you and your childhood friends were so desperate to see. You're here now, Brothers Warren, so tell me—*what do you think?*"

"You're...dead..." The words creaked out of me.

"For some, death is but a malleable state of being, Mr. Warren."

"Why did you bring us here?"

"That wasn't *me*." There was a hard edge to his voice. But my God, I *remembered* it—the way he *sounded*, the way he *spoke* to us back then. That charismatic hypnotist's lilt. "That was your...*Black Mouth*...intervening."

"Those children outside..."

"They, too, exist in a malleable state," the Magician said. "Irrevocably gone from your world, yes, but subsisting here now. With me."

"In hell," I said.

"In the *well*, Mr. Warren." And the son of a bitch affected a wide grin.

"Did you kill them all? Did you kill—"

"*I've killed no one.*" His voice shook the towers of hay and caused the fire to momentarily burn with an unnatural greenish hue. His face appeared to grow dark, as if storm clouds were building just behind the bulwark of his skull. Then he grinned again, chilling me to the core of my being. "I am merely a bystander. Those children out there did what they did of their own volition."

"No. Children don't do that. They don't *kill* like that."

The Magician chuckled. "Of all the people to make such a declaration," he said, then spoke no more.

"What are you?" I kept my voice firm, and rephrased it as a demand: "Tell me what you are."

The Magician's grin faltered. "That's a dark bit of business."

"You said that to me once before. I think it's time you come clean."

Something rippled beneath the surface of his face. It was subtle, but I caught it. I think Dennis did, too, because I sensed his big body stiffen beside me in the darkness. That face beneath a face. Behind him in the black, I sensed something shift about as if in discomfort.

"I died once, by accident, when I was a younger man," he said. "Lost an eye, suffered a failure of the heart. Quite tragic. Ultimately, I was brought back to the Land of the Living, but I assure you, Brothers Warren, that it wasn't due to the prowess of those in the medical profession.

"I do not remember dying. I remember the accident, of course, and then I remember waking up *here*. It did not look the same back then—in fact, it was just a dark void when I first arrived—but you must trust me when I say that *the place is the place is the place*.

"I wasn't alone when I got here," the Magician continued. "There was a...*thing*. An angel? A devil? I don't know. It sat in the middle of this void, right here in a hole in the ground." He pointed down to the hole he was now, himself, standing in. "This angel or devil or whatever it was, it had been waiting for me, or for someone *like* me. It asked me what was my trade, and I told it—*magic*. This seemed to please the creature.

"It then asked me if I preferred to stay dead, or if I wished to return to the Land of the Living. Well, the choice was obvious, wasn't it? I chose life. And this, too, seemed to please the creature."

I recalled Roger Kowalski's story about this very man, and how he'd come upon him one evening in his tent, sitting cross-legged in a hole in the ground. I thought, too, of all those countless drawings of black circles Dennis had given me while I was incarcerated in that institution all those years ago. There was some dark symmetry in all this, yet I could not work it out. A destiny unfolding...

"The creature reached into my side and removed a rib." The Magician's widening smile exceeded the confines of his face. "I believe you've even seen the scar, Mr. Warren."

"Yes," I told him, recalling that jagged serration that twisted along his pale flank. "That's your other dark business. I remember."

"The creature gave me my own rib and then gave me a *mission*. I was to become a collector of the young and the impressionable, and to keep them here, and use their life force to build this place. Their essence would keep the creature sated—fed, you might say, though not in the crude way you may think of it—and it would allow me to exist in perpetuity. But, see, there was one caveat," he added, chuckling again, and wagging a gloved finger at us. "I couldn't collect them *myself*. I couldn't actually *kill*, Brothers Warren. That was the catch. There were ceremonial rules to be followed, you see. Rules that have existed long before the creation of this world by... well, let's say a higher authority. The devil can only *tempt*, it cannot *act*. Therefore, to build this place, I had to rely only on the cold, callous brutality of mankind. Fortunately, there is so much of it. Even in *children*."

"That's bullshit," I said. "You're a predator, just like Clay said. A manipulator. You targeted innocent children and made them do terrible—"

"*Innocent children?*" And he laughed, a sound that rolled like thunder throughout the cave. "I think you have me figured out *inaccurately*, Mr. Warren! Innocent? Did you not hear the stipulation placed upon me? The caveat that I cannot do anything with my own hand? My only tool is temptation! I am limited in what I can do, from traveling from...shall we say, hole to hole? Cave to cave? The places where the underworld breaches the Land of the Living? A *thing* constantly moving, and searching out the juicy bits awaiting me. I am but a mere *parasite* clinging to the fauna of a particular event. I am no different than a man who watches a fire burn and settles down beside it to warm himself. I did not *cause* that fire, I am merely benefitting from its warmth.

"And since I've shed my mortal coil, my existence in your world takes the form of a mere whisper in the ear of the apprentice who cares to listen. That is all! You yourself have heard my whispers from the well from time to time, Mr. Warren. After all these years, our bond remains strong, doesn't it? Ah, but I'm waxing poetic!"

"Those children—"

"Were already ruined before I got to them," he said, curtly. "I saw them, *sensed* them. Stalked them? Call it what you like, but it was an *attraction* to their dark fates that drew me into their lives. Don't you see? They were *destined*, Mr. Warren, to take dark paths. Just like they all are. Just like *you*. I am only there to hasten the deal and feed off the bones…"

"The things you had us do—"

"Were *nothing*! You did not do *anything* at my behest! You set a forest fire out of anger and malice, and two people died. You went away to an institution because of your actions, and what do you do when you return to your…*Black Mouth*? You murder your *father*, Mr. Warren! Ha! Is that blame to be put on me, as well? When a shark attacks a seal, do you fault the small fish for picking at the bloody morsels? Use your head, Mr. Warren! Put things into perspective, sir! Everyone has *free will*. Everyone makes their own destiny."

I took a step back. I struggled to say something, but he had rendered me speechless.

"Let's examine *your* destiny, shall we, Mr. Warren? A life wasted in a fog of booze and drugs and suicidal tendencies. Failed relationships and failed careers. A coward at his core. A man who could have had all the power of heaven and hell at his fingertips, but decided to *walk away* instead."

"You're a liar." The words tumbled out of me even though I didn't think I had the strength to speak them.

"Your friends matured into confident, respectable, successful adults. I might argue that I'd even instilled in them some of those very attributes all those years ago. Would you be so cruel as to deny that of me?"

No, I couldn't deny him that. In fact, Clay had told me something eerily similar one night in the motel room: *Despite all his twisted games that summer, he actually gave me some confidence. Can you imagine that? Something good coming from a monster like him?*

I pressed the heels of my hands into my eyes, shook my head. Tried to clear the fog that had been building inside my skull. "You...you just tried to trick us...just like you've been...tricking kids for years... but you *failed*. You were *wrong* about us..."

"Was I, Mr. Warren? Was I wrong? You *did* send a brother to the well that night, did you not? You *did* take the life of your father. But let me be perfectly clear—*those things were all a part of your destiny*. They would have happened in some fashion or another whether I visited you that summer or not. I was just there to *feed* off the *bones*."

"Stop saying that!" I shook my head and took another step back. I looked down at my hands and saw how badly they were shaking. I looked over at Dennis, who seemed eerily calm.

"And here you've been blaming me all this time," he continued, "afraid of the thing you turned me into inside your own head. Making me into some kind of monster just so you could keep lying to yourself and avoid personal responsibility for your actions. *I* am not the monster, Mr. Warren. The monster is *you*."

I screamed, and the fire fanned out across the ground.

"But you don't have to do that to yourself anymore," he said. "As I recall, you wanted to come with me all those years ago. Am I correct in my recollection, Mr. Warren?"

I shook my head. But yes, he was correct, and he knew it.

"Well…it seems you're here with me now. I think our best course of action for this evening is to send Brother Dennis back home, to the Land of the Living, and I will allow you, Mr. Warren, to remain here with me, just as you wanted all those years ago."

I fell to my knees. Tears were filling up my eyes and my hands were starting to shake.

"My most excellent apprentice." He spread his arms wide. I watched a petal fall from the carnation in his lapel and seesaw lazily to the ground. "Look how your body trembles, how your mind is a jumble. How you sweat in your skin and stink perpetually of the bottle. My, what that world has done to you. How cruel people can be to themselves. How they *hurt* themselves. Stay here with me and you will *never…hurt…again…*"

And in that moment, that's exactly what I wanted.

He reached down and withdrew the bone-handled knife from his boot. The blade gleamed in the firelight, and I imagined I could see the countless flickering firefly eyes of the dead children in that cold black steel. As if our having freed them with card tricks had only been a temporary reprieve, and their souls were locked up forever in that blade.

He tossed it over to me, where it landed on the ground with a substantial thump.

The thing behind him in the dark made a sound like a motor.

"You know the truth, Mr. Warren. There comes a point when you've exceeded your welcome among the Land of the Living. I found myself there once, too. I gave my final performance, and then inserted that very blade that lies before you into my side. In that moment, Mr. Warren, I became a thing more powerful than some mortal man. I was *transcended.*"

I stared at the knife on the ground in front of me. The handle that

was clearly a rib. The blade that looked ancient and deadly and yet...
somehow empathetic to my plight. Warm as an embrace. I reached
for it—

"*Yessss*, Mr. Warren," the Magician hissed. "Pick up the *knife*, Mr.
Warren..."

He wasn't wrong. I had done this to myself. All my problems, all
my horrors. All the grief and the guilt. All the people I had alienated.
I had hurt *myself*. I had hurt *Dennis*.

Do you blame the small fish?

I reached out and wrapped my trembling fingers around the knife's
bone handle. It was warm as an organ to the touch.

"*Yessss*," the Magician hissed. His single eye became impossibly
wide. "*Right...into...your...belly...*"

Something fluttered through the air. I looked up and watched its
descent as it wafted lazily to the floor of the cave.

The two of hearts.

A second card twirled through the darkness. It landed on the
ground beside the other one. The joker.

I looked over and saw Dennis holding the deck of cards in one
hand. As I stared at him, he peeled a third card off the top of the deck.
He held it between his index and middle fingers. Then he flicked his
fingers, and the card spiraled through the air. It fluttered to the ground
about a foot away from where the Magician stood in his hole.

I didn't know what he was doing, but I remembered him doing this
exact same thing the night I picked him up from the police station in
Sutton's Quay. He'd been sitting in his cell, flicking cards through the
open cell door, and onto a circle that had been sketched in chalk on
the cement floor...

"Dennis Warren does magic tricks," Dennis said, and launched a
fourth card into the air.

This one went farther than the others, as if carried by an invisible current of wind. It was the six of clubs—I could see it clearly as it tumbled through the air—and it alighted on the right-hand cuff of the Magician's black jacket.

The card burst into a green flame. The flame faded quickly and cast a helix of pale smoke up into the air, leaving a residue of ash on the Magician's sleeve. The Magician brushed it away, then looked sourly at me. "Save your brother this indignity, Mr. Warren," he said, "and own your own destiny for once."

Another card spiraled down lazily, landing on the pointed toe of the Magician's black leather boot.

That green flame again…only this time it persisted, growing in potency as it burned. The Magician lifted his leg and shook his foot, dampening the fire. It finally went out, and a sprinkle of ash snowed to the ground.

When the Magician looked up again, I thought I caught a flicker of fear behind his eye.

I looked down once more at the knife in my hand.

"Do the right thing!" the Magician shouted at me now. The presence behind him twisted about in the dark. "Don't miss your chance again! You cannot afford another mistake! *Look at yourself!*"

Brandishing his bloody sword, the king of hearts—my destiny card—landed on the Magician's carnation. That green fire ignited the flower, and sent it sizzling like a firework. The Magician patted it out with one long-fingered, white-gloved hand, dampening it to smoke. There was a look of irritation on his face now.

"Enough," he growled at my brother.

The flame reignited, burning strong along the lapel of the Magician's tuxedo jacket. He patted at it again, but this time he only fanned the flames. That green fire raced up to his shoulder and burned down along his left arm. He cried out, swatting at it, patting frantically. In his panic, he fell out of his hole and struck the ground. Instead of dampening the flames, the fall sent a fireball roiling toward the ceiling of the cave.

The Magician scrambled to his feet. He stripped out of the burning jacket and tossed it to the ground, where it smoldered in the dirt.

Another card was twirling in the air. Two cards. *Many* cards. Dennis was whipping the whole deck at him now, and each one that landed on the Magician exploded in a spark of green fire. His shirt began to burn, his drooping red suspenders, the hems of his frayed black pants. He kept slapping at the flames with his white gloves until they, too, caught ablaze, and then he began shaking his hands and screaming.

"*Do it!*" the Magician shrieked at me as those green flames crawled up the sides of his face. He was retreating as he screamed, back toward his hole, like something hideous about to escape down a drain. "*Run that blade into your belly! Run that blade into your—*"

I lunged forward and planted the blade of the knife into the Magician's chest. As I did so, he gripped me about the shoulders with hands that were on fire, and I started screaming right along with him.

A tracer of green flame ran up the side of his face. The strap on the eye patch burned, and then the eye patch itself was on fire. The Magician released me, and I staggered back, gagging on the smell of him as he burned. He dropped to his knees in the hole in the ground and pawed at his face with hands that were ablaze. The eye patch fell away, and I saw something impossible in that eye socket—a swirling galaxy of planets and stars, of light shooting out in all directions, of vast, endless seas filled with all manner of hungry, terrible things, of—

(an angel or demon crouching in the dark)

The scream that erupted from him as he burned was Sarah Patchin's scream, was Milo Patchin's scream. I'd listened to those screams for over twenty years, every time I closed my eyes. They were here now, with me, and I kept screaming right along with them.

The Magician lunged for me, grabbing me about the ankle with one fiery hand. He was still impossibly strong, and he was pulling me now toward him, into that hole with him, while his face continued to ripple and shift and melt and *change* beneath the fire.

Then Dennis was there, a big shape behind the wall of smoke and green flame rising off the Magician. He came up behind the Magician and wrapped him up in one of his big Dennis Warren bear hugs. The Magician's fingers were stripped away from my ankle, and I quickly scurried back on my hands and feet until I struck the far wall of the cave. Pain resonated up my right arm, and I held it against my chest.

Dennis wrenched the Magician off the ground, squeezing him in his steely arms. A moment after that, and they were both engulfed in flames.

"*Dennis!*"

I rushed at them, not thinking, just wanting to *get there*, then falling flat on my face. I looked up and saw the fire intensify to the point that it looked like they both might explode—

—and then the flames faded, leaving nothing but a column of black smoke twirling toward the ceiling of the cave.

Dennis stood beyond the smoke, smudged with ash and glistening with perspiration, but seemingly otherwise unhurt. He had that faraway look in his eyes, which told me he'd retreated inside his turtle shell. As I stared at him, he lowered himself to the dirt, keeled over on his side, and drew his legs up to his chest.

The hole in the ground where the Magician had been sitting when we'd first come in here was between Dennis and me. I crawled over to it and peered down. The bone-handled knife was in there, lying on a dingy heap of green, foul-smelling ash. It was all that was left of the Magician.

I got up and went over to my brother. I shook him gently, repeating his name over and over again, just like I had always done when we were kids. It was how I'd always got him to come out of his turtle shell.

He didn't come out of it this time.

Whatever was back there in the darkness crept closer; once more, I sensed rather than saw it. The idea of whatever it might be caused my throat to tighten.

I heard a sound like sand spilling in an hourglass, followed by a *whomp!* that made my ears pop. I looked over at the hole in the ground in time to see the bottom of it collapse. The ashes fell away with a barely audible hiss. I reached out for the bone-handled knife, but I was too late; I watched it tumble down into that pit of sudden darkness.

An icy air emanated from the opening. It wasn't a wind or even a breeze—in fact, there was something terribly stagnant and motionless about it—but I could still feel its chill running up and down my sweaty arms and across my face.

I peered over the side of the hole, expecting to see another smaller tunnel having opened up, but that's not exactly what I saw. A hole is still *something*; what I saw when I looked down was the *absence* of everything—a solitary black eye of nothingness through which that icy air radiated. I scooted back, thinking I had gone too close to the hole in the ground, when in actuality the *hole* had come too close to *me*: It was widening, and taking pieces of this world with it.

Suddenly, there was a loud, drawn-out moaning sound from above. I looked up and dirt fell into my eyes, stinging them. A second later, a beam came crashing down from the ceiling of the cave; it planted itself like a javelin into the dirt, then tipped over and struck the cave wall. More dirt fell from above, along with rocks the size of softballs.

The thing in the darkness inched closer still…

I pressed the side of my face against my brother's. His skin was furnace hot and I could feel his heartbeat vibrating through the bones of his skull. In his ear, very calmly, I repeated his name over and over again until his slate-colored eyes slid over to meet my own.

"We have to leave now, Dennis," I whispered, glancing at the hole in the ground that was growing wider, wider.

This world was coming apart at the seams.

2

I thought we'd be safe now outside, but I was wrong. As we burst out of the cave, I heard what sounded like some prehistoric roar. I looked across the clearing and realized it was the sound of the iron girders of the Ferris wheel giving way.

The children were no longer on the rides; they stood now in the clearing, confused and lost. Their wounds were no longer visible, and their eyes looked normal. But they were still clearly whatever remained when souls got trapped in this place.

The carousel slowed to a stop, the calliope music winding down. It began sinking deeper into the soil. The other rides were crumbling apart and being sucked down into the earth, too. Massive craters—

(circles holes circles)

—appeared along the ground, where the earth surrendered and opened up.

"Come on!" I shouted, tugging at my brother's hand.

We hurried beneath the sign that arched over the clearing, the heavy steel letters dropping like mortars all around us. Trees were coming down, too, from every direction. We climbed over a fallen redwood only to find the massive purple hippo dead on the other side, its spine crushed by a fallen tree trunk, a bloody froth bubbling from its gaping maw.

I didn't see the entrance to the mineshaft at first, but then I saw the tapestry of vines that had covered it. The strange flowers had dried up and the vines themselves had turned brown and brittle. I let go of Dennis's hand and began tearing those dead vines out of the way.

Just as I finished, I felt a peculiar sensation creeping up my spine. I turned and saw the earth behind me tumbling away into a bottomless black void. The sight of it caused a scream to rupture up my throat.

When I turned back around to the mineshaft, I saw the children, all of them, standing around Dennis, staring up at me.

"Go!" I shouted at them, pointing to the mineshaft. "Hurry! Get out! All of you!"

They ran into the shaft, so many of them that my heart broke. Their sneakers sounded like war drums as they trampled the ground.

When they were gone, I shoved Dennis toward the opening of the shaft. He went forward with a dreamy stumble, that distant look still on his face.

"*Move, Dennis!*"

I pushed him hard, and he staggered into the mineshaft.

I went last, and even though I knew it wasn't a smart thing to do, I paused and looked back out over my shoulder at what was becoming of the well.

The trees and the sky and the land was gone, having been replaced by a deep and unfathomable *nothingness*. A void, though not empty, for the last thing I saw before turning and running back down that mineshaft was a creature in the middle of that void sitting in a hole.

3

I crawled up out of the hole first, then reached down to help Dennis out. He just gazed dully up at me, not fully there.

Something crashed to the ground behind me. I looked over my shoulder and saw that one of the beams in the barn's ceiling had fallen. An unsettling *reeeeeek* sound, and I actually *felt* the barn begin to pitch to one side. It was going to come down on our heads if we didn't get the hell out of there.

"Dennis!" I shouted at him, thrusting my hand down the hole in his direction. "Take my hand and climb up!"

That blank stare...

I closed my eyes, took a breath, and in a calm voice, said, "Dennis. Dennis. Dennis. Dennis. Dennis," while pieces of the barn crashed and exploded all around me.

Dennis blinked his eyes. He wiped sweaty grime from his forehead...then smiled up at me.

"Come on, buddy," I told him, still holding out my hand.

He gripped my hand, then crawled out of the hole in the ground while I pulled at him with both hands wrapped around his large one.

"Jamie Warren is ho—"

The rear section of the tin ceiling buckled, broke through the joists, then began sliding toward the earth. The sound was like a jet flying too low to the ground.

I shouted for Dennis to run, and he obliged, chugging along at my heels until we burst through the barn doors. We didn't stop until we were halfway across the field, and the sound of an earthquake, a tornado, a tsunami caused us both to whirl around.

Standing before a roiling cloud of dust, Dennis and I watched the barn crumble into the earth. The shockwave from its collapse blasted right through me, whipping the sweaty hair off my forehead and injuring something less tangible that was buried deep inside me. The ground upon which it sat bellied downward, creating a giant sucking crater. It pulled down most of the barn, some nearby trees, and a portion of the alfalfa field with it.

Dennis and I watched as it all sank into the ground, where, for all I know, my father's blood continues to seep to this day…

Down the unforgiving throat of Black Mouth.

CHAPTER TWENTY-FIVE

AFTERMATH

1

Clay Willis was recovering in a private room at the Braxton County Memorial Hospital in Gassaway. He'd been there for the better part of a week, where he had drifted in and out of consciousness and undergone a series of surgeries. He'd suffered injuries to his stomach, liver, left lung, and abdominal muscles, and he'd lost a lot of blood. It was touch and go when the paramedics arrived at the motel, but now, days after the event, Clay was mostly out of the woods. Yet while the injuries themselves were no longer life-threatening, doctors were closely monitoring him for any signs of infection.

Mia hadn't left Clay's side since the incident. She'd ridden with him in the back of the ambulance that night, and had spent the past few days camping out in a chair at Clay's bedside. The hospital was ordinarily strict about their visiting hours, but given the circumstances, none of the nurses working that ward wanted to rouse the sleeping woman from her chair and tell her to go home for the night. So Mia had stayed.

She looked hung out to dry when Dennis and I met her in the hospital cafeteria near the end of the week. We'd spoken previously on the phone, so I knew what had happened to them, and what Clay's status was day to day. (I would have gone sooner, but I'd suffered a setback of my own after the events at the farmhouse, to include another seizure brought on by acute alcohol withdrawal, and had been admitted to a separate hospital across town for forty-eight-hour observation. The hospital staff monitored me for signs of delirium tremens—irregular heartbeat, elevated blood pressure, tremors, disorientation. When one of the nurses asked me if I felt I was suffering from hallucinations, my shrill, humorless cackle did little to set her mind at ease. Prior to my discharge, a doctor came and checked my blood pressure one last time. "Keep this up and you'll be dead by forty," he told me, then he looked over to where Dennis slept soundly in a chair with a stuffed rabbit tucked under one arm.)

Mia and I embraced. She was careful of my right arm, which was currently in a sling. I'd broken my elbow, most likely the night I fell down the stairs at the farmhouse. Come to think of it, I probably looked no less worn out than she did. Less explicable were the strange burns running up and down my arm, burns in the distinct shape of small fingers. If Mia noticed them, she had the good sense not to say anything.

She hugged Dennis, too, as he stood there swaying on his feet with his head cocked to one side, his eyes foggy. He didn't even bring up his arms to hug her back, he was so exhausted. Much like Mia had hunkered down at Clay's bedside, Dennis had done similarly with me during my own hospital stay, though only because he had nowhere else to go and couldn't be left alone. Still, there had been at least one moment when I'd jolted shrieking from a nightmare in that hospital bed, only to find my brother right beside me, clutching my trembling hand in both of his.

I set Dennis up with a bowl of Froot Loops at one end of a long table, then grabbed a couple of coffees for Mia and me. We sat far enough away from Dennis to keep him out of earshot, though given his current state, I didn't think it mattered.

"Doctors said he should be out of surgery within the hour," Mia said. She cradled her paper coffee cup in both hands, as if to divine some strength from it. Lowering her voice, she said, "He's here, too, you know."

I knew whom she meant. Wayne Lee Stull. He'd also survived that night at the motel, though his condition was much more dire than Clay's.

"He's in a coma," Mia said. Much like Dennis, her eyes had grown distant, and I wondered if she kept reliving that night in the motel room, a video clip on a never-ending, repeating loop. "Nurses tell me there's likely some severe brain trauma, though they won't know the extent until he wakes up. If he *ever* wakes up."

"I'm sorry," I told her, then immediately wondered if there existed a less useful phrase in the whole of the English language.

"Police found latex masks in his briefcase, and he'd even worn an eye patch when he attacked Clay. I knew something was off with that guy when Clay and I met him at that restaurant. I mean, his whole demeanor was off, but he said something that night that bothered me, only it didn't click until later. He said that the Magician had killed his brother, but—"

"But the Magician doesn't kill," I finished for her.

"That's right." She nodded her head. "Bound by ceremony, just like Roger Kowalski told us. Whatever that means."

I thought I knew what it meant, or at least grazed the surface of knowing, but I wasn't prepared to go there. Not just yet. "So what do the police think?" I asked instead.

"Well, they're not saying much at this point, but I'll bet it's the same thing *I* think. That he and his twin brother *did* come across the Magician when they were kids, but that it was Stull who killed his brother, not the Magician. Only he never got caught. And what happens to somebody who does something like that and never gets caught? Someone who could kill their own brother in the first place? I mean, who knows what else he's been doing for all these years?"

I glanced over at Dennis and watched him shovel a spoonful of Froot Loops into his mouth.

"There's a detective from Sutton's Quay who's been checking in here every afternoon, asking about Clay and making sure I'm all right, and he's been feeding me tidbits I guess I wouldn't ordinarily be privy to. Nice guy. Big black mustache."

"Detective Aiello," I said.

She looked surprised. "You know him?"

"He's the cop who found my brother walking up the highway after Mom died."

"Something else that'll probably make the news in a day or so," she said, lowering her voice further, even though we were currently the only people in the cafeteria, aside from Dennis. "Last week, a woman was beaten to death outside a bar in Indiana, about forty-five minutes from Stull's house in Evansville. Stull's fingerprints were found on one of the woman's shoes. Not to mention police found a piece of rock or something in the trunk of his car, wrapped in a plastic bag and covered in blood. Most likely the murder weapon."

"Jesus Christ. What is...*who* is this guy...?" But I thought I knew that, too. *My existence in your world takes the form of a mere whisper in the ear of the apprentice who cares to listen.* I absently touched one of the burn marks along my arm.

"I don't know for sure," Mia said, "but he might just turn out to be the guy I photographed at that carnival in Lexington. The same guy Molly Broome described to Clay. Our Magician's replacement, you might say." She sighed, and sounded instantly tired. "It's all just speculation right now, but those masks he made, they look very much like the Magician's face. I've seen photos. Add in the eye patch? It's frightening, man. He even used a knife with a bone handle on Clay.

Just like he'd given Molly to use on Charlotte Brown. That detective told me the police are looking into it, and that they've also been in touch with Ashida Rowe to connect some of the dots. There's still a lot they don't know about the guy, but it sounds plausible. I mean, what other answer is there? The *real* Magician is dead. Is it so hard to believe this guy Stull lost his mind and just took over for him? Wears his face, his eye patch? Uses his knife? The perfect apprentice."

I thought about this in the context of what had happened back at Black Mouth. Or what I *thought* had happened. Only days later, and even with those burn marks on my arms, I was already questioning all Dennis and I had supposedly gone through. It didn't help that I'd spent the next couple of days after that ordeal hallucinating in a hospital bed while doing the Detox Boogie. Now, sitting here across from Mia beneath the stark white tract lighting of the hospital cafeteria, I wasn't sure what had happened. I wasn't sure what I believed. The human mind has a talent for misdirection.

I must have had a certain look in my eye, because she asked me what happened when Dennis and I went back home that night.

If I say it out loud, she's going to think I'm a crazy drunk. That I hallucinated the whole thing. That I've got nothing but poison in my DNA. And even if she doesn't think that about me, I'm afraid that I'll think that about myself…

"Nothing," I told her. "Nothing happened. You were right. Those ghosts were all in my head."

Smiling, she reached across the table and squeezed my hand.

2

We got to see Clay after his surgery. He was still woozy from the anesthesia, so we only peered in at him through the window of his recovery room at first. Tubes hooked up to his face and limbs, machinery beeping and blinking all around him. This was his fourth surgery in so many days, and he'd come out of it like a champ. The surgeon, who looked like a young Elliott Gould, assured us Clay would be fine.

Propped up on a mound of pillows, Clay repositioned his head when he noticed the three of us staring at him through the glass partition of his recovery room. He smiled. Then he raised one hand—there was a heart monitor clipped to his index finger—and beckoned to us.

We filed quietly into the room and gathered around his bed. When he spoke, his voice was weak and raspy. "Boy, I hope I don't look as awful as you three…"

I couldn't help it—I laughed. Tears spilled down my face, and I kept laughing. Clay smiled warmly at me, and I could see his sleepy brown eyes filling up, too. This man, who had traded in long-sleeved shirts for ugly Hawaiian ones, and who had cast off that grubby trucker's hat, now lost to the sands of time.

I turned and looked at Mia, who was smiling down at Clay, and my God, Mia, she was a kid again for a moment, right there in front of my eyes. I could see her with her hair pulled back in that severe ponytail, the sweat shining in tiny droplets along the delicate curve of an ear, the macaroni necklace that left blue paint stains on her oversized white undershirts. The first girl I'd ever loved.

She opened her mouth to say something, but Clay gently shushed her. "Just let me look at you guys awhile longer," he said, and he extended his white hands toward us. Mia took one, I took the other, and then she and I both took up Dennis's hands. We formed a circle that way. A wheel of destiny.

Because friendship, too, is a certain kind of magic.

3

Before Dennis and I left for Ohio, I drove us back to the farmhouse. I told Dennis it was so he could pack some of his clothes and things, and that was partially true, but in reality it was because I wanted to see what the place looked like. I wanted to see if that barn was a heap of boards and tin, or if I'd find it still standing on the edge of the field.

It was a gray afternoon, with a barricade of storm clouds hanging over Black Mouth. As I pulled the car up the driveway, I found I wasn't sure what I would prefer to find there—the barn still standing, or the barn reduced to a pile of rubble in a sinkhole. One would mean I was crazy, the other would mean something darkly unfathomable.

The barn was not standing. Pieces of it poked from the earth, like the site of an explosion, and there was a perceptible sloping of the ground surrounding where it had once stood. I was surprised to find myself relieved at the sight of it.

I parked in front of the house. Before shutting off the engine, I turned to Dennis, who was leaning out the open passenger window and staring at the place where the barn had once stood.

"That really happened, didn't it?" I asked him.

He said nothing, but he *did* glance down at the burn marks on my arms. He had similar marks on his.

"At least he's dead now," I said, and shut down the engine.

"No," said Dennis. His voice was quiet. He drew his big head back in through the window, his dark hair a wild mop, and looked at me. There was a clarity in his eyes that I'd never seen before. "He is not dead. He is just trapped."

"Trapped where?" I said, feeling my skin begin to prickle.

"In my turtle shell," said Dennis.

4

The house was different now. The oppressive heat was gone, and there was a hopeful quality to the daylight that hung in all the windows. As Dennis pounded up the stairs to pack some of his things, I wandered from room to room, sensing the emptiness of the place. The unused mustiness of it all. I listened for the *thhhk-thhhk* sound of baby Milo, the soft whisper of his mother's feet along the hardwood floors. But there was nothing left for me to hear. The house was just a house now. Mother and child, I knew, had finally gone off to someplace better.

Is Black Mouth the hero of this story? I wondered. *Did it draw us all back here under the guise of fate? Was it pulling the strings all along? Did it use the Magician's own black magic to suit its own purposes?*

Upstairs, as Dennis rummaged through his dresser drawers, I eased open the door to the master bedroom. There was the stripped bed, the dusty footprints on the floor, the curtains drawn over the windows. I called out to each of my parents, then held my breath as I waited for a response. But the only sound I heard was the metronomic ticking of my own heartbeat.

Now that the monster has been vanquished, has Black Mouth gone back to sleep? Has it finally put those old ghosts to rest? Is that what this all comes down to?

There came a loud thump from across the hall.

"Dennis?"

No answer from him, so I crossed the hall to see what had happened.

Dennis was lying on the floor of our childhood bedroom, clutching at his chest and rocking back and forth. I rushed to his side, my hands swimming frantically in the air above him, confused and terrified, unsure what I should do. I saw the aggrieved, constricted look on his face, his seawater eyes squeezed shut in pain, his small, square teeth clenched tight. A dim whistle escaped his throat.

I cradled his head in my hands and didn't know what to do. *Heart attack*, my rational mind concluded, but I found I couldn't reconcile what that actually meant in the real world. *What does that mean?*

"Dennis! Dennis! Dennis! Dennis!"

My tears fell on his forehead.

Then he went still, and his eyes went wide. Not unfocused, though, but trained on me, as if seeing me—*seeing* me—for one last time. His fingers closed around one of my wrists. There was little strength left in him. He opened his mouth, his tongue working.

"*He.* Is now. Dead," Dennis said.

And then my brother was gone.

A GRAND AND UNSPEAKABLE MAJESTY

1

A social worker once recommended I write down my thoughts in a notebook as a way of coping with the events of my past. At the time, I wasn't ready. More recently, another social worker, Clay Willis, suggested I do the same thing, although for a slightly different reason. Not just to cope with the events of my past, but as a way to move forward, clearheaded and sober. A rope to climb out of the hole. This time, I followed the advice.

Sometimes, parts of this story come out on the page. It's an exorcism of sorts, I suppose. A climb up the rope, with one hand steadily gripping over the other, until my progress—slow as it may be—becomes discernible. Other times, I find I'm only able to write one damnable sentence—

I have done terrible things

—before I set down my pen and quake in my chair. On more than one occasion, I have filled an entire page with only three words, forever repeating, like an echo lost in space: *one more minute, one more minute, one more minute...*

Because it never really stops, does it? You can never strip away past trauma, you can only learn to live with it and move past it. Alcoholism works the same way: Once you're an alcoholic, you're *always* an alcoholic. You can't strip it away. You learn to live with it and move past it. Or you don't, and you fall deeper into that black mouth until it swallows you up.

It's been one year since Dennis's death. His ashes sit in an urn on my bookshelf, in my shitty apartment in downtown Akron. I've got Dennis's red bandana with the eye holes cut into it, which I've tied around the urn. It makes me think of the Ninja Turtles every time I see it. It makes me think of Dennis, too.

It would be nice to say that I've been straight and sober for the past year, and that Dennis's death made me connect with a strength inside myself that has kept me on a path of sobriety ever since that day. But that's not the truth. There's an old AA saying that goes *There is no magic in recovery, only miracles*, and do you know what? That's pretty much the truth of it. No magic. Just miracles.

The *truth* is that sobriety is a magic *trick*. It's full of mystery and misdirection. It comes easy to some and remains elusive to others. There are those who perfect it, and those who will forever fumble the cards. The secret of the trick is to *acknowledge* it's a trick, to not be fooled by the sleight of hand, and to take it all in due course. Moment to moment, day by day, just like that dude at the foundry used to say—*one more minute, one more minute, one more minute*. Staying sober is no different than practicing those old card tricks all those years ago. I got pretty good back then, but I still fumbled from time to time. So, yeah, I've fallen off the wagon twice since Dennis's death, but each time, I get back up, dust myself off, and steady my hands for the next trick.

My friends are there to help me. Emily Pearson and George Epperson are available if I need to throw out a lifeline, and they know I'm available for them, too. The three of us have dinner together once a week. George isn't as stern as he sounded that one night on the phone, and he's got some pretty funny proctology stories (believe it or not). Emily got me a job in the mailroom at the accounting firm where she works. It's a mundane job, but I'm grateful to have it. And for the past year, I've managed to keep it.

And then there's Mia and Clay, of course. Always just a phone call away. And sometimes, even closer than that…

It's time, I tell myself, and I take the urn down from the shelf.

2

As of this moment, Wayne Lee Stull is still in a coma. He's not expected to recover—to return to the Land of the Living, I could say—but there are legal reasons why the state of West Virginia keeps him alive and hooked up to machines. Primarily, it's because law enforcement is champing at the bit to interrogate him regarding some terrible things that have come to light. There are a handful of homicides they've connected him to—the woman beaten to death outside that tavern near Evansville for one, but also a couple of prostitutes from Indianapolis and Bloomington. Police have also reopened his brother's cold case murder investigation.

A little over a week after the events of that night in the motel room, police were dispatched to Stull's childhood home, which was the farmhouse on Slaughterhouse Row. I cannot say what they expected to find when they got there; what I *can* say is that they walked into a nightmare. What looked like human faces hung from clotheslines throughout the house, hundreds of them. Most of them were made out of latex, each one a slight variation on the Magician's face, as if to suggest Stull had attempted to get the man's face down perfectly over the years from memory. A few of the others were actual *faces*. People he'd killed and skinned and left to dry like flaking brown cuts of jerky.

In the basement, police found the withered remains of a human corpse. The body had been dismembered, and many of its bones were missing. My understanding, based on the minimal information I've procured from Mia (who got *her* information from Detective Aiello), was that strips of brittle flesh, delicate as ancient parchment, were folded like laundry in an old metal washtub. Mason jars filled with formaldehyde stood on a shelf above an old washer and dryer, the peeling remnants of a face in one jar, fingers in another, female genitals and reproductive organs in yet another. The remains were ultimately identified as belonging to Shirley Stull, Wayne Lee Stull's mother. A medical examiner reckoned that she'd been dead for years, and wouldn't estimate a specific timeframe. At first, there was a question about what had happened to her bones, but then police uncovered a cache of hunting knives, each one with an authentic bone handle, in one of the back bedrooms of that farmhouse, and that question was quickly put to rest.

Ashida Rowe subpoenaed Stull's time and attendance records from Halcyon Elder Care, where he'd worked, and found that Stull had taken leave during the time the Happy Horace Carnival was traveling through Kentucky. This wasn't proof that Stull was *in* Kentucky, of course, but it added another layer to the onion. When Ashida asked Stull's former supervisor if he could tell her anything particularly unusual about Stull, the man said he believed Stull had gone to his house one afternoon and blinded his dog. Since that day, Ashida Rowe has begun the arduous task of comparing Stull's time and attendance records to the murders of any children that may have happened while the Happy Horace Carnival was in town. To date, I've learned of no additional connections, but Ashida Rowe continues the search.

The mere possibility of Stull's involvement in Charlotte Brown's murder was enough to save Molly Broome from a life in prison. The prosecution offered Molly a plea deal, and Ashida Rowe took it. Molly was sentenced to three years of incarceration in a juvenile facility for the murder of her best friend. If that seems like a light sentence for her crime, I'm here to say with no uncertainty that she'll carry the guilt around with her for the rest of her life. In that regard, she was doomed to a life sentence from the very beginning.

Mia is gathering all this information for a documentary she wants to produce about the Magician and his deranged protégé. It'll focus on what happened to the four of us as children, and then what happened to us last year, as the four of us reunited and began our search for the one-eyed man. It's my understanding that she's been given a lot of information from Detective Aiello (under the table, as they say). When she told me about all this on the phone, I suspected she was testing to see if I'd have some issue with it. But I just wished her luck. She's promised me anonymity, which is pretty much all I could ever ask for at this point in my life. In more ways than one.

Clay has been working closely with Ashida Rowe, studying cases where children have been incarcerated for similar crimes. In a sense, it's what he's always done. But when I talk to him now, there is a renewed fire in him. Like Mia, he's also been digging doggedly through Stull's history, trying to find irrefutable proof of Stull's connection to Charlotte Brown's murder, as well as any number of other murders where a man with an eye patch has been mentioned. Like Mia, he believes that Stull was the real-life monster who'd lost his mind and ultimately took over doing what the Magician had begun. An apprentice, but also just a man. Just a person doing terrible things. Nothing supernatural about that. Nothing magical.

I've had a year to reflect on what happened to Dennis and me that night in Black Mouth, and to consider what I believe. Was it all an hallucination? Some misfiring in my brain as I went through the early gyrations of the Detox Boogie? As the burns on my flesh healed, I found it easier to distance myself and to pretend that maybe none of that had happened. It was saner that way, wasn't it? Or was I just fooling myself? Had we actually traveled to the well where the Magician, even in death, still pulled at the strings and manipulated his most heinous apprentice to kill for him? Had it been a dream, or had we truly defeated the Magician with our unique brand of brotherly magic?

To this day, I'm not sure what's true or not. But I will say this—if it *did* happen, then the one thing that still terrifies me is the memory of what I saw just before Dennis and I fled back through that mineshaft and returned to the Land of the Living: a *thing* with many faces— faces upon faces beneath faces—and a singular gaping mouth in which flickered an entire distant universe. Floating in a void, sitting in a hole, waiting patiently for its next apprentice...

3

A house like a blood clot. I stare at it from my car, which is parked a distance away on the main road. There is a noticeable concavity to the field behind the house, and in the place where the barn once stood. Mom's Econoline van is gone, having either been towed away by some local entrepreneur, or sunken so low into the earth that it is no longer visible.

Black Mouth is slowly reclaiming it all.

I wait awhile. Dennis's urn sits on the passenger seat beside me, braced behind the seatbelt. The red bandana is still tied around it.

When two other vehicles arrive, I unbuckle the belt and take the urn with me as I get out of the car.

Clay is standing beside his Toyota, shielding his eyes from the sun with one hand as he watches me approach. It's late summer, hot as hell, and he's wearing one of his awful Hawaiian shirts. He's leaning on a cane, something that's necessary after all he's been through. He won't need it forever—that's what the doctors tell him—but he needs it now. The sight of him makes me smile, laugh a little, shake my head. But it does my heart good that he's here for this.

Mia comes up behind him, and the first thing I notice is she's grown her hair out and has it pulled back in a tight ponytail. She's got on a plain white T-shirt, too—what looks like a man's undershirt— and she's wearing a macaroni necklace. The macaroni is painted blue, and while it seems like an impossibility, I'm suddenly certain it's the same one Dennis gave to her on her eleventh birthday.

Anyone driving by the farmhouse at that moment would see three adults standing on the shoulder of the road, locked in an embrace. But no one ever drives out here anymore. This place is now as desolate as the dark side of the moon. Ours was the last farmhouse standing, and now that it's empty, Black Mouth has become all but forgotten by those who live in Sutton's Quay. Perhaps it's best that way.

Together, we cross the property. We go slow so that Clay, with his cane, can keep up...but also because it's all too much for me to come upon all at once. I feel like a different person coming here now. Mostly, that's a good thing. But it also means I'm greeted as a stranger, which makes me feel funny somehow.

I slow down even more as we draw closer to the old farmhouse. Habit has me searching the windows for ghosts as something tightens inside my chest. I think of my father, swallowed up by the black mouth of alcoholism, and the monster he ultimately became because of it. Even now, the weight of him is huge. It brings me to my knees, right there in front of the farmhouse. It's a thing I know I'll never escape. Yet Mia and Clay are there to help me rise again.

"I'm okay," I tell them, and in that moment, I believe it. Or at least I try to.

We carry Dennis's ashes down into Black Mouth. We take our time, because it's a steep descent, and Clay's got that cane. But we also take our time because we're in awe of what we find. We expect a pit of ash, but to our surprise, we see small trees and tiny shrubs have started to grow. There are furtive patches of greenery wreathed around the rim of the great crater, and flowers bloom in the culverts that crisscross down to the heart of the Mouth. Bees strum through the air and there is a smell of *life* down here once again. Things *thrive*. The sight brings me pause, and for a moment, I'm unable to move. Both Mia and Clay appear awestruck, as well.

The memory of our younger selves still haunts this place. We can all feel it. As we go deeper, Mia runs a hand along the branches of a sapling, quietly chanting, "Touch the Wicker Witch tree, touch the Wicker Witch tree," and I catch Clay more than once reaching for the brim of a trucker's hat he no longer wears.

Are you down here, Sarah Patchin? Are you down here, baby Milo? Do you still haunt this dank and empty chamber?

Had they ever?

I look around, thinking, *You are the hero of this story.* And I let the world around me define what that means.

When we arrive at the mouth of the old mineshaft, I'm accosted by a conflicting tumult of emotion. There's magic here, all right, but I don't sense that it's dark magic. I don't sense anything that characterizes it in any way at all, in fact—only that it hums faintly below the surface like a ley line. Duller than it was in my youth, but still here, no doubt about it. And I'm surprised to find that this knowledge carries with it a strange kind of comfort for me now.

"Do you feel it?" Mia is looking up and around, too. Her black eyes sparkle and there is white ash from the ground caught in her eyelashes and in her ponytail. She doesn't need to explain it; we can *all* feel it.

I open Dennis's urn, and shake his ashes out into the wind. They swirl and almost seem to shimmer as they travel throughout the heart of Black Mouth. The three of us stand there, watching the display, lost in our own personal silence. And for one fleetingly brief moment, Dennis is right here with me—with all of us—and I can sense not only his consciousness, but the snippets of consciousness he collected like breadcrumbs from everyone he ever met. In that moment, I'm in Mia's head as she speaks to a girl behind the back alley of a theater in Van Nuys; I'm in Clay's head as he talks with Molly Broome; I even catch glimpses of the living nightmare that was Wayne Lee Stull as he goes about his dark deeds. I look at my friends and see that they've glimpsed these things as well; most specifically is the look on Mia's face that suggests she *sees* what Dennis and I accomplished down in the well, and she appears instantly heartbroken, terrified, and proud all at once. I look to Clay and see that he senses it, too; he is weeping silently and smiling at me as he braces himself against the headstock of his cane. *All of this, coming out of Dennis's turtle shell...*

But then those breadcrumbs scatter and float off into the air, and I'm left wondering if I just imagined it all.

Before we leave, Mia drapes her macaroni necklace around a branch of the Wicker Witch sapling. She smiles at me, touches my arm. I can't tell if it's pain I'm seeing in her eyes now, or just the residue of a lifetime of healing. Clay puts his arm around her waist, and she does the same for him, helping him walk toward the crest of the wooded hillside. He glances over his shoulder, catches me staring, and nods his head, as if to let me know he's proud of me.

I'm the last to leave Black Mouth that day. Before I do, I pause to take in the soft moan of the wind through the underground tunnels, the flurry of ash as it blows across the ground, the grand and unspeakable majesty in the air all around me. I'm no longer listening for the suckling sound of an infant; no longer holding my breath for the whisper of feet through the loam. It's just me, hoping one last time to hear his voice, and all the magic that it held...

Jamie Warren is home.

Substance Abuse and Mental Health Services
Administration's National Helpline US:
1-800-662-HELP (4357)

FRANK (National Drugs Helpline UK):
0300 123 6600

ACKNOWLEDGEMENTS

I keep getting myself into this mess. Here are some of the people who helped me get out: my wife, my dad, Kevin Kangas, Greg F. Gifune and Tyre Lewis.

Sophie Robinson, Katharine Carroll, Sarah Mather, Steve Gove, Julia Lloyd, Hayley Shepherd, Fenton Coulthurst and anyone else toiling away within the spirit of the glorious creature that is Titan Books—thank you!

Cameron McClure, Katie Shea Boutillier and Matt Snow are the agents extraordinaire. Tireless, they are.

Joe Hempel and the good folks at Tantor—thanks for getting in people's heads.

Lastly, thanks to my family—particularly my wife (who bears a repeat mention) and my kids—for being a part of this story, and all the others, even if they don't realize it.

RONALD MALFI
January 29, 2022
Annapolis, Maryland

Ronald Malfi is the award-winning author of several horror novels, including the bestseller *Come with Me*, published by Titan Books in 2021. He is the recipient of two Independent Publisher Book Awards, the Beverly Hills Book Award, the Vincent Preis Horror Award, the Benjamin Franklin Award, and his novel *Floating Staircase* was a finalist for the Bram Stoker Award. He lives with his wife and two daughters in Maryland.

ronmalfi.com
@RonaldMalfi

For more fantastic fiction, author events,
exclusive excerpts, competitions, limited editions and more

VISIT OUR WEBSITE
titanbooks.com

LIKE US ON FACEBOOK
facebook.com/titanbooks

FOLLOW US ON TWITTER AND INSTAGRAM
@TitanBooks

EMAIL US
readerfeedback@titanemail.com